COLD
REDEMPTION

GALLOW
COLD
REDEMPTION

NATHAN HAWKE

The right of Nathan Hawke to be identified as the author
of this work has been asserted by him in accordance with
the Copyright, Designs and Patents Act 1988.

First published in Great Britain in 2013
by Gollancz
An imprint of the Orion Publishing Group
Orion House, 5 Upper St Martin's Lane,
London WC2H 9EA
An Hachette UK Company

This edition published in Great Britain in 2013
by Gollancz

1 3 5 7 9 10 8 6 4 2

A CIP catalogue record for this book
is available from the British Library

ISBN 978 0 575 11510 1

Typeset by Deltatype Ltd, Birkenhead, Merseyside

Printed and bound by CPI Group (UK) Ltd,
Croydon CR0 4YY

The Orion Publishing Group's policy is to use papers that are
natural, renewable and recyclable products and made from wood
grown in sustainable forests. The logging and manufacturing
processes are expected to conform to the environmental
regulations of the country of origin.

www.orionbooks.co.uk

And each man stands with his face in the light of his own drawn sword. Ready to do what a hero can.

Elizabeth Browning

PROLOGUE – IRONSKIN

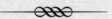

The man on the table in front of the Aulian was dying. The soldiers with their forked beards crowded around, full of anxious faces, but they knew it. He was past help.

'I'll do what I can.' The Aulian shook his head. 'Leave him with me.' When they did, that too was a sign of how little hope they had. A prince of the Lhosir left alone with an Aulian wizard. The Aulian opened his satchel and bag and set about making his preparations.

'Who are you?' The dying man's eyes were open. The skin of his face was grey and slick with sweat; but there was a fierce intelligence behind those eyes and a fear too. A fork-beard prince who was afraid to die, but then who wouldn't be when dying looked like this? The Aulian didn't answer, but when he came close the Lhosir grabbed his sleeve. 'I asked you: who are you?'

'I'm here to heal you. If it can be done.'

'Can it?'

'I will try, but I am ... I am not sure that it can. If you have words to say, you should say them.'

The Lhosir let him go. He was trembling but he seemed to understand. The Aulian lifted his head and tipped three potions into his mouth, careful and gentle. 'One for the pain. One for the healing. One to keep you alive no matter what for two more days.' Then he unrolled a cloth bundle and took out a knife and started to cut as gently as he could at the bandages over the Lhosir's wound. The room already stank of putrefaction. The rot was surely too far gone for the Lhosir to live.

'I left him. I left my friend. I abandoned him.'

The Aulian nodded. He mumbled something as he cut, not really listening. The Lhosir was fevered already and the potions would quickly send him out of his mind. Soon nothing he said would mean very much. 'Even if you survive, your warring days are over. Even small exertions will leave you short of breath.'

'I was afraid. I am Lhosir but I was afraid.'

'Everyone is afraid.' The Aulian lifted away a part of the bandage. The Lhosir flinched and whimpered where it stuck to the skin and the Aulian had to pull it free. The stench was appalling. 'I'm going to cut the wound and drain it now. This will hurt like fire even through the potions I've given you.' The Aulian dropped the festering dressing into a bowl of salt. As delicately as he could, he forced the Lhosir prince's mouth open and pushed a piece of leather between his teeth. 'Bite on this.'

The Lhosir spat it out. 'The ironskins took him.'

The Aulian stopped, waiting now for the potions to take the Lhosir's thoughts. 'Ironskins?'

'The Fateguard.'

The Aulian looked at the knife in his hand, razor sharp. 'Then tell me about these iron-skinned men, Lhosir.'

So the Lhosir did, and the Aulian stood and listened and didn't move, and a chill went through him. 'There was another one like that,' he said when the prince was done. 'Long ago. We buried it far away from here under a place called Witches' Reach. It was a terrible monster. Its power was very great, and very dangerous.'

The Lhosir started to talk about the friend he'd left behind, the one he said the ironskins had taken. The Aulian listened until the Lhosir's words broke down into a senseless mumble. The potions were taking hold. He turned his knife to the wound. The Lhosir screamed then. He screamed like a man having his soul torn out of him piece by piece. Like a man slowly cut in two by a rust-edged saw. The Aulian worked quickly. The wound was deep and the rot had spread deeper still and the stink made him gag. He cut it out as best he could, drained the seeping pus away, cut until blood flowed red and the screaming grew louder still. When he was done he tipped a handful of wriggling creatures onto the dying Lhosir's bloody flesh and placed their bowl over the wound.

The door flew open. Another Lhosir, with the dying prince's bodyguards scurrying in his wake. They ran in and then stumbled and turned away, hit by the reeking air. The Aulian didn't look up. He wrapped cloth over the wound as fast as he could, hiding what he'd done. The first of the soldiers was on him quickly, gagging. The dying prince was quiet now. Fainted at last.

'Wizard, what have you done?'

The Aulian cleaned his knife and began to pack away his bags. 'If he lives through the next two days he may recover. Send someone to me then.' He looked at the forkbeard soldier. 'Only if he lives.'

But the Lhosir wasn't looking at him; he was staring at the hole in the dying prince's side – at the blind thing wriggling from under the cloth. The Aulian frowned. He'd been careless in his haste. He turned back to the soldier. 'It will—'

'Sorcerer!' The forkbeard drove his sword through the Aulian. 'Monster! What have you done?'

The Aulian tried to think of an answer, but all his thoughts were of another monster. The monster with the iron skin. And, as he fell to the floor and his eyes fixed on the dying Lhosir's hand hanging down from the table, how the Lhosir seemed to have too many fingers.

BEYARD

1

THE AULIAN WAY

Addic stopped. He blew on his hands and rubbed them together and took a moment to look at the mountains behind him. Hard to decide which he liked better: the ice-bitter clear skies of today or the blizzards that had come before. Wind and snow kept a man holed up in his hut with little to do but hope he could dig himself out again when it stopped. A clear day like this meant working, a chance to gather wood and maybe even hunt, but Modris it was cold! He stamped his feet and blew on his fingers again. It wasn't helping. They'd gone numb a while back. His feet would follow before much longer. Cursed cold. He looked back the way he'd come, and it felt as though he'd been walking for hours but he could still see the little jagged spur that overlooked the hut where he'd been hiding these last few days.

Up on the shoulder of the mountain beyond the spur a bright flash caught his eye, a momentary glimmer in the sun. He squinted and peered but it vanished as quickly as it had come and he couldn't make anything out. The snow, most likely, not that snow glinted like that; but what else could it be so deep in the pass?

Snow. Yes. Still, he kept looking now and then as he walked, until a wisp of cloud crossed the mountain and hid the shoulder where the old Aulian Way once ran from Varyxhun through the mountains and out the other side. The Aulians had fallen long before Addic was born, but that didn't mean that nothing ever came over the mountains any more. The winter cold was a killer, but shadewalkers were already dead and so they came anyway.

He quickened his pace. The high road was carved into the mountainside over the knife-cut gorge of the Isset. It was hardly used at the best of times, even in summer when the snow briefly melted. No one had come through since the blizzards, and so he was left to wade thigh-deep through the snow on a narrow road he couldn't see along a slope that would happily pitch him over a cliff if he took a wrong step. It was hard work, deadly tiring, but he didn't have much choice now and at least the effort was keeping him warm. If he stopped to rest, he'd freeze. And it probably *hadn't* been another shadewalker high up in the mountains, but if it was then he certainly didn't want to be the first living thing it found.

By the time he ran into the forkbeards, hours later, he'd forgotten the shadewalker. By then he was so tired that his mind was wandering freely. He kept thinking how, somewhere ahead of him, one of the black lifeless trees that clung tenaciously to the gentler slopes above would have come down and blocked the road completely and he'd have to turn back, and he simply didn't have the strength to go all the way back to his safe little hole where the forkbeards would never find him.

And there they were: four of them, forkbeards armed to the elbows and riding hardy mountain ponies along the Aulian Way where they had no possible reason to be unless they'd finally caught wind of where he was hiding; and the first thing he felt was an overwhelming relief that someone else had come this far and ploughed a path through the snow so that he wouldn't have to, and how that was going to make his walking so much quicker and easier for the rest of the way. Took a few moments more for some sense to kick in, to realise that this far out from Varyxhun the forkbeards had come to hunt him down, winkle him out of wherever he was hiding and kill him. He might even have been flattered if he'd been carrying anything sharper than a big pile of animal pelts over his shoulder.

The crushing weight of failure hit him then, the futility of even trying to escape; and then a backhand of despair for good measure, since if the forkbeards had learned where he was hiding then someone must have told them, and there weren't too many people that could be. Jonnic, perhaps. Brawlic, although it was hard to imagine. Achista? Little sister Achista?

His shoulders sagged. He tried to tell himself that no, she was too careful to be caught by any forkbeard, but the thought settled on him like a skin of heavy stone. He set the pelts carefully down and bowed in the snow. The forkbeards seemed bored and irritable, looking for trouble. 'My lords!' They were about as far from lords as Addic could imagine, but he called them that anyway in case it made a difference. Maybe they were out here on some other errand. He tried to imagine what that might be.

'Addic.' The forkbeard at the front beamed with pleasure, neatly murdering that little glimmer of hope. 'Very kind of you to save us some bother.' He swung himself down from his pony, keeping a cautious distance. It crossed Addic's mind then that although the forkbeards had horses, they were hardly going to take the High Road at a gallop in the middle of winter when it was covered in snow, nor even at a fast trot unless they were unusually desperate to go over the edge and into the freezing Isset a hundred feet below. And if they knew him, then there *was* only one reason for them to be out here. He turned and ran, or tried his best to, floundering away through the snow, not straight back down the road because that would make it too easy for them but angling up among the trees. The snow shifted and slid under his feet, deep and soft. As he tried to catch his breath a spear whispered past his face.

'Back here, Marroc. Take it like a man,' bawled one of the forkbeards. Addic had no idea who they were. Just another band of Cithjan's thugs out from Varyxhun. They probably looked pretty stupid, all of them and him too, not that that was much comfort. Struggling and hauling themselves up through the steep slopes and the drifted snow, slipping and sliding and almost falling with every other step, catching themselves now and then on the odd stunted tree that had somehow found a way to grow in this forsaken waste. The forkbeards were right behind him. Every lurch forward was a gamble, a test of balance and luck, waiting to see what lay under the snow, whether it would hold or shift. Sooner or later one of them would fall and wouldn't catch himself, and then he'd be off straight down the slope, a quick bounce as he reached the road maybe and then over the edge, tumbling away among the rock and ice to the foaming waters of the Isset. Which for Addic was no worse than being caught, but for the forkbeards it was probably a worse fate than letting him get away. Perhaps desperation gave him an advantage?

But no, of course it was *him* that slipped and felt his legs go out from under him. He rolled onto his back, sliding faster and faster through the snow, trying to dig in his feet and achieving nothing. He could see the road below – with two more forkbeards standing on it right in his path – and then the great yawning abyss of the gorge. He threw out his arms and clawed at the slope but the snow only laughed at him, coming away in great chunks to tumble around him, past him. He caught a glimpse of the forkbeards on the road looking up. Laughing, probably, or maybe they were disappointed that the Isset and the mountainside were going to do their work for them. Maybe he could steer himself to hit them and they could all go over the edge together?

Two forkbeards on the road? He wondered for a moment where they'd come from, but then he caught a rock which sent him spinning and flipped him onto his front so he couldn't see where he was going any more. A tree flew past, bashing him on the hip; he snatched and got half a hand to it but his fingers wouldn't hold. Then he hit the road. One foot plunged deep into the snow and wrenched loose again with an ugly pain. His flailing hand caught hold of something and tried to cling on. *The forkbeards, maybe?* Again a moment of wonder, because he could have sworn he'd only seen four forkbeards with their ponies and they'd all been chasing him, so these had to have come the other way, but that couldn't be right ...

A hand grabbed him, and then another. He spun round, tipped over onto his back again, felt his legs go over the edge of the gorge and into the nothing, but the rest of him stopped. The forkbeards had caught him, and for one fleeting second he felt a surge of relief, though it quickly died: the forkbeards would have something far worse in mind than a quick death in the freezing waters of the Isset.

A cloud of snow blew over him. When it passed he brushed his face clear so he could see. He was right on the edge of the gorge, the Isset grinning back up at him from far below. Two men stood over him. They'd let go and they weren't hitting him yet and so his first instinct was to get up and run, but getting back to his feet and avoiding slipping over the edge took long enough for his eyes to see who'd saved him. He had no idea who they were or what they were doing out here on the Aulian Way in the middle of winter, but they weren't forkbeards after all.

The bigger of the two men held out a hand to steady him. They weren't Marroc either. The big one, well, if you looked past the poorly shaven chin, everything about him said that he *was* a forkbeard. Big strong arms, wide shoulders, tall and muscular with those pitiless glacier eyes. The other one though ... Holy Modris, was he an Aulian, a real live one? He was short and wiry, wasted and thin and utterly exhausted, but his skin was darker than any Marroc and his eyes were such a deep brown they were almost black. He was also bald. Their clothes didn't say much at all except that they were dressed for the mountains.

The four forkbeards were picking their way down from the slopes above, slow and cautious now. The two men who'd saved his life looked at him blankly. They were half dead. The Aulian's eyes were glassy, his hands limp and his breathing ragged. The big one wasn't much better, swaying from side to side. Addic thought of the flash he'd seen from the mountain shoulder hours ago and for a moment wonder got the better of fear. 'You crossed the Aulian Way? In winter?'

The forkbeards were almost down now and they had their shields off their backs. The first one slid onto the road in a pile of snow about ten paces from where Addic was standing. He pulled out his axe but didn't come forward, not yet. He watched warily. 'Hand over the Marroc.'

The big man stood a little straighter. 'Why? What's he done?' He was breathing hard and his shoulders quickly slumped again. He looked ready to collapse. *An ally, maybe?* But against four forkbeards? Addic glanced down the road, back the way he'd come.

'Pissed me off,' said the forkbeard with the axe. 'Like you're doing now.'

The stranger growled. The Aulian put a hand on his arm but the big man shook it off. 'Three years,' he snarled. 'Three years I'm away and I come back to this.' The other forkbeards were on the road now, the four of them grouping together, ready to advance. The stranger drew his sword and for a moment Addic forgot about running and stared at the blade. It was long, too long to be a Marroc edge – or a forkbeard one either – and in the winter sun it was tinged a deep red like dried blood. 'Three years.' The big man bared his teeth and advanced. 'Now tell me how far it is to Varyxhun and get out of my way!'

'Three days,' said Addic weakly, bemused by the idea of anyone telling four angry forkbeards to *get out of my way*. 'Maybe four.' The forkbeards were peering at the stranger's shield, an old battered round thing, painted red once before half the paint flaked off. It had seen a lot of use, that was obvious.

'Move!' The stranger walked straight at them.

'Piss off!'

Addic didn't see quite what happened next. One of the forkbeards must have tried something, or else the stranger just liked picking fights when he was outnumbered and exhausted. There was a shout, a red blur and a scream and then one of the forkbeards dropped his shield and bright blood sprayed across the snow. It took Addic a moment to realise that the shield lying on the road still had a hand and half an arm holding it.

'*Nioingr!*' The other three piled into the stranger. Addic wished he had a blade of his own, and if he had might have stayed. But he didn't, and there wasn't anything he could do, and so he turned to flee and ran straight into the Aulian.

'Hey!'

'Out the way.' He pushed past. The darkskin had a knife out but obviously didn't know what to do with it. 'If I were you, I'd run!'

The Aulian ignored him and took a step toward the fight. 'Gallow!'

Addic heard the name as he fled. It stuck with him as he ran. He'd heard it somewhere before.

2

ORIBAS

'Gallow!' The knife Oribas had was for stripping bark and carving wood, not for stabbing mad armoured men with forked beards, and even if it had been, he wouldn't have known how to use it.

The man Gallow had saved ran off down the road, back the way he'd come. Oribas watched him go. He ought to do the same – that would be sensible – but he didn't. It would be nice to think his decision had something to do with honour or loyalty or friendship but the truth was crueller: he simply didn't have the strength. He could barely even stand, and that was after Gallow had half carried him for the last two days through blizzards and snowfields deep enough to bury a man. Oribas couldn't understand how Gallow was still on his feet, never mind spoiling for a fight.

One of the forkbeards slammed Gallow with his shield and he stumbled. Oribas wanted to shout at them that it was hardly fair, taking on a man who'd just walked the Aulian Way in winter, but instead he put his knife back where it belonged and sat in the middle of the road and closed his eyes. His legs had had enough. Besides, the forkbeards probably didn't care about what was fair, not after Gallow had chopped off their friend's arm – he was lying in the snow, clutching his stump.

They were both as weak as children from crossing the pass but it still surprised Oribas when Gallow went down. A second forkbeard was out of the fight by then, sitting in the road rocking back and forth, holding his guts. But then Oribas saw the red sword fall from Gallow's hand and disappear into the soft snow at the big man's feet. He saw Gallow stumble, one of the forkbeards jab the butt of his axe into his face before he could find his balance again, and that was that. The forkbeard who'd knocked him down went to look at his comrade who was now lying still in the road. He wrinkled his nose and prodded the body with his boot. 'Fahred's gone. Bled out.'

The other one still on his feet stamped through the snow to Oribas and picked him up by his shirt. 'The Marroc! Where'd he go?'

Oribas pointed down the road.

'And you didn't stop him?' The forkbeard snorted with contempt. 'To the Isset with you then!'

He didn't so much throw Oribas over the cliff as simply let go and push. Oribas stepped back to catch himself, screamed when his foot found only air and kept on going, and down he went, spinning as he fell. The rest happened with blurring speed. For a moment he was looking towards the river far below, seeing that the cliff was actually more of a steep and jagged mess of stumps and skeletal branches and sharp prongs of stone waiting to smash him to pieces. There was a dead tree sticking out below him that probably wouldn't take his weight but he reached out a hand for it anyway. His satchel slipped off his arm as he hit a boulder, flew down ahead of him and snagged on the tree, and then his fingers closed around the wood and his other arm was swinging around to grasp the bark as well, and his shoulders felt like they were being torn out of their sockets ...

The wood let out a horrible crack, shifted and shook him loose. Now he wasn't falling as much as sliding, and a hundred fists punched him in the chest and the thighs as he spread-eagled over the stones and scrabbled for purchase. His foot hit something solid, twisted him sideways and drove his knee up into his ribs, almost pitching him out into the void again. His fingers were like the talons of an eagle, grabbing hold of whatever was there. And then he was still. By some miracle, he wasn't falling any more.

For a time he stayed exactly there, gasping, arms and legs ablaze with the effort of it but not daring to let his grip go even a fraction. His lungs were burning. Waves of pain washed over him. He tipped his head back and rolled his eyes as far as they'd go, looking up, half expecting to see the forkbeard who'd pushed him staring down, ready to drop rocks on him. But there was nothing, only sky. He shifted, trying to get himself more comfortable, then levered himself up onto the ledge that had caught him. The road was about twenty feet above. The boulder that he'd hit was half that. The dead tree would be a mere handspan beyond him if he got to his feet and stretched for it, but a handspan was still a handspan. His satchel hung off the end. It was all so close but all desperately beyond him.

He hugged the ledge, listening, waiting for the forkbeards to see him when they finally threw Gallow's corpse off the edge too, but they never did. He heard snatches of their talk for a few minutes, taut and angry, but neither came to the side of the road, and then he heard them mount their ponies and move away. He supposed they must have gone, but he waited a while longer to be certain. He had a good long look at the cliff above him. Gallow would have scaled it without a thought, like he was bounding up a flight of steps. Oribas summoned his courage and called out but got no answer. Gallow was dead or unconscious or the forkbeards had taken him then. In his mind he saw the big man lying helpless in the snow, slowly bleeding out. He'd have to climb up by himself. Ought to. Ought to right now. Get up onto the road and see what had happened but his arms and hands didn't have the strength, his legs weren't long enough.

He sat and wondered what to do, and after a time he felt

the cold creeping in through his furs, making him dopey. He'd fall sooner or later. Even if he kept awake through to nightfall, the cold would kill him before the next morning.

'Hedge-born forkbeards!' The shout came from close by on the road, probably loud enough to reach right through the valley. '*Nioingr!* All of you!'

If there was more, Oribas didn't hear. By then he'd taken a lungful of cold air and was yelling as loud as he could, and he kept on until a face peered over the edge and stared at him in wonder. It was the Marroc the forkbeards had been chasing.

'You're alive! What happened to your friend?' The Marroc's face was screwed up in confusion. 'Do you need help?'

'Yes.'

The man disappeared and came back a moment later. 'Forkbeard whelps took all my furs,' he said. He looked at Oribas expectantly.

'Have you got any rope?'

The Marroc shook his head. 'No.'

Gallow had been carrying both their packs, had been for days. 'My friend had some,' he said. 'Is he still up there? They didn't throw his body over the edge. If he is, he has some.' He closed his eyes and bit his lip.

The face disappeared and then came back for a second time. 'No, no body up here. Plenty of blood over the snow, but that's all. Someone got hurt bad. You sure they didn't throw him over?'

'Yes.'

'Then they must have taken him with them.' The Marroc frowned. 'Why would they do that?'

'I don't know.'

'Why do they do anything? Because they're forkbeards. Why'd you help me?'

'*I* didn't.' Oribas looked miserably away. 'I just stood and watched. As for Gallow? I don't know. It's what he does but I never understood why.'

The Marroc peered closer. 'Gallow? That his name?'

'Yes.'

'Funny. They were looking for a Gallow in these parts a few years back. Is he one of them? A forkbeard?'

'A Lhosir. Yes.' Oribas felt his heart sinking. Neither of them had any rope. This man was going to leave him here because there was nothing else he could do. The cold was chilling him deep now. His fingers and his feet were numb. He could feel himself slowly shutting down.

Another pause. 'Are you an Aulian?'

'I suppose, if that means anything any more. Look, there are some trees on the slope above the road. You could cut some strips of bark and make a rope with those if you haven't got any.' His hands were turning stiff even stuffed down inside his furs. His legs were going too, not from the cold but just from having nothing left to give after the bitterness of the mountains.

'I don't know about that. Actually, I reckon you can just climb up from there unless your arms and legs are broken.'

'No, I can't.'

'Yes, you can. It's not even that hard.'

Oribas shook his head and turned away. 'I barely have the strength to stand, my friend.'

The next thing he knew, snow was falling around him and the Marroc was climbing down. He made it look easy. A moment later he stood beside Oribas on the ledge. 'See. Stand up.'

'I don't think I can.'

'Then how were you going to climb a rope?'

Oribas shrugged forlornly. The Marroc shoved him sideways, almost tipping him off into the river. Oribas swore. 'Are you mad?'

But for a moment he'd forgotten how tired he was. The

Marroc nodded. 'Better. Now how about you either stand up or I push you off this ledge and into the river. Either your legs get you up there or I do you a mercy.'

It was the sort of thing Gallow would have done and it made Oribas feel pathetic and stupid. The Marroc coaxed and cajoled and threatened him until he wrapped his arms around the Marroc's neck and his legs around the man's waist, and then the Marroc climbed the slope for both of them as though he was half mountain goat. He swore a lot and called Oribas all sorts of things that Oribas didn't understand and a good few that he did, and it took what felt like most of the rest of the day; but he did it, and when they got to the top they both fell onto the snow-covered road and lay there panting and sweating.

'Thank you.' Oribas had lost count of how many times he'd already said that.

'Your friend saved my life. Modris put him there. He wouldn't look very kindly on me leaving you after that. You all right now?'

Oribas sat up. Standing was too difficult. 'I will be. I just need a moment.'

'Lhosir turd-beards.' The Marroc wandered around the churned and bloodstained snow where Gallow and the Lhosir had fought. He chuckled to himself and shook his head. 'You and your friend were heading for Varyxhun, were you?'

Oribas nodded.

'That's another three or four days on foot. Those fork-beards came all this way looking for me and then they let me go and took your friend instead. What happened?'

Oribas told him as best he could remember it. By the end the Marroc was grinning. 'Took two of them down, did he? Good for him. But what were you doing out here?'

'Gallow was on his way home. He never said much about it.' Which was a long stretching of the truth but he didn't

23

know this Marroc who'd saved his life, not yet.

The Marroc was poking around in the snow. 'There's a few farms between here and there. You should get to Brawlic's place before it's dark. Knock on his door and give him a penny and tell him that Addic pulled you off a cliff and sent you to him. He'll put you up in the warm for the night and feed you a bowl of something. You look like you could do with it.' The Marroc paused and began digging in the snow. 'Hello, hello? What have we here?'

Oribas felt himself rocking back and forth. He didn't mean to; it was just … happening. And though he tried to look up, his head kept dropping towards his chest. The Marroc was burrowing into the bloodstained snow where Gallow had fallen. 'O sweet Modris!' He lifted out something long and dark that looked a lot like a sword, but now Oribas couldn't lift his eyes to see properly. 'Your friend. Gallow, was it? He ever call himself anything else?'

Oribas nodded. His eyes slowly closed. Then the Marroc was shaking him, hauling him up, propping him under one shoulder. 'No no no, Aulian, you don't go and stop working on me now.' He slapped Oribas with a handful of snow. 'Fine. I'll take you to Brawlic's farm myself. Good a place as any to go. This sword, is it what I think it is?' There were a lot of names for the sword he had in his hand. The red sword. Solace. The Comforter. The Edge of Sorrows. Oribas might have added a few of his own but he only shrugged and started to slip to the ground. The Marroc lifted him up again. 'What *were* you doing out here anyway, Aulian? What were you *really* doing here?'

'Oribas,' said Oribas. 'My name is Oribas. It's a very long story.'

'I want to hear it, Aulian. All of it.'

3

THE LORD OF VARYXHUN

Cithjan of Varyxhun rose late. He dressed himself in Marroc finery and stroked the two braids of his forked beard and drank a bowl of warm honeyed milk that a Marroc serving girl brought to him. She had a frightened face, but so did all the Marroc in Varyxhun these days. He paid no attention as she took out the chamberpot from beneath his bed. When he was good and ready to face the day, he left his room and walked out into the dark passages of the castle. As he left, the iron-masked Fateguard that King Medrin Sixfingers had sent to watch over him fell in behind. The Fateguard made everyone nervous, even Cithjan. The iron-skin almost never said a word but you always heard him coming, clanking in all that iron he wore. And then he'd stop and become utterly silent, and that was when you knew he was right behind you. Cithjan shivered.

He broke his fast with warm bread and cold meat and more honey, too much of all of them which was why he'd been getting steadily fatter ever since he'd crossed the sea to serve his new king after old Yurlak had finally died. The Fateguard stood behind him, silent, watching. You couldn't argue with him as a bodyguard, but Cithjan quietly wondered whether the ironskin needed to be there *all* the time. It meant no one ever wanted to talk to him, and that wasn't particularly useful when he was supposed to be the governor of a province permanently on the brink of revolt. The ironskin was almost certainly a spy, too. King Sixfingers was always watching. The ironskins had stayed in their temples before Yurlak had died. Then Sixfingers had gone and struck his bargain with the witch of the north and now, for whatever unholy reason, they were his.

Once Cithjan was done eating, he took his time walking to the Hall of Thrones where old King Tane had held his court for a few weeks, back when the Screambreaker had been whipping his Marroc arse all the way from the sea to the mountains. Varyxhun was as impregnable a place as Cithjan had seen, layered up the side of a mountain in tier after tier of walls and gatehouses over a single winding road, and that was before you got to the castle proper. If the old Marroc king had held fast, Cithjan reckoned the Screambreaker would still be outside, trying to winkle him out. But Tane had headed off down the Aulian Way looking for Maker-Devourer-knew-what. He'd cut himself and the wound had gone bad and he'd died.

The Hall of Thrones was a big room, gloomy and foreboding. The way it picked up and echoed every noise had everyone walking around on tiptoe and talking in whispers as though someone had died. It was like that all the time, every bloody day.

'Well?'

The Marroc they'd given him to deal with all the other Marroc slid up to the throne and fell to his knees. Cithjan had given up telling him not to do that.

Clank clank. The Fateguard standing at his shoulder shifted slightly. The Marroc seemed to shrink into himself. Grisic. He was a weasel. You never knew with any Marroc quite where their loyalties were, and Cithjan had dark suspicions about this one and so he set little tests now and then. Grisic hadn't given himself away yet, but maybe that accounted for his nervousness.

'There are two farmers from Pottislet, your highness ...'

26

Cithjan rolled his eyes. *Highness.* Another habit the Marroc refused to break. 'Governor.'

'Yes, sir. Governor, sir.' *Fawning creep.* 'Two farmers from Pottislet come to beg for your aid your high— Governor. They say that ice wolves have come out of the mountains and are ravaging their herds.'

Ice wolves? Had anyone ever *seen* an ice wolf? 'Really? Another feeble effort to lure Lhosir soldiers out into the wilderness where they can quietly disappear?' Maker-Devourer knew they'd had enough of that.

'They beg you—'

'Send them away, Grisic.' They were under siege here in Varyxhun. Men vanished every few days, just disappeared without a trace, but everyone knew exactly what happened to them. If they were Lhosir they had their throats cut and vanished down the Isset into the Crackmarsh. If they were Marroc the options were more varied: some simply vanished down the Isset like his own men did; others turned out to be alive and well and living out in the wilds where they happily murdered Lhosir if the chance came their way; a few of them had been hauled off to the villages deep in the hills where no one gave a stuff about threats and reprisals and had been ripped to pieces by horses for being collaborators – or, as Cithjan looked at it, for having gone on with their lives as best they could without murdering anyone. A few, the really lucky ones, got to be strung up in Varyxhun Square itself in the middle of the night. Each morning they were waiting for him. If his eyes hadn't started to go a bit dim, Cithjan might have been able to see them from the castle walls. It took time to erect a gibbet and hang a man and cut his belly for all his entrails to dangle out, and yet no one ever saw or heard a thing. They'd done it to a Lhosir once last summer. Cithjan had seen to it that they never did it again. *Do what you like to each other. Touch one of us and you all pay dear.* It was a simple message.

Clank clank behind him. He shuddered. Grisic flinched as he rattled on through other irritations that should never have come to Cithjan. More ice wolves. A shadewalker seen in the forests around Haradslet. An irate plea from Tevvig Stonefists at Boyrhun for more arrows, since his previous messages had been ignored and now he didn't have any left and there were Marroc rebels openly shooting at his men. Yes, of course, three thousand arrows, and by the way what previous messages? But no need to ask Tevvig about that since it happened all the bloody time. A Lhosir messenger alone on the road? By the sound of things, this one had ended up disguising himself as a Marroc woman to get through to the Aulian Bridge and cross to this side of the Isset. Now there was a thing – a Lhosir disguising himself because he was afraid – Sixfingers would have his head if he ever heard about *that*. So yes, three thousand arrows and fifty armed men from Varyxhun and half the garrison out of Witches' Reach to make sure the arrows arrived safely, and Stonefists was welcome to keep the men as long as he made sure the Marroc around Boyrhun learned a lesson or two. A hundred of them hung along the roadside should do the trick. Rebels for preference, but any would do because the rebels got their food and shelter from somewhere, right? Grisic did a good job of keeping a straight face at that. He barely winced at all.

Boyrhun was thirty miles away as the crow flew, but since it was across the other side of the Isset gorge, it might almost have been in another country. The whole west bank of the river was virtually in open revolt and there was no pretending that Varyxhun would stay quiet if he left to sort it out. If he marched down the valley, crossed the Aulian Bridge, marched up the other side and set about murdering enough Marroc to make them get the message, then yes, he'd get all that done right enough, and then he'd have a fine view across the river as Varyxhun went up in flames.

Sixfingers might put up with a little unrest, but he wouldn't put up with that.

Clank clank. Did the Fateguard ever get tired? He'd never seen this one rest, or eat, or do anything other than what he was doing right now, standing like an angry statue, putting the shits up everyone.

'There's one other thing.' Grisic's smile was ashen. 'You put a bounty on the Marroc bandit Addic Snakefeet.' Cithjan frowned and then nodded as though he remembered. He put bounties on so many Marroc these days that he'd long ago lost track of who and why. 'Fahred and three of his men went out to bring you his head. They've come back.'

Four Lhosir out on the road? And they'd come back at all?

'They were set upon and—'

Cithjan rolled his eyes. 'How many of them are dead?'

'Just Fahred himself. They say they were set upon by an Aulian and –' he hesitated '– a Lhosir with no beard.'

Clank clank. 'A Lhosir?'

Grisic was bobbing up and down like a frightened hare. 'They killed the Aulian. They brought the Lhosir here. They said …' He frowned. 'They thought you might want to see him. He was carrying a shield of the Crimson Legion.'

Now there was a thing. 'One of Medrin's men? Stolen, most likely.'

Grisic bowed. 'Yes. As you say.'

'Well we can't hang him with all the Marroc. Send him to the Devil's Caves.'

Clank clank. Cithjan turned, ready to snap at the ironskin fidgeting behind him, but the Fateguard had moved around beside him and was leaning over. Cithjan couldn't help himself from shrinking back. The black iron crown and mask would do that to anyone, wouldn't they? The ironskin hissed, 'I would like to question this Lhosir first.'

Cithjan stared at the Fateguard. After a moment he

blinked a few times and nodded. 'Yes. Well. You can do that. If you want.'

Clank clank clank. The Fateguard stalked across the Hall of Thrones, the echoes of iron on stone freezing everyone in their tracks. No one moved. When he was gone, Cithjan let out a deep breath – for some reason he'd been holding it. He stared after the ironskin and then at Grisic. 'You'd better show him where to go then, hadn't you?'

The Fateguard in his iron mask strode through the doors of the Hall of Thrones. Eyes cast his way were full of dread. Marroc ran at the sight of him and even Lhosir tautened their faces and gritted their teeth and waited desperately for him to go away; and that was but the smallest of the curses on those who served the Eyes of Time.

The Marroc snake Grisic slithered out of the hall behind him and trotted on ahead, bowing and scraping and beckoning as though he wasn't quite sure whether he was leading a man or some sort of animal. He wore his mask of servility well, but the Fateguard had blessings to go with their curses, and one such blessing was to see the truth of a man's heart. Good or evil, kind or cruel, the men of iron cared little, but liars made the ice-cold blood burn in their veins, and this Marroc had a yellow streak of treachery to him.

He ignored Grisic. Varyxhun was an ancient castle, carved out of the mountainside by Aulian miners, comforting in its darkness and its age and its deep old roots tunnelled far into the stone. He crossed the courtyard, past gates that had never been sundered by any foe, not even the all-conquering Screambreaker. Below them, the gatehouse stairs wound down. There were tunnels here forgotten even by the Marroc, tunnels that reached all the way to the town of Varyxhun and perhaps further, as far as the old Aulian fortress at Witches' Reach or even the Aulian Bridge, the great span that crossed the gorge of the Isset before the river tumbled through cataracts and rapids into the swamp of the Crackmarsh.

The Fateguard embraced the gloom. He took a candle to light his way, but when the Marroc weasel took a torch for himself, the Fateguard gripped it in his iron-clad hand and crushed it out. Gloom and darkness were an ironskin's friends. They were where he belonged, in the shadows with the shadewalkers; but then he'd been to this place so often he could have done with no light at all. The place where prisoners came and were broken and made to talk, where he would listen and hammer a nail into a man's flesh for every lie that he heard.

He passed two cells without bothering to look. The smell was of old rot and filth. He stopped at the third. Here was the Lhosir. Beardless, weak and thin and pale and beaten, but here he was.

There's only one way into the valley of Varyxhun for a Lhosir, and that is to cross the Aulian Bridge. Yet not for you. The Fateguard stared hard at the man in the cell. He had an air to him. A meaning. A significance felt even in the Hall of Thrones, but there was something else, something the Fateguard had not expected. 'Gallow? Gallow Truesword. Gallow Foxbeard. Gallow the thief of the red sword.'

The Lhosir looked up and stared. He seemed neither frightened nor pleased, merely resigned. Slowly the Fateguard lifted off his mask and crown. Light burned in the beardless Lhosir's eyes and then at last a flash of recognition. 'Beyard?'

The Fateguard curled his lip. 'Hello, old friend.'

4

UPRISING

Oribas had little memory of his last few miles down the Aulian Way. The cold had reached inside him by then, the sunlight was fading and he was as close as he could be to dead without actually dying. He had some hazy notion of being dragged off the road and along a track between the black leafless bones of winter trees, of climbing and climbing, step after remorseless step up some steep winding path, of being hauled through a doorway, of light and heat and a delicious warm fire, and then he'd been asleep.

He thought he might have been asleep for a whole day, but only an hour or two passed before he woke again. Now there were half a dozen Marroc in a big open room that, as far as he could see, was their whole house. A young woman was waving a pot of something warm and delicious-smelling under his nose. Oribas stared at her. Maybe he was delirious with fatigue or with disbelief that he was somewhere warm, but she had the most beautiful elfin face and he couldn't stop looking at her.

She reddened and looked away. 'I know you want rest,' she said, 'but you need some food first to give you back your strength.'

Behind her, the other Marroc were looking at him. Addic smiled but the others were less friendly. They were passing the red sword between them, the Edge of Sorrows. His eyes strayed back to the woman. She looked small and young and determined. Her smile, when it came, was a shy fragile thing. 'Who are you?' he asked her.

She shook her head. 'Eat.'

'You have beautiful eyes. Full of sadness and steel and passion.'

She laughed at him, and he had to smile back at the way her face lit up. 'And you have a mind addled by the cold.' She fed him one spoonful at a time, and it very likely wasn't even remotely the best food he'd ever had, but that was how it seemed.

'My friend,' he asked when his eyes started to close again. 'What happened to Gallow?' But she only smiled and nodded some more and he wasn't sure she even heard him, and after that he must have fallen asleep again, because when he woke up it was the middle of the next morning and the house was empty and he felt deliciously wonderfully warm.

'Drink.' The woman was squatting beside him. She must have woken him again. His head felt clearer now, sharp and focused, not all blurry like the night before. He remembered what he'd said and cringed and felt stupid.

'I'm sorry.' He sat up and looked at her, properly this time. She was offering him a warm bowl of something brown and lumpy and full of grease, and even if it was the same as whatever she'd given him yesterday, a night over the warm embers of the fire hadn't done it any favours. He wrinkled his nose and tried not to gag; he *was* hungry, though, and ached all over. And she *was* pretty, in a boyish sort of way.

'Addic says you were in the mountains.' She shook her head as though at an errant child. 'In the winter? You're lucky the cold didn't take you.'

'I know. But there were two of us. What happened to my friend?'

'Addic's outside.' She smiled. 'I'll tell him you're awake once you've eaten.'

'No. My other friend.' The food wasn't so bad when he

managed not to think about it, not to look at it and not to let it linger in his mouth any longer than necessary. 'The one who came with me across the mountains.'

'Like you?' She touched his cheek and it took him a moment to realise why – she'd never seen someone like him before. 'Where do you come from?'

'Somewhere far away. I lived in a desert on the other side of what was once the Aulian Empire.'

'Then it must have been something very important to make you come all this way and cross the mountains.' Somehow, without realising it, he'd emptied the bowl.

'I came because my friend asked me to.'

'I'll find Addic.' She rose and left him and he watched her go, eyes following her to the door with an unexpected longing until she was gone. Fate had carried Gallow all this way with her sweet false promises of family and friendship, and Oribas had followed; now he was trapped by the winter in this land with nothing and no one, and Gallow was surely dead. Cruel and unkind to bring a man so far and then cut him down so close to home.

Three Marroc came in. Two had knives in their hands. A broad brawny one with a straggly beard and a thin-faced clean-shaven one with a mean look in his eye. The third was Addic. The brawny one grabbed him by the arm. 'Aulian, I should cut your throat!'

Addic put a hand on the brawny one's arm. 'This one's not a sorcerer, Brawlic. He didn't summon the shadewalkers.'

'Three already in one winter and the forkbeards do nothing!' The thin-faced one tutted and shook his head. 'No wonder people are so restless. I'm sure they'd love nothing more than an Aulian they could call a sorcerer, just so they could hang him in Varyxhun square.' He walked slowly to the corner of the room and picked up the Edge of Sorrows from where it stood, propped against the wall. They had no scabbard for it – that was still hanging from Gallow's belt, or perhaps some other Lhosir now. The thin-faced one lifted the sword and swung it a few times. The air whistled and moaned as it parted before the rust-red steel. He looked at Oribas. 'So you came over the mountains with a Lhosir with no beard who fought some of his own on the Aulian Way and saved Addic's life. That right? Addic says you called him a name: Gallow. What was his deed name, Aulian?'

'His what?'

Addic stepped between them. 'Forkbeards give themselves names. What was the rest of his name?'

Oribas blinked, confused. 'He said he was Gallow Foxbeard among his own.'

The thin-faced Marroc turned to the other two. He brandished the sword and his face had a greedy gleam to it. 'The Foxbeard. Then you know what this is, Addic? You know ...'

Addic held up a hand but his eyes had a hungry glitter to them too. Yes, he knew all right. He crouched down beside Oribas. 'The forkbeards came here hunting one they called Gallow the Foxbeard three summers ago after Andhun fell to the Vathen. They were after a sword. Did he ever call this sword by a name?'

Oribas shook his head. He felt weak and stiff but his wits were back where they should be now and they were saying that they didn't much like the looks on any of these Marroc faces right now. They knew the red sword for what it was, or they thought they did. The Edge of Sorrows if you were Aulian. Other names to others.

Addic smiled but the glitter in his eyes was made of daggers, not of laughter. 'I'll tell you what I've heard of Gallow the Foxbeard, Aulian, and then you can tell me if this is the man who kept me from falling into the Isset and stood and fought four of Cithjan's bastards. He was a forkbeard who never went back across the sea after old Tane died. When the Vathen swept out of the east with the Sword of the Weeping God, he was there when the forkbeards met them outside Andhun and they slaughtered each other. The forkbeards say the Widowmaker slew the Weeping Giant and took his sword, and that Gallow was at his side when he fell and that he stole it for himself. They say it was because of him that Andhun fell to the Vathen and that he's why their king is Medrin Sixfingers where once he had twelve. Most tales say Gallow drowned in the seas below Andhun's cliffs, but others whisper he came this way, looking for the Marroc family he'd left behind. Either way, neither his body nor the sword were ever found.' Addic bared his teeth. 'Is this the Gallow who crossed the mountains with you, Aulian? Because if he is then we've all heard a great deal of his deeds, good and ill. And this sword is Solace, the red sword of the Vathen, taken by the Widowmaker and whose edge our forkbeard king greatly desires.'

Oribas licked his lips. 'I'll tell you of the Gallow I knew. Decide for yourself if he's the same Gallow Foxbeard of whom you speak, for I cannot say, and he never called his sword by any name that I recall. I come from a desert at the far edge of what was once the Aulian Empire—'

'You speak our tongue,' interrupted the thin-faced one.

'Where I came from I was a scholar. I learned many tongues. Many years ago a monster came to my town. It wore the guise of a man, though it was not, and we didn't know it for what it was, not for many weeks. It brought ruin and murder and much worse. You speak of the ghosts of the old empire, of the shadewalkers. This creature was a thousand times more terrible. Rakshasa, it was once named. When finally it was revealed, it left us all but destroyed. I followed its trail but I could never find it, nor find a way to destroy it. In my despair I prayed to the old gods in a place we call the Arroch Ilm Daddaq, the Tainted Well. They sent me a vision and I followed that vision to the shores at the end of the world, and there I found Gallow, washed up from some shipwreck with others of his crew. He told me he had come from a place the Aulians knew long ago as the Glass Isles, to which the gods sailed after Mouth Catht split asunder. I understood: now the gods had sent him back to me. They had listened to my prayer after all and here was their answer. Together we hunted the Rakshasa that destroyed my town. We hunted it for many months and in the end we found it and put an end to it. All these things you speak of?' He shrugged. 'The gods sent Gallow to me. All he ever asked of his fate was to be allowed to return to his home across these mountains. He told me he was once the Gallow Truesword who fought beside the Screambreaker, but that that man was long gone.'

'What about the sword, Aulian?'

'I have a name, Marroc. I am called Oribas.'

Addic nodded. 'And I'm Addic. My surly friend here is Brawlic and this is his farm. His wife Kortha has cooked the food you've eaten and my sister Achista has fed it to you. My other friend here is Second Jonnic.' He laughed. 'The last of six brothers, Second, and his poor father ran out of names. There are some who call him Vengeful Jonnic instead, though, and with good reason.'

Second Jonnic watched Oribas coldly. 'My brother who shared my name was killed by the forkbeards in Andhun.' He turned to Addic. 'He's only telling us half the truth. He knows more and I'll have it out of him.'

Addic raised a hand. 'Brawlic has given him food and shelter and the forkbeards would have thrown me into the Isset were it not for this man and his friend. He's no enemy.'

Oribas looked from one to the other. 'I thank you for your kindnesses. If there is a way to repay you, I will do what I can.'

Jonnic spat. 'If the forkbeards get hold of him, they'll find out about all of us now.'

'I've no wish to be a part of any of your troubles.' Oribas kept his voice calm and quiet. 'If you could tell me where the Lhosir will take Gallow ...'

'Your friend is certainly dead. And once they know who he is, the forkbeards will be back, looking for this sword.'

Addic shook his head. 'If they killed him then how will they know his name? And if they don't know his name, how will they know there's a sword to find?' He grinned.

Jonnic ground his teeth. 'All the more reason this one can't stay where the forkbeards might find him. We know perfectly well what the best thing would be.'

'I do, but he's clearly not fit to cross the pass again, not in this state.' Addic's eyes narrowed on Oribas. 'You hunted a monster worse than a shadewalker? And defeated it? How?'

Oribas struggled to his feet. His legs felt as though they were made of wool. For a moment his head spun. He looked around the room, searching for the woman Achista, Addic's sister, but she wasn't there. Then he searched for his satchel for a while before he remembered where it was – hanging from the dead stump of a tree dangling over the Isset. The thought of trying to get it back made him shudder. He fiddled at the pouches on his belt instead while the Marroc watched him suspiciously. 'The ruins of old Aulia were beset by shadewalkers after the empire fell. There were those who took it upon themselves to hunt them. Shadow-stalkers and sword-dancers. I am neither of those things but I have seen them work.' He walked stiffly to the fire and threw a pinch of powder from one of his pouches into the flames. The fire flared, leaping out of the hearth and high towards the roof for a moment. The Marroc gasped and recoiled. 'Creatures like those have their weaknesses. Salt. Iron. Pure ice-cold water. And fire.'

'He's a witch,' hissed Brawlic. 'Get him out of my house!'

Addic put a hand on the farmer's arm. 'He's not a witch. Are you, Aulian?'

'I'm a scholar. In my hunt for the monster that destroyed my home, I studied such things. I don't begin to understand the magic that brought them to be, but I understand how they may be sent back where they belong.'

Addic pulled Jonnic aside. The two whispered to one another while Brawlic stared with open hostility at Oribas. Whatever decision the other Marroc reached, Jonnic didn't like it. Addic held up his hands. 'Shadewalkers cross the mountains now and then. When they come, all we can do is step out of their path. Even the forkbeards fear them. Can you defeat one?'

Oribas shook his head. 'Not alone, for I'm no warrior. But I can show you how.'

Addic started to laugh. 'You see, Jonnic. And imagine what the people of Varyxhun and beyond will say when a Marroc comes among them carrying the sword Solace and slays a shadewalker. *That's* how we'll have our uprising.'

Jonnic snorted. 'I say we take it to Valaric the Mournful in the Crackmarsh. Or across it and back to the Vathen. Let *them* fight the forkbeards.' He stared at Oribas. 'You came over the mountains. Across the Aulian Way after the first winter snows. Why?'

Oribas shrugged. 'It was Gallow.' He smiled faintly. 'He wanted to go home.'

5

GALLOW

In the gloom under Varyxhun, in Gallow's cramped and dank stone cell, Beyard picked up the empty cess bucket. He turned it upside down and sat on it. Gallow squatted in a corner, watching.

'Seventeen winters,' said the ironskin. 'Eighteen soon.' His voice was like grating metal, not the voice that Gallow remembered, and his face was pale and hollow, his eyes rimmed red and steeped in shadows. But he was still unmistakably Beyard. 'I heard about you, but not for a long time. No one knew who you were until you stole King Medrin's sword.'

'It was never his sword,' whispered Gallow.

Beyard's lips drew back. His teeth were a perfect white. He made a noise that might have been a laugh but that came out more like a wet cough. 'We both have our reasons not to like our king. I never gave away your names, either of you. Look at me now, Gallow. My reward is a skin of iron punishment to atone. For what? For being the only one with the courage to stay and stand fast when we all three broke the old laws? Why did you come back?'

'I never meant to leave.' They stared at each other in silence. Gallow took in the man who'd once been his friend, back when they were both filled with boyish bravado. The armour of the Fateguard, the iron strips and plates, covered him from head to toe. The Fateguard were the holy fists who guarded the Temple of Fates and enforced the will of the Eyes of Time, both cursed and blessed. They were rarely seen outside a temple and Gallow had never heard of one taking off his mask. More often than not they were the worst *nioingr* who would never have any other chance to atone, but that wasn't Beyard. Beyard had never been a coward. 'Are you my executioner?'

That wet coughing sound again. Beyard shook his head. 'Not I. But there will be one, have no doubt. Who will you have to speak you out when you hang?'

'I doubt there's a single Lhosir who'd do that now.'

'Then I will do it.' Beyard shifted. Metal ground on metal. 'What happened to you?'

The iron man looked down at himself. 'To me? See it for yourself. After you ran—'

Gallow bared his teeth. 'I did not *run*, Beyard! I would have stood beside you. Willingly. Do you not remember how it was?'

For a moment a light flashed in the Fateguard's bloody eyes. 'I remember, Gallow. We each paid our own price for our foolishness. I saw Medrin cross the sea; but fate found him out and I saw him back again with a wound that should have killed him, that left him crippled and for many years but half a man. I saw him rise each day with barely the strength to walk. I saw him fight for every scrap of strength. He came to the temple daily for a time. Suddenly a very pious man when it looked like he might never again lift a sword. Sometimes I wonder how loud he screamed when you crippled him for a second time. Medrin Sixfingers. Perhaps his punishment is finished now. But you? I never told them your name, just as I never told them his. The Eyes of Time searched for you and found nothing. And when neither of you found the courage to step forward, the punishment fell on me alone. I was made as you see me because I wouldn't betray your names. And because of what we'd done.'

'We did *nothing*!'

'But we had intent. We should not have been where they found us.'

Gallow looked away. 'I shouldn't have let you face them alone.'

Beyard rattled and shook with grinding laughter. 'Then we would *both* be men of iron. What difference would it have made? Besides, fate has its ways. Fate found Medrin without my help. The Crimson Shield was at the bottom of the sea with the Moontongue by then and its other thieves long forgotten. What did fate find for you, Gallow the smith's son?'

'I crossed the sea,' said Gallow. 'I fought with the Scream-breaker and after a time he named me Truesword. When it was done and Yurlak looked as though he was going to die and Medrin would take his crown, I stayed behind. I meant to cross the mountains into Aulia to be as far away as I could be but I never even reached Varyxhun. Before I knew what had happened, another eight years passed and I was a husband with a Marroc wife and a father with two sons and a daughter.'

'Truesword. I heard that name but you're Foxbeard now. I know about the Vathen and how you fought them and how you found the Screambreaker half dead and carried him back to Andhun, how you sailed with Medrin to reclaim the Crimson Shield and how you and the Screambreaker stood side by side in his last battle against the Vathen. They say you killed him there and took Solace, the red sword of the Vathen, from his hand as he fell.'

'I took his sword when he fell but I didn't kill him.'

'No.' A baleful look settled on Beyard's face. 'You turned on your own kind and cut off Medrin's hand as the Vathen swept through Andhun. I know you threw yourself into the sea and I know it was the Screambreaker himself who hauled you out of it, so I know you didn't kill him and I know the the Vathen didn't either.' Another wet hack of a laugh and

Beyard cocked his head. 'You were meant to come to us, Gallow. You were owed to us, you and Medrin both. Fate granted the Screambreaker a year and a day beyond what should have been his death to bring you back to us. He'd earned it. He dragged you from the sea when you should have drowned and told you your fate, yet you refused it.'

Gallow shook his head. 'I remember his words, old friend: "It's the nature of men like us to fight our fates."'

A coldness filled Beyard's eyes. 'I'm not your friend, Gallow. Not any more and not for many years. And you are Lhosir. You should know better than to turn against your fate.'

'I wanted to go home, Beyard.' Gallow's shoulders sagged. 'To see my sons. To be with my wife. To make more. To work the fields and the forge. Simple honest things, building a home. That's all.'

'But it was not your fate, Gallow.'

'No.' This time Gallow spat out a bitter laugh. 'The Marroc fled Andhun in a hundred ships. It was a calm day, clear, a balmy sea. And then in the night a storm came and scattered us and when the sun rose we were alone and lost, and ever since, with every step I've taken towards my home, fate has carried me ten away. Three years, Beyard. Three years and I've crossed half the world.' He looked around the cell, overwhelmed by despair. 'And here I am. Three years. I don't even know if she's still alive. Or my children, and if they are then they must certainly think I'm dead. She probably has another man. I suppose I hope for her that it's so. And now I'll never know, will I?' He looked up and touched his shirt. Beneath it, against his skin, an old locket hung on a worn chain. A little piece of Arda he'd taken with him into battle when the Vathen had come. The one thing over all that time he'd never lost. That, his shield and the cursed red sword.

'You should know better than to fight fate.'

'Medrin is king now, is he?'

'Yes. King Medrin One-Hand. Medrin Sixfingers. Medrin Ironhand, or Silverhand if you prefer. Yurlak scoured the world before he died for any who could make his son whole again. An Aulian came, a dark one, but it was the Eyes of Time who gave Medrin the hand he has now, one of iron and silver. A poor substitute for flesh and bone. Yurlak lived long enough to see it and then he died.' Another wet laugh. 'Yurlak scoured the world for you as well, Gallow Foxbeard. I swear it was his fury that kept him alive so long. But Ironhand? He means to cross the mountains and rebuild Aulia itself. He sees himself an emperor.' Beyard shook his head, a savage snarl on his face. 'Medrin, eh? Fool he is, but he's not the man either of us knew. He's a leader as his father was before him. A king with an iron hand.' Beyard rose. He picked up his mask and crown. 'I'm glad, Gallow, to have set my eyes on you one more time. I'll not tell Cithjan who you are. He'd send you to Medrin in chains and Medrin would bring down every world of pain that he knows upon you. He'd find this wife and these sons of yours and make blood ravens of them while you watch. So no, I'll not tell Cithjan. You were a better man than that. You will be Gellef Sheepstealer and you will merely hang for the two men you killed.'

'Two?'

'The other will die in a few days. I am ironskin, so I know his fate.'

'What of the Aulian who was with me?'

Beyard put the mask and crown back over his head. 'You should know how it is with our kind. They threw him into the gorge of the Isset.'

Which left him with nothing. Gallow held his head in his hands. 'All this way. I brought him all this way. I told him he didn't have to follow.'

'A man can't escape his fate. I'd plead for you, for the

sake of the friendship we once shared, but you turned on your kin, Gallow. You should not have done that.' Beyard stood in the door of the cell and turned, face hidden now behind bars of iron. 'Does the red sword swim beneath the waves below the cliffs of Andhun? Did you lose it on the other side of the world?'

Gallow froze, head bowed and eyes filled with tears for those he'd never see again. The sword. Solace, the Comforter, the Peacebringer, all those names the Marroc and the Vathen had given it, and it had done nothing but mock him from the moment he'd held it in his hand. Oribas called it by its Aulian name: the Edge of Sorrows, for the Aulians had always seen the truth of the curse it carried. 'I never lost it, Beyard,' he said, slowly looking up as he did. 'I carried it out of the sea of Andhun and I carried it across the world and back again. I carried it across the ruins of Aulia and along the length of the Aulian Way. The men I killed? It tasted their blood.'

Beyard stiffened. 'It's here? In Varyxhun?'

'If the men I fought didn't think to bring it back then it's lying beside the Aulian Way. In a place where only I will find it.'

The Fateguard stepped back inside and stood over Gallow, eyes boring down into him. 'Where, old friend? Where is it?'

Gallow shook his head. 'I'll not give it to Medrin. Not for nothing.'

Beyard's iron-gloved hands reached around Gallow's neck and tore the locket with the snip of Arda's hair away from him. 'I will find them. Whoever they are. I will punish them until you show me.'

Gallow met his eyes, unflinching. 'Will you? You were my friend once and a far better man than that. Has the iron skin of the Eyes of Time taken the Beyard I knew?'

'I am Fateguard,' Beyard hissed, but his eyes flicked away in a flash of shame.

'All I ask is to know whether my family lives.'

'And what use is that knowledge? If you find they're all dead, if your woman has another man, if your children are scattered and gone, will you go to the hangman more easily? For these are all likely things. Or if you find that they wait and still mourn after all this time and all is as it was and could be again, will you die at peace?'

'Let me see them and I'll show you where the sword is hidden.'

Beyard shook his head. 'Take me to the sword and you'll live until you have what you came here for.'

'For your blood oath, Beyard, I'll do that.'

Again Beyard shook his head. 'I'll swear to you on the Fates themselves. For my kind that is an oath cast in iron, but I cannot give you a blood oath. I am Fateguard, Gallow. I have no blood to offer.'

6

THE SHADEWALKER

The Marroc let Oribas rest for three days, eyeing him watchfully, talking among themselves in careful huddles while Oribas took care never to pry and spent his time staring into the fire and helping around the house as best he could – simple chores that needed little strength or skill. They fed him plenty of greasy stew and he held his nose and smiled and tried not think too much about the delicate care that his own kin put into the feasting tables of his homeland. The big Marroc Brawlic still made the sign of evil when he thought Oribas wasn't looking and the thin one still wanted to murder him. Sometimes Oribas caught Achista looking at him and then looking quickly away with a smile, but she was rarely in the house and it was the older woman who brought him his food now, Brawlic's wife Kortha. But on the third evening when Achista came into the house, she looked at him and didn't smile and instead pulled Addic and Jonnic away from the fire where they'd been whittling wood. The three of them talked in urgent whispers until Addic nodded and slipped his whittling knife back into its sheath. Then he came and sat beside Oribas. 'Aulian, there's a shadewalker.' He stared at Oribas hard. 'It's been seen again. Near Horkaslet. If you still say you can lay it to rest, then you and Jonnic and I can leave to hunt it in the morning.'

Oribas stretched out his hands. When the Marroc talked to him, they talked of little but shadewalkers and sometimes the Edge of Sorrows and what he knew about both. They'd been waiting for this. 'Salt? Iron? Water? Fire? You have these things?'

'You have the fire. Water is all around you. Iron and salt we have. Jonnic?'

Jonnic disappeared outside. When he came back, he was holding a sword in a scabbard crusted with snow. He looked Oribas in the eye and leaned into him and drew out the blade. It was old but clean and meticulously oiled. 'Not a forkbeard sword, this. An old Marroc one. Hard iron.' He slammed it back into its scabbard and handed it to Addic.

They left not long after the next dawn on the back of three mules, ploughing a path through the fresh snow down the little valley from Brawlic's farm, following a small fast river until it turned to run between two peaks towards the valley of the Isset. Jonnic led them to a place where one of the great Varyxhun pines had fallen across the water. He dismounted and gingerly led his mule across the giant trunk. Oribas and Addic followed, and together they climbed a steep twisting trail that rose up the other side of the valley towards the next ridge. The Marroc didn't talk, and by the end of the day they were across a high snow-bound pass and into the next valley along. They spent the night in the barn of some farmer that both Addic and Jonnic knew, the Marroc leaving Oribas with the mules while they went into the house. Addic came back out with a bowl of stew despairingly similar to the ones Oribas had so happily left behind. They slept not long after sunset and rose again early in the morning, reaching a hamlet by the middle of the day that was little more than a dozen houses and barns. Addic talked to one of the Marroc, who nodded and pointed and made a sign against evil, and Oribas didn't need to hear a word to understand perfectly. *Shadewalker. That way.* So they set off across snow-covered fields, all of them more upright in their saddles now. Jonnic held his head craned forward, making little jerking movements from side to side. Addic's foot twitched. About a mile from the hamlet they stopped at the edge of a dense stand of pines, black against the mottled mountainside, and Addic pointed. 'It's in there.'

'I've never faced a shadewalker before,' Oribas told him. 'I know what they are and I know what will stop one but I've never faced one.' Shadewalkers preferred dark places. Places with no sun, which was why they rarely came to the desert.

'You should have told us that before we left, Oribas.' Addic slipped off the back of his mule.

Jonnic stayed where he was. He spat. 'If we were going to get rid of this Aulian, here would do. Far enough away from old Brawlic that the forkbeards would never suspect even if they found him.'

Addic snorted. 'And bring them down on Ronnelic and Jonna and Ylya and Massic and the rest? Why, have they done something to offend you?'

Oribas yawned with a careful precision. 'In Aulia it is considered impolite to discuss a man's murder while he's standing right in front of you. I would hate to inconvenience your friends with my death. Perhaps it would be more convenient for us all if I were to stay alive?'

Addic laughed. 'I'm sorry about Jonnic. He hasn't quite grasped the idea that there are people in the world who are neither his Marroc friends nor forkbeards out to hang him.'

'I've quite grasped the Vathen,' snapped Jonnic. He glared at Oribas. 'When I cut a man's throat, his body goes in the Isset. Won't be a trouble to anyone. No *inconvenience*.'

Oribas spared him a smile. 'Then I shall remain glad that it's Addic and not you who carries the iron sword.' He turned away from Jonnic with as much bad grace as his Aulian manners could muster. 'An iron sword driven through the shadewalker's heart will kill it. Steel will sometimes work but more usually the creature appears to have been slain only to rise again in the days or weeks that follow. I've heard of the same shadewalker being put to rest four times before it stayed at peace, but when you truly kill it, you will know. There will be no doubt.' Just saying the words made him think of the Edge of Sorrows and all the names that the Marroc and the Lhosir had for the red sword. Was *that* what it was for? Putting shadewalkers to rest? 'Shadewalkers were knights once, soldiers of the Aulian emperor. They remember little of who they were but they have not forgotten their skill. Most still carry their old swords and armour.'

'We know.' Addic's lips were pressed tight together. 'We've seen them. Too many of them.'

'The sword-dancers learn to fight with such skill that they can cut the armour from a shadewalker's skin and pierce its dead bones with one thrust. The shadow-stalkers learn ways to make a shadewalker so weak that it can barely move. We have neither here, but we will confront it as though we have both. Whoever takes the sword must make the final thrust, but you must also defend us while I weaken it. Where's the salt?'

Addic jerked his thumb at a sack strapped to the back of his saddle.

'Addic, if you carry the sword then your friend Jonnic will need a torch and some of the salt as well. The shadewalker cannot cross a line of salt. I'll trap it in a circle. Once that is done, the rest is much easier. I will throw furnace powders over the creature and Jonnic will set his torch to it. When it flares you must all stand back, but be ready, for it will only burn a moment. As the flames die we throw pure water and more salt. If we strike well, it will fall as though dead, but don't be fooled. The iron sword must finish the creature. Is your point good and sharp?'

'You know all this but you've never faced one of these creatures?' Jonnic looked ready to run.

'I've seen it done. Where I come from there were men

who would hunt them and bring them to my school just so that we could be shown.'

They entered the trees on foot, the pines packed too closely for mules and so dark that they would quickly be lost. Addic took the lead, Jonnic came at the rear. They moved slowly and with care, squeezing between the branches.

'You'll need to lure the creature into open ground,' Oribas whispered. A circle of salt would be almost impossible amid these trees.

'And how will I do that?' hissed Addic.

'My understanding is that shadewalkers are very easily lured.'

'Lured how?'

Oribas tried to sound unconcerned, as though he was talking about trapping a badger or a hare. 'As with any hungry animal, one baits one's trap with food, Addic.' They all knew he meant them.

'Have you ever see a man taken by a shadewalker, Aulian?' whispered Jonnic behind him. 'Their faces are ...' His words faded. Oribas understood. The faces of their victims were the worst. They were unrecognisable. Thin and stretched as though they'd been sucked to nothing from the inside.

'Yes,' he said quietly. 'I have. I lost a friend once and I've seen other victims too.' The friend had been more Gallow's friend than his but they'd travelled for many miles and many days together. He'd died in the foothills along the Aulian Way and Oribas hadn't been there to tell Gallow and his sailors how to fight them. Too busy chasing a monster of his own.

The trees shivered and rustled ahead of them. Too much for a small forest creature and something as large as a deer wasn't likely to come into a wood like this. A bear? Oribas wasn't sure but the idea of a bear frightened him even more than a shadewalker. Salt wouldn't stop a bear. His fingers drifted to his belt, opening the pouches lined with waxed paper that held his saltpetre and the fierce-burning powdered grey metal that came from the alchemists near his old home. Would a flash of fire scare off a bear? He had no idea. Deserts didn't have bears. From the way Gallow had talked, probably not.

A branch cracked. A shape emerged from the gloom ahead, ragged clothes hanging over rusting mail, an old round wooden shield, scarred and stained, and a long notched sword almost trailing in the blanket of needles that covered the forest floor. Face as pale as the snow, eyes wide open, skin taut over the bones of its face, the shadewalker came towards them at a steady pace, without a sound save for its footsteps and the whip of a branch now and then as it brushed across its shield. In front of Oribas, Addic froze.

'Modris protect us,' he croaked.

'Diaran!' cried Jonnic behind them. He took a pace back and then another. As the shadewalker advanced, he turned and ran. Jonnic, who held the torch and so their fire. Oribas stumbled as Addic backed into him.

'What do I do?' the Marroc quavered.

Oribas backed away too, grabbing a fistful of salt from the bag over his shoulder. A man could always outrun a shadewalker if his legs were good. Why were these Marroc so afraid?

The shadewalker lifted its sword as it came closer, one of the old blades of the Aulian emperor's guard. Fine swords if you could find one in good repair and they reminded Oribas of the long-bladed Edge of Sorrows. The Marroc had left the red sword at home and he thought now they might wish they hadn't. Addic lifted his shield to defend himself, but he was still backing away and he was white with fear.

'It's just a man who forgot when to die,' hissed Oribas. He stepped around Addic and threw a handful of salt at the shadewalker's face. It rained down in a fine dust. The shadewalker stopped and hissed; for a moment its guard was down but Addic was too gripped by fear to strike at it. Oribas threw down a line of salt across the earth between them. 'It cannot cross!' He shifted around between the trees, laying down more salt, trying to encircle the shadewalker.

The creature cleared its eyes. It advanced on Addic again and then reached the salted earth and stopped. Its head whipped around to Oribas as though it understood exactly what the Aulian was doing.

'Get your friend Jonnic back here!'

'Jonnic!'

The shadewalker turned. It walked quickly now, straight at Oribas, swinging its sword in its hand. Oribas laid another line of salt. 'Can you make fire? Do you have what you need?' He watched Addic fumble in his bag and then shake his head. The shadewalker stopped abruptly again a few feet from Oribas, held by the salt a second time. Its eyes were white and a blue like water from a glacier. Oribas hadn't even known what a glacier was until Gallow had dragged him over the mountains, but he'd seen eyes like these before. Gallow had them. Ice-man eyes they called them in the desert, always had, even long ago, and now he wondered: where had these shadewalkers come from, these men who'd once guarded the old emperors of the world? Too tall and broad-shouldered to be Marroc, too pale-skinned to be Aulian. Or did the pale skin and those eyes simply come as a part of what made them?

They stared at one another. When Oribas walked toward the end of the arc of salt, the shadewalker moved with him. It kept moving, stepping gingerly along the line until it found its end and looked up. Its dead face didn't change but perhaps its eyes gleamed a little brighter as it sensed its victory. It advanced quickly. Addic cried out, turned and ran while Oribas simply stepped over the line of salt to be on the other side. The shadewalker came at him, stopped abruptly at the salt and began to walk along the line again, looking for a way past. Oribas tracked the arc of salt he'd laid out, slowly and carefully, trying not to look at the shadewalker stalking the edge of his barrier. He moved from one end to the other and laid down another line. The shadewalker ignored him until it found a way through, but Oribas stepped calmly over the salt a second time and then stood and waited. The arc was three quarters of a circle now. 'One more dance, restless one?'

As soon as the shadewalker started looking for a way past again, Oribas ran, dropping salt as he went. When he was done he stepped back and watched. For a time the shade-walker followed the line. After it had gone round the inside of the circle three times, it stopped and turned to stare at him.

Oribas bowed. 'Can we both agree that you will wait here while I find my friends?'

7

THE RAVINE

Beyard demanded Gallow's oath not to run away and so Gallow gave it to him. Now he was in his mail and with his shield and helm, sitting on the back of a borrowed horse with the ironskin and a dozen Lhosir around him. Two were the men he'd faced on the Aulian Way – Arithas and Hrothin – and they stared at him with open hatred and spat at his feet and growled *nioingr* to his face. Gallow wondered at the return of his mail and his shield and helm, but those were in case of Marroc archers hiding in the woods. It seemed that among the villages in the high hills the Marroc were almost in open revolt.

'We know about you, *nioingr*,' snarled Hrothin.

'That's twice, Hrothin. Call me that a third time and you'll have to give me a sword and let me kill you,' said Gallow coldly. Beyard snarled and the two Lhosir backed away, their surly glances raking over him.

'Those two will be your watchers.' Beyard watched them go. 'One of the men you killed was Hrothin's brother. He has a blood feud with you now.'

'You're going to hang me, old friend. Hrothin will be disappointed.'

Beyard dangled Gallow's locket in the air between them, the one with a snip of Arda's hair inside. 'A feud is settled between families, Gallow, not just the men who start it. I can give him yours if I choose.' There was little of Beyard's face to see through the iron mask and crown he wore. Certainly not his eyes. 'They're only Marroc.'

Gallow's voice dropped. 'The Beyard I once knew would never sully himself like that.'

'But I am of the Fateguard now. I serve other ends.' Was that a glimmer of resentment lingering in there for whatever the Eyes of Time did to make the servants of fate as they were? 'I know you didn't slay the Screambreaker, as so many say you did, but you still led Marroc men against their king, you struck Yurlak's son and took his hand and now you've killed two of your kinsmen without cause. What would your old friend say to that, Gallow?'

'He'd ask why I did each of those things and he'd listen as I told him. Perhaps he might even agree I was right.'

They spent three long days plodding up the Aulian Way through ice and trampled snow. The fourth took them up into the start of the mountain pass where Gallow had first met Addic. The snowfalls since had been light but it still took hours of searching to find where Gallow had killed Fahred, walking their horses slowly along the road, Hrothin and Arithas pointing to features of the landscape here and there – *No, it was further than this; I remember that stone on the way back; No, too far* – but it was the horse tracks that settled it, for the Lhosir had dismounted to fight and no one else had been foolhardy enough to take a horse up the narrow path of the pass in deep snow. They found the place where they'd run up the slope after the Marroc, the snow still pockmarked by their steps, and then the scar in the white where the Marroc had fallen and slid and almost gone over the edge. They found where Gallow had killed Hrothin's brother and, as they burrowed into the snow, the stains of his blood.

Gallow watched. There were other tracks here. Someone had come back after the fight. Hard to say whether it was one man or two, certainly not more, but the way the snow had been scattered about made it clear they'd been looking for something. The Lhosir poked about until Beyard pushed them all away.

'Back! Before you make it worse!' He turned to Gallow, face hidden behind his mask. 'Are you lying, Foxbeard? Was the sword never here?' But he knew better. Arithas and Hrothin hadn't paid it much thought at the time but they'd noticed the blade he'd drawn was longer than they were used to and remembered it falling into the snow. They'd been there and they'd seen it, even if they hadn't known the Edge of Sorrows for what it was.

The Lhosir untied him from his saddle and pulled him down and Gallow walked up the road, tracing the fight in his head. Arithas and Hrothin had beaten him down where Beyard was sniffing at the snow. One Lhosir had come further past, a few yards on to where Oribas had been. The snow there was churned and trampled, most of it pushed over the edge. A struggle, perhaps. The Marroc they'd saved must have run but Gallow couldn't see any other prints. He'd run through his old tracks then, which made sense because he'd have been quicker that way too.

Gallow looked over the edge. Trails of snow lay in broken lumps down the side of the ravine, but when he looked up the snow was pristine. It had fallen from the road then. Someone had gone over. Oribas, as Beyard had said; and then he saw the Aulian's satchel still hanging from the dead branch of a broken tree, a dozen feet below him.

When he turned, Arithas and Hrothin were right behind him. He looked them up and down. 'Which one of you threw him over?'

Arithas sneered. 'He didn't even—'

Beyard had tied Gallow's hands in front of him so he could knot them to his saddle. Gallow grabbed two fist-fuls of Arithas's furs and dropped to his knees. He drove his head into the Lhosir's groin and pulled, hard. Arithas doubled up and pitched forward onto Gallow's back. Gallow straightened, pulled him off his feet and let go. By the time Arithas even knew what was happening, he was over the edge. He shrieked once and then Gallow heard the crack of him hitting a boulder and the rattle of falling stones over the echoing hiss of the Isset below.

Hrothin grabbed him. 'And over you go too, *nioingr*!'

Gallow's fingers closed on Hrothin. 'Third time. Shall we go together then, brother?' he hissed. They were face to face, nose to nose.

'Hrothin!'

Beyard was too far away, though, and Hrothin's blood was up. 'Filthy *nioingr*!'

'Fourth time.' Gallow spat in his face. 'You have to stand by those words with steel now.'

'I have to stand by nothing for you, Marroc!'

'Hrothin!' This time Beyard's shout was so loud and deep that it seemed to rumble through the ground itself and at the same time shake the air. Beyard was stamping through the snow towards them.

'You must get cold out here under all that iron,' Gallow said.

'Where's Arithas?'

Hrothin snarled. 'The *nioingr* threw him over the edge.'

The iron mask turned to Gallow. Beyard's voice shook with cold fury. 'You'll hang for what you are, Gallow. A *nioingr*. No one will speak you out. No one will say your name. You'll be spat upon and dogs will eat the scraps of you and you'll be forgotten. You'll not cheat that fate. I'd thought you a better man, but Ironhand was right to name you Foxbeard. Leave him, Hrothin. Arithas was an idiot.' He pushed the two Lhosir apart and then punched Gallow in the face, the iron gauntlet smashing his nose and jarring loose a tooth. Gallow hardly saw it coming. He staggered back. As he did, Beyard stooped and snatched one foot from under him, tipping him over onto the road. The Fateguard dragged him by his foot through the snow and dumped him by the other Lhosir riders.

'Two men came here after the fight. They've already taken what we're looking for. They walked down the road and now we've trampled their tracks. One of them was hurt. He was leaning on the other.' He drove a boot into Gallow's ribs. 'Put this one back on his horse and tie him to it. We're hunting for Marroc now. If he gives any more trouble, cut off a foot. Or a hand. Yes, a hand. The king would like that.'

Gallow spat blood into the snow. 'I gave no oath about not killing your men, my friend. And that one murdered Oribas.' But quietly he wondered. *Two* men walked away? One of them was surely the Marroc. But the other?

8

THE BURNING

Oribas took his time leaving the wood, partly to give his heart a chance to stop beating so fast, and in part because he managed to get lost on the way out and wander through a lot more trees than he had on the way in. The Marroc were waiting in the middle of the field, sitting on their mules, watching like a pair of scared starlings ready to take flight the moment anything came out. They looked at Oribas in amazement.

'I have it trapped,' he said as he reached them. 'I'll need your help to kill it. Fire and cold iron. I'll need your sword.' When neither of them moved he poked Addic in the leg. 'Well? Shall we put a shadewalker to rest or shall we wait for the next rain or snow to take away my salt and let it go?'

Addic dismounted. Jonnic stayed where he was at first, but when Oribas reached the edge of the trees, he got down and followed. They let Oribas lead the way this time and he heard them whispering, cautiously but not cautiously enough, in the stillness under the trees. *What if he's leading us to it? But that's exactly what he's doing! But what if it's a trap? Have you lost your head? I mean he's an Aulian too: what if he's in league with the shadewalkers? Idiot.* At least there was no talk of throwing him into a ravine this time.

The shadewalker was where Oribas had left it, standing as still as a statue as though it had grasped the futility of trying to break the circle of salt and was simply waiting for it to go away. Addic and Jonnic crowded behind Oribas, who still wondered at their fear: if his circle of salt had failed then the shadewalker wouldn't be here. The hard part came when one of them had to step inside to finish it.

'Now what?' asked Addic.

'Light a torch.'

Jonnic fumbled with a tinderbox, dropped it, picked it up, struck a few sparks and burned his hand. He couldn't take his eyes off the shadewalker.

'Give it to me.' Oribas reached out but Jonnic jumped away as though the Aulian was a snake. Eventually the Marroc got a flame going and lit a brand. Oribas took careful steps closer, looking for the line of the salt. Salt and snow. Belatedly he realised how lucky they were that the trees here were dense enough to keep most of the snow off the forest floor. Out in the fields under their blankets of white his circle of salt would never have worked.

The shadewalker stepped back as though daring him to cross. It was watching him. Oribas took a fistful each of saltpetre and powdered metal from his pouch and crossed the line. The shadewalker sprang at him at once but Oribas was ready. He threw the powders in its face and stepped smartly back, stumbling a little as its sword swung past him. 'Now burn it!'

Jonnic stood frozen. Addic snatched the torch and threw it, straight and true. It hit the shadewalker in the chest and a whoosh of flame shot up. It dropped its sword and staggered, stumbling this way and that, trying to get away from the fire. Oribas picked up a lump of snow and hurled it. 'Cold pure water.' The flames were dying already, the metal and the saltpetre enough to scorch it but never enough to set it alight. He'd heard of some people using oil to burn the creatures, and Gallow said the Marroc of Andhun made an oil from fish which ran like warm honey and burned as easily as dried grass, but so far he hadn't seen a drop of it among the Marroc of the mountains.

Addic gave him a bemused look and then he and Jonnic began to pelt the shadewalker with snow. Oribas filled his hands with salt again. As the shadewalker reeled he stepped back into the circle and threw both handfuls. The shadewalker hissed and crackled, its skin blackening. A terrible smell knotted Oribas's stomach. The creature's struggles stopped. It fell to its knees and pitched forward and lay still on its soft bed of fallen needles and sparse trampled snow. The Marroc stared at it.

'Is it dead?'

'It was already dead,' said Oribas. 'That wasn't as much flame or salt as there should have been. It must have been weak already. It'll be still for a while now. An iron sword through the heart will end it for ever.'

Neither Marroc moved. Oribas rolled his eyes. He crossed the line of salt and knelt beside the prone shadewalker and started pulling at its mail. The Marroc just stared and backed away, and it was hard work doing it on his own because the shadewalker was big and heavy and stank enough to make him gag, and there was always the nagging worry that maybe his books were wrong and everything he'd heard wasn't quite as he remembered it and the shadewalker wasn't in a torpor that would last for hours, and what, exactly, was he going to do if it started moving again before he was finished?

He rolled it over, tipped another handful of salt over its face and went back to struggling to haul its mail high enough over its chest for someone to stab it through the heart. Addic came to help him at last and then Jonnic, both of them ashen-faced and quivering like squirrels but at least they had an urgency to them. When it was done, Oribas stood up. The two Marroc scuttled back, scuffing his circle of salt to ruin, a carelessness that would have earned Oribas a week of cleaning chores back when he'd been learning his craft. The three of them stood together, looking. Underneath its mail, the shadewalker's clothes were rotten and ragged and stained.

'Where do they come from?' asked Jonnic. Oribas shook his head.

'Aulia. The end of days, but no one knows for sure how they came to rise. The armour, their swords, their clothes, all these say they were the emperor's guard at the fall. No one knows exactly what happened. Not the start of it. When the city of Aulia itself died, it was no surprise that the rest of the empire collapsed. But as to *how* Aulia died?' He shrugged. 'As the histories I learned tell it, a black mist fell over the city that lasted for three days, and when it lifted, every single creature was dead. The few who escaped before it engulfed them say the mist swept outward from the imperial palace, but as to its cause?' He crouched down beside the dead thing, screwed up his face, fingers pushing down into ragged clothes and the cold dead flesh, searching for the gap between the ribs. 'Aulia was built on the slopes of a volcano. The emperors were ever digging tunnels under their palaces, always deeper. It's said the last one was searching for an entrance to the underworld, looking for his wife and sons lost at sea ten years before, but the Aulians were always diggers, always tunnelling under the earth. My teacher thought perhaps they broke open a monstrous cave filled with poisonous gas, for such things do occur and there had been times before when the mountain leaked fire from its summit and belched poison from the many caves and tunnels that riddled its flanks.' He stared at the shadewalker. Fumes, his master had always insisted. Poisonous air from the mountain that found a way from deep inside the earth through the emperor's tunnels; but Oribas knew of no gas that would make a dead man rise and walk the earth and neither did anyone else. 'Some say the emperor's tunnels finally reached the underworld and that a part of the underworld spilled out as a result. A punishment from the gods.'

'Modris and Diaran protect us,' whispered Jonnic, and both the Marroc made little signs to ward away evil. Oribas had seen Gallow do the same. He'd always laughed at such superstition, but not now, not with a dead shadewalker right here in front of him.

No, not dead, not yet. 'You need to finish him.' Addic handed Oribas the iron sword without even looking at him. Oribas waved him away. 'I've never held a sword in my life save to carry it from one place to another and I do not intend to start. You can do it. A simple thrust.' He poked himself in the chest over his own heart and then poked the shadewalker. 'Here. Between the ribs. Drive it deep and hard.'

Addic offered the sword to Jonnic. Jonnic shook his head and backed hurriedly away as though Addic was mad. Oribas stayed where he was, kneeling beside the shade-walker with fingers held where the sword would need to go. His hands were shaking. Addic lifted the sword and held it, point down and *his* hands were shaking too. He let the tip rest on the shadewalker's chest.

'There.' Oribas backed away. Addic's knuckles were clenched white. The Marroc muttered a prayer and rammed the sword hard down into the dead thing's flesh. At first nothing happened. The shadewalker didn't move or make a sound save for a twitch as the sword drove into it.

'Is it dead?' Addic stayed where he was, staring. Oribas found he didn't know. All he'd learned on shadewalkers and how to bind them and confine them and put them to rest but no one had said what happened afterwards. Some sort of release of the energy that held them between life and death seemed expected.

'Look!' Jonnic pointed. The shadewalker's flesh was starting to darken, only a tinge at first but then spreading rapidly. Its belly swelled up and then collapsed in on itself. Addic reeled away at the smell, the spell broken. Oribas caught a lungful of it and threw up, staggering away, scuffing the circle of salt himself this time.

'Gods preserve us!' He threw a handful of snow in his face and drew in lungfuls of clean air well away from the shadewalker. It was the sort of smell he was sure he would carry with him for ever, just a whiff of it, always in his clothes and his hair and on his skin. They gathered themselves together and went back to look, hands held over their mouths. Where the shadewalker had lain was now no more than a collection of bones. A skeleton dressed in rotten cloth and rusted mail.

'I'd swear that was a forkbeard when it was alive,' muttered Jonnic, and Oribas wondered if he might be right.

'Best forkbeard I've seen for a while then,' said Addic. 'Wish they were all like that.' He turned and a smile broke over his face and he grabbed Jonnic by the arms and shook him. 'Look! Look at it! Look at what we did! We killed a shadewalker!'

'*You* killed it, you mean,' said Jonnic. He looked distant and thoughtful, then a smile settled on his face too. 'We did, didn't we? We really did.'

Addic grabbed Oribas. 'They can be killed! They can!'

'Put to rest,' said Oribas mildly.

'Aulian, don't you see what this means? We can send the shadewalkers away!'

'I'm hoping it means you're not going to throw me into a ravine now,' said Oribas, and then he smiled too, because the flowering of understanding in another man was always a joy to see, whoever they were. 'Also food and shelter for the rest of the winter would be nice. Until the snows clear and I can make my way back over the pass. Do you think you could do it again now you know that it can be done?'

They rode back to the half-dozen houses that made up the hamlet of Horkaslet. Since no one would believe what had happened until they saw the evidence with their own eyes, Jonnic dragged the Marroc out of their houses and their barns to come across the fields. And after that, when they'd seen it, they forgot what they'd been doing and broke out the best food they had and got roaring drunk on mead and ale, both drinks that Oribas had never met before and hoped very much to meet again. The Marroc ate until their bellies were swollen. They sang songs and talked the stupid talk of drunk men, about how Addic and Jonnic would ride and rid the mountain valleys of the shadewalkers and then rid them of the forkbeards too while they were at it, until they all passed out in a stupor.

The three stayed another day and spent that evening doing more of the same before Addic decided they ought to be going back. They took their time about leaving, and as their mules plodded down the valley, Addic asked all manner of questions. He asked where to get the powder that made them burn – which Oribas didn't know, this side of the mountains, but he described the fish oil, and Addic nodded – and about shadewalkers and what had made them and about Aulia and about what other magic Oribas knew, until Oribas had to tell him there was no magic to it at all, but if they could find a way to get back his satchel from where he'd left it hanging over the Isset then he'd be happy to show them a trick or two.

They sheltered for the night in another barn with another farmer who knew Addic and Jonnic well enough but laughed heartily at their stories of killing a shadewalker. He told them they should drink less and looked askance at Oribas and his strange skin. After they left him, Addic was sombre. 'Three, this winter. Three seen already and the real cold hasn't come yet,' and Oribas had no answer to that; but later another thought crossed his mind.

'There's one thing I would ask of you. I'd like to know what happened to my friend, the Lhosir who saved your life, Addic. I would like to know if Gallow is still alive. Is there a way, do you think, to find out?'

66

9

BRAWLIC'S FARM

Beyard led the Lhosir from Varyxhun back down the high mountain pass. He rode at the front and now and then stopped and got off his horse and knelt down in the snow and pushed his face towards it and sniffed. Men left traces. Not only the tread of their boots but a deeper mark. It was said among the Lhosir that no one could evade the Fateguard once they had the sight of the Eyes of Time upon them, and it was true. Beyard closed his eyes behind his mask and touched the iron to the snow and knew, without knowing how, that two men had passed this way days ago, the two men that he was following. The essence of their presence remained.

He did it over and over again until he lost count of how many times, but as the light was starting to fade he did it once more and found they were not there, and knew that they'd left the Varyxhun Road. He turned the grumbling Lhosir around and led them back until he found a winding twisting track where men had passed since the last heavy snows. He sniffed again. This was the way.

He knew where they were going now. The track wound back and forth over a ridge and down into one of the higher valleys. From the top he saw smoke a few miles away. Chimney smoke. He stopped and pointed. 'That's where we sleep tonight.'

The Lhosir moved with purpose now, hurrying down the ridge before the day ended and plunged them into the deep quick darkness that came after a mountain sunset. They wove between stands of towering Varyxhun pines, across the uneven ground and the thick drifts of snow. They lost sight of the smoke, and when the last rays of the sun sank below the horizon they started to mutter among themselves. All of them knew how cold the mountainsides became at night and how quickly any warmth faded. Beyard snarled at them. Cold? He felt nothing else. Out here in the snow and ice and the falling dark, or in a warm summer meadow with the sun blazing down, or standing in the flickering orange glare of a funeral pyre. Always the same. Always cold.

He whipped them with words and it wasn't quite full dark when they spied the farmhouse ahead of them again, large and welcoming with its warmth, firelight flickering between the cracks in the shutters and sparks rising into the night from the chimney. One house for one family of Marroc, a couple of barns for the animals. Beyard felt the mood around him change. An easy fight, a full belly, mead and a warm place to sleep – yes, the Lhosir weren't muttering now – they were eager, but the coldness inside Beyard only bit deeper. None of those pleasures were his any more. Pleasures were forgotten things among the Fateguard. Cold and iron and the weave of fate were all he'd know for the rest of time. The Beyard of long ago yearned for something else, but that Beyard was a distant voice now, all but lost in a blizzard of howls.

The Lhosir dismounted and left their horses far enough from the farm not to be heard. They argued about what to do with Gallow, whether to leave him with a couple of men to watch him or to take him with them; and in the end they took him because they couldn't agree on who'd stay behind to do the watching. Beyard undid his bonds and tied him again, this time with his hands behind his back. 'So you don't throw anyone into something that's not good for them, *nioingr*.'

'That's the second time you've called me that, old friend.' Gallow's voice was as cold as the snow. 'A third time and it's axes and shields.' Under his mask the old Beyard stirred at that. Might even have smiled. Axes and shields. The right way to settle matters, not some spiritless hanging.

He pushed the Foxbeard on, letting the other Lhosir lead the way. The deep twilight was perfect. The Marroc would be inside and huddled around their fire. They'd probably eaten and they'd be sleepy. Might be as many as a dozen living here but only a handful would be fighting men. If it came to that then it would be bloody and short and swift, and the women and children would answer his questions, not the men. The women always knew all the secrets; and they always talked when you held their children over a fire for long enough. And once they'd talked, Beyard let them go. Lhosir didn't make war on women and children.

They were almost at the house, creeping through the snow, voices dropped to whispers, swords already out of their scabbards. The Lhosir at the front were creeping around the wall towards the door, peeking in through the cracks in the shutters when Gallow turned. 'If the Aulian is here, he's done nothing wrong, Beyard.' He stopped.

Beyard pushed him on. 'There was an Aulian. Arithas threw him into the ravine.'

'Two men came down the Varyxhun Road. There was only one Marroc that day. Oribas knows Solace for what it is. He'd know to take it and hide it.' The Foxbeard didn't believe in his own words though. It was hope without conviction.

'Your Aulian is a witch, is he? A man who can fly?' But Beyard frowned under his mask as he spoke. No way to know who made the tracks he was following, but it *was* a long way to climb just to go back for a sword unless you knew exactly what it was you were looking for. And how would some Marroc know the Comforter when he saw it?

'Did you truly bring it back?' He didn't need to ask, not really. In the snow where Gallow had said to look, he'd felt the residue of something that wasn't a man. The remains of a strand of fate that belonged to something other.

'I did.'

'Why?'

The Foxbeard looked at him as though the question had never crossed his mind. 'What else would I do with it, old friend? Who else should carry its curse?'

The Lhosir were at the farmhouse doors now, waiting for his signal. 'Kneel.' Beyard pressed Gallow down into the snow. He took another piece of rope and bound Gallow's wrists to his ankles. 'I have your oath that you won't run.'

'You do.'

'What does your Aulian look like?'

'Like an Aulian. Short and dark to our eyes.'

Beyard looked up and down the valley. Even if Gallow broke his oath there was nowhere for him to go. Hobbled as he was he'd never get back to the horses, and out here at night a man would freeze to death and Gallow wasn't strong, not now, not after crossing the mountains. 'If I don't find you here when I come back then I will hunt out your family. If they're still alive, I'll give them to Hrothin.'

He left Gallow there and headed for the farmhouse, waving at the Lhosir to break in. Dressed in all his clanking iron, a Fateguard was never good for stealth. Being noticed was what they were for after all; and so he left the other Lhosir to smash in the door to the Marroc farm and start the shouting and the screaming and, even though he ran after them, by the time Beyard crashed in, they were almost done. Three Marroc men lay dead or dying. Women wailed. One of them ran for a window and hurled herself at it, bursting through the shutters. A big man with an axe threw himself at the Lhosir going after her and got himself skewered for his troubles. The last man went down a moment later and

Beyard was left with a couple of Marroc women huddled quivering in a corner together and four children. The dead men scattered around the farmhouse floor were armed too well to be mere farmers.

'Bordas, Torjik, go and get the woman back. She can't have gone far. Niflas, go with them. Bring the Foxbeard in here before he freezes.' He turned to the cowering women and children and crouched in front of them, the iron mask of the Fateguard looming in their faces. They were terrified and they were right to be. 'Listen well, Marroc. Tell me what I want to know and I'll leave you be. Deny me and I will turn my back and let my soldiers do as they will. Two men came here some days ago. One of them may have been hurt.' He paused, watching their eyes, all of them. There was always one face to give the truth away; and yes, they knew the men he meant. His eyes settled on the one who gave away most. A boy a few years short of being a man. 'They had an unusual sword. Long and with a touch of red to its blade.' Yes. Solace had come here. 'And was one of them perhaps a stranger? A foreigner? A darkskin?' Yes to that too, but something was wrong. There were no glances towards the bodies as he asked his questions. The men and the sword had been here, that was clear, but now they were gone?

There was only so far they could answer with their faces. He walked to the fire and pulled out a burning branch. The flames licked over his iron gauntlet as he reached into the blaze but he never felt the heat, only ever cold. Between them the Marroc told him everything with an honesty born of fear. The bandit Addic had come with a half-dead Aulian he'd found on the road and, yes, the red sword too. They'd stayed a few days and then gone with another to hunt a shadewalker. Beyard took a while to believe that, but in the end he did. As for the sword, none of them knew. The men had taken it with them when they'd gone, or else they'd hidden it in the barns perhaps. The burning branch never left

Beyard's hands. It never once touched their skin.

Fear gives birth to truth. He rose when he was done, oblivious until then to the other Lhosir moving around him, tearing the house apart, helping themselves to food and mead or else simply standing, watching.

'The men we're looking for will return,' Beyard told them. 'We wait for them. These ones are not to be touched.' The Lhosir didn't like that but they could live with it. The Fateguard were joyless souls. He looked about, missing something. 'Where's Gallow? Where's the other woman? Where's Niflas?'

But it was a while longer before Niflas came back and when he did he held up a handful of tangled rope and dropped it at Beyard's feet. 'Bordas and Torjik are still looking, Fateguard, but they're gone. Both of them. Gone and taken our horses too.'

10

ACHISTA

In the failing light Gallow struggled with the ropes around him. He tried to bunch his legs to pull his hands in front of him, to bring the bonds to where his teeth could work on them, but Beyard had tied them too tight, and so he lay in the snow, rolling helplessly back and forth. Shouts and screams echoed from the farmhouse and then one of the shutters slammed open with a crack of wood and firelight spilled out into the night. A figure struggled from the snow-drift beneath the window.

'Marroc!' he cried. 'Marroc, here!'

The figure glanced his way, turned a moment, hesitated and then turned back. 'Who's there?'

A woman's voice. Gallow answered, 'I can lead you to the forkbeard horses.'

The figure ran towards him, arms and legs flailing through the deep snow. Yes, a woman. She stopped when she saw him though. 'You're one of them!' She turned away and started to run.

'Have you seen an Aulian? His name is Oribas!'

He couldn't think of anything else to say but that was enough. She stopped again. 'What's *your* name?'

'Gallow.'

The woman came back. She had a knife in her hand. She looked him over, face filled with indecision while the rest of her twitched with the desire to run far and fast before the Lhosir came after her.

'I can take you to their horses!'

'You're the one who saved Addic?'

The Marroc on the road? Gallow shook his head. 'I never knew his name.' He rolled and turned his ropes towards her. 'Quickly!'

'Addic brought your Aulian friend here. He spoke of you. Fine words.' The woman knelt beside him and took her knife to the ropes that hobbled him. *She'd seen Oribas!* Somehow he'd been thrown off a cliff and lived!

'We crossed the mountains together. Is he hurt?'

The rope snapped free. The Marroc woman shook her head. She kept glancing back at the farmhouse. The crashes and cries from inside had been muffled by the snow but now they'd fallen quiet. The Lhosir hadn't yet come out to chase her down but maybe that was because they didn't think she'd get far in the dark. The need to run filled her eyes as she sawed at the rope around his wrists. 'Gallow. I've heard of you. Everyone has. Gallow the Foxbeard, who turned on the forkbeard prince and cut off his hand and stole away with the Sword of the Weeping God. No wonder they have you all trussed up.' She gave him a hard look. 'How do I know you won't cut off mine?'

'You don't. But I won't.'

'Forkbeards were everywhere looking for you a few years back. Murderous mad they were about what you did. Still are, I expect.' The rope split and Gallow's hands flew apart.

'I had my reasons.'

She looked him up and down, the knife held between them, the point at his belly. 'You can keep them. Forkbeards murdering forkbeards is good enough for me.' She took a wary step away. 'Lead then, Gallow Foxbeard, and move fast. Don't you worry about me following. I'll be there, just not so close in case you lead me false.'

'Why would I do that?' Gallow picked himself out of the snow and set off at a run, following the Lhosir tracks back the way they'd come. The moon gave enough light; the woman would have seen them easily enough without him.

'Forkbeards are forkbeards, that's why.'

The horses were exactly where the Lhosir had left them, stamping their feet and snorting at the deepening cold. Gallow let them all loose and mounted one. He watched the Marroc woman throw herself at the back of another and scrabble and pull herself up until she was sitting upright. She didn't look like she'd ever been on a horse before. 'If you can't ride then you should come up with me.'

A derisive snort answered him. 'We go our separate ways now, forkbeard.'

Gallow shrugged. With a kick he urged his horse into the others, chasing them away and scattering them. Anything to make it harder for Beyard to follow. The Fateguard would, though. That was what they did. When he looked around, the Marroc woman was lying in the snow.

'*Nioingr!*' A shout from the farm pierced the night. 'Now we're going to kill you, Foxbeard.' The Lhosir had discovered his escape. They were coming. The woman looked at him, brushing the snow off her. Gallow reached out a hand.

'Get up behind me!' She was shivering already. The shouts from the farmhouse were getting closer and quickly. They weren't stupid. The horses were the first place to look.

The woman hissed at him. 'Go your own way, forkbeard!'

'Then I thank you for setting me free. Go back to your house, woman.' He turned his horse away from her. 'You won't escape these Lhosir on foot.'

'So sure?'

'They have a Fateguard with them. He'll find you.'

She ignored him, tried to mount her horse a second time and ended up flat on her back in the snow again. Gallow unwrapped his fur cloak and threw it at her. 'Take this at least! You'll not last the night out here without it.' And without it *he'd* likely freeze too. He'd have to kill the horse.

75

Find a deep drift and dig in until the morning. Kill the horse and climb inside its carcass like Hostjir had done in the old sagas. Was that even possible?

The woman looked at the furs and then looked at him. 'Damn you, forkbeard.' She picked them up and threw them back at him and then stood beside his horse and held up her hand expectantly. 'Well, help me up then.'

As soon as she was pressed up behind him and Gallow had wrapped the furs around them both, he felt a jab in his ribs through his mail. 'I still have a knife, forkbeard. You might have saved my brother Addic and you might have helped me out but that doesn't make us friends. I'll fillet your liver if you even blink wrong.'

Gallow almost smiled but then a bitterness welled up inside him. Arda might have said the same, the wife he'd left behind. She'd come from the mountains too. Did they make all Marroc women like that up here? He missed her. Three years spending every day trying to find a way back to her, and now he'd come so far and was so close to what had once been home, and ...

But now wasn't the time. He pushed the horse on and drove it as hard as he dared through the night, following the trail the Lhosir had made back to the ridge and winding down the other side, back to the Aulian Way, the Varyxhun Road as the Marroc called it. The snow here was only a few inches thick. Older falls had been piled into embankments on either side and had half melted in the afternoons and then frozen like granite each night, over and over until there were ice walls on either side of the road half as tall as a man. He pushed on and on down the gorge of the Isset towards Varyxhun while the night grew ever colder. The woman stayed slumped against his back. He thought she was asleep until she suddenly shifted and poked him. 'Here! Stop! Go up that trail there.' In the dark he could hardly see it, but when she pointed, there it was, a break in the ice wall beside the road and a narrow path up through the trees. The horse was close to the end of its legs, breathing hard, fighting against the cold. His own hands and face were numb too.

'Where are we going?'

'Never you mind. It's not far and that's all you need to know.'

The last ten minutes were slow. The black branches of the trees blotted out the sky and the stars and the moon flickered between them. The track wound back and forth, climbing up the slope. It was hardly a track at all in places and Gallow had to stop more than once to see which way it led, but it ended at a tiny log hut, empty and with no door. The Marroc woman slipped out from under their furs and went inside. Gallow blew on his hands and rubbed them together, trying to find some feeling in them again. The horse snickered and butted him as he got off. He patted its neck. 'Sorry. No blankets.' Likely as not the cold would kill it before the morning and then they'd be on foot and Beyard wouldn't be far behind.

The Marroc woman was building a fire. 'Woodsman hut,' she said as he came in. 'No one comes here this time of year.'

'Except Marroc hiding from forkbeards?'

She gave him a sharp look. 'I still have my knife. Don't you try anything.'

Gallow looked at the door, at the roof. Too small to coax their horse inside. He went back out and tied it as close to the door as he could, then stripped the saddle off its back and tied his fur cloak around it instead.

'What are you doing?' The Marroc woman looked at him as though he was mad. 'We'll need that!'

'How far is it to Varyxhun on foot?'

She shrugged, striking sparks now at a little nest of tinder. 'Three days, give or take. Depends how fast you walk.'

'Beyard will catch us before then.'

'Never heard of him,' She cupped her hands over the first tiny flame and blew softly, fanning it.

'The Fateguard.' Which didn't mean anything to her, so he added, 'The one in the iron mask.' *That* did. She looked up sharply and made the sign of Modris the Protector. 'So we need the horse.'

She snorted. 'People see you riding a forkbeard horse in Varyxhun, they'll have you off the back of it and hanging from a gibbet before you can blink.'

'And why shouldn't I ride a forkbeard horse? I'm a forkbeard.'

She straightened and looked at him long and hard. 'Yes.' Her fingers tightened on the knife. 'Yes, you are.'

He helped her to build up the fire, careful to stay away from her as best he could in the cramped space of the hut. When it was done he curled up as close as he dared and let its warmth seep into him. The Marroc woman sat on the other side, watching. Her eyes drooped but never quite closed; and why would they, when all the Lhosir had done among the Marroc was a litany of rape and slaughter and carnage? No, he understood her wariness. In her place he'd feel the same.

He closed his own eyes and rubbed the feeling back into his face and fingers and listened to the silence of the woods, and then suddenly light was streaming in through the door and it was morning. He blinked and sat up. The Marroc woman was fast asleep, snoring gently. He stoked the embers and then went outside and there was their horse, still on its feet, pressed against the wall of the hut with his furs wrapped around it. It gave him a baleful look and nudged him as he searched the Lhosir saddlebags for anything to eat. Back inside he shook the Marroc woman; as soon as he touched her she jumped and scrambled away, one hand going into the fire in her haste, the other grabbing for her knife. Gallow backed off as far as the walls would let him.

He sat down and tore bread from the Lhosir saddles in two and threw her half of it. She snatched it out of the air, then looked at her hand and winced. 'Forkbeards are full of lies!'

'Oribas would have something for that.'

'The Aulian.' The anger fell out of her face. 'What do you forkbeards want with him? What's he done?'

Gallow shrugged. 'It's not Oribas they're looking for, it's the sword I was carrying.'

She stared at him, and for a moment the mistrust vanished into wonder. 'Gallow Foxbeard and the Sword of the Weeping God. So it's all true, is it?'

'Was Oribas there? And the sword? Has Beyard got them both now?'

The old look of suspicion settled back over her face. 'There was a shadewalker. Your Aulian claimed he could put an end to it. Addic went off with him to see if he could.'

'Where did they go? How do I find him?'

The woman took a deep breath and then seemed to come to some decision. 'Horkaslet. They went across the ridge to Horkaslet.' Then her hand flew to her mouth. 'We have to stop them from going back to the farm! The forkbeards will be waiting for them!' She still held the knife and now she waved it in Gallow's face. 'You! You have to take us there. Quick! Before it's too late!'

11

A WARM WELCOME

The Marroc were cheerful as they rode the last miles towards home. Oribas tried to let the mood take him with it, but there were too many glooms weighing on his mind. Gallow, his strange and unexpected friend for the last year. Whatever he'd told the Marroc, whether or not the gods had sent Gallow as an answer to his prayers, he was still just a man returning to his family. Harsh of fate to let him come so close to what he so wanted and then take him. And then there was his own fate too, hanging loose in the great weave now the Rakshasa was gone, flapping in the wind. The monster had given him a purpose and a direction and now that was over.

He stopped and got off his horse while the Marroc wandered on. They were riding beside a stream, rustling its way down from the mountains, swathed in ice but not so frozen that the water didn't break through here and there. He cleared a patch of snow, plucked a blade of grass and tied a knot in it and set in the water. 'If you've killed him then you've done wrong. You should have let him have his last years among those he loved. If not, if you truly sent him to me to kill my monster, leave him be. Give him his peace.' They were words spoken to gods, though the only gods Oribas knew were the old gods of Aulia and they were far away. As an afterthought he set another knotted blade adrift. 'If you've killed him then I would like to go home now.'

Jonnic waited up the path. Addic walked slowly back. 'Have you found something, Aulian?'

Oribas shook his head. 'A little prayer, that's all. To wish us all to our homes in warmth and safety.' He pushed past Addic and mounted again. The desert where he'd been born was littered with temples to the Aulian gods, all empty and desolate now, abandoned just as the gods themselves had been after the empire fell. To the desert child in Oribas, water was the sacred goddess and always had been. Quiet and unassuming, asking little save that she be nurtured with love and care, fickle though, and deadly when she withdrew her blessings.

'Amen to that.' Addic followed him and together the three rode in silence over the rise to Brawlic's farm. Smoke rose from the chimney. There was no one about. Maybe that was to be expected late on a winter afternoon. Oribas's world had little to say about farms, nor about mountains or winter or all this cold and snow and how men set about living in the middle of it.

The Marroc left their horses in the barn and called out, and suddenly there were armed men everywhere, soldiers like the men in the road that Gallow had fought, big and tall, cloaked in thick heavy furs with mail underneath, with axes and shields and swords at their sides and helms that hid half their face but not the braids of their forked beards.

'Forkbeards!' Addic had his iron sword in his hand as the Lhosir reached him but they didn't stop to trade blows. The first charged into him, taking Addic's sword on his shield, and battered him back, and before he could find his balance, the next one crashed in and knocked him to the ground. Jonnic was already running with three more Lhosir chasing after. Oribas simply stood where he was, helpless and with no idea what to do.

'Alive!' A monster came out of the farm behind the soldiers, a terrible golem made of black iron, or so it seemed at first until Oribas understood that this was simply a man, huge and fierce perhaps, but a man clad in metal. He wore a crown on his head and a mask over his face. 'Alive, you dogs!' he cried again, and then he saw Oribas and came straight towards him. There were more Lhosir behind him, swords drawn, watching. Addic cried out, a scream of fury and fear, as the forkbeards pinned him to the ground. The metal man strode closer.

Oribas turned to flee but barely managed a handful of strides before an arm with fearsome strength caught his shoulder and spun him round and a palm smashed into his face and knocked him flat. He blinked, bewildered by the brightness of the sky, and then darkness fell as the shadow of the iron man loomed over him. The mask was a twisted visage, as though of a demonic man burned deep by fire. Between vertical slits in the metal, deathly pale skin hid among the shadows. Oribas squealed, 'Shadewalker!' It was the first thought that came into his head. His hand was at his side, resting on the shoulder bag where he kept his salt – he scrabbled back in terror and scraped out as much as his fingers could claw together and threw it at the iron mask. A moment later a boot stamped on his arm, hard enough to bruise bone, and pinned him there. A spear point came to rest against his throat. The Lhosir soldiers around him laughed.

'Not a move, Aulian,' the spearman growled.

The iron man tore off his gauntlets and the mask and crown and clawed at his face. His skin was sallow and greasy, his hair lank and ragged, but he was no shadewalker.

The spear point dug into his skin. 'What have you done, Aulian?'

'Salt,' gasped Oribas. 'Only salt. I thought he was a shadewalker!'

The Lhosir roared with laughter and the spear withdrew a little. 'Salt in the eyes of a Fateguard? Maker-Devourer, but that's a thing. You have a fierce heart in there, Aulian.' The Lhosir's eyes gleamed and the spear waved over his face again. 'Stay right where you are if you want to keep it beating.'

The iron-skinned man rubbed snow in his face. He took his time and then slowly replaced his mask and crown and his gauntlets. He turned to Oribas, who squirmed with fear again, not sure which looked worse, the iron man or the spear that would skewer him if he moved. The iron man growled. 'Let him up, Niflas. If he runs, catch him.'

Niflas lifted his spear and backed away, laughing. 'This one? He couldn't run from a flock of angry birds.'

'If he gets away from you I'll make a cloak out of your lungs.' The iron man came closer.

Oribas stared up as the Fateguard towered over him. 'What are you?'

The iron man ignored his question. 'Aulians don't come over the mountains any more. You're the first that isn't a shadewalker for twenty years. But you didn't come alone, did you?'

The Aulian didn't even blink but Beyard saw the answer in the sparkle of his eyes. He nodded, as much to himself as to anyone. 'No, I know who you are. You came across the mountains with Gallow the smith's son, Gallow Truesword, Gallow the Foxbeard.'

Foxbeard. The Aulian's eyes flinched and gave him away. So Gallow had called himself Foxbeard, the name King Medrin had given him.

Beyard looked over his shoulder. They had the second Marroc now. He'd take them inside and deal with them properly: show them their women and their sons and daughters, still alive and unharmed, and tell them exactly what they would have to do to keep them that way. There would be no mercy for the men and they'd know it. Pointless to pretend otherwise, but he'd send them back for Cithjan's judgment for the sake of things.

He turned to the Aulian again and held out Gallow's locket. 'The Foxbeard. He's still alive.' Strange, the flash of glee he felt at that, same as when Gallow had thrown Arithas into the ravine. 'Why did he come back. Because of this?' He waved the locket. Wide eyes said yes. Sixfingers would never believe it but Beyard did for he'd seen the same answer in Gallow's own eyes. All this way for a woman. For his sons, and so that was how Beyard would find him again. He looked at the Aulian, peering hard as if he could look inside the man. 'And you? Will he come for you?' The Aulian thought not. Beyard's eyes bored harder in, searching the twisted skeins of fate that ran though him and finding strangely little. 'What have you done, Aulian? What is your crime?'

The Aulian shook his head. 'None ... nothing.'

'Then why are you are afraid?'

'You ... I am afraid of you.'

Underneath his mask Beyard's face didn't change. *Of course you are, Aulian.* 'But there's more. What are you hiding?' The Aulian shook his head. 'But I smell a death on you, Aulian. You have killed.' A strange death, though. Not fresh but old as stone.

The Aulian closed his eyes. His head drooped as though he was announcing his own death. 'A shadewalker. I helped to lay a shadewalker to rest.'

Beyard sat back on his haunches. So it wasn't the red sword. Killing a shadewalker – that wasn't what he'd expected at all but the Aulian wasn't lying. The Fateguard cocked his head. 'You're a brave man to face one, Aulian, and a clever one to win. You should be proud, but all I see is fear. Why so afraid?'

He asked about the red sword but all he got was confusion. The Aulian knew exactly what it was but he had no idea of the where and so Beyard let him be, telling the Lhosir to treat him well. He'd go back to Cithjan with the others, but as far as Beyard could see he'd done no wrong. He might even take the Aulian back to Varyxhun himself and let him go; and then he wondered at that. Why? For the Foxbeard? Yes, but then still, why? Why did Gallow's return trouble him so?

No matter, not now. He would get to work on the Marroc. They knew where the sword was hidden and it wouldn't take long to convince them to share their knowledge. As for Gallow, there was only one place he was going. Fate whispered patience in Beyard's ear and so he took his time. He settled himself in front of what would have been a pleasantly warm fire for any but a Fateguard and stared at the two Marroc. He still had their women and their children, all well and unharmed, all with their fingers and hands still attached in all the right places and none of them scarred by burns, not yet. He showed the Marroc his mercy and explained with slow and careful patience how their womenfolk and their sons and daughters might stay the way they were, and though the Marroc refused to say a word, in the end they gave themselves away, eyes darting here and there, answering his questions without a sound, looking to the place where the sword was hidden. Beyard had his men rip up the floor, had them pull back the skins and furs and dig in the remains of an old firepit beneath. They didn't have to go far to find a wooden crate half-filled with bundles of arrows and a few old swords underneath. He looked at the Marroc askance when the Lhosir showed him what they'd found and gave a little nod. The Marroc men had sealed their fate and they knew it. Varyxhun would see two more gibbets.

The red sword wasn't in there with the rest, but all he had to do was look from the stash of arrows to the quivering women and children and they were telling him before he even said a word, confession flowing out like he'd broken a dam. Hidden under the hay in the barn, and five minutes later he had it in his hand. He swung it in arcs and listened to the air moan as the red steel cut it. The wailing of ruined souls, perhaps, or maybe simply the way the steel had been forged.

12

VARYXHUN

Her name was Achista. He got it out of her after the second night when they were sneaking into the barn of some Marroc farmer she didn't like. 'Forvic has a loud mouth when there are none of you forkbeards around but he's happy enough to take your coin when he thinks there's no one to notice. It'll be a pleasure to make some trouble for him.' Gallow simply nodded and told himself that he wanted no part in this, that it was none of his concern what Marroc did to forkbeards or forkbeards did to Marroc. All he wanted was to go home.

He touched a hand to his chest, to the locket he'd carried there for the last three years, only to remember that Beyard had it now.

'Praying to your uncaring god, forkbeard?' Achista settled into farmer Forvic's hay. Gallow kept carefully away from her. 'Or are you looking for your heart? Wasting your time there. You lot don't have any.'

She didn't want to hear his story, not at first, but for some reason he needed to tell her. He said little about the early years, fighting in the Screambreaker's army, killing Marroc left and right. He'd been the same as the rest of them then. They'd none of them seen any wrong in it – just the way of the world, the soldier's way, the strong taking from the weak – and he could say he was sorry as much as he liked; it changed nothing about what he'd done and she'd never believe him anyway. So he told her the truth and left it that, and then how after the war was done he'd turned his head towards Aulia; how he'd met Arda on the way and all the little things that sparked between them. How she'd shouted as he'd left her to fight the Vathen, how he'd sailed with Medrin to bring the Crimson Shield of Modris back to Andhun, the bargain he'd struck with Corvin Screambreaker and everything that had followed. Years adrift, and now all he wanted was to go home to Nadric's forge and make nails and wire and horseshoes.

He thought perhaps she'd fallen asleep long before he finished and perhaps she had, but in the morning when she looked at him he found her face was softer than it had been the night before and she put a hand on his arm instead of poking a knife at his ribs. He saw the fear in her eyes, the almost-knowledge that they were too late, and that was when she told him her name.

They reached Horkaslet late in the afternoon to find that the Marroc and their strange Aulian friend had left the morning before; and since there was only one trail to be followed for the last few hours to Horkaslet and they hadn't crossed paths, they both knew it was pointless to go in pursuit. They did anyway, Achista's face tight with grief amid the joyful Marroc of Horkaslet, still drunk at the slaying of their shadewalker. They rode on into the night and found the farm where Addic and Oribas had stayed only the night before, and in the morning they rose with the dawn and set off for the mountain trail over the ridge into the next valley and Brawlic's farm. Their Lhosir horse fell lame that afternoon and so they walked the last of the way along the mountain stream, back to the farmstead they'd fled together three nights before. Perhaps the walking was as well, for by the time they saw the gibbet they were both too tired to run. Achista stared while tears ran down her cheeks. Gallow's stomach clenched with an old anger. At least the hanged man hadn't been ripped open to have his lungs splayed like wings from his back. Then she ran and Gallow turned his head, not wanting to see any more. Beyard had done this. His oldest friend had hanged this man and Gallow couldn't bring himself to see what else he'd done inside. He wished he had a sword with which to follow her in case Beyard's Lhosir had lingered; but in time she came out again and there were others with her, Marroc women and children, and they stopped at the threshold and stared at him. They were too far away for him to read their faces but he felt their hate.

'Go!' Achista snatched the reins of the horse from his hand. 'Filthy forkbeard. Just go!'

Gallow stared at the hanged man. 'This is why I did what I did. This and far worse.'

Achista spat at him. 'That was Brawlic. This was his farm. Those are his sons and his daughters. Would you like to see them weep for him?'

'I'm sorry about your family.'

A useless thing to say but he couldn't think of anything else. Her stare was a hard one and he deserved all of it. She shook her head. 'They weren't my family, but Brawlic was a good man. Then again, he's not the first good man you forkbeards have murdered and he won't be the last either. The iron devil of Varyxhun has taken my brother Addic and your Aulian friend too and I *will* avenge them, and if you see him before you die, you tell him that.' She spat again, at his feet this time.

'Where?'

Achista turned away, leading the Lhosir horse towards the barn. Grief had made her older.

An animal growl built in Gallow's throat. He went after her, grabbed her by the shoulder and spun her around, and for a moment she was afraid of what she saw in him. '*Where*? Where did he take Oribas?'

She pulled herself free. 'You don't change, do you?

Forkbeards for ever, whatever you say. Addic and your Aulian friend were here the night before last. The iron devil left for Varyxhun with a dozen forkbeards at first light this morning. Two days from now they'll be in Varyxhun castle. The day after that Cithjan will hang them. They're dead, Gallow. Your friend. My brother.'

Half her face cried out to him in pain. The other half saw just another forkbeard and looked at him full of furious murder. She walked away, and Gallow knew better than to follow.

'Varyxhun.' He nodded to himself. 'Very well, old friend. I was heading that way anyway.'

They'd left the Marroc women and children alive and untouched, and that, Beyard knew, was right and decent. The Lhosir didn't make war on women and children but the Marroc men were a different matter. He hanged the farmer and had the others bound and hooded. The Aulian he allowed to ride free. The Aulian, as best he could see, had done nothing wrong and the man made him curious.

'Gallow was a friend once,' he said, but the Aulian always had eyes full of terror and dread whenever Beyard looked at him and he soon gave up. No one ever had words for a Fateguard, only screams.

The road up to Varyxhun castle split from the Aulian Way a mile from the city gates and zigzagged back and forth up the mountainside, six tiers of it, through six impassable gates beneath six murderous walls. There Beyard handed over his prisoners for Cithjan to do as he wished, for they were his problem now. Gibbets for the Marroc at the very least, but the Aulian seemed valuable and, as far as Beyard could see, innocent; and so it came as a surprise some days later when he found the Aulian had been sent off to the Devil's Caves with all the rest. The waste troubled him but he had other business.

'So many years, old friend, but we are not ones to forget.' He took off his iron gauntlets, opened Gallow's locket and sniffed at the tiny snip of hair that lay inside. 'I will find them, old friend. I will be waiting.'

13

THE CRACKMARSH

Reddic ran fast through the cold muddy water meadows of the Crackmarsh. The sunlight was fading. His lungs burned and his legs too, but he ran anyway because no amount of pain was worse than stopping, not with what was following him. He'd come into the swamp with an axe on his hip and a shield on his arm and two other men he barely knew. All those were gone now. The ghuldogs were all that was left.

He reached a small island, a low hump of sodden earth rising out of the shallow water, a few sickly old trees clutching it tight among a withered web of roots. He stopped for a moment, had no choice any more, just couldn't go on without a moment to rest, leaning against hard wet bark before his legs gave way beneath him. Back through the haze of rain he couldn't see anything except dull grey water and the scattered ghost shapes of other tree-crowned hummocks like watching sentinels. The ghuldogs were there, though, not far. Following him, steady and patient. Waiting for the dark. Waiting for his strength to fail. Waiting with their cold clammy limbs and their heartless rending claws and biting fangs.

A splash whipped his head round, desperate eyes searching for the source of the sound and finding nothing. He whimpered and pushed away from the trees, back into the water to run again. The clouds grew darker. The sun behind them sank further. The rain grew heavier. He was soaked.

Freezing water ran against his skin and down into his sodden boots.

'Modris!' The wail burst out of him as his legs failed. He stumbled and slip-sprawled into the water. They were behind him, close, and they'd eat him if they caught him, and so he forced himself onto his hands and knees and looked up. Somewhere there had to be strength left in him.

Shapes moved through the haze. Bent and hunched. Two, then three, then half a dozen. They came slowly, sniffing him out. They fanned around him and he knew this was the end. He had nothing left. When he tried to stand, he couldn't. On his hands and knees he watched them and wept his misery out. The ghuldogs sniffed closer. Cautious now that he wished they'd simply take him and be done with it. The closest of them stopped a stone's throw away, near enough to see it clearly through the rain. The relic of a man, sallow and gaunt, but with the head of a savage wolf, patches of mangy fur clinging to its skull, eyes burning red, fangs bared, saliva dripping from its jaws into the swamp. It took a pace closer and then another, each step slow and delicate and precise. Stalking him, though the time for stalking was long past.

Reddic closed his eyes. He fingered the sign of Modris the Protector hung on a loop of leather around his neck. Begged the god of the Marroc to save him though there was clearly no salvation to be had. A haunting hooting cry rang through the wind and the rain. Something between the howl of a wolf and an anguished cry of despair. He waited for the end.

A hand took his shoulder. He flinched and whimpered and screwed up his eyes, but the hand was just a hand – no talons, no fangs – and when he opened his eyes and looked up it was a man standing over him. A hard-faced Marroc man in mail with a spear, and when Reddic rose shaking to his feet, he saw that the man wasn't alone, that there were a dozen more in a cautious circle. The ghuldogs were still there as well, shapes in the rain-haze, watching.

The soldier helped him to his feet.

'I was looking to find Valaric's men.' Reddic couldn't keep the quaver out of his voice. 'I want to fight.'

There and then he didn't sound much like a man who'd picked up his axe and left his home to join the last free Marroc in their stand against the forkbeards but the soldier only nodded. There might even have been a hint of a grim smile. 'Well, you found us. Welcome to the Crackmarsh, Marroc.'

14

THE DEVIL'S CAVES

Oribas had told Gallow a lot of things when they'd crossed the desert together. More were forgotten than remembered but Gallow knew that the Aulians had come over the mountains once. Oribas said they'd never reached far into what were now the Marroc lands because the mountain valleys were too cold and wet for their liking, but they'd made their mark. Gallow had seen their work for himself: the fortress of Witches' Reach at the far mouth of the gorge, the impossible span of the Aulian Bridge across the Isset beneath it, the road that reached as far as Tarkhun, halfway to the coast, and of course the unconquerable stone of Varyxhun castle, etched into the bluffs that overlooked the city.

They'd built the first town of Varyxhun too but there wasn't much left to see of their handiwork now. It hadn't ever been much to the Aulians, but then the Marroc had come to the valley, drawn by the peace the Aulians had brought, and the town had grown. Gallow passed silently through the open gates. Aulians had stood here once, and later King Tane's huscarls, but now the soldiers who leaned on their spears and glowered at everyone who passed were Lhosir. They stared openly at Gallow's shaven chin and he heard their muted growls. *Nioingr.* One of them spat at his feet as they passed. He let it go. Had to. For Arda. For Oribas.

He stopped and looked past them. The main street of

Varyxhun ran straight as an arrow from the gates to the market square in the middle of the town. It was a river of half-frozen mud and slush, piles of dirty snow pushed up against the walls of the wooden houses that lined it. He'd come through here once long ago with the Screambreaker and his army, chasing after the fleeing Marroc king. They'd stopped for a while to throw a few spears and arrows at the walls of Varyxhun castle, perched up on the crags of the mountainside overlooking them, but not for long. Assaulting the castle was impossible. They'd already fought their way across the Aulian Bridge and then past the fortress of Witches' Reach that defended the entrance to the valley. They'd been tired and battered and bloodied by the time they reached the city, and there had stood the castle as it did today, staring down at them from hundreds of feet of sheer rock, the single narrow road winding back and forth beneath a slaughter of walls, defended by gatehouse after gatehouse after gatehouse. They'd settled for helping themselves to the town, feasting on its food and its mead and its women. They hadn't burned much, but then the Screambreaker had grown more thoughtful towards the end of his campaign. It was Tane he wanted, not the castle, and that meant making Varyxhun his home. They bled it dry but they hadn't killed it, and then it turned out that Tane had slipped out right under their noses and died somewhere in the mountains, weeks earlier while he was looking to escape along the Aulian Way. The war was suddenly finished, and when the Screambreaker turned his eye to the castle once again, he'd found the gates hanging open, the huscarls who'd defended them dead by their own hands. And that had been enough. The Lhosir had quietly melted away. They'd gone to Andhun, the last Marroc stronghold, and after that most of them had gone home.

Now Lhosir in mail and helms walked through the mud of Varyxhun once more. Marroc hurried past them, eyes down. Gallow hadn't been keeping track of the days, but Midwinter was surely close. In Middislet they'd celebrated for days, burning effigies of the Weeping God on Midwinter night and drinking mead until dawn to toast the birth of the sun and the first sunrise of the year, all of them roaring drunk. There were no hanging effigies of the Weeping God in Varyxhun though. Perhaps they had little to celebrate this midwinter.

Gallow wrapped himself in his furs, covering his face as best he could. The last time he'd been here had been in summer and these fringes of the town had been a sea of mud. The cold had changed that into hard frozen dirt covered in an inch of treacherous slime made of mud and animal dung and melted snow. At least the smell wasn't as bad as he remembered. Along the street by the gates, hanged men dangled from gibbets, blackened and withered by time, skin pecked to shreds, twisting languorously back and forth in the wind. There were half a dozen of them, Medrin, or whoever ruled here in his name, always reminding the Marroc of their lords and of the price of dissent. There was a tavern by the gates. It had been the Horn of Plenty once, with some of the best Marroc ale in the valley, but it had changed its name now – to the King's Hand, with a crude wooden six-fingered hand painted black hanging over the door. Whether the Marroc meant that as homage to their king or as mockery Gallow couldn't guess. He looked further along the road towards the market square where traders and travellers congregated. If there was any word to be had of Nadric the smith or Fenaric the carter it would be there. But when he asked, the Marroc all saw his Lhosir face and shrugged or turned away. As far as he could tell, no one knew the names. If they did, they kept their knowledge to themselves.

He slept in a hen house and left Varyxhun the next morning, alone and on foot with nothing more than the clothes he wore – mail and a helm under thick furs. He stared up at Varyxhun castle, wondering if Oribas was there, if the Aulian was already dead or whether he was still alive and in a dungeon, waiting to hang. Stared and wondered what he could possibly do, alone against so many, then looked with his fingers for Arda's locket around his neck and remembered again that it was gone. He bowed his head. No. There was nothing to be done. Alone he could make no difference.

I'm sorry. But I came here to go home, not to die.

He didn't give much thought to where he'd sleep or what he'd eat. He'd come this far. Fate would provide, and if he had to chop wood every night for a barn to sleep in and a bowl of soup, that's what he'd do. Middislet was maybe a dozen days away, fewer if he crossed the Crackmarsh. If Nadric had left Varyxhun then Arda would have gone with him and that's where they'd be. After three years of trying to get home, a few more days didn't seem like it should be too much bother, but he felt her closeness now, an urgency that grew quietly inside him. Every time he touched the place where her locket had once sat warm against his skin and found it missing, its absence felt like a fresh wound.

He avoided the Lhosir he saw on the road. The Marroc in turn steered away from him as soon as they saw his face and his eyes and knew what he was. He spent the first night in a barn and chopped wood even though the Marroc farmer was clearly terrified and desperate for this strange beardless forkbeard to go away. While he had an axe to borrow, he cut himself a staff for walking. A new pair of boots would have been nice. The old ones had seen him across the Aulian Way and the desert before. They leaked and had holes in their soles and his feet were wet and freezing.

Every time he stopped, he looked back, thought of Oribas and almost turned around, then thought of Arda and made himself go on. It felt wrong though. Weak. When one day he stood before the Maker-Devourer's cauldron and faced the challenge *Did you live your life well*? what could he say? Yes, I did, except for the day when I turned my back on a friend.

But I have a wife who needs a husband. Children who need a father. And one man against a castle? Even the Scream-breaker didn't try it and he had a whole army. Yet it still seemed wrong to simply leave. It was enough to make any man weep, a choice like that, but he knew he'd chosen what a Marroc would choose, not a Lhosir. He'd lessened himself.

On the third morning out of Varyxhun a pair of Lhosir warriors on horseback trotted by. They shouted as they came, warning him off the road, and a few minutes later he saw why. A heavy wagon appeared, a great creaking wooden cage of a thing pulled by six plodding oxen. Another Lhosir sat at the front, shouting and cursing at the beasts. In the back a dozen men were penned in the cage. Gallow stood off the road to watch them pass. The captives were mostly Marroc, shivering and freezing in nothing but rags despite the biting wind and huddled all together, but in their midst he saw another face, darker than the rest. Unmistakable. An Aulian.

'Oribas!' The Aulian looked up as the wagon drove on. Another Lhosir rider came past, bringing up the rear. He stared at Gallow for a moment, eyes lingering on the furs obscuring Gallow's clean chin before shifting deeper into the trees and snow along the roadside. His head kept darting this way and that as though he was looking for something. Gallow ran after him, caught up and trotted alongside him. 'What chance for a brother from across the sea to take a ride on your wagon?'

'You're better off walking,' snapped the soldier. 'And if you have deeds yet undone, get off the road well before the sun sets.'

'Why's that then?'

The soldier looked at him as though he was mad. 'New

to the valley, brother? Marroc, that's why.' That was what he was looking for. Marroc with bows, hiding in the trees.

'These prisoners – where are you taking them?'

'If you don't already know then it's none of your business.' The soldier stared hard at Gallow for a moment then curled his lip and went back to eyeing the trees. Gallow let him go, but as the wagon and its riders pulled away, he picked up his pace and kept it in sight. Oribas! It was as though the Maker-Devourer had heard him weep and had given him a second chance. No Lhosir could ignore a sign like that.

He tried to think. The Lhosir would want a place with stone walls and a good strong door. Witches' Reach was the obvious, yet in the middle of the afternoon the wagon turned off the Varyxhun Road and onto a track that was almost too narrow for it to pass, winding among the black bones of trees beside one of the thousand nameless freezing streams that ran off the mountains to join the Isset. Out of sight of the road, it stopped. The three Lhosir riders clustered with the wagon driver around the cage. The driver opened it, poking the prisoners out into the snow while the riders stayed mounted, eyes scanning the slopes for danger. They were nervous, all of them. The prisoners huddled together, backs against the wind until the riders waved their spears and herded them further up the track. The driver stayed where he was. He unharnessed his animals, whacking them with a stick to get them to move. Gallow watched a while longer as the soldiers hurried the shivering Marroc away up the track. The driver was turning his cart. Gallow racked his memory. There was nothing up here, nothing he could remember, only some caves, not even a village.

He stepped out of his hiding place and walked briskly along the track. The wagon driver was swearing at his animals so hard that he didn't even look up until Gallow spoke. 'Why not turn the wagon round on the road?'

The driver jumped almost a foot up into the air. He had a knife in his hand in a flash. Then he looked Gallow up and down and saw he was Lhosir and relaxed a little. 'Maker-Devourer! A brother should know better than to creep up on a man!' He frowned. 'What's a brother doing up here? This track doesn't go anywhere.' He didn't put his knife away.

Gallow shrugged. 'Hard place to turn a wagon this size. Want some help?'

The Lhosir stared. Gallow's furs were wrapped across his face, hiding his chin. Finally the driver put away his knife. 'That would be much appreciated.'

'But why not turn the wagon back on the road?'

The driver glanced up the track. The riders were almost out of sight. 'Last time we did that, three of the sheep collapsed before we even got this far. It's better if they can walk at least to the caves. I mean it's all the same in the end, but having to pick them up and drag them all that way …' He shook his head as he finally got all but two of the oxen separated from the wagon. 'Let's get this turned then. If you want to help, push on that side there.'

'Where you taking them?' Gallow asked, careful not to let his fur slip.

'Devil's Caves.'

Yes, that was the name, remembered from more than a decade past. 'And what do all those filthy Marroc do up there that's better than hanging from a gibbet?'

The driver laughed. 'Well …' He grinned and drew a thumb across his throat. 'Same thing, really. Just without …' He frowned, sudden caution in his eye as though he'd seen a thundercloud slide cross Gallow's face. 'Name's Fraggas. I don't recognise you, brother, and I know most of our kin who travel these roads.' His hand was slipping to his knife again.

'I think you've heard of me though.' Gallow let the fur slide off his chin. 'Gallow. Gallow Foxbeard.'

Fraggas the carter had just enough time for his grin to turn sour at the edges before the end of Gallow's staff hit him in the face and knocked him flat in the snow. 'You kill them, do you? Where no one sees. Is that it?' He didn't wait for whatever answer might bubble out of the carter's shattered nose along with all the blood but helped himself instead to the knife and the axe from Fraggas's belt. Then he ran up the path, following the trail in the snow. If the caves were close he needed to catch the other Lhosir quickly, before they started cutting throats. Somewhere a god was laughing at him. Fraggas had boots that looked fine and new and were just the right size, but Gallow had no time.

15

THE ICE CAGE

He ran hard, scrambling up past cascades and waterfalls until the track levelled again in a snowy ravine whose walls rose fast and grew quickly steep. The Lhosir soldiers saw him just as he caught sight of the caves where they were heading. The Devil's Caves, marked by piles of stones and bones. One of the riders turned and charged. Gallow lifted his walking staff as though it was a javelot, hurled it and threw himself into the snow, rolling under the rider's thrust. The staff caught the Lhosir in the face, knocking him backwards. Gallow didn't wait to see whether he fell. He ran on towards the other two who were already cutting down the scattering screaming Marroc. 'Oribas!' He could see the Aulian. Three Marroc were already dead, sprawled crimson streaks across pristine white. The rest were floundering through the snow, running as best they could with their hands tied behind their backs.

Oribas threw himself down beside one of the dead Marroc. The two remaining Lhosir riders split. One skewered the nearest Marroc while the other turned his spear at Gallow and charged. Gallow twisted away from the thrust. He grabbed the shaft of the spear and levered the point down into the snow and the earth beneath until it jammed against something solid and wrenched out of the rider's hand. As he passed, Gallow snapped around and hurled the spear with every ounce of his strength into the man's back. It caught the Lhosir between the shoulders. He arched and fell off his horse, howling. Gallow ran at him before he could get up, but now the first rider was coming back, his face smeared with blood from Gallow's staff and he still had his spear. The second was getting to his feet, swearing a storm and trying to shake the spear loose from his back where it was caught in his furs. He held himself crookedly. The spear might not have pierced his mail but it hadn't been wasted.

'*Nioingr!*' The first Lhosir spurred his horse at Gallow. Gallow watched the tip of his spear, looking to see which way to dive, but at the last minute the Lhosir's eyes flicked away from him to something further up the valley and he veered away. The second Lhosir had dislodged the spear and now lurched at Gallow, axe in hand. He held his shield awkwardly, his arm pressed in against his body as though he couldn't lift it any further. His face was strained with pain. With a shield of his own, Gallow would have laughed at him. As it was, he backed away.

The third rider hurtled past, cantering down the valley after the first. Something flickered through the air after them. He jerked in the saddle but kept riding.

'Give me your name,' hissed the Lhosir with the axe.

'Gallow,' said Gallow. 'Truesword to some, Foxbeard to others.'

'Truesword.' The Lhosir nodded. 'I heard the Scream-breaker gave you that name. I was at Andhun when he fell. I saw you there. I know your deeds both of that day and the day that followed. Not so true to our king, were you? Nothing but a Marroc-loving *nioingr* now. Pity. It would have been a fine thing to die by the hand of the old Truesword. Why did you do it?'

Gallow backed further away. 'Give me your name, brother of the sea. I'll speak you out after I kill you.' But The Lhosir didn't get a chance. As he opened his mouth, an arrow took him in the throat. Gallow threw himself flat and looked towards the mouth of the cave. Two men with bows were coming slowly towards him, arrows nocked, strings partly drawn. If he ran they'd both get a shot before he could reach any cover. His mail and his furs would probably be enough to keep out an arrow, but then there was Oribas.

A third archer was moving among the Marroc prisoners, calling back the ones who were still running and cutting loose each man as they reached him. Gallow scrabbled up to the dying Lhosir. The Lhosir's mouth moved but the only sound to come out was a choking cough as blood poured out into the snow. Gallow pulled at the Lhosir's shield. 'Maker-Devourer, I don't know this man but he faced me in battle and he fought well and he did not run. There is bravery here. I offer him to you for your cauldron.' He took the Lhosir's hand and pressed the dying fingers tightly around his sword. The soldier's eyes held his. *Thank you*, they said, then rolled back and he was gone. Gallow gave the spirit a moment to separate from the flesh, then took the man's shield off his arm and the sword out of his hand and rose to a crouch to face the archers. They'd stopped, thirty paces short, arrows at the ready.

'I don't care who you are,' he said. Behind the shield all they could see of him was his face. 'The Aulian prisoner is my friend and I'll take him. The rest is none of my business.'

One of the archers lowered her bow, but it was only when she spoke that Gallow recognised her. Achista! He knew her voice. 'What were you doing to that forkbeard?'

'I was speaking him out, Achista. It's our custom. He was brave. He didn't run.'

'But you should. If you had any sense.'

The other Marroc swore. 'He knows your *name*?'

Achista laughed. 'This is the one who helped me escape the iron devil. The Foxbeard.'

Gallow turned back to the dead Lhosir and unbuckled the man's belt. He eased it out then rose and slipped it on under his furs. Next he started on the boots. They weren't as nice as the wagon driver's but they looked good enough and were certainly better than his own. 'I don't have any business with you, Marroc. I came for the Aulian and now we'll leave with no blood spilt between us. You can have this one's mail and his helm. I'll have his furs.' Oribas would need them. The Aulian hadn't even seen what snow was until they'd reached the edge of the mountains. 'You won't see us in Varyxhun again.'

'You're not going anywhere,' said the other archer.

Gallow finished stripping the boots off the dead man. They were tight but they'd do. He slipped the shield back onto his arm and picked the sword out of the snow and turned back to face the Marroc with their bows. 'If you were going to shoot me then you should have done it when I had my back to you. I have mail under these furs. Your aim had best be sharp, because if you don't take me down with the first arrow then you'll not get another.'

'Achista!'

One of the prisoners was running towards her, another trotting less happily in his wake. Achista turned and her voice changed, suddenly filled with delight. 'Addic! You're alive! Thank Diaran! You stupid clod! And Jonnic! How did you let them catch you?' Gallow squinted at them. The first was the Marroc from the Aulian Way.

The Marroc slowed and stared at Gallow and his eyes widened. 'You? Has Modris sent you to be my guardian?'

Achista's eyes flicked over to Oribas and lingered just a moment longer than they needed to. They moved back to Gallow. 'Addic, what do we do with him?'

The other Marroc, the one who'd come up behind Addic, snarled, 'He's a forkbeard!'

'Jonnic, I wasn't asking you!'

Gallow didn't move. 'Among my people I'm a traitor with no name or honour. I will go. Let that be enough.'

The Marroc Jonnic spat, shivering in his rags. 'Addic,

Cithjan sent us both up here to be killed in the caves where he thinks no one will know. I say we put the forkbeard there.'

Addic was shivering too. No surprise, since the Marroc prisoners were wearing little more than shirts or tunics and half were barefoot in the snow. Gallow reached carefully back, never taking his eyes off the archer, and tossed him the furs from the dead soldier. 'No point saving your life just to let Father Winter have you.'

'No, Jonnic. Let him go.'

'He'll go and—'

Addic put a hand on the other Marroc's shoulder. 'It doesn't matter. A life for a life.' He let go, picked up the furs and nodded to Gallow. 'Debt paid, forkbeard. You can go.'

The archer behind Achista growled and bared his teeth as he lowered his bow. Gallow ignored all four of them. He strode and then ran towards Oribas, loosening his furs as he went. 'Aulian!'

Oribas was shivering like a leaf in the wind. Gallow threw him his furs and the Aulian dived into them. Gallow grabbed him by the shoulders and shook him. 'The Lhosir said they'd thrown you into the river! I saw your bag! How by the Maker-Devourer's beard did you end up here?'

Oribas's teeth were chattering. 'Well, they did throw me over the edge but not quite into the river. And after that, by way of the Marroc man whose life you saved and then a shadewalker and a devil in iron. Not to mention the coldest wind that has ever scoured this cursed earth. I tell you, Gallow, I might just be a simple man from the desert but I cannot see what woman in any land could be worth living in this when you could have the warmth of the sun on your skin.' He looked up at the sky, his eyes poking out from Gallow's furs. '*Is* that even the sun, or is it some feeble candle dropped by one of the gods as he passed in his chariot of clouds?'

'Cheer up, desert man. How many times have you been thirsty in my land, eh?'

'Do not speak too soon, Gallow – I might yet die of thirst because my jaw is frozen shut!' Oribas stepped back from Gallow and punched him on the shoulder. 'I thought you were dead, my friend.' His smiled faded. 'Like your friend in iron.'

'They were going to hang me but they found out about the sword. They took me with them to look for it and I escaped. I'm sorry, Oribas. I thought *you* were dead, and so I led them to you. Did they find it?' Oribas nodded. Not that it mattered to Gallow. Let Medrin have the Comforter.

He looked down the valley. The two Lhosir riders who'd fled were long out of sight. It would take more than a full day for them to get back to Varyxhun but Witches' Reach was closer. Behind him the Marroc were arguing among themselves. 'We can't stay here, Oribas.'

Oribas snorted. 'Gallow, I can't even feel my feet. I need a warm fire and some boots. And some clothes. And possibly to live in a different country. One that doesn't freeze my lungs with every breath.'

The Marroc were moving into the shelter of the caves now. Two of them walked off towards the trees, carrying axes. While Gallow watched, Addic came over. He was shivering and his face was blue with cold. 'I owed you my life, forkbeard, and now I've paid it back. I'd like to let you go, but …' He shook his head. 'You're a forkbeard. The others are afraid you'll lead your kin back here. We can't leave before the morning – the cold will kill us. Jonnic and Krasic will be back with what we need by then, and you go your way while we go ours. No blood. Will you share our fire in peace, forkbeard? Do I have your word?'

Gallow looked at Oribas. The Aulian was still weak from their crossing of the mountains, never mind everything since. He nodded. 'You have my word, Marroc.'

Addic turned to Oribas. 'Oribas of Aulia. We killed a shadewalker together. I won't easily forget that. You too are welcome to join our fire.' He looked back at Gallow. 'And you, forkbeard. I'll not call you an enemy but others might. I'd ask you leave your sword and axe aside.' A frown crossed his face. 'Why did you do it, forkbeard?'

'Do what?'

'On the road when the other forkbeards ...' He sighed and smiled. 'On the road. Why didn't you just let the Lhosir have me and walk on by?'

Gallow frowned as though the answer was obvious. 'Because when the strong do nothing, the wicked prevail.'

Addic nodded. 'Come on then. Even if they ride straight for Witches' Reach, no one's going to come looking for us until morning. We'll be long gone before anyone gets this far up the road.'

16

FRAGGAS THE CARTER

Fraggas didn't stay with his cart to see what happened after the *nioingr* smashed his face. He counted himself lucky to be alive and ran, leaving it turned half across the track and four of his animals wandering free. A Lhosir warrior wasn't supposed to run from anything but there were plenty enough Lhosir who did anyway, and even some who called themselves warriors. Maybe it was breathing all this Marroc air but, truth was, Fraggas had never been much of one for fighting.

It didn't help that he wasn't even back at the Varyxhun Road before two of the soldiers who'd been his escort came riding past, both at a gallop like the Maker-Devourer was nipping at their arses. They didn't stop, didn't even slow down, and so he ran as fast as he could until he reached the road and then wondered which way to go. He had maybe three hours of sun left before it got dark, three hours to get himself to some shelter, and it suddenly dawned on him that he was a Lhosir, alone, unarmed and on foot in country filled with hostile Marroc. The Marroc farms along the road were friendly enough places to their own kind, always ready to offer up a piece of floor and share their fire, but not to a forkbeard, and Fraggas was used to arriving at them with armed men at his back. The soldiers who'd come with him had been jumpy as rabbits from the moment they'd left Varyxhun. He'd heard their talk. It was getting worse. Marroc bandits on the roads, shooting Lhosir with their hunting bows and then vanishing into the woods. If you came away from Varyxhun then you came in numbers, with mail, helm and shield and preferably a horse, and Fraggas had none of those things.

He stood at the end of the track up to the Devil's Caves, wondering which way to go. Back towards Varyxhun meant slipping into a farmer's barn for the night and hoping not to be seen, but maybe there was some chance of meeting Lhosir coming the other way. Heading on towards the Aulian Bridge meant walking on after nightfall. He wouldn't get to Witches' Reach until long after dark but there was a garrison there, a few dozen men who kept watch on the bridge for Marroc robbers and highwaymen, and for the Vathen too. The soldiers on their horses would have gone that way. Maybe they'd send men back for him?

So he hurried down the road towards Witches' Reach, walking as briskly as he could. His furs would keep him warm enough in the day, but not once the night started to bite. He'd seen too many men out here lose their fingers and even their feet. Marroc mostly – maybe half the prisoners he'd carried to the Devil's Caves were losing pieces to frost by the time he got them there – and he had no intention of following their example. Sign of the times it was, that Cithjan sent Marroc off to be killed in secret. They hadn't had any of this last winter. It had been gibbets then, lining the road outside Varyxhun, but instead of breaking the Marroc it only seemed to make things worse. The valley men had never taken well to being ruled by a forkbeard and more and more Marroc kept coming over the bridge from other places, every man with an axe to grind, men who'd lost a friend or a son – and that was if they didn't go into the Crackmarsh to pledge themselves to Valaric the Mournful, although Fraggas quietly thought the Marroc of the Crackmarsh had their hand in the troubles of the valley too.

Yes, Varyxhun had become a magnet for all the resentment of the Marroc. The whole valley simmered like an angry pot. When you travelled the road you saw these things. You saw who came and who went. You heard it in the taverns among the other carters, the snips of conversation from tables on the other side of the room, and you saw the glances and the murderous anger, more and more of it. He'd heard the soldiers talking. There were men dying on the road every other day. They were bewildered by the Marroc. Across the sea a man had something he wanted to say then he said it, and if that meant a fight then that's what there was. He didn't say it with an arrow shot from the shadows and then vanish into the mountains. More and more the older Lhosir were talking of home and going back to their farms. None of them much understood why Medrin Sixfingers wanted to be king over all the Marroc. Even Fraggas couldn't see the point to it.

He never would either, because as he was wondering that, a cart came struggling through the muddy snow the other way, a creaking farm cart with three Marroc men sitting on the back who saw a forkbeard walking in a hurry on his own and saw too that the road was empty. As Fraggas passed them, they jumped off and pulled him down and gave him the good stabbing they thought every forkbeard deserved. They took his furs and helped themselves to his unexpectedly nice boots and rolled him into the snow at the side of the road and drove on, pleased at what they'd done.

Later, the same farmers passed the track up to the Devil's Caves without much interest, although everyone from these parts knew what the forkbeards did up there. They stopped at another farm as twilight fell and exchanged greetings with the men who lived there. They all knew each other, at least a little, and as a payment for their food and shelter they gave the furs they'd taken from Fraggas. Good warm forkbeard furs, if a little bloody, but blood could be brushed out once it was dry. Their hosts wanted the boots too but the farmer's son who'd put them on was less than keen because they were good and warm, and so he kept them and left not long after the sun rose.

The same boots meant they were dead an hour later, skewered by twenty Lhosir horsemen coming the other way and led by the iron devil of the castle. Fate had it that one of Beyard's forkbeards knew Fraggas well enough to know his fancy boots. As the last Marroc slowly died, Beyard leaned over him and asked him where he'd found them, and then thought it strange that a carter who was supposed to be on his way back from the Devil's Caves should have been alone on the Varyxhun Road, on foot and hurrying to the Aulian Bridge instead of on his cart back to Varyxhun with his escort of soldiers riding beside him. He thought about this and then changed his plan and followed the track towards the caves. He had the red sword, Solace, the Comforter, hanging at his hip, and wondered if he might soon be using it.

17

SPIRES OF STONE

The Marroc looked at Gallow with grim dislike. He couldn't blame them. Many of their kin had died on the end of his spear and he saw in their eyes how these ones hated him for that. But he told them about the wars when they asked and he spared nothing, and then he talked of the coming of the Vathen and how he'd tried to save Andhun from Medrin Twelvefingers, how he'd fought him in the Marroc duke's own rooms and cut off his hand and made him into Medrin Sixfingers instead, and how afterwards he'd fled the city before the Vathan horde. Their faces changed at that. Gallow the Foxbeard, the *nioingr*, hated among the forkbeards, hunted for years. Several of them had heard of him, but nothing good. The forkbeards had turned Varyxhun on its head searching for him. They knew his family was somewhere hereabouts but they didn't know names and so they'd asked and searched and they hadn't much liked it when they hadn't found what they were looking for.

Gallow lapsed into silence as he listened to the Marroc talk. Beyard. The Fateguard had the snip of Arda's hair he'd carried all this time. He had her scent. The Edge of Sorrows alone wouldn't be enough for Medrin. He had to get to her first, before Sixfingers. Before Beyard, if he could.

He left the Marroc to their fire and wandered further into the caves, carrying a brand with him to light the way. The back of the cave, wide and flat-bottomed as though it had once been a river, rose into the mountainside. It wound steadily upwards for several minutes, a good wide passage, and then led him to a stone balcony over a vast amphitheatre, too large for the light of his brand to even touch the other side. Shadowy columns rose from the floor to the roof. Dim spikes of rock grew upward, and when he followed them he saw that more hung like icicles, dripping out of the darkness above, hundreds of them. When he held up his brand and peered across he still couldn't make out the other side but his flame flickered. He felt cold fresh air, just a wisp of it blowing over his face.

Then he looked down. A few feet below him lay a mound of bodies. He'd seen piles like this after battles when the dead were heaped together to be burned. There must have been a hundred of them. They hadn't rotted and there was no smell. They were frozen.

He went back, and there must have been something about the look on his face because the Marroc stopped their chattering and stared, and then Achista snatched a brand of her own and ran back to see, and Oribas and Addic too. Gallow kept his silence.

'Bastards.' Achista's face was pinched when she came back.

Addic looked at Gallow and shook his head. 'It was your kind that did this,' he said. 'Remember that.'

'Surely they were guilty of some crime?' said Oribas.

'The crime of being a Marroc!' snapped Addic.

'No, no!' Oribas raised his hands and shook his head the way he always did when he was about to explain to someone why they were wrong using arguments forged from unshakeable calm and rational logic, and which more often than not ended with him being dumped on his backside.

'Yes.' Gallow stopped him with a glance. There was no place here for a scholar's debate. 'Even Medrin never killed without a reason, but whatever that reason was makes no difference. When a man is put to death then his passing should be seen. It should be heard. Men might speak against him and others might speak for him. No matter the guilt, a death should carry a weight. A significance. My brothers of the sea would never treat one of their own like this, not even one they splayed apart and hung as the bloody raven of a *nioingr*. What they've done here is for animals, Oribas, not for men.' He glowered at the fire. 'Medrin. It wasn't like this before Medrin.'

No one spoke. Gradually the Marroc settled to sleep, but as Gallow closed his eyes, Achista crouched beside him. She hissed in his ear, 'It wasn't King Sixfingers, forkbeard. It was your precious Widowmaker. He was the one who started this.'

At dawn they rekindled the fire at the mouth of the cave and sat around it in glum silence, waiting for Jonnic and Krasic to come back with furs and boots and food for all of them. When two men leading a donkey came through the snow at the end of the ravine, the Marroc cried out and waved their hands. Two of the prisoners even ran out into the snow. Addic stood and stared and frowned. Achista too. The hairs on Gallow's neck prickled.

The first Marroc reached the newcomers and the men leading the donkey drew swords from under the furs and ran them through. Shields followed and then they charged. Addic snarled and took up the axe from the Lhosir Gallow had killed the day before. Achista strung her bow.

'Wait!' Gallow gripped his sword. 'There are more of them. There must be.' And a moment later they saw he was right. More Lhosir on horseback came over the rise, riding fast towards the caves, squashing into the mouth of the ravine. There must have been a score of them, more perhaps, all armed, and lumbering at the back on a great black horse came a man in iron. Beyard. And though for the Marroc to stand and fight was sure death, the sight gave Gallow a strange surge of hope, for if Beyard was here then he wasn't somewhere else and he hadn't gone hunting for Arda, not yet, and there was a chance to stop him or for Gallow to die and make his hunting pointless.

Achista let fly an arrow. It struck one of the Lhosir shields. Addic clenched his fists. 'I won't lie down and die! Every one of them we kill is a victory.'

He looked ready to charge out into the snow in his rags but Achista stilled him. 'There's a way through the caves, Addi.' Addic turned and stared at her as Gallow thought of the wisp of wind he'd felt back where the bodies of the murdered Marroc lay. 'Krasic led us though. That's how we were waiting for the forkbeards inside.'

'They'll follow us.'

There wasn't much to be done about that, but at least through the caves the Lhosir would be on foot and not on horseback. 'You lead,' said Gallow. 'I'll hold the rear.'

'You?' Jonnic snarled. 'And how do we know you won't turn your coat to save your skin?'

Gallow bared his teeth. 'Because I took King Medrin's hand off his arm, Marroc. What forgiveness do you imagine there could be for that? Besides, if I mean to turn against you, would you rather have me in your midst?' He pushed Oribas deeper into the cave. The Lhosir at the front were getting close and the Marroc were taking too long to get going. 'Go, Aulian. Get away.' He pushed Achista too. 'Dither and they'll be on us.'

He drew his sword and wished he had a spear, but at least he had a shield again and the Lhosir were in their winter furs, which would make them slow and clumsy. The Marroc ran into the depths of the caves, grabbing burning sticks from the fire to light their way. Gallow stamped out what they left – no reason for the Lhosir to see where they were going. And then the first two were at the mouth of the cave with the others on their horses only a moment behind.

Gallow kicked the embers into their faces and ran at them. He brought his sword down on one man's helm, dazing him, and barged the other with his shield, staggering him so he tripped and fell and dropped his spear. Beyard and the rest of the Lhosir were almost on him now. No time to finish either of these then, but he took the dropped spear. If the caves grew narrow then a spear might serve better than a sword.

'Foxbeard! *Nioingr!*' Beyard dismounted outside the cave. The rest of the Lhosir paused as Gallow backed away.

'That's three, Beyard,' Gallow shouted back. 'You have to fight me now.'

'I know that, old friend. So let's be at it.' The Fateguard drew a long dark sword, too long to be either a Lhosir or a Marroc blade, and Gallow knew it at once. Solace. 'First blood drawn, shall we have? Or to the death? Make it easy for yourself. Face me here and be done with it. Sixfingers will have to settle for gloating over your head and I'll have no reason to go hunting for those who share your blood.'

Gallow almost threw the spear; but even if Beyard wasn't quick enough to dodge, the point would never pass through all that iron. 'Why don't you call me by name, Beyard? Have you forgotten it? We'll have our reckoning but I'll be the one to choose the ground for it. That's my right and it'll not be here.' He turned and bolted into the cave, following his memory of the twists and turns of the tunnel until it spilled him out into the great underground cathedral again. He had no light to see by but across the darkness torches burned, bobbing up and down, the Marroc finding their way to the other side. The closest were a full spear's throw ahead of him. Maker-Devourer but the place was huge!

And dark, but he'd seen before that a ledge ran down from the balcony and that it was a twenty-foot drop to the floor below. And he'd seen where the Marroc bodies lay piled. He jumped into the blackness, landing on their frozen limbs and sliding down among them, then fumbled blindly towards the flickering of the torches, hands out in front of him feeling for the pillars and spires of stone, feet groping warily for pits and chasms. He couldn't see his hand in front of his face, nothing but the distant torches, and he hadn't gone far at all when the Marroc ahead started to climb some slope he couldn't see while the Lhosir reached the balcony behind him. He didn't see them but he heard, heard one of them pitch over the edge among the murdered Marroc and shout and curse his luck. The thought came to him then that a man could hide in this place. Simply slip to one side and let the Lhosir pass after the Marroc and none of them would ever know until they came out the other end. He could go back, take their horses and whatever else he fancied and vanish on his way to Middislet. Be there before Beyard could possibly catch him. He turned the thought over in his head without stopping, then tossed it aside. Oribas would probably tell him he should do it, and Arda surely would, but he'd given these Marroc his word. Besides, there was Beyard. He was Fateguard and not so easily fooled.

He felt the floor of the cathedral rise beneath his feet as he crept on. The Marroc lights were almost gone, all that was left of them a soft glow shining out of some passage high in the wall of the cave. The Lhosir behind him had torches of their own now. They were coming, jumping down from the balcony and running through the stone spires. They were gaining. With his own light to guide him, a man could run faster.

He slowed. Let Beyard keep his sword. Let the Lhosir and Marroc kill each other without him. Three years wasted. Three years and he hadn't seen his sons, and even a Fateguard's senses weren't perfect, and he'd still get back to their horses before Beyard knew for sure what he'd done.

'Gallow?' A hiss came from one of the spires as he passed. 'Oribas?'

An arm from the shadows grabbed his own, pulling him. 'The others wouldn't wait for you. I'm sorry.'

'I told you to run!' But now they could both stay! They could hide, the two of them, and yet he let the Aulian lead him on, not towards the fading orange glow further along the wall but in and out of spires of stone. There was some sort of path here, one that Gallow would never have found on his own in the dark. It twisted and turned and then they were at the brink of some depthless fissure, invisible in the blackness but Gallow could feel the space at his feet. Oribas led him on to where one of the stone columns had snapped and fallen. Tucked behind it was a narrow bridge, little more than a thick branch laid across the void. Oribas crawled across. 'It was easier with a torch.'

It would be a fine place to hold, a little voice said – one man against many for a time. He might kill a good few before they took him down. Or he still might hide as he'd planned and let Beyard and his Lhosir pass. But Oribas was leading him on, hurrying him, no thought of anything except to follow the Marroc, and so Gallow followed too, and the moment when outcomes might have been different was gone. He knew what drove Oribas on. When Achista had looked at the Aulian with that one lingering glance, it had landed like a perfect snowflake, and Oribas had caught it, impossible to resist, and of everything that the world took and gave, here was a thing that Gallow's heart understood without question.

Back across the cavern the dancing lights of Beyard's Lhosir were getting closer.

18

THE WIZARD OF THE
MOUNTAINSIDE

Achista waited at the mouth of the passage. She had a bow. She could hold the forkbeards up and keep them at bay and maybe send one or two of them back to their uncaring god; and when she spoke her thinking aloud, she almost believed it, almost believed that she hadn't stayed simply because of the Aulian wizard.

He killed a shadewalker. Addic spoke of it with awe and it was nothing short of magic. The Aulian had caught her staring at him too, and he'd smiled and she'd scowled and looked away, but she couldn't pretend that her heart hadn't been beating faster, nor now as she waited watching the torches of the Lhosir dip and bob their way across the floor of the cavern. Her own light was guiding them, but it was also guiding the Aulian and his forkbeard friend.

She hurried them past when they finally reached her, pressing her torch into their hands while she waited on, alone and in the dark. She had her bow trained on the spot where the forkbeards would cross the fissure. As they reached it she let fly, her aim guided by the flame of their brands. The first arrow must have missed but she heard the forkbeards call out. The second drew a yell of pain and the third a flurry of shouts and movement. Some of the forkbeards dropped their torches. She'd slowed them, daring them to come onward in the face of a Marroc with a bow, and that, for now, was enough. She turned and crept away, fingers and toes feeling along the tunnel. Around the first bend she saw a glow of orange light. She'd asked him not to, but the Aulian had been waiting for her.

'It seemed only polite to return the favour.' He smiled and her heart jumped. The forkbeard Gallow muttered something in his surly way and took off ahead, running over the stone with the torch held in front of him while she and Oribas followed, eyes down, careful not to look at the brightness of the flame but only at where each foot would fall; and after a time that felt like an age, with their torch burned almost down to a stub, the walls of the caves gleamed daylight white instead of fiery yellow and they were at the end, out among snow-covered crags and jagged lumps of black stone.

Below them the mountain sloped steeply down and disappeared over the edge of yet another ravine. The Marroc ahead had already cut a path across the pristine deep snow to where lumps of stone broke through the white once more. They'd gouged a great furrow, and now they were picking their way down among snow-drenched outcrops, descending with laborious care towards the edge of the precipice. Achista watched Oribas. She pointed and he nodded as he saw the bridge of three long ropes that spanned the ravine to another precarious path on the other side. As he started to follow she put a hand on his shoulder. 'Tread lightly, Aulian. The snow here is unstable.' She pointed to where a swathe had already come loose lower down the slope, sliding off the mountain to reveal ice and the rock beneath. Oribas took a step and almost fell as the snow swallowed him. He reached out to catch himself. His hand caught her arm and her hand caught his. She held it fast.

'Thank you.' He smiled again and she thought his smile might have been the kindest she'd ever seen. Simple and honest. None of the bitterness that festered among all the Marroc men she knew. 'I've seen this in sand,' he said. 'Sometimes it makes a crust. If you disturb it, it will give way beneath as you walk and the whole slope will slide.' He looked down thoughtfully. 'And in this case take you over the edge into that ravine. We should each follow the tracks of the others then.' He put a hand on the forkbeard's arm. 'Let Achista go first, Gallow. You, my friend, are far less delicate. You're more likely to upset the balance at work here.'

The forkbeard snorted. 'A desert man lecturing a Lhosir of the Ice Wraiths and a Marroc of the Varyxhun valley on the dangers of sliding snow?'

He let her go first though, and the Aulian was right, even if he *was* from the desert. She followed the trail left by the other Marroc, cutting high across the snowfield instead of down and straight for the bridge. She reached the rocks without the snow shifting under her feet and looked back for the forkbeard and the Aulian. The forkbeard was following, but Oribas had scrambled higher up where the slope was steeper still and the snowfield ended and black gnarls of mountain jutted out from the white. As she watched, he began digging in the snow under the stones as if he was looking for something.

Achista picked her way down to the edge of the ravine. When she reached the bridge Oribas was still up there and now Addic was already on the other side, shouting at them to get across before he cut the ropes. She waited for the forkbeard to catch up.

'What's he doing?'

Gallow stared back in bewilderment. 'Oribas!' The shout was loud enough to shake the snow off the mountain, but if the Aulian heard then he gave no sign of it. Even when the forkbeard bellowed his name louder, all Oribas did was raise and shake his head and turn back to his foraging. He moved from stone to stone, pushing at each and excavating until at last he found one that pleased him. He crouched and began rummaging through the pouches on his belt. The forkbeard shook his head. 'Go across! I'll wait for him. Tell the rest of them to go. I'll stay to cut the bridge.'

Achista tried not to look down at the tumble of boulders beneath her as she walked across the bridge, or at the sprinkling of snow that covered them. She could hear rushing water but she couldn't see it, lost as it was under the ice. Two dozen steps, give or take, to cross the ravine, and for that time everything else fled her thoughts. Just slow steady breaths and slow steady steps, each foot sure on the rope, one after the next. When she reached the other side and looked back the Aulian was on his way down. The forkbeard was still waiting but the others were already off and away along the path that climbed up the other side along the next ridge, all except Addic with his knife. Oribas picked his way through the stones and crossed as she did, slowly and carefully, muttering to himself as he came. He was halfway when the iron devil and the first of the forkbeards finally emerged from the caves. Achista waved at Gallow: 'Forkbeard! They're here.'

Gallow waited for Oribas to reach her and then crossed with sure quick strides, growling forkbeard prayers and oaths. As soon as he was across, Addic began sawing at the ropes. The forkbeard's eyes were wide as though he was about to go into battle and the bulk of him shook with each huge breath.

Oribas put a hand on Addic's arm. 'There's no need for that.' But Addic paid no attention and the forkbeard quickly set to helping too. Across the ravine the iron devil was following the path the Marroc had made. Oribas came to stand beside her. 'Do you see the stone where I stopped? The one I marked with the snow in the sign of your god Modris?'

Achista stared. Yes, she saw it now, the sign. She hadn't before.

'Where I dug out the snow underneath, do you think you could hit it with an arrow?'

She nodded. On the far side of the ravine the other fork-beards were coming out of the cave now. They must have realised they had no chance of reaching the bridge in time but they came anyway, some of them ignoring the Marroc path and cutting down the slope as fast as they dared. Achista watched while Addic and Gallow hacked at the last rope. 'Why?'

Oribas leaned and whispered in her ear. She almost jumped at how close he was. 'Another little Aulian trick, that's why.'

Addic let out a cry of triumph. The last rope snapped and whipped through the air as the end of the bridge fell. The forkbeards out on the snowfield stopped to watch but the iron devil kept on until he was standing on the far side, straight across from them. He saluted. 'Why cut those ropes, old friend? We could have fought in the middle of that bridge. Swaying from side to side over a pitiless drop. They would have written a song to us for that, Foxbeard, whatever the ending.'

Gallow laughed back at him. 'The ending would have been of two forkbeards plunging to their deaths as the Marroc cut the bridge and skipped away whooping in triumph. The Marroc would sing a song about that, right enough, but you'd not hear it across the sea.'

'Your Marroc not as friendly as you thought?'

'More friendly than my friends, old friend.'

Achista drew back her bow. The iron devil cocked his head at her. Oribas whispered in her ear. 'Wait! Wait until they're all close.'

The forkbeards were spreading across the slope now. They'd seen the place where the snow had sheared away and plunged over the edge and understood the danger now. Achista had to remind herself sometimes that the forkbeards came from a place of ice and cold too, that the Varyxhun valley was close to what they knew as home. It was easy to forget, but perhaps that was why so many of them came. She looked at the boulder Oribas had marked. 'What do you mean to do? Knock it over and then hope he doesn't see it before it bowls him into the ravine like an iron skittle?'

The Aulian smiled. 'That would do, wouldn't it? If you could get the iron-skinned one, that would be best. Although I admit I was hoping for somewhat more.'

'But he's not in its path.'

The iron devil drew his sword, the deep red sword that Addic and the Aulian had brought to the farmhouse. He pointed it at Gallow. 'The Marroc tell me it's cursed. I'm beginning to think they're right. Maybe you should keep it, Foxbeard.'

Gallow called back across the ravine, 'The Marroc are right, old friend. If Medrin wants it so badly, let him have it. No good comes of the red blade.'

'Now would be perfect,' murmured Oribas.

Achista took aim and let her arrow fly. The forkbeards out in the snow all cringed behind their shields. The arrow hit the underside of Oribas's boulder but nothing happened. The forkbeards turned to look. One or two started to laugh, but not the iron devil. His head whipped round. He looked up, looked across at the forkbeards all out in the open and roared, '*Get back!*'

'Again.'

She loosed a second arrow. This time there was a flash of light and a whoosh of flame and a loud crack where the arrow struck something Oribas had left behind. A stone the size of a small child tipped and slid and then tumbled, bringing a few others with it, rolling towards the forkbeards out in the open snow. They scattered, scrambling out of the way of the falling boulder, all except the iron devil who stayed absolutely still. Snow tumbled around the boulder's wake. Achista caught a glimpse of something very smug in the Aulian's face and then half of the slope across the ravine

126

began to slip at once. The forkbeards wailed and screamed and down they went, caught in the sliding snow. The ones still close to the mouth of the Devil's Caves and outside the reach of the avalanche watched in helpless horror. For the others there was no hope, nothing anyone could do as a great cloud of powdery snow crashed over the edge of the ravine, enveloping everything in its path, rumbling and roaring, filled with cries that quickly faded as half the forkbeards were swept over the edge. Achista watched the iron devil stagger and fall and then he too was lost in the plume – a moment later a wall of fine ice and snow swept over her, stinging her face, buffeting her hard enough that she stumbled and fell onto her backside. As the cloud slowly sank into the ravine, she picked herself up. The forkbeards left by the cave mouth hurled dire curses. Two lucky ones lay in the jumble of broken snow at the edge of the slide, struggling to their feet, but the iron devil was gone and half a dozen others who'd been closest to him. Vanished. She looked into the ravine but all she could see was a cloud of settling snow. There were no cries or wails or screams. The forkbeards were dead and Oribas was smiling. She couldn't help but take a step away from him. Witchery. There wasn't anything else it could have been.

His smile faded. He frowned and peered into the ravine as though looking for something. Over on the other side of the slope one of the forkbeards was stringing a bow. A thing she could understand. She took aim at him before he could nock an arrow: he saw her and hid behind his shield; Achista shot her own arrow into it to make her point and grabbed Oribas by his arm. 'Come on!'

Gallow was shaking his head. He wasn't smiling at all, although he didn't seem surprised by what Oribas had done. 'The ironskin was my friend once,' he said. 'We were almost brothers.'

Achista pulled at Oribas. 'You had an iron devil for a

friend, forkbeard? Well, now he's gone, and good riddance!'
She ran after Addic and the other Marroc, dragging Oribas
in her wake. The forkbeard with the bow was stringing it
again so she stopped and took another shot at him and then
at a couple of the others, sending them cowering behind
their shields once more.

'Gallow, the ironskin stopped being your friend when
they put the mask and crown on him,' said Oribas.

'And what would you know of the Fateguard, Oribas?
They never crossed the mountains. What does an Aulian
know of those who serve the Eyes of Time?'

'Little enough, my friend.' Oribas shrugged and shook his
head and Achista saw the look in his eye. He knew something more, something painful, a burden he was keeping to
himself.

'You never killed a man, Oribas.' The forkbeard looked
grim. 'In the year we hunted your Rakshasa, you never once
even lifted your hand to hurt another. There were times
when you could have, times when perhaps you should
have, but you never did, not once. The chase was ended, the
bridge cut and gone. Why, Oribas? Why do that? Was there
truly a need?'

The Aulian looked sombre as they trotted along the path
in the snow in the wake of the others. His eyes didn't flicker
and his face gave nothing away but Achista slowly realised
that she knew the answer.

He'd done it for her.

19

THE BATTLE OF JODDERSLET

Addic sat beside a fire, warming his naked feet. It had taken the rest of the morning for them to reach Jodderslet, the nearest hamlet amid the isolated valleys nestled in the mountains around Varyxhun. He looked at the sky, hoping for clouds that might bring snow to cover their tracks, but the air was clear and the sun was bright and warm. The Aulian might have swept half a dozen of the forkbeards into the ravine but that still left near a dozen of them on the other side of the bridge. They'd find a way across. Half the little hamlets and farmsteads in the high valleys had never even seen a forkbeard before and it would surprise him if there was a single forkbeard who'd ever heard of Jodderslet, but that would change now. The forkbeards would follow. Forkbeards always did.

The other Marroc former prisoners were huddled around him, rubbing their icy skin, trying to get warm. They were hardly fighters. The farmers of Jodderslet milled around, bemused as much as anything else by the sudden arrival of so many strangers. *They* were hardly fighters either and they stared in bewilderment at Oribas. None of them had ever heard of Aulia, never mind seen a man from over the mountains. Half thought he was some sort of monster and made the sign of Modris every time they saw him. But they'd heard of forkbeards, and when Addic said that a band of them would be coming, they were none too happy. They collected whatever might pass for weapons: axes, a few forks, a spear or two and a couple of hunting bows, if you included Achista's. Addic looked around. Not a piece of armour among them. Not a single shield, not one helm, except on the forkbeard Gallow. Between the farmers and the prisoners there were two or three Marroc for every forkbeard they'd left on the mountainside but the forkbeards were soldiers, armed and armoured, while most of these Marroc were ordinary men who'd never fought with anything more than their fists.

'Maybe they won't come,' said one of the farmers, but Addic knew better. When did the forkbeards ever not give chase when a Marroc ran?

He left the farmers and the other Marroc to pick their weapons. Addic supposed they could keep running instead of fighting, but he and the others from the caves had no boots, only rags for clothes and there was nothing but snow out here. They were half frozen and exhausted already. Better to try and take a forkbeard or two with them. He crossed the barn to Gallow. 'And what about you? Will you fight your kinsmen a second time?'

'It's not my fight.' Gallow's face was pinched and bitter. He stood by the door to the barn, staring out into the snow, oblivious to the bustle behind him.

'No.' Addic turned away and then stopped. 'But it wasn't your fight back when you stopped me going over the edge of the Varyxhun Road and into the Isset either. You'd make a difference here.'

'By killing more men who were once my friends?'

'By saving those who might become new ones.'

Gallow stared at him with those ice-blue eyes that jabbed like spears. 'None of you will ever call me friend, Marroc, no matter what I do. There was only ever one of you who looked past where my forked beard should be. It's time I went to find her.'

Addic shook his head. 'When the strong do nothing, the

wicked prevail. Your words, forkbeard, not mine.' He left Gallow to his gloom and sought out his sister instead, sitting in a corner of the barn with Oribas. The Aulian was drawing in the dirt with a stick and it took a moment for Addic to understand: he was drawing Jodderslet, a map of it. 'What are you doing?'

'I'm no warrior,' he said, 'but I studied all the great generals of the early empire – Kunessin, Loredan, Cronan and Allectus. I can't say it much interested me but we were obliged to study the history of war as much as we were obliged to study poetry and alchemy.' He poked at the dirt with his stick. 'The enemy will follow our trail. They'll emerge from the trees on the slopes above us. They'll have to cross this open space to reach us. The snow will slow them down. They'll be exposed.'

'And will you bring the mountain down on them again?' asked Addic sourly. The Aulian shook his head. Achista shot her brother a sharp look.

'No. But General Tullinus lost a thousand men crossing a swamp against savages armed with little more than knives and bows. While they're in the open ...'

'We have two bows; the forkbeards will advance behind their shields and we have no time to dig pits or built barricades.' Addic turned away and left them to it and went back to look for Gallow, to ask the forkbeard to at least leave them his sword, but the big man was gone and Addic couldn't find him. After that there didn't seem much to do except sharpen his axe, wait for the forkbeards and warm himself by a fire. Might as well be comfortable before he went out into the snow to die.

Achista watched him. Her brother, whom she loved more than any other man. He thought that by staying here they were all going to die, and he was probably right. She touched Oribas on the back of his hand. 'You should go with your forkbeard friend,' she said, 'before he leaves without you.'

Oribas shook his head. 'Gallow has a reason to go; I have a reason to stay.' Her hand was still touching his. He took it and squeezed it, and since Addic was likely right and they were going to die today, Achista leaned across the Aulian's maps and kissed him.

'For what you did at the ravine.'

Oribas turned away and let her hand go. He looked sad. Ashamed even. 'I feel no pride in that. Gallow is more right than he knows. Until today I'd never killed, neither man nor beast. I've slain monsters and showed others how, and I will show you, as best I can, how to fight the Lhosir when they come. But I'm no soldier and nor do I wish to become one. What I did at the ravine I did for my own reasons. Give me a spear and I'd probably hold the wrong end and stab myself in the foot.'

'You have no reason to be ashamed.' She spat. 'They were forkbeards! Every forkbeard who died in that ravine is a forkbeard who won't be coming here to spill more Marroc blood.'

Oribas touched his fingertips to her face. 'Victories that last are not won by blood but by words and by forgiveness, Achista.'

'Then find your words, Aulian, and make the Foxbeard stay. Make him fight for us!'

Oribas shook his head. 'The gods sent him to me to defeat the terror that gripped my home. Perhaps they've sent him here to defeat yours now, or perhaps not. But either way we must all choose our own fates.' He leaned over and whispered something in her ear.

One of the farmers brought out a cask of ale. Addic and the other Marroc from the caves drank eagerly, lighting a little fire inside their bellies and talking among themselves of the tiny victories each had scored over the forkbeards before they'd been caught. A purse cut here, a horse stolen, a household made ill with rancid milk, a drunkard felled with a bottle and kicked in the street. None of them had ever killed. None of them had stood face to face with a forkbeard and taken up arms against him, nor even stared down the shaft of an arrow. Those were the men who hung from the gibbets in Varyxhun or lurked like angry shadows in the deep woods and the snow. These men were the ones who might have been branded or whipped or perhaps put to work as slaves back when the lord of Varyxhun had been a Marroc. Now the forkbeards simply got rid of them.

'Forkbeards! They're here!' Addic jumped up and looked for his sister, but she was gone and Oribas too. He ran outside. The forkbeards were coming out of the wood higher up the slope, just as the Aulian had said. The snow there was deep, up past their knees. Deep enough to make them wade and stop them from mounting a charge as they came in among the houses. Addic took a fork. That would do. Close enough to a spear. He stood. 'Face them!' he roared and farmers and prisoners alike came and stood beside him, near thirty men against about a dozen. They were going to die but they'd do it defending their homes and their families. 'Don't fear them!' he cried. 'They're just men! They die like any other. They have their armour and their shields but there's more of us, so grab them and take them down and be in at them with your knives. If you have the courage to stand then you can win!' He almost believed it himself. He looked around for Achista and the other Marroc who had a bow but they were nowhere to be seen. On a roof out of sight if they had any sense, waiting for the forkbeards to get close so they could pick their spots. Make each arrow count.

The forkbeards started down the slope. They walked quickly at first, shields loose by their sides. Then the one at the back pitched over into the snow and the one beside him cried out and turned and they all stopped and looked behind them. Addic counted. Thirteen of them. Twelve if you passed over the one who'd fallen. He didn't look like he was getting up again.

At the top of the slope, out of the trees, two figures emerged holding bows. Addic's heart skipped a beat. Achista! And the forkbeards were between them! Oribas appeared beside him. 'Out in the open, Addic. Exposed. Now they have to wonder how many more of you there might be waiting in the trees.'

'One dead forkbeard hardly makes a difference, Aulian.' The forkbeards were on the move again, coming down the slope more slowly now, their shields raised behind them against the two archers. They clustered together.

'Every battle must have its first man to fall. If only we had some fire.'

The forkbeards came on. Achista and the other archer followed them down, keeping their distance but still shooting arrows now and then, pinning them in their tight circle of shields and keeping their heads down. 'Work in twos and threes,' Addic told the others. 'Pick a forkbeard and pull him down. One of you takes his sword hand and holds it fast, one of you pulls away his shield, the third one goes in with the knife. Brothers together! Fathers and sons! It's like bleeding out a pig. Midwinter was just days ago. You do that?' There were was a murmur among the farmers he took to mean yes. 'Just the same! Best way to think of it.' And they could win, they could! If they held their nerve and didn't mind a few of them dying, the way the forkbeards never seemed to care.

At the bottom of the slope the forkbeards broke their circle and started to run. Another fell to an arrow and then they were close, and Addic felt the Marroc around him waver. 'Don't!' he cried, beginning to despair. 'Don't run! Stand!'

But beside him Oribas turned and fled. 'Don't listen to

him. Run after me!' And the Marroc were only too eager as the forkbeards reached the edge of the deep snow and picked up speed. They turned and ran and Addic had no choice but to run with them, and they all fled together among the houses and barns of Jodderslet. The Aulian led the way. He kept glancing back as if to see whether the forkbeards were still there, as if something might have happened to make them change their minds. As if such a thing was possible.

They reached the space in the middle of the hamlet where the farmers let their pigs, their chicken and geese out during the summer. The Marroc scattered. Addic bolted past a house with a howling forkbeard right behind him, only to have a door open almost in his face. A stick holding a pot of steaming water swung out. The forkbeard ducked the stick but not the scalding water that poured over his head. He screamed and slowed, clutching his face. Addic turned. He didn't have much but he had his fork and now he swung it. The forkbeard lurched away, getting his shield up barely in time. A woman came out, still holding the stick with the pot on the end of it. She swung it at the half-blind forkbeard, cracking it across his helm and staggering him again. He stabbed at her wildly and this time Addic caught his arm and the three of them fell down into the snow together. They wrestled, and now the shield and the helm and the mail that were a soldier's friends in war became unwieldy weighty things that kept the forkbeard from rising. All three of them were howling and cursing and screaming in each others' faces. Addic had the forkbeard held down but now he couldn't move and the woman was bashing at the forkbeard with her stick and doing nothing more than making him even angrier than he was. Addic looked up for any other Marroc. Out in the open two forkbeards were fighting a third. It took him a moment to realise the one fighting alone was Gallow.

Another forkbeard ran towards him. Addic stared up

helplessly, but the man staggered and fell with an arrow in the back of his leg. Before he could get up, another Marroc appeared, one of the prisoners. His rags were bloody and he had a pitchfork in his hand. 'Need some help?'

Addic nodded, and grinned because he finally saw. The Aulian had drawn the forkbeards apart. He'd made them scatter and destroyed their invincible wall of shields before it was ever made. And the Marroc were going to win.

20

PARTING WAYS

Gallow watched as the Marroc broke and ran. He felt pity for them because that was what Marroc always did. The Lhosir charged without thought to how many they were and how many stood against them and the Marroc wavered and broke. It was the same every time.

He stood in the centre of the hamlet and watched it happen. The track out of the valley was marked with cairns of stones. If he followed it for long enough, it would take him to the little town of Hrodicslet. Three days in summer on a mule, the Marroc had told him, although they weren't so sure about in winter and on foot because none of them ever left their farms once the snows set in. Hrodicslet was on the far eastern fringe of the Crackmarsh, which meant it was a way out of the mountains without crossing the Aulian Bridge over the Isset. He knew Hrodicslet. Fenaric the carter had gone that way a few times. A week winding through the hills would take him home, but if he crossed the Crackmarsh he could be there in two days as long as the ghuldogs didn't get him.

Yet even though he knew the way, he didn't leave, not yet. He watched Oribas, perhaps his last friend in the world. The Aulian was here because he'd sworn an oath – sworn that if Gallow helped him to kill the Rakshasa then he'd take Gallow to the Aulian Way which crossed the mountains to Varyxhun. And after he kept his oath, he'd still stayed even though Gallow had tried to send him away. *Where shall I go? I have nowhere else to be.* Crossing the mountains had almost killed them both and yet now here he was, holding hands with a Marroc woman. So perhaps it was right that Oribas had come to this land. Perhaps it had always been his fate to find Achista and her people, as it had been Gallow's to wash up on that far southern shore where Oribas had found him; as it had been fate for Beyard to find him and for one friend to be the end of another.

Oribas wouldn't leave her. He'd fight for her in his own way, a thing Gallow understood above anything else. So he stayed as the Lhosir emerged from the wooded hill and smiled at the Marroc archers harrying them from behind, and then the smile faded as he watched the Marroc turn and run and an old bitter sadness welled up inside him. The weight of who he'd become. Always just one more battle before he could go home. He waited for the Lhosir to pour into the space in the middle of the hamlet; and as they did he stepped out from the open barn and roared out his challenge: 'I am Gallow Truesword! The Foxbeard! Fight me if you dare!'

The first Lhosir ran after Marroc prey but the next one slowed long enough to realise Gallow wasn't just another one of their own. Gallow put an end to the question by hurling his spear straight into the Lhosir's face. A spear was fine in a battle line, but up close and spread out like this he much preferred an axe or even his sword. Something short that struck from the side instead of a straight thrust.

'You!' Two more Lhosir were striding towards him. He charged them down, right in the middle of the farmhouses where everyone could see, and swung at the first, hard and fierce. 'All I wanted was to go home!' There was an anger inside him now, growing with every blow. Anger at the Marroc for needing him, for not standing on their own just one time. At the Lhosir for being here where they didn't belong. At Beyard for having once been his friend and at

Oribas for killing him. At himself for not letting things be and leaving the Marroc on the Aulian Way to fall to his death. But most of all at fate. Fate had cursed him from the moment he'd picked up the Edge of Sorrows. Fate that had sent storms and pirates and demons and hurled him so far from his home. Fate that had taunted him year after year and pretended to relent only to spit in his eye. Beyard had known him. Other men had seen him. In time Medrin would learn that Gallow Foxbeard was back, the man who'd taken his hand, and then Medrin would turn the world on its head to find him and he wouldn't know one single moment of peace until one of them was dead. Fate.

His axe bit into a shield so hard that the Lhosir almost wrenched it out of his hand. Gallow snarled. Beneath the cliffs of Andhun the Screambreaker had fished him and the red sword out of the sea, and as he'd opened his eyes and coughed and spewed out the water that filled his lungs, the Screambreaker had offered him a choice. The Vathen had shouted and cursed and thrown their spears and shot their arrows, which splashed in the water around the Screambreaker's little boat but never struck true. The Screambreaker hadn't seemed to notice. He'd held out the red sword. 'No use to me. Not where I'm going.' And he'd looked at Gallow hard and then away to the Marroc ships fleeing from burning Andhun and then last to where a single Lhosir ship was setting sail from the shore. 'You didn't think you really got away all those years ago, did you?' His lips had curled and, for perhaps the first time, Gallow had seen the Screambreaker smile. 'But then it's the nature of men like us to fight our fates. I'll let you choose. After all these years I've earned that and so have you. Which way, Truesword? Which way will it be?'

And so Gallow had turned his back on fate, and fate had punished him ever since, for every single day, and now a rage broke inside him, for he could see that there would be no escape; and he screamed at these men in front of him, a cry of rage and anguish enough to make even two Lhosir warriors falter before him; and as they fell back, his axe kissed the face of one and cut the thread of his life; and the other, seeing a thing too terrible to defy, turned and ran; and Gallow stood there alone, quivering, murderous, eyes searching for any who dared stand in his path; and when no one did, he fell to his knees beside the man he'd killed and wept. He tore away the dead Lhosir's furs to be his own and put them on and walked through the bloody mayhem of Marroc falling on forkbeards and forkbeards slaying Marroc. Turned his back on them all and left.

The Marroc gathered slowly in the open space between the barns where Gallow had stood. It was done. The forkbeards were dead and none of the victors could quite believe it. Oribas darted around until he saw that Achista was still alive and her brother Addic too. He stared open-mouthed at the dead. Not that he hadn't seen dead men before – he'd seen far too many – but he'd never been death's architect. Not until today.

'How did you do it?' Addic fell in beside him. 'Because you did. It was you.' And it was.

'You always run. That's what Gallow said.' He saw Addic wince, though he hadn't meant it as anything more than a simple statement of the way things were. 'But I spent a year with him and what I learned was that your Marroc women can be every bit as fierce and terrible as a Lhosir. So I went to them and told them that their men would run, even though they could win this day if they wanted it, and I told them to make their own stand. These are their homes, their lives, their sons and daughters. Why shouldn't they fight? With ropes to trip, and sticks and yes, pots of scalding water, but most of all they shouldn't run and they shouldn't cower, and when their men saw this then they'd turn and stand and fight too. The Lhosir win because they aren't afraid to die, but there aren't so very many of them, and men are men wherever they are born, and all can be brave if they have the will put inside them. So that is what I did.'

'Truly, you're a wizard.' Addic shook his head, full of disbelief, and Oribas understood his wonder because he hadn't really thought it would work either. But the truth was all around them. The Lhosir were dead, and yes, a good few Marroc too, but far fewer than would have died if they'd simply run.

He wondered then whether he might have made a beginning of sorts, whether he might one day look at what he'd done here and know that he'd had a hand in making some consequence he'd never foreseen, and whether it would be for good or for ill. But he didn't have very much time to do anything with that thought before Achista threw her arms around him and hugged him and then hugged Addic too. 'Look,' she said. 'Look what we did! We won!'

Oribas was already looking. 'Yes,' he said, and felt a touch of dread at the joy in her voice.

She looked him in the eye and kissed him. 'Addic is right. You *are* a wizard, Aulian. A magician.'

'No. I ...' He shook himself. A dozen Lhosir, that was all. They'd have killed the Marroc too and so he'd saved more lives than had been taken, hadn't he? He gently let Achista go, still uneasy. Gallow. Gallow would know. He'd never met a man with such a sure sense of what was right. But when he looked, Gallow had gone.

21

THE EYES OF TIME

Under the snow Beyard stared at the past. The Scream-breaker was across the sea, basking in his shattering of the Marroc King Tane outside Sithhun. The Crimson Shield of Modris the Protector had been carried to the Temple of Fates in Nardjas and three boys had slipped inside in the dark to steal a glimpse of it before it vanished far into the icy north. But the stealing had not gone well. He remembered the room where the Fateguard had cornered them, the air ripe with fear, shaking at the sharp crack of metal slammed into wood and a door pushed half open. And he was the one who'd turned to the others to ask if they'd stand and take their punishment like men.

Medrin was gone so quickly that Beyard had to blink to remember he'd even been there. Out through a narrow window covered in moon-shadows as sharp as a blade, friends betrayed to a fear that would one day cost him dear. Medrin Twelvefingers, defying his father in those years when that's what all boys did.

Which had left the two of them. Him and Gallow, parading their courage, shouting their defiance, holding their fear deep inside. Metal groaning, wood cracking, splinters flying. The iron-skinned men of the Fateguard were coming and they'd spat in fate's eye. 'My dead grandmother could push harder than that.' 'They'll never catch me!' 'You go!' 'No, you!' 'I'm too fast for them.' They were both wrong. He knew that now, now that his own skin was sheathed in iron too.

He'd been the oldest and so he'd stood his ground the hardest. He remembered Gallow's hesitation. The fear in his moon-caught face. They'd both known they'd never see each other again. Both been so sure of it.

How wrong.

'I will not forget.' They weren't Gallow's words in the end but his own after Gallow was gone. For the brief moment he stood, before the ironskins smashed through the door and he tried to run and they caught him with ease and took him off to the frost winds of the north, winds birthed by ice wraiths, and abandoned him there. He remembered the wind most of all, a cruel gale that flayed any thought of kindness, that moaned and screamed like the ghosts of the ever-hungry dead and wailed like the widows they left behind as it tore at cliffs that were hard as iron and bitter as juniper.

'I will not forget.' He clung to it. In a wagon of old weathered wood and fat sausage-fingers of rust, pulled by unicorns born burned and blackened and twisted, he held it in his heart and spoke it out, over and over. 'I will not forget.' They weren't alive, those nightmare horses, and when at last they stopped and stamped their feet, no steamy breath came with their snorts and even the snow and the stone shivered at their cold.

The Eyes of Time had been waiting. And then, for a long time, nothing.

In the ravine littered with fallen snow and broken Lhosir, Beyard understood that fate was not done with him yet. His life belonged to it and always had. Inside his case of battered iron something stirred. The Eyes of Time had made him what he was. He'd sworn vows that couldn't be broken, even by death. The Fateguard were cursed men and he knew it, and fate didn't choose to let him go. Metal grated as he moved, the fingers of his sword hand opening and closing, reaching for a blade he no longer held. His eyes opened and saw nothing but darkness, buried in snow. His lungs, which had been still, took a new lurching breath. His muscles creaked and strained, his bones groaned and shifted and the snow heaved and crumbled as he rose. He stood unsteadily amid the wreckage and looked about him. Up and down the ravine at the dead men who had served him. To the bridge that had almost saved him, the tangle of ropes to which he'd clung as others fell around him. Pieces of it lay about him now, broken where they'd snapped under their unwonted burden and pitched him down to the snow and stones below. He stumbled and staggered among them, lost and wondering who he was and where and how he he'd been the lucky one and clung to the severed ropes of the bridge and hadn't been smashed like all his kin. The Eyes of Time would know the answer, and perhaps the Aulian who did this, and even, deep down, a part of him knew it too. Knew it and feared it enough to know he never wished to hear it.

He shied away from the thought. The snow fell past him as he clung to the severed bridge and so was there to break his fall. Snow and his iron had saved him. Let it be so.

He began to dig, looking for the sword he'd held as he fell, the red sword of the Weeping God which must one day face the Crimson Shield again and repeat the old story of the Marroc, of Modris the Protector and Diaran the Lifegiver and the Weeping God who must bear so much pain. He pulled it from the snow and stared at its blade and then he sheathed it and stared at the thing held tight in his other iron hand, still safe. An amulet on a chain. A locket. He took off his iron gauntlets and held it in his cold white fingers, opened it and sniffed and then put it away and donned his crown once more and began to walk up the ravine, patiently looking for a way out.

'I will not forget.' His words were soft as the broken snow. They'd sealed their destiny by what they'd done, all of them. The others simply didn't yet know it.

ORIBAS

22

WITCHES' REACH

The tower of Witches' Reach was a crumbling old thing of stone built two hundred years before when the Holy Aulian Empire had been at the height of its power. Traders had found the way across the mountains. A legion of soldiers had crossed in their wake and for a time the Varyxhun valley had been a part of that empire, the furthest the Aulians had ever reached to the north. They brought engineers and architects and felled the mighty pines and built their bridge across the Isset, perhaps planning a great conquest of the plains to the north, but the invasion had never happened and fifty years later the last of them had withdrawn back across the Aulian Way to warmer climes. As well as their great bridge and the impregnable Varyxhun castle, they'd left behind them two watchtowers that looked down on the entrance to the valley from the heights over the bridge: Dragons' Reach on the far side of the river and Witches' Reach on the near. Dragons' Reach was a tumble of broken stone after the mountain beneath it had crumbled in the great Ice Winter sixty years later, but Witches' Reach remained, commanding the road to Varyxhun. The Aulians hadn't known the paths and trails of the high valleys and thought nothing could come into the valley without being seen by the garrison there. The forkbeards apparently thought the same. Cithjan had put a hundred men into the tower at the start of the winter, charged with keeping the Varyxhun Road and the bridge clear of Marroc outlaws, and so far the fifty of them that hadn't ridden off to Boyrhun to kill Marroc over on the other side of the valley instead were doing a fine job of it.

Which was why Oribas was crouched beside Addic halfway up a mountain, squinting at the fortress.

'I want to show you something.' Achista squatted next to him holding what looked like a scrunched-up bedsheet. She flapped it open to reveal a crude picture of a battle hammer daubed from corner to corner. 'The banner of King Tane. When this flies from the top of Witches' Reach, every Marroc crossing the Isset will see it! Varyxhun will rise and turn on the forkbeards!'

Oribas had no idea whether or not she might be right. He'd certainly met a lot of angry Marroc after Jodderslet. He'd also seen the insides of Varyxhun castle and knew that anger wasn't much substitute for mail and steel. 'If you took the tower, it would take two days for word to reach Varyxhun. Another two or three for the Lhosir to come. They'll surround you. I don't see how you can escape once they arrive. Your flag will not fly for long.'

Addic stood behind them. 'While it does, every Marroc and forkbeard leaving the valley will see it. Sixfingers himself will hear of it. We'll make Cithjan look a fool.'

'Men made to look fools can become mightily fierce.'

Achista rolled the flag into a bundle again. 'We can't run away when the forkbeards come! That's the point! We'll hold the tower as long as we can. Up and down the valley Marroc will rise to our standard and tear them down!'

'And if they don't?' Oribas raised an eyebrow.

'They will.' Addic put a hand on his shoulder. 'But if they don't then the forkbeards will kill us. You don't have to come with us when we seize it, Aulian. You'd be most welcome, but this isn't your war.'

Oribas looked to Achista. 'I will come.' He took her hand. They walked down the mountainside into the saddle below the tower and then away from the gorge of the Isset and into a thick wood of Varyxhun pine. Deep among the colossal trees Addic led the way to a clearing carpeted with dark blue autumn flowers where a camp of some fifty Marroc men waited for them. The Marroc here were grim-faced. Some had mail and helms and shields stolen from the Lhosir. A few had swords. Most had axes and nearly all of them had bows.

'Here's my Marroc army, Aulian.' Addic smiled. 'The first part of it.'

'How will you convince the Lhosir to open their gates?'

'Don't I have a wizard, Aulian?'

'Most of what tricks I had fell into the ravine on the day we first met.'

Addic vanished later that day and he didn't return for several more, but the first part of his plan was soon clear enough. The Marroc in the forest made no effort to hide their presence. They lit fires to keep warm and the smoke climbed up above the trees for the Lhosir in the tower to see. With each day that passed more Marroc arrived. Perhaps only a few, and mostly farmers with nothing but axes or a spear or a fork, but they all had bows and Achista drilled them for hours every day, making them whittle their own arrows and fletch them and shoot them into bales of straw, and for every arrow that missed its target, each archer was forced to make another. It taught them to shoot with care and thought over haste, though Oribas wondered how well that teaching would survive when their targets changed from bales of straw to screaming Lhosir. An armoured man with a shield wasn't as easy to kill with arrows as many archers liked to think.

He'd been in the camp for less than a week when the Lhosir made a sortie out of the tower to see what was happening in the woods. He was on the edge of the treeline when the Marroc lookouts came scurrying down from where they kept their watch. A score of Lhosir soldiers were coming on foot. The Marroc spoke with fearful glee and then raced back to the camp deep inside the trees. Oribas stayed where he was, hunkered down among the shadows and the snow. A man who chose to hide in a place like this and kept still and quiet would never be found unless those searching for him almost trod on him. More Marroc came running by. Oribas watched them rushing back and forth, leaving a confusion of tracks and trails. A few ran back the way they'd come, leaving fresh furrows in the snow. But not all: others picked their way back through their own tracks and crouched down to hide with their bows and their arrows. As long as the Lhosir didn't look too hard, it would seem as though a dozen or so men had fled into the deeper woods.

As the Lhosir came into view, one last Marroc burst from cover, full of shouted warnings and movement as he fled. Oribas watched the Lhosir break into a run. They were like hunting dogs. They had the scent of a fight and could hardly hold themselves back. They ran in among the trees and Oribas tensed, for the greatest danger was now, and it only took one of the hidden Marroc to lose his nerve and bolt and the trap would fail. None of them did. Oribas waited until the Lhosir were gone, lost to sight but not to sound, then rose and hurried after them. He was the signal. The rest of the Marroc emerged from where they'd lain hidden.

The other part of the ambush belonged to Achista – Oribas wasn't there to see it happen but he knew how it would go: the Lhosir would follow the trail until it stopped at a huge fallen tree that barred their path. Then Marroc would rise from the shadows beyond and throw their spears. Archers on either side would pepper the Lhosir with arrows, and after that it would fall to a confusion of fighting. In the thick forest the Lhosir wouldn't be able to make a shield wall and muster a charge. There would be three or four Marroc for every Lhosir. Achista would repeat the victory of Jodderslet.

That was how it would be, and so when he heard the first shouts go up, the Lhosir roars and battle cries and the Marroc screams, Oribas dropped out of sight into the snow beside the trail. The sounds of the fighting rose to a peak and then petered away into the shouts of wounded Marroc calling for aid and a few furious roars of the last battle-mad Lhosir as they scythed down as many Marroc as they could before they fell. And then finally what he was waiting for: the sound of men running, the last Lhosir following their own trail back, racing out of the trees. *Legs. Shoot them in the legs.* That's what he'd told the bowmen. They'd be soldiers in mail coats, with helms, carrying shields, armour too thick for an arrow to puncture, but they had nothing to protect them below the knees.

They came, two of them, running fast, still with their axes and their shields even in their rout. Oribas willed the Marroc arrows to fly true but the Lhosir were moving fast and were hard to hit. A flurry of shafts zipped across the trail. One of the Lhosir staggered but kept his feet as an arrow hit him in the side and stuck out of his furs. Oribas gripped a rope lying beside him in the snow. He watched the fleeing Lhosir and then jumped up and pulled with all his might and snapped it taut across the trail. It took the legs of the first Lhosir and he sprawled in a flurry of snow. The rope jerked out of Oribas's hands. He staggered forward. The second Lhosir lurched sideways, half tripped over the first and stumbled on. Without thinking Oribas hurled himself, crashing into the last Lhosir's side and knocking him down. They flailed at each other in the snow for a few seconds but the Lhosir had twice the strength and twice the weight of Oribas and threw him off with ease. For a moment Oribas lay floundering on his back like an upturned beetle. The Lhosir pulled himself up. His face was a rictus of fury. He lifted his sword and there was simply nothing Oribas could do about it, no words or clever plans that would make the slightest difference; but before the Lhosir could strike a Marroc arrow hit him in the back, knocking him off balance, and then another Marroc flew out of the trees and bore the Lhosir down, hacking at his face with a knife, and then another and another, and by the time Oribas found his feet, the Lhosir was dead, a crimson pond of blood dripping out of his savaged throat. Oribas stared. Most of the dead he'd seen before had been half ripped to pieces, stinking and rotting and savaged by vultures under the desert sun, so it wasn't the torn flesh and the blood that held him. It was that he'd never seen a man dead at his feet who'd been trying to kill him only a moment ago.

He was still looking at the Lhosir when Achista and the other Marroc came jogging up the trail. Some were dressed in freshly scavenged mail, others carrying new swords and shields. They stripped the man at Oribas's feet with the speed of jackals. Achista pressed a sword into his hand. She was dressed in mail now, a hauberk that was too long for her and far too wide and made her look ridiculous, but it also made him want to take her and hold her long and tight because she was going into battle now and the death he'd seen made him realise that it was all horribly real. Before the day was out, it wouldn't only be Lhosir who were dead.

23

THE DRAGON'S CAVES

The Marroc pushed quickly through the forest and onto the slopes beneath Witches' Reach. Achista didn't lead them towards the saddle between the two mountains; instead she took them across the craggy snowbound slopes, picking a way between them until she reached a crack in the mountainside, a slit of a cave only a few feet wide but as tall as a house. A trickle of water ran out the bottom. Oribas bent to sniff at it and recoiled. Achista laughed. 'Where do you think the cess from the tower ends up?'

Inside the cave, far enough to be out of sight, a handful of wooden brands wrapped in cloth lay beside coils of rope and two small kegs of fish oil. The Marroc broke the seals on one of the kegs and dipped their torches. One of them got a tiny fire going and lit the first, then they lit one from another until every other Marroc had a burning brand. Through the orange flicker of the flames Oribas saw a path worn in the floor of the cave.

'This cave leads up into the tower?' he asked with a wry smile. 'Surely the Lhosir will have barred any such tunnel?'

'You Aulians built this tower.' Her eyes gleamed in the firelight.

'We do like to dig.' That old fascination with reaching down into the earth, to the shades that dwelt there. The last emperor might have dug the furthest, but Aulians had been delving into the soil and rock since before the empire was anything more than a town with grand aspirations.

'When the Aulians left they barred the tunnel with two

seals. One was opened a long time ago. No one ever found a way to open the other. The forkbeards think they're safe.'

'But you've found a way?' Her eyes bored into him and he understood. He shook his head. 'I'm not a wizard, Achista.'

'Addic said you'd know how to open the seals.'

Oribas laughed. 'Even if I did, how long ago were these tunnels closed? How many hundreds of years? Metal rusts, Achista. Stone crumbles. I will try but I very much hope you have another way.'

The passage rose into the heart of the mountain, the crack in the stone petering out into a tunnel, roughly hewn and so narrow that even Oribas was forced to hunch his head into his shoulders. The Marroc shuffled along in the feeble near-dark of their torches, creeping like spiders in the night through puddles and rivulets of foul-smelling water. The walls glistened with damp slime and the stink got worse the deeper they went. After an hour of climbing into the mountain's heart, the Marroc stopped. The passage opened into a round shaft twenty paces across that rose towards the mountain's peak and delved to its root. Below where they stood, the shaft was filled with scummy water. A narrow ledge circled it.

'This part is slippery.'

Achista sent one Marroc around the walkway to the far side. Metal rungs bolted into the stone rose into the darkness of the shaft. Oribas stared at them in horror. 'And how old are those?'

'Addic and I climbed them months ago. We marked the loose ones.'

They brought more torches. Oribas looked up. The shaft disappeared into darkness. 'How far does it go?'

'As far as the tallest tree in the forest.'

Oribas shrugged. Some of the trees in the Varyxhun valley were as tall as fifty men. He followed her around the walkway and started to climb behind her. He wasn't sure why he was suddenly at the front of the Marroc, but it seemed natural to be at Achista's side. 'Where's your brother?' he asked. 'Shouldn't he be leading this?'

They were twenty feet above the water now. 'I found this, Oribas, not Addic. If anyone should be here to lead ahead of me then it's Rannic, but he's with Modris now, casting his shield over us.' She tapped the rung just above her feet. 'This one's loose. Make sure you tell whoever comes behind you.'

They climbed only another few feet when there was a howl from below. Oribas turned his head in time to see a Marroc splash into the water, fallen from the treacherous stone walkway. The Marroc cried out once more and then sank like a stone. A second man fell after him as he crouched to try and reach his friend. He scrabbled at the wall of the shaft and managed to grab another Marroc around the ankle, but his hands kept slipping and there was no way anyone standing on the walkway could bend down to help him without pitching themselves into the water as well. He fell back and then lunged again. His fingers clawed at the stone.

One man already drowned, just like that, out of nothing. The pointlessness of it made Oribas angry. 'You have ropes!' he shouted at them. 'Use them! Pull him out!'

It took three Marroc to haul the second man out. It was as though the foetid water in the shaft clung to him, trying to drag him down.

They climbed on. Oribas didn't know how far. He counted the rungs for a while when his arms started to tire and got up to somewhere close to a hundred before he lost count because it now took all the will he could muster just to keep going. He'd climbed ladders and stairs aplenty in his time but none like this; and when they finally reached the top, his arms and his shoulders felt like lead. Achista held her torch out over the edge and waved it so that those below could see the end was in sight, then, when there were a half-dozen of them safely up, she pulled Oribas to his feet and led him on. They were in another passage now, wider and made with more care, typical Aulian work lined with bricks and tiles, though the floor was still rough bare rock. Oribas looked for inscriptions or engravings or murals but everything was crusted in filth. When he stopped to scrape some off, Achista pulled him on again. She dragged him to a wall with a circular stone door in the centre. To the right of the door four bronze wheels dark with verdigris stuck out of the stone, each engraved with symbols that had almost disappeared over time. Oribas took her torch and inspected them. There were six signs on each wheel, animals, the totems for each of the six Ascendants who'd once stood guard over the empire. A chill ran over his skin right to his feet and back again and wouldn't leave him alone. He'd been to places like this before. He brushed a little of the dirt aside, nodded to himself and then walked away. 'And now we turn back,' he said to Achista as he passed her.

'You can't open it?' Her look was tragic.

'I probably can but I certainly shouldn't. I'll tell the others. No need for the ones still climbing to come up all this way for nothing.'

Achista darted in front of him, stopping him with a hand pressed to his chest. 'Please.' He opened his mouth, but before he could even begin to tell her why he shouldn't, why none of them should even go near a place like this, why the Lhosir in the tower were taking their lives to the edge of the abyss simply by being here, she put her other hand on his cheek and stared at him with such wide, hopeful eyes that she killed his words dead. He stood agape. 'Please,' she said again. 'It's the only way in. We have to! We have to try. If we don't try, what are we?'

Gallow would have said the same. And if Gallow had been here and told him to open it then he would have done so even while he was explaining exactly why no man alive should ever enter a place that had been closed with a seal of the Ascendants. 'This isn't a seal to keep us out, Achista. It's a seal to keep something in.'

'Whatever was inside has been dead and gone for hundreds of years now.'

'Yes,' said Oribas, turning back to the door. 'It has. And it should stay that way.'

She took his hand and held it tight. 'After the Aulians left, they say the Reach became the home of a Marroc prince. They say that beneath it he found an Aulian treasure vault. For twenty years he tried to open it until at last he solved its puzzle. They say he found the answer written on a nearby rock. The day after, he left with all his men and headed north and was never seen again. After that, no one lived in Witches' Reach until the forkbeards came.'

Oribas shook his head. 'I have another story for you. A long story for another time, of the Rakshasa that killed my home, my town, my people, my family and many others besides. I prayed and the gods sent Gallow Truesword and together we destroyed the creature.' He turned to face her and looked her hard in the eye. 'But before Gallow, I tracked the Rakshasa back to the place from which it came. I found a seal like this that had been opened. Thousands of lives, Achista.' He went back to the wheels beside the door and gave one an experimental tug, half hoping that it wouldn't move, that the mechanism inside had corroded solid. And the wheel didn't turn, but even as he shrugged his shoulders ready to walk away again, Achista had an unlit torch pushed through the wheel to make a lever and was pulling on it with all her weight, and with a jerk it shifted. The sound of grinding stone and metal echoed through the passage. She looked pleased with herself and started to push at the round stone door. Oribas pulled her away. 'The seals are held closed by a riddle, Achista.' He brushed dirt from the stonework on the other side of the door. 'There are four mechanisms inside the stone. Each wheel must be set to the sign of the correct

Ascendant to move the bars that prevent the door from opening. When all four are set correctly, the stone can slide aside. They are not easily made and so are not made lightly. Something on the other side of this seal was not meant to be found. And to be sealed here, in a place so remote from the heart of the empire ...' He shook himself. 'If I open this for you, Achista, you must promise me: no one will touch anything on the other side unless I say it is safe.'

Achista set to work on the other wheels, loosening each until she could turn all four. Oribas finished clearing the dirt from the inscription beside the door. The words carved into the stone were old and worn but still deep enough to read: '*Here buried under the mountain lies the iron witch, drowned in the river and laid out in salt where the wind and the sun shall be guardians amid this place of snow and ice.*'

Achista squinted at the wheels. The other Marroc were crowding close now, drawn in by their curiosity. 'But these are just animals.'

'The six Ascendants are the Earth, the Sun, the Fire, the Sky, the River and the Night. Each has its totem.' Oribas frowned. 'Buried under the mountain. A statement of fact, but the mountain is also the Earth.' He skipped to the other side of the door and turned the top wheel to the sign of the bear, the totem animal of the Earth. Without a torch for a lever it took the two of them to make the wheel move, Achista's hands pressed onto his. 'The iron witch?' He shrugged. 'Laid out in salt? Not sure. Drowned in the river is obvious, and the wind and the sun are simple enough too. Guardians in this place of snow and ice. Cold could be the earth again but it's always four different Ascendants. Winter is the season of Night, so maybe that.'

'There are only four wheels, Oribas.'

'I don't think Night is right, not for a place like this. Earth, River, Sky, Sun. Those are the clearest. Bear, fish, bird, dragon. We'll try that first.'

They wrestled with the wheels. As the final one ground into place, the stone groaned and shifted. The wall shook and a deep rumble echoed through the passageway. Oribas backed away. 'If you can move it, I think the door will open now. Have a care, Achista. I have no idea what lies beyond.'

'I know.' She nodded at several of the Marroc, who started to lever the stone aside. Her smile was a weak one.

The Marroc pulled the stone back far enough for someone to squeeze through. They all looked at Oribas expectantly. He shook his head. 'Did any of you bring salt? No? Thought not. Well don't expect me to go ah—' But Achista was already worming her way through and so he didn't have any choice but to follow her. 'The old Aulian priests made these seals to keep the very worst of their demons locked away,' he hissed. 'Things worse than any shadewalker. Believe me when I say I know what sort of creatures they were. If there's a way into the tower, it may have another seal like this one, one that can't be opened at all from the inside.' Whatever they'd put here, there would be other wards though, surely. *Laid out in salt*, and salt was a ward to those creatures. Perhaps they could creep through and creep out the other side and …

'It's the only way to the forkbeards, Oribas.' She held up her torch. 'Besides, look!'

His skin was a-prickle from head to toe but at last he saw what Achista was trying to show him: the tomb wasn't a tomb at all. It was a Lhosir storeroom. They were in the cellars of the tower.

'I told you there was another door, one already opened,' said Achista. 'Some say the Marroc prince who lived here took the treasure he found and went north, and others that something terrible came out and everyone died. And there's some who say he wasn't a Marroc at all. But it was all hundreds of years ago, and whatever was here is long gone. Today there are only forkbeards.'

24

THE ROAD TO MIDDISLET

Gallow didn't look back. Not once. He walked away in stolen boots from the Marroc victory and from the last friend he had left to him after three years of searching for his home. He wore the furs of a dead kinsman and the mail and helm that the Screambreaker had given him outside Andhun. He carried a spear and a sword and an axe and a shield all scavenged from battlefields, and three years of longing in his heart.

The Marroc farmers' trail was marked by cairns of stones that rose from the snow so that even in the winter a traveller wouldn't lose his way. As the light fell he sought shelter where he could find it. A woodsman's hut the first night, the next at a farm among the animals where frightened Marroc stared wide-eyed at his steel, prayed to their gods that in the morning he'd be gone and then thanked them when he was. The only tracks he saw in the snow were of animals crossing from the shelter of one stand of trees to another. The path wound down a sharp-sided valley through stands of giant Varyxhun pine that towered over everything, around boulders strewn about a stream that danced through its heart. Twice he had to wade through snow as deep as a house, cutting a path through a great broken swathe of it that had tumbled down from the slopes above. He had nothing he could use to make any fire and so when twilight fell and there was no shelter to be found he simply walked on through the darkness, guided by the stars and the moon, the only way to keep warm. The cold nipped and bit at him like an angry puppy but it held no fear. He'd crossed the Aulian Way after all, higher and colder and longer than this.

The sides of the valley broke apart. The slopes became more gentle. The stands of pine became a great forest of lesser trees and the stream beside him swelled to a river as other waters joined it. The air grew warmer, the snow under his feet thinner and more broken. He reckoned on being a day away from Hrodicslet when he came to a camp beside the road where the embers of a fire were still warm under his fingers. He sat down beside it and rubbed his hands and blew at the ash but it was too old to glow and light into flames again. There was nothing else to see save for a few marks in the snow where men had sat not long ago and a simple shelter made of branches, a place for a man to sleep out of the wind and the snow. He felt eyes watching him but nothing more. He didn't go looking.

Cold and exhausted and hungry, he reached Hrodicslet. Now at every farm Marroc slammed their doors in his face. They were hospitable folk to their own kind, or so the carter Fenaric had once said, but no one had shelter for a forkbeard.

'I'll pay you! I'll work for you!' he shouted at their doors, but none of them opened again. When the sun began to set and yet another barrage of curses turned him away, he kicked the door open again before the Marroc inside could bar it. There were three of them, an old man and a younger one and another who was little more than a boy. 'What Marroc turns a starving freezing man from their door?' The words sounded hollow even as he spat them to the floor. Any Marroc, that was the answer, if the starving man was a forkbeard.

The men backed away from him. Animals milled around, pigs and goats and chickens all driven inside for warmth and shelter. The young one snatched up a lump of firewood. The old one yelled a curse through gritted teeth, never taking his eyes off Gallow. 'What do you want, forkbeard?'

A dog like a wolf padded out from between the hanging furs that separated the night room from the rest of the house, sending the chickens squawking and flapping away. It bared its teeth and growled at Gallow.

'Make your dog be still or I'll kill it!' But the Marroc didn't move. The dog snarled and drew back to its haunches and still the Marroc did nothing, and then the dog sprang. Gallow lifted his shield. The dog scrabbled for purchase, bit at the wood and then fell. It crouched, glowering and snarling, and then launched itself again, this time at Gallow's arm. Gallow raised his axe out of the dog's reach and twisted to let it fly past. It snapped at him, seizing his furs in its jaws and almost spinning him around.

He brought the axe down on the back of its head and the dog fell dead. The Marroc boy screamed and threw himself at Gallow, swinging his lump of wood. Gallow bashed him away with his shield and there was his hatchet again, singing through the air straight at the boy's head. He pulled the blow at the last but for a moment he'd meant it. For a moment he'd happily have killed the lot of them.

He shoved the boy away. They all stared at him in hatred.

'Damn you, Marroc!'

'Damn you too, forkbeard,' hissed the old man. 'Take what you want and be gone.'

'I'll do that. Where are the women and children?'

The old man glanced at the night room. The younger one clenched his fists and shook his head. *So that's what they thought of forkbeards, was it?* And then he thought of the way it had been with the Screambreaker's army and wondered how he could possibly blame them. 'Make sure they stay there. You two go and be with them.' He pointed his axe at the old man. 'Not you. You stay.'

'What do you want, forkbeard?'

Gallow growled and raised his fist and they did as he asked. He made the old man show him where they kept their food. He took as much as he could carry and a leather bag with a strap to carry it. Everywhere he went would be like this until he was home. There'd be no shelter, no charity, nothing for the hated forkbeard. Fate again, laughing at him. 'I didn't want to kill your dog, old Marroc. I have nothing against dogs.' The old man's face stayed as it was, a mask of hidden fear and sullen hate. 'I'll take my rest in your house tonight. You'll stay in your night room, all of you. If you do as I say then I'll be on my way in the morning and you'll not see me again. If you come out, if you seek help, if any one of you raises a single hand or word against me, I'll kill every person here. I'll burn your farm. I'll go back to my kin and they'll burn your neighbours. We'll hunt you until every single Marroc here lies bloody in the snow. Do you understand me, old man?'

The words hissed out of him. 'I understand you, forkbeard.'

'Then go to your night room and keep your kin there with you, close.'

He pushed the corpse of the dog outside and closed the door behind it. After nights in the mountain snow the house was deliciously warm. In the morning he left with a clutch of fresh eggs. The Marroc had seen just another forkbeard and so that's what he'd become. The realisation haunted him. This was how it was for the Lhosir here; and what if some forkbeard happened upon Nadric's forge, hungry and desperate? Would Arda have the sense to keep her peace?

He skirted around Hrodicslet to the edge of the Crack-marsh, the quickest way home. The fringes of the marsh were boggy but not waterlogged, not like the water meadows they became each spring. The ghuldogs were mostly quiet in the winter, hiding in their burrows. Nothing much came out into this dead open landscape with its stands of twisted trees, not at this time of year. He crossed it without trouble, walking on through the night to keep warm, dozing in the warmest hours of the day, surviving on the food he'd stolen.

Stolen. He'd never been a thief before. At least, he'd never seen himself like that. The Screambreaker's army had plundered the Marroc lands, taking what pleased them, burning whatever caught their eye to burn. The spoils of war though, not thieving, although from where he stood now it was hard to see the difference.

The edge of the Crackmarsh took him to the caves and the woods where the villagers of Middislet had hidden when they'd thought the Vathen were coming, all of them except Arda, who'd stayed alone to defend Nadric's forge because she was fed up with soldiers coming and taking everything that was hers. He remembered that day well, as clear as he remembered the day he'd first seen her, and the memories made a longing that drove him onward, heedless of the pain in his feet and his legs, the weariness in his bones. He couldn't be sure that she was there, whether any of them were even still alive, but each time he closed his eyes he saw her, waiting all this time.

One way or another, he was coming home.

25

WHAT HAPPENED TO TOLVIS LOUDMOUTH

'There's something else I want from you, Loudmouth.' Three years ago Tolvis Loudmouth had stood beside the Screambreaker. It was the morning before the battle that would see the Screambreaker take the red sword from the dead hands of the Weeping Giant and then fall in his turn. Tolvis was hardly ready to be asked for any other favours, given what the Screambreaker had just told him about keeping Twelvefingers from burning Andhun, but you didn't say no to the old man so he'd kept his mouth shut for once. 'If I die tomorrow, take my body and speak me out in secret. I'll have no great celebration for all the things I've done. Then take this where it belongs.' He'd handed over a fat purse of silver. Tolvis knew exactly what it was because it was the same fat purse he'd given to Gallow Truesword a couple of weeks earlier when he'd traded it for Truesword's plundered Vathan horses.

A hundred men saw the Screambreaker die later that same day, moments before the Lhosir broke the Vathan army. Afterwards, when they couldn't find his body, they built a pyre to him anyway and spoke him out. And then Twelvefingers turned on Andhun and the Marroc there, and Tolvis had led a band of the Screambreaker's men to stop him, and Gallow had chopped off Medrin's hand and turned him into Sixfingers instead of Twelve; and then the Vathen had turned out not to be as broken as everyone thought and by the next sunrise half of Andhun belonged to the horsemen, someone burning the bridge across the Isset was the only thing keeping them out of the other half, and Sixfingers was on a ship back across the sea, hovering somewhere between life and death. Tolvis had watched Gallow fall from the cliffs into the sea and thought maybe he'd seen a man with a boat trying to haul someone out of the water or maybe not, but either way it was hard to be sure because the air over his head had been full of Vathan arrows and javelots at the time and mostly he'd been trying not to die.

He hadn't gone home nor sought the remnants of the Lhosir army. By then he'd had enough of it all, and so he'd gone inland instead, all on his own, because Gallow had been a friend, and being a friend had to be worth something. He'd gone to Varyxhun and poked his nose around for Arda Smithswife and eventually found her and gave her the purse full of silver that Gallow had always meant her to have, and she'd taken it with thanks. And maybe it came from living with a Lhosir for eight years or maybe it was simply the way she was, but it didn't seem to trouble her much that he was a forkbeard. He'd stayed a while because he wasn't quite sure whether Gallow was dead or alive, but if he was alive then he'd certainly find a way back home from Andhun and it seemed only right that he should keep an eye on his friend's family until then. A week grew into a month and then two. Varyxhun filled with Lhosir looking for Gallow Foxbeard, the traitor, the *nioingr*. Tolvis kept away. They'd have been happy enough to hang Loudmouth too.

Two months turned into three. By then they all knew that Gallow wouldn't be coming back, though none of them said it; and he still stayed, and Arda never minded about that as long as he made himself useful, and none of them said anything about the Lhosir looking for the Foxbeard. When the Fateguard came, they left, quietly, going back to Nadric's old forge in Middislet, and the months turned into a year without any of them quite noticing. Nadric was getting too old to earn his living at his forge but Tolvis knew how to work a farm and he had a strong arm and a quick enough wit to learn the simple things. As that first winter came, Arda took to being away for days at a time. Tolvis never asked, not then, and she never said, but she came back with food, and more than they needed. There were Marroc in the Crackmarsh, bandits and renegades sworn to fight the forkbeards. He knew that was where she went, but it wasn't his business and so he left her to it. The villagers in Middislet weren't that keen on forkbeards just like all the other Marroc, but Middislet wasn't Varyxhun or Andhun and they'd never had blood ravens lining the roads. Mostly everyone got quietly on with their lives, and if Arda had swapped one forkbeard for another, so what? Loudmouth had a quiet suspicion that half the Marroc thought he was Gallow just come back from the fighting with a big mess made of his face. Besides, that first winter was a hard one and there were plenty of people grateful for the food Arda brought out of the Crackmarsh.

A year turned into two and Arda came to him one day and told him that if he was staying he might want to cut off his beard, and it hadn't surprised him greatly either when, after he did it, she'd taken him to the night room alone. There wasn't any ceremony about it, but she was lying with him and laying Gallow to rest both at once, and he'd been happy enough with that. Some of the Marroc said things behind her back and others said them to her face, but she only shrugged and pointed out that people had always said things behind her back even before she'd married Gallow, and that she had no truck with anyone whose life was so joyless they had nothing better to do than make misery for others, nor did she care in the least as long as there was food for her family. Gallow's silver made her rich in the village, she still vanished off among the Crackmarsh men for whole weeks at a time, and it wasn't as if there were baskets full of spare men going at the market who'd look after her and her half-forkbeard children. She made Tolvis laugh, and he made her laugh too, and when Sixfingers came back across the sea with a new hand made of witch's iron and set about raising armies to fight the Vathen, Tolvis kept to himself, not wanting anything to do with it.

'Loudmouth!'

He looked up from where he was supposed to be cutting nails for Nadric. There weren't too many Marroc who bothered to talk to him in Middislet. They were used to him, tolerated him with grudging reluctance, but no one said they had to like it. But now and then Fenaric the carter came by, and Fenaric didn't seem to care who Tolvis was, even though Arda made it plain that she couldn't stand the carter and wouldn't spare him a word.

'I've got news, forkbeard. You might want to hear it.' He looked from side to side as though there might be someone lurking in the shadows of the forge.

'What's that then?' Tolvis was careful to be civil with the carter. Varyxhun was turning bad. Tolvis quietly thought that if there wasn't an uprising in the spring then he'd eat Nadric's forge, and if there *was,* well he wanted to be far away from it. And then there was Sixfingers. He hadn't forgotten Gallow, that was for sure. Probably thought of him every time he looked at the stump where his hand used to be. Probably hadn't forgotten that Gallow had had a family. So yes, he gave Fenaric the time of day, careful to keep an ear to the ground.

Fenaric sat himself on a log beside the forge fire. 'Could do with new tyres for the wagon,' he said.

So he was short of money. Tolvis nodded. 'I'll talk to Nadric and see what's to be done.' That's how it went. Little favours for snippets of the world outside the village.

'Was up at Issetbridge.' He sniffed and looked about as though he was bored. 'Heard a story that a dozen forkbeards

168

got killed up in the high valleys. Not the only story like that, either.'

'Glad that's not near here then.' Cithjan had a fondness for hangings from what he'd heard. Thought if you hanged enough Marroc everything would be sorted out. Maybe if he hanged every last one of them, it would.

'Reckon it's going to get bloody, forkbeard.'

'Reckon so, carter.' Tolvis went back to cutting nails. If that was all Fenaric had then he could pay for his tyres.

The carter stayed where he was though, so there was clearly more. Funny thing about the trouble in Varyxhun – it made the Marroc in Middislet more unsure about Tolvis. Reminded them how much they were supposed to hate all forkbeards; but at the same time Tolvis knew it set them thinking about how it might not be such a bad thing to have one living among them if the trouble spilled over the Aulian Bridge. 'There was one other thing I heard. Something about a sword. That sword the Vathen were supposed to have with them at Andhun, the one you forkbeards took off them.'

Tolvis stopped cutting. 'Oh yes?'

'Well I don't know for sure what's true and what's not, but what I heard was it went missing when the Vathen kicked you lot out of Andhun.' He cocked his head. 'You know different?'

'No, that's about the right of it.' Tolvis tried not to look interested.

'There's a rumour going around Issetbridge that the iron devil of Varyxhun has found it again.'

Tolvis almost choked. 'Anyone say how?'

Fenaric stuck out his bottom lip and grunted, and Tolvis knew him well enough to know this wasn't just the carter trying to get some tyres hammered for nothing. After a bit Fenaric stood up. 'That's about it.'

'That was news worth having, carter. I'll see about those tyres.'

'No hurry. I'll be good for another month. If they're ready for the next time I roll through, that would be fine.' He walked away.

Tolvis Loudmouth sat and stared at the forge for a very long time and hardly cut any nails at all after Fenaric left. The carter had earned his tyres but Tolvis wasn't sure what to make of it, because if the red sword hadn't drowned off the cliffs of Andhun then maybe Gallow hadn't drowned there either, and a pang of something came with that thought. Not fear, exactly. Sadness, and that was when he realised how content he'd become here, doing nothing very much and being in no way important.

He didn't tell Arda. The return of the red sword wouldn't mean anything to her, but he took to sleeping with his own blade kept in the corner of the night room, which she noticed and gave him all sorts of grief for until he made up some story after Fenaric had gone about outlaws roaming the Fedderhun Road. And then the day after that Vennic came screaming through the village with some wild tale about a man made of iron riding the fringes of the Crackmarsh. Vennic hadn't seen it himself but he'd heard from another shepherd out in the hills and now he had it in his head that a shadewalker was coming. The rest of the village laughed in his face. Shadewalkers never rode horses and they didn't wear iron or venture out in the middle of the day, and anyway this was Vennic, who saw ghosts in the moon and devils in the shadows and thought Modris talked to him through his sheep.

Tolvis kept his mouth shut. He'd seen enough to know it was a Fateguard that Vennic's friend had seen, the iron devil of Varyxhun. After that he took to sleeping with his shield in the night room too, and with one eye open, and that was probably why he sat up in the small hours of the morning a few nights later, wide awake and quite sure there was someone outside. He slipped his sword out of its scabbard and slid his shield onto his arm and crept to the door to the yard and opened it a crack, and right there in front of him was the shadow of a man swathed in metal and with a shield of his own on his arm. Tolvis let out a cry and jumped back, ready for a fight, but the iron devil in the yard didn't move.

'Tolvis Loudmouth?' Iron grated on iron. 'Well I certainly wasn't expecting to find *you*. Still, Sixfingers keeps a special place in his heart for both of you.'

26

THE IRON MAN

Middislet was still miles away when the sun set but Gallow kept walking. Perhaps there was shelter to be found in the hills that edged the Crackmarsh but he wasn't looking for it, not now. He knew how close he was and he knew this land, and besides there were Marroc in the woods and caves here. He'd seen them. Bandits or thieves, he didn't know which, but it didn't matter. He was a forkbeard alone and so he kept on going. He could almost have walked these last miles blindfold and still found his way home.

Snow started to fall, muffling the darkness and silencing the wind. The night was black as ink when he reached the forge and the house was still. Everyone inside would be sleeping. He listened at the door and heard nothing, no snores, no snuffles, no wheezes. But this was home, still the way he remembered it, and his heart was beating fast. Three years. Anything could have happened. He didn't know whether to knock or simply open the door and creep inside.

He was still standing there when he heard movement, the scrape of wood across the floor and then the chink of metal and a footstep and the door opened, and in the night Gallow stared. There was a man. He was holding a candle. Not Nadric, not Arda, but ...

'Tolvis Loudmouth?' Gallow stared. The side of Loudmouth's face was a mass of scars from that last fight in Andhun. He looked fatter and his forked beard was gone. But most of all Gallow simply couldn't understand what he was doing here. Here in Middislet at Nadric's forge. It made no sense. Words started and then faltered.

'Gallow?' Tolvis couldn't find anything to say either.

Gallow couldn't think, couldn't think of anything at all except that Tolvis had been a friend, one he'd never thought to see again. He offered his arm and Tolvis took it and they clasped each other. 'Loudmouth?' He shook his head in disbelief again. 'Your beard ...'

Tolvis was laughing, almost weeping with joy and surprise and dismay. 'The silver I got you for those horses in Andhun. The Screambreaker.' He shook his head. 'There didn't seem to be a particularly good moment for giving it back, what with the whole chopping Medrin's hand off and being chased through the castle by a Vathan horde. And then you didn't come ... You held the Vathen long enough that we got away. I couldn't keep all that silver if it wasn't mine and so I went to Varyxhun after Andhun fell and I found her, and then I stayed in case you came back and weren't dead after all, and then I never quite ... left ...'

'Loudmouth.' Gallow shook his head. Now he looked closer there were bruises and a bloody gash on Loudmouth's face. Fresh, no more than a day old. 'What's wrong?'

Tolvis looked over his shoulder. He glanced at the night room. 'Maker-Devourer, Gallow, I'm so sorry.'

Gallow's heart beat even faster. 'What, Loudmouth? What is it?'

He had tears in his eyes. His hands grasped Gallow's arms. 'I looked after your family, Gallow. I've done what I could but Sixfingers never stopped looking.'

'My sons?'

Tolvis looked away. Gallow grabbed his shirt and shook him.

'Arda? What, Loudmouth? *What?*'

And then the furs around the night room shifted and a shadow moved out of them and a rasp cut the night. 'This was always where you'd come, Foxbeard. I've been waiting for you.'

The scrape of metal on metal and then a shape unfolded itself from the darkness behind Tolvis, a man cased in iron, and Gallow knew, though he couldn't see the face that lay beneath the mask in the moonlight, that this was Beyard. Who else? Gallow hissed, 'You're dead!'

'Did you weep for me, old friend? Did you build a pyre for me and speak me out?' Between them Tolvis hung his head. Beyard held out the amulet with the lock of Arda's hair and threw it at Gallow's feet. 'You were quick, Truesword, but I was quicker. Across the Crackmarsh and the bandits and the ghuldogs knew enough to leave well alone. I watched her. Your children too. I know why you came home.' He pushed Tolvis aside and offered out his hand. 'Come, old friend. No need for Sixfingers to know. You understand what he'd do if he did.'

Snap their ribs from their spines and pull their lungs through their skin and fly them like wings, suspended from gibbets and wheels. Blood ravens. Gallow's hand gripped his sword. He shook his head. 'Where are they, Beyard? What have you done?'

'They're in the cellar. Unhurt. Aren't they, Loudmouth?'

Tolvis bowed his head. He nodded, eyes closed.

'I have no interest in them, Truesword. Medrin need never know. You can't escape your fate but no one else has to share it.' His face turned a fraction to Tolvis. 'Even this one. We'll leave, you and I, quietly in the night. Loudmouth here will lie with your woman and raise your sons as his own. We both know he'll raise them as he should.' Beyard made a wet rasping sound that might have been laughter and tipped his head to Tolvis. 'After all, I didn't make you stay, Loudmouth. You could have left me alone with them if you'd wished. But you couldn't do that, could you?'

Tolvis seemed to fold in on himself. He shrank back into

the darkness of the house. 'I looked after them, Gallow. We thought you were dead. I kept them safe.'

Gallow hesitated. He looked from Tolvis to Beyard and back again. 'I'll kill you, old friend, if I have to.'

Beyard nodded. 'As I will you, old friend. I will kill who I must.' His sword was already in his hand. The red sword, Solace, and now he levelled it at Tolvis. 'This one tried already. He fought well, but I am Fateguard now and my skin is iron.'

'Swear on your blood, Beyard. No harm to my wife and my family. Swear you won't come back for them. Swear you won't come back for Loudmouth.'

'I told you in Varyxhun, Gallow: I can't swear on what I don't have.' Beyard dropped to one knee, though the sword remained pointed at Loudmouth's throat. 'They think you dead, Truesword. The family you left, they belong to another now. I've watched. Your sons call Loudmouth father. Your wife calls him husband. Your fate lies elsewhere and always did. Leave them be, Truesword. Let us go into the night, the two of us alone. I've not forgotten that Sixfingers fled and left us once long ago. I've no love for him, only duty.'

Tolvis hissed, 'Then don't serve him!'

'I must.'

Gallow slowly slid his sword back into its scabbard. He looked at Loudmouth and sniffed the air and looked at Beyard again, standing once more with the red sword still in his hand. Three years of searching and now the last gift he could give them was to leave? Let them go? 'I'd see them one more time. I'll not wake them. Then I'll come with you.'

'It's best they don't know, Truesword.'

'I know.'

Tolvis turned and gripped Gallow's arm. 'They're strong and filled with life. That much I did well.'

Gallow walked inside, treading lightly. The smells were such an old familiar comfort that they almost made him weep. He crept down the steps into the stale warmth of the cellar and crouched down beside each of the sleeping figures there. His sons: Pursic, who'd grown into a boy in the years he'd been gone, and Tathic. His daughters: Feya, who was losing the baby looks he remembered, and Jelira, the daughter who wasn't his but whom he'd taken to be his own, almost a woman now. And Arda. He crouched beside her for the longest time of all, drawn by the temptation to wake her. She looked exactly as he remembered. No one who glanced at her in the street would have said she was beautiful but to Gallow she was perfect. He swallowed hard and forced himself to rise. Beyard was right: what good did it do for her to see him now? She'd shout and scream at him for not coming home and she'd wake everyone else, and then she'd probably go up and start throwing pans at the ironskin.

Three years across half the world to be here though. Tears blurred his eyes. They were alive. Well. Safe. Perhaps if he went with Beyard then they might stay that way. Loudmouth would take care of them and Tathic and Pursic would grow to be fine young men who didn't remember too much of their real father. Perhaps that was for the best. What did he have to offer them now? A life of being hunted, that's what. And Arda, in her cold harsh practical way, would tell him the same, no matter how much she was screaming inside, and no one would ever see her weep except maybe Loudmouth now and then.

He climbed quietly back up the steps. 'Thank you, Beyard. Thank you for that.'

'You were my friend once.' The iron man beckoned, eyes on Loudmouth. 'Come, Truesword.'

Gallow followed Beyard outside. Every step felt as though he was walking through stone, as though he was wading up the steep slope of one of the great dunes from the desert that Oribas called home. It seemed such a long way to come only to end like this.

'It is your fate, Truesword. Set for the three of us all those years ago.'

Gallow thought about that for a bit. 'I turned my back on that fate once.'

'And look what it brought you.'

'You two talk too much.' Tolvis hurled himself at Beyard. A sword flashed in the moonlight, cutting at Beyard's face. The Fateguard stepped back. Neither of them carried a shield but Beyard was in his iron, covered head to toe in it, while Tolvis had a thick sheepskin night shirt and nothing else.

'Must we do this again?' Beyard lashed out, fast as lightning, but Tolvis danced away, quicker still and too quick for Beyard to catch. The air moaned. The Fateguard still carried the red sword.

Tolvis howled like a wolf. 'Come on Gallow! There's two of us now!'

There was no reading Beyard's face under his mask but his voice was low and cold. 'I was kind to you last time, Tolvis Loudmouth. I won't be kind again.'

'That's the sword that cut off Medrin's hand, is it?' Loudmouth jumped away as Beyard swung again. 'As good as any to take my head.' He flicked a glance at Gallow. 'Help me, Gallow. I can't fight him on my own. Tried that already. If he kills me, who looks after the others?'

Beyard glared. 'Stand your ground, Truesword. I'll keep my word if you keep yours.'

'And I've always wanted to kill a Fateguard,' shouted Tolvis. 'Everyone says you can't. Everyone says the Fateguard don't ever die but that can't be right. You're just men under there.'

'Stop, Tolvis!' Gallow lunged to pull Loudmouth away but he was too quick.

'And what, Truesword? Stay here and hide while you go meekly to Medrin? Damn you! I told you to make an end of him there and then.' He shook his head. 'I came here to give your woman your silver and watch over your sons as a true friend might do, but I've broken that friendship.' His sword clattered off Beyard's iron arm. 'I stayed too long. I've lain with your woman and called your sons my own.' The air screamed as Solace sliced an inch in front of Loudmouth's face. 'You were the one who stayed to hold the Vathen. If one of us must die today then let it be me, Truesword, not you, not this time.' He caught Beyard another ringing blow, this time on the hip. The Fateguard lunged, untroubled. The tip of the Edge of Sorrows stabbed into Loudmouth's side as he danced away.

'Stop!' Gallow had his axe in his hand. Beyard swung the red sword's tip towards him at once.

'Stand your ground, Gallow Truesword!'

Through the open door into the house the cellar swung open with a crash. Arda. Gallow turned away, hiding his face. He roared at Tolvis again but neither of them would listen. Tolvis slipped inside Beyard's guard. His sword skittered sparks from the Fateguard's iron crown. Beyard cuffed him away.

'You! Forkbeard pig-poker!' Arda ran out behind Gallow. He knew what was coming and stepped away and had to turn. She had a half-full chamber pot, ready to crack him over the head with it, and then she saw his face and froze and the chamber pot fell from her fingers and crashed between them, spilling itself over their feet. 'You!' Her mouth fell open. He'd never seen her eyes so wide. 'Gallow?'

'Arda!' He wanted to reach for her but his arms wouldn't move and he had an axe in one hand and a shield in the other. She didn't move either. Just stared and stared as though she was seeing a ghost; and perhaps to her that's what he was.

Loudmouth whooped as his sword clattered on Beyard's armour again. 'Sooner or later, Fateguard, I'm going to find a hole and slide this into you.' He jumped into the shadows of Nadric's forge. Beyard moved slowly after him.

Now it was Nadric at the top of the cellar steps, squinting. 'Gallow?'

Tolvis kicked a plume of ash from the forge's firepit into Beyard's face. The Fateguard stepped back and Tolvis lunged, stabbing at the iron man's eyes, but Beyard caught his blade with the Edge of Sorrows and for a moment they were pressed together. Beyard's knee slammed up. Tolvis squealed and doubled over, threw himself back, slipped and fell.

'Dada?' More faces were peering up from the cellar, squeezing past Nadric and running to the open door, staring out into the yard. Pursic, the smallest of them staring at Tolvis, not at Gallow. 'Dada!' Nadric tried to push the children back inside but they wriggled through his hands.

Beyard took a quick stride and stood over Tolvis. 'Brave, Loudmouth, but stupid.' He lifted the Edge of Sorrows ready to drive it down.

Gallow threw his axe as hard as he could, straight into Beyard's side. It bit into the Fateguard's iron and staggered him sideways. Beyard roared. His head snapped to Gallow and his face lowered. 'You've sealed all our fates now, old friend. None will be spared.' He kicked Tolvis and came at Gallow, the scattered embers of the forge fire crunching under his iron boots. Gallow drew his sword and lifted his shield and braced himself ready for the Edge of Sorrows to come.

27

A SIMPLE VICTORY

The Marroc gathered in the cellars of Witches' Reach, waiting until they were all up the shaft. Oribas looked at what the Lhosir had stored in the cellar-tomb. Kegs of ale and mead. Sacks and sacks of flour and dried peas and beans, strings of onions. A few baskets of nuts. Certainly enough to keep a hundred Marroc fed for a few weeks. He looked at the stone door, rolled right back now. They could close it behind them but there was no way to seal it from the inside; nor was there a way to open it again once the four seals had been locked. Oribas found a second door like the first, the way out into the rest of the tower, wide open and half smashed apart. Whatever the Aulians had buried here was long gone. Still, he checked through the sacks and the crates and baskets until he found some salt and filled the bag over his shoulder.

Achista beckoned the Marroc on. Beyond the second seal a staircase spiralled up into the bottom of the tower. They went up. Oribas recognised the room at once. It was hexagonal, with the stairs in the centre and six stone benches set one into each wall. They would have been altars once, one for each of the Ascendants, but now the Lhosir used them for tables and the whole room was piled with more crates and sacks.

Voices echoed down the staircase. Lhosir. Achista crept forward, finger to her lips and her bow in her other hand. She nocked an arrow and began up the steps. Other Marroc crowded around her, the ones with mail and helms; when Oribas tried to follow she pushed him gently away and shook her head and so he watched anxiously as the Marroc silently inched their way up until the first alarmed Lhosir shout came ringing down. The Marroc all started yelling and running and the men around him let out whoops and charged up the steps. Oribas found himself joining them, carried away in the rush. They burst out into a kitchen where three Lhosir already lay dead, riddled with arrows. The Marroc rushed on, most pouring out of a door into the yard between the tower and the wall that surrounded it, some pushing on up a flight of steep wooden steps. Sounds of fighting came from both. Oribas took the door. It was easier. He had no idea which way Achista had gone but he wanted to be near her. It didn't make any sense since there wasn't anything he could do except get in the way, but he wanted it anyway.

The curtain wall of Witches' Reach encircled the summit of the mountain with the tower built into it on the very peak. Half a dozen wooden huts and outhouses had been propped up against the stonework: stables and a small forge and storehouses, perhaps, or hanging sheds, or maybe the Lhosir slept out here. Oribas had no idea. The gates to the road down the mountainside and the Aulian Bridge hung open. A dozen Lhosir – some in mail, some not – were fighting twice that many Marroc. Most of the Lhosir had formed themselves into a circle of shields and the Marroc were keeping them occupied while they brought down the ones who'd been cut off from their fellows. A wide flight of steps rose to another door, the main door into the tower. Aulian steps. Indeed, everything about the tower was jarringly familiar. It looked like the towers Oribas knew from the desert, with their finely jointed walls in which every stone was different and no join ran straight for long, fitted together like a jigsaw with hardly room to slip a knife blade in between them. The outer wall was more recent and a much cruder thing, stones piled haphazardly together and thick with crumbling mortar.

The door at the top of the stairs burst open. Four Lhosir in mail hurtled out, smashing through the Marroc in the yard, cutting two men down as they went. Another dozen Marroc came after them, shouting and screaming and waving axes. The Lhosir punched through the Marroc surrounding the circle of shields and joined it and Oribas watched in admiration: the circle opened to receive them and closed again around them and then grew a little as the new Lhosir joined the wall. It was seamless.

'Take them!' screamed Achista. She stood at the top of the steps and loosed an arrow at the Lhosir. It stuck into a shield and quivered there.

The Lhosir held their ground and the yard fell still for a moment, some Marroc finishing off the men they'd caught alone, the others standing back from the Lhosir shield wall. The Marroc outnumbered the Lhosir three or four to one but they were the ones afraid, and now that fear was turning against them. They started to back away. Oribas saw one or two Lhosir glance at the open gates and then back at the Marroc in front of them. 'Let them go!' he shouted. 'Let them run.' That's what Achista wanted, wasn't it? For word to spread of their defeat?

And then, gods preserve him, there she was, shouldering her bow and snatching an axe from the Marroc beside her and walking towards the Lhosir shields. She looked so small in her outsize mail shirt against the men in their furs with their forked beards. They'd kill her in a blink and he couldn't do anything, not a thing! He didn't have a weapon, and even if he had, he wouldn't have had the first idea what to do with it.

One of the Lhosir pointed at her and laughed; and then all the Lhosir were shouting, taunting the Marroc around them that they were afraid and had to send a woman to do their fighting, and Achista had pushed her way to the front of the Marroc and stood there for a moment, holding her axe, staring them down. Any moment now she'd charge them, he knew it, and then ...

He couldn't think what else to do. He snatched up a fistful of snow and scrunched it into a ball, let out a high-pitched cry – it probably didn't sound frightening at all but it was meant for his own courage – ran through the Marroc to stand beside Achista and hurled his snowball at the Lhosir. It was a good throw. It clipped a shield and broke apart into the face of the Lhosir holding it. A few of the Marroc laughed. He grabbed another handful and hurled that too, and then another and another, and now some of the Marroc joined in, pelting the Lhosir with snow as they stood behind their shields; and then in the midst of that someone fired an arrow and the Lhosir didn't see it coming. It hit one in the face and he staggered back, and then other arrows came; and perhaps one of them came from a Marroc who'd been with Oribas in the woods, for it flew low beneath the shields and struck a Lhosir in the leg. The wounded Lhosir howled and broke from the wall, charging as best he could, flailing his axe; and again the Marroc might have lost their courage if it hadn't been for Achista, who ran straight back at him. He batted her away with his shield and ignored her, but now two of the Marroc in mail ran at him. The three crashed together. The Lhosir took one of the Marroc down with a huge swing of his axe and then fell a moment later to the other. Achista picked herself up, and at that rest of the Lhosir charged. Oribas had no idea whether they were charging for the gates and escape or still thought they could win the day, but the Marroc split and let them through, and the Lhosir must have taken that as a sign that these Marroc had no stomach to fight, for the shield wall broke apart and they fell upon the Marroc as though they were a broken enemy, but the Marroc weren't broken at all. They surrounded each Lhosir as they'd learned in Jodderslet. They took them down one by one, pulling them into the snow and finishing them off with their knives; and every time a Lhosir cut one Marroc down, two more surged into him, leaping on his back, grabbing his shield, stabbing and hacking and slashing.

The Lhosir fought to the bitter end. The last two stood back to back behind their shields and whirling axes and killed three men before the Marroc withdrew and peppered them with arrows until they fell. Carnage filled the snow-covered yard. To Oribas it was a vision of horror but Achista was jubilant. She ran among the dazed Marroc from one to the next, grabbing them, shaking them, showing them what they'd done. The invincible forkbeards! Beaten! Again! She went to every single one of them, to the ones who crouched beside friends or brothers whose blood now stained the snow, touching them all. Then to the wounded, doing nothing useful except telling them how Modris would protect them and reward them for their courage. Oribas shook his head. Wounds from Lhosir spears and swords were savage things but here were Marroc men laughing and talking through their pain, covered in their own blood, men who wouldn't last the night.

He picked himself up and busied himself among them – treating wounds was one of the first things he'd learned. There wasn't much he could do for some and for others he lacked the medicines that might have saved them. But the cold of this place was his ally now. He pressed snow into wounds to staunch the blood and sent those Marroc who seemed to have nothing better to do into the tower to look for needles and thread and to get a fire going. The axe cuts were the easiest, ragged and bloody and horrible to look at but rarely deep. He set them aside to be stitched and cauterised. The men wounded by stabs from spears and swords were probably going to die but he did what he could for them. The Marroc watched with a mix of awe and horror when he packed wounds with snow then stitched them half closed but still open enough to drain. A few muttered under their breath about witchcraft, but they let him be. He was the Aulian wizard, after all, who'd laid a shadewalker to rest and opened the seal between the caves and the tower; and he was, they whispered to each other, sworn to serve the Huntress Achista who'd led them to victory at Jodderslet and now twice more. Oribas didn't remember swearing anything to anyone but he wasn't going to argue. Besides, if Achista had asked him there and then for an oath he might just have given it.

They let him work, and by the time he was finished with the easier wounds the sun had set and the Marroc had raised their banner from the top of the tower just as Achista said they would, had lit a great fire and were feasting on Lhosir food. Achista kept them busy carrying the bodies of their own dead away, deep into the woods where the Lhosir would never find them, and coming back with bundle after bundle of firewood. They'd have until the morning, she said, before the forkbeards knew what they'd done, and after that the gates would be closed and they'd hold the forkbeards at bay for as long as it took the Marroc to rise across the valley and throw them out.

That night she was alive with energy. She set watches and then picked two dozen men to creep down to the Varyxhun Road. They dragged out the bodies of the dead Lhosir, already stripped naked and scavenged for anything the Marroc could use. Oribas stayed in the tower so he didn't see, but he heard in the morning that they'd beheaded every one of them, scattered the bodies along the trail that led from the Varyxhun Road up the mountainside to Witches' Reach and left the heads piled on the Aulian Bridge. The Lhosir would know what they'd done. Everyone would know, and the edge of the Crackmarsh wasn't far away, where the outlaw Valaric had his hideaway with five hundred Marroc soldiers, all of whom had taken a blood oath of vengeance against Medrin Sixfingers for what he'd done in Andhun.

Oribas was glad to have no part of such dealings – instead he took a torch down to the old Aulian tomb. Not that he thought there was anything left to fear if the Lhosir had lived here for so long, but he wanted to be sure and he was curious to know what was so terrible that the Aulians had built a tomb so far from their homes. There were histories of all sorts of creatures, sorcerers and monsters hunted down and sealed inside these tombs. He knew of at least a dozen but he'd never heard of anything so terrible that it had been carried across the mountains to be so far away from the empire.

He moved through the crates and sacks, searching for the old Aulian crypt that was surely there. He found it eventually, a narrow crawlway that he could only get through by lying down and wriggling forward, holding the torch right out in front of him. There were strange scorings in the stone, deep grooves with no particular pattern to them. The crawlway was unpleasantly tight, as if deliberately too narrow for a large man to escape. It went on for a few feet and then opened into a small round chamber. In the centre stood a flat stone block large enough for a man to lie flat on top. Rising out of the block were six iron rods as thick as his thumb. They were stained and brittle with rust and all of them had snapped, but the rods had clearly once reached from the slab to the ceiling. Broken pieces of them lay on the floor, and there were deep holes in the stone of the roof matching the stumps below. The floor was covered in a pale grit. Oribas touched a few grains of it to his tongue. Salt.

He crawled around the chamber and found something else: two pieces of iron armour, a chest plate and a back plate. Each had three holes punched through them, sized and spaced to match the iron rods. He tested them against the width of the crawlway. They wouldn't fit, no matter which way round he tried them, but there were scratches on the inside of the chamber as though someone else had tried the same and had been much more persistent in their efforts.

He sat and stared for a while, wondering. It looked for all the world as though a suit of iron armour had once been pinned to the stone slab by six iron rods. An inscription even read *the iron witch*. What was it they'd had here?

There were no bones. That bothered him. After the tomb was opened someone might have come in and taken the armour for its iron, but why take their bones? Another thing bothered him too: the breastplate looked familiar. It looked like the armour of the iron devil who'd taken the Edge of Sorrows from Brawlic's farm. The Lhosir Fateguard.

He scraped around the edges of the stone slab for more inscriptions. Aulian priests liked to bind their prisoners with words and symbols as well as stone and metal and salt, but he found nothing, and that was strange too. There were places where inscriptions might have been, places where they ought to have been, but they looked as though they'd been scraped clean, the walls rubbed and scratched until no trace of words remained, only gouges in the stone.

He must have been there a long time but he didn't really notice. He dug more fistfuls of salt out of the bag on his belt because it never hurt to sprinkle salt over a place like this. He spilled half of it over the pieces of armour and spread the rest over the slab. Nothing happened, which was something of a relief. Afterwards, when he'd crawled back out of the crypt, he felt a little foolish and in need of some rest.

On his way up the stairs he found Achista coming the other way. She looked surprised to see him.

'I was looking for you,' she said, but he knew she wasn't. He smiled anyway.

'You found me.'

'What were you doing?'

'I was looking at the tomb. Just curiosity.'

'I wanted to thank you for what you did with the wounded men.'

Oribas wasn't sure that all the Marroc felt the same, and they'd thank him even less when some of the wounds turned bad, when he started to drain fluids from the deeper ones, when the ones he'd known right from the start he'd never save began to die. That would be in the morning. Two of them, if he was right. He forced the smile back onto his face. 'And what were you really doing coming down here, Achista? After something from the Lhosir stores?' But the way her eyes suddenly wouldn't meet his forced him to think elsewhere. 'The seal?'

She nodded. 'We should close it. What if the forkbeards find it when they come?'

'If it's closed then it can't be opened again from this side. You'd trap us here. You know that, don't you?'

She couldn't look at him. He understood – this was what she and Addic had planned from the start. They'd hold for as long as it took. Either the Marroc of Varyxhun would rise or the Marroc of Witches' Reach would die to the last man. There'd be no running away because there was nowhere to go. 'Someone could always slip out and open the seal again from the outside. If the forkbeards hadn't found the cave and it was time for us to go.'

'Someone who understood how to make it work.' She meant him.

'Yes. I thought … I thought perhaps you could wait somewhere nearby. And watch for our signal to come.' A signal that would never happen, or would be a column of flame as the tower burned with Achista and the last of the Marroc trapped inside, set on martyrdom. Oribas took her hands.

'As you wish.' He had to blink the tears from his eyes. 'But not today, Achista. Not today. When the Lhosir find the cave then we'll close the seal. But until then there's no hurry, is there?'

Her eyes shone in the torchlight, brim-full with sadness and joy. She leaned into him and rested her head on his shoulder. 'No, Aulian. I suppose a few more days can't hurt.'

28

THE FORGE

Deep under Witches' Reach Oribas poured his salt.
Far away in the icy north the Eyes of Time shrieked
in white burning agony. In the Temple of Fates in Nardjas
and in Sithhun at King Medrin's side the iron-skinned men
of the Fateguard staggered and howled. And in Middislet
Gallow held his sword high, ready for the Edge of Sorrows
to come down, but the blow never fell. Beyard clutched
his head, fell to his knees and screamed at a pain he didn't
understand. The Edge of Sorrows slipped from limp iron
fingers into the snow.

Tolvis pulled himself to his feet and lifted his sword
but Gallow stilled him. He stooped and took the Edge of
Sorrows. Beyard knelt, breathing hard. He slowly raised his
head and looked up. Gallow held the point of the red sword
to his face.

'Go on,' whispered Beyard. 'Do it. I will not stop you.'

Loudmouth laughed. 'Don't you dare let him—'

Gallow cut him off. 'Get Nadric and the children back
inside! Keep them away and leave this to me.' He tapped
Beyard several times on the crown with the Edge of Sorrows
and felt a tingle in his arm with each touch, a tiny shock
with every tap. 'In the forge, old friend. In the shadows and
out of the snow. Get up.'

'No!' Loudmouth was clutching an axe now. For a
moment Gallow almost turned the red sword on him. It
would be easy. Simple. One cut, and didn't he deserve it for

what he'd done, stealing another man's wife and sons?

But that was the sword up to its old tricks and Gallow was wise to them. 'He was a friend for far longer than you were, Loudmouth. Just keep away. And you, old friend, take off that crown and that mask. I'd see your face one last time to remember you as we both once were. Young and stupid.'

Beyard lifted the iron helm from his shoulders. He stared at Gallow with pale dead eyes. 'How did you do it, Truesword?'

'Fate.' Gallow shrugged. Even with the mask gone he couldn't read Beyard's face. Sadness. Nothing more. Flakes of snow drifted down between them. Where they landed on Beyard's hair, Gallow saw, they didn't melt.

'Do it here, Gallow. Under the sky.'

Gallow hesitated. As he shifted, the candlelight from the house caught Beyard's face again. He looked as pale as a dead man.

'I swore I would not forget, old friend. I did not. I am Fateguard now but I gave no one your name then and nor have I now. Sixfingers will look for the sword but not for Gallow Foxbeard, nor for his wife and sons, not from me.' For a moment Beyard smiled. 'Piss-poor gang of thieves we turned out to be.'

'Piss-poor.'

'You saw the shield in the end. As did I, in time. Hardly worth it, was it?'

'It wasn't seeing it that mattered. It was the getting that close.'

Beyard rasped, or maybe laughed. He nodded. 'Yes.' Gallow tried to lift the red sword to finish it but his hand wouldn't move.

Arda strode out of the house in her winter furs and her boots. She hit Beyard in the face with a pan and he sprawled back into the snow. 'Three years, you pig!' she snapped, turning to Gallow. 'Three years and then you come back and you bring *this* with you!' She stamped on Beyard's iron-skinned fingers. 'Trees think better than you do! Now either finish this pasty-faced forkbeard or give me that sword so I can do it.' She snorted. 'Or you can give it to Loudmouth, not that he'd be any better.'

Gallow didn't know whether to laugh or cry. The first time he'd heard her voice in three years and it was exactly how he remembered it. He shook his head at Beyard. 'Sorry, old friend.'

'So am I.' Beyard rolled in the snow and kicked Arda's feet from under her. He caught her as she fell, staggered up and away from Gallow, and Gallow didn't dare strike because now Beyard had Arda held between them, one iron-gloved hand wrapped around her throat. 'Stay where you are, Truesword or I will break her neck.' Arda hammered furiously at Beyard but he was a man cased in iron. Her fists and feet rattled against him and did nothing. Beyard's fingers squeezed. 'Put the sword down in the snow. The others can still go.' His fingers tightened. 'You can't win, Truesword. There are men coming. Around the Crackmarsh instead of through it but they'll be here by the morning. Fight me and she dies. If somehow you win you'll still have twenty men hunting you by sunset.'

Gallow took a step away. 'Then I'll run, and you'll get neither me nor the sword and you can kill her if you wish. Just another Marroc, after all.'

Arda stopped struggling and stared. Beyard shook his head. 'No, Truesword. That's not who you are.'

'She's taken another man.'

'You were dead!' snapped Arda.

Gallow ignored her. Beyard was still shaking his head. He was smiling. 'That's still not who you are, Truesword.' He squeezed tighter, so tight that Arda couldn't breathe. He was strangling her, his eyes fixed on Gallow. 'Her corpse will be my shield if you fight me, Truesword.'

'Gallow!' Loudmouth. 'Ironskin, if you hurt her, I will cut you to pieces and feed them to pigs. I will piss on your corpse.'

'Wait!' Gallow let Solace fall by his side. 'Beyard, this is not who you are either. Let her go.'

The iron man's fingers loosened. 'You for her, Gallow?'

Arda pulled herself out of Beyard's grip. She hissed at Gallow, 'Just run when you have the chance, you stupid forkbeard.'

Beyard laughed. 'I can see why you chose her, Gallow. I'll keep her safe.' He caught Arda's hand before she could get away. 'You and Solace for all the other Marroc here. Her to keep you to your word.' He dragged Arda slowly back into the darkness of the forge. Gallow stared after her, eyes full of sorrow while her own thoughts were kept so tightly pressed inside that she was the same mystery to him as she'd been from the moment he'd met her. 'I will be here, waiting for you, old friend.'

In the house Loudmouth and Nadric were packing bags. Loudmouth gripped Gallow's shoulder. 'Nadric can take the children to the Crackmarsh as soon as it's light. Between us we'll kill the Fateguard. We'll wait here, and if he's not lying and more brothers of the sea come tomorrow, we'll fight them too. The two of us.'

Gallow shook his head. 'Beyard's not a liar. Take them now.'

'It's freezing cold and dark as soot!'

'By sunrise you'll reach the Crackmarsh. They'll be safe there.'

Tolvis shook his head. 'Feya's too little. She'll freeze. And Nadric's too old to—'

'Carry her.'

'But I'm not—'

Gallow had Loudmouth by his shirt, pulling him up close and almost lifting him off the ground. 'You want to stay here

193

at my side and fight Beyard? I've seen you fight him once already. In the morning Medrin's men will come. My family will be long gone. You will see to that. What's between me and Beyard is none of your trouble. Get them ready. When you're gone, Beyard and I will settle this between us. I'll follow when it's done or else I'll be dead.'

'It should be me,' gasped Tolvis.

'But it's not you he wants, Loudmouth.' He let go. 'You cared for my family when you thought I was dead. Care for them now.' He turned and walked back outside, not wanting to meet the stares of his children. They hadn't seen him for years. What good did it do for them to see him now?

Back in the forge Beyard had Arda sat on the floor, tied and with a sack thrown over her head. He squatted beside her, still and silent, and for a long time Gallow stood there too, watching them both, remembering the days before he'd crossed the sea, and afterwards, roaming the Marroc lands with the Screambreaker's band, fighting, burning, killing, every unkindness that came with war.

'Did you miss it, Beyard? Not crossing the sea and going to war with the rest?'

Beyard took so long to answer that Gallow wondered if the Fateguard was asleep, but eventually he stirred and turned his head. 'No. And that seems strange even to me. Those of us chosen by the Eyes of Time, we serve ...' He seemed to struggle. 'We serve a different purpose now.'

'You serve Medrin.'

'That is a passing thing.'

They stood and watched without words. From the house Loudmouth's angry shouts crept out through the falling snow. Arda bawled insults at Beyard and Gallow alike from under the sack and told Gallow how much he was a fool and how much she hated him and how much Tolvis was a better man until Beyard gently laid an iron hand on her and told her she could say what she liked, there was nothing that would drive Gallow away because he wasn't here for her. He spoke quietly, telling her how Gallow had been brought to him in Varyxhun and what had passed between them, and the locket Gallow carried and how he'd used it to find her. When he was done she still swore and told Gallow he was useless, but her words had an edge to them, a touch of despair, and when she stopped, Gallow saw that she was shaking. Sobbing.

They heard Tolvis and Nadric and the children leave. For a time after that Gallow stared at the roof of Nadric's forge, listening to the darkness. Beyard remained silent. He didn't move, didn't creak or shift, and Gallow couldn't even hear him breathe, until suddenly he twisted and his arm flashed out. He threw one of Nadric's hammers so fast and so out of the blue that Gallow didn't even move. It hit him in the head, and the next thing he knew he was lying on his back in the snow outside the forge and Beyard was standing over him. The iron man was holding the red sword again, and there was a black horse in the forge yard with Arda struggling and yelling blue murder slung across its back.

A cold hand of iron touched his shoulder. 'It is true, Truesword. We do not sleep.' Beyard stood up and backed away. 'Get up.' As Gallow sat up, Beyard tossed him his helm, scored now by Nadric's hammer, and climbed onto the back of his horse. 'For a time there I thought I'd killed you. You were out like the dead.' He shook his head. 'Perhaps that would have been better. Damn you, Truesword. I'll give you a day. I won't hurt her. I swear that by the Eyes of Time. But I'll keep her so I know you'll come. I'll let Medrin have his sword, but we're not done, you and I. Find me when you're ready.'

Gallow struggled to his feet. 'Just take me. Let her go and take me.'

'No.'

They stood and faced one another, eye to eye. 'Why? Let her go!'

'No.'

'Curse you, Beyard, why? It's me you want!'

'Why? Fate. Memories. Who we once were. Because if I take you meekly back in chains then I'll have to give you to Sixfingers. Does it matter? All this way and here I am letting you go, but it was hardly fair throwing that hammer. Don't hide from me too well, Truesword. Come for me when you're ready.'

Gallow shook his head. 'I'll come for you. I'll come for both of you.'

Beyard smiled. He stepped back and raised the red sword in salute. 'I know you will.' Then he shook his head and glanced at the sky where the first light before dawn was beginning to grey the night. 'Medrin's men will come soon. I'll keep them away from your precious Marroc. When the time comes, fight well, Truesword.'

For a long time Gallow stayed where he was. Tolvis and the others were gone but he knew exactly where they'd be. Nadric would lead them to the edge of the Crackmarsh and the caves in the woods, to the place where the villagers of Middislet had always hidden when war swept towards them. He knew the way.

The sun began to rise. Cocks crowed. The people of Middislet would be waking and Beyard was gone. Gallow bowed his head and turned to the south, towards the Crackmarsh. He walked and ran as fast as he could, determined to find Loudmouth and the Marroc he'd seen in the hills and take them back with him, his own little army, and slay every one of Medrin's men if that was what it took.

But perhaps the years had made him careless, or perhaps his mind was too much on Arda or on seeing his children again after so long and what he might say to them. And so he didn't see the Marroc slip out from among the trees in the darkness behind him with a bowstring in his hand, nor hear him until the string looped over his head and pulled tight around his neck and he started to choke. He threw himself down, but two more slipped from the night and pinned him while the bowstring drew tighter and tighter.

'Well well. Another stinking beardless forkbeard,' hissed one. 'Take him with the other one. Valaric's going to want to see this.'

Valaric?

Gallow's eyes dimmed. But there were probably lots of Marroc called Valaric.

29

WHAT HAPPENED TO
VALARIC THE MOURNFUL

After he'd set fire to Teenar's Bridge and scrambled up the cliffs into the western half of Andhun, Valaric had sat and stared over the Isset and watched the eastern half burn. There was no way to know whether the Vathen had done it or whether it was the forkbeards or whether it was no one in particular and just one of those things that happen when two armies rampage through someone else's city at the same time. He watched the last of the Marroc boats sail out of the harbour and tried to remind himself that he'd made sure at least *some* people had had enough time to get away from the slaughter. He'd seen that coming, the vengeful forkbeards. The Vathen, though, he hadn't seen *that*. Not that it made a difference. Forkbeards and horse-men fighting each other was just fine. If they could have found somewhere else to do it then it would have been perfect.

He waited until nightfall to see who would win, but it wasn't until the next morning that he saw the Vathen moving at the other end of the ruined bridge. Knowing that the forkbeards had probably been killed to the last man didn't make him nearly as happy as it should have. He didn't know the Vathen but they weren't likely to be much better. He made up for the disappointment by turning on the forkbeards who'd been in the western half when the bridge burned. There were only a handful, and by the time the fires had died in the harbour, the western half belonged to the Marroc again. The Vathen wouldn't be crossing the Isset at

Andhun, nor anywhere else on its lower reaches without a lot of boats, but anyone could simply ride and march across the Crackmarsh, so that was where he went, and quickly, gathering men around him as he did. They became a grim band, Valaric's Crackmarsh men, fighting the bestial ghuldog half-men night after night until they learned to leave them be; and then when the Vathen did finally come their way, Valaric murdered them in every way he could imagine. His men were never far from the Vathan camps. Sentries vanished. Scouting parties sank into the marsh under hails of arrows. His Marroc crept among them at night and spoiled their food and poisoned their water. They crippled horses as often as men. They learned to communicate with the ghuldogs in the most basic way and used them, drawing the ghuldogs to the Vathen, showing the half-men that the Vathen and their horses were easier prey, seeing to it that the Vathen had no doubt the stories were true and the Crackmarsh was full of monsters. It was an ugly bloody summer of murder and knives and honour had no part in it, but the Vathen never crossed the Crackmarsh.

Months passed. Summer turned to autumn. The Isset fell to its lowest and the Vathen tried one last time. They lashed together a fleet of rafts into a giant floating bridge, but by then the forkbeards had come back. Even in the Crackmarsh they knew that Yurlak himself had crossed the sea. Marroc fought alongside the forkbeards now, but not Valaric. He sat in his marsh and watched, waiting to pick off the winner.

The battle, when it came, made the slaughter outside Andhun look like a skirmish. Valaric didn't see it but he heard soon enough: the Vathen had beaten Yurlak. Then they beat him again and this time they killed him for good measure, but by then the winter was setting in and the Crackmarsh men had turned the ghuldogs into their own horde. There were thousands of the feral creatures, half dog and half man. Valaric led them out of the marsh one late autumn night and they swept in secret along the banks of the river, the ghuldogs sinking into the Isset in the daylight, the Marroc vanishing among the trees. They caught a new Vathan horde crossing the river, so many it would take them days. On the first night Valaric sent the ghuldogs into the camp of the Vathen who'd crossed while he and his Crackmarsh men cut loose the rafts that made the bridge and set them adrift and then melted away back to their swamp. Stories trickled to them of how the Vathan camp had been turned into a bloody horror. Ghuldogs took a man down, they ripped him apart and usually partly ate him, and even the men who got away with only a bite generally died or even worse. They were only stories, especially that last part, but living in the Crackmarsh Valaric came to know the truth.

The ghuldogs didn't come back – they stayed along the Isset, preying on whatever came their way – but the Crackmarsh was huge and there were always more.

The Vathen fared badly that winter. When they came again in the spring, Medrin Sixfingers was waiting for them, and Valaric wished he hadn't crushed the Vathen after all, for Medrin loved his blood ravens and hated every Marroc ever born. He came with more forkbeards and this time he came to stay. He hanged every Marroc who said a word out of place and drafted the men he didn't murder into his army. He wasn't like the other forkbeards. Valaric heard that much. He only cared about the winning of a fight, not the way of the winning, and he won that year against the Vathen on the back of his Marroc archers.

Some said it was the year after that the horror began – after Sixfingers broke the Vathen and drove them back across the Isset at last and set his mind to ruling his new kingdom – but Valaric knew better. The Crackmarsh began not far from where the Isset tumbled out of the Varyxhun valley gorge, close to the Aulian Bridge and Issetbridge. He knew that Medrin had sent the very worst of his forkbeards into the valley looking for the Sword of the Weeping God and for Gallow the Foxbeard. He knew about what they'd done there, the blood ravens. Varyxhun became as Andhun had been, as the rest of the old kingdom of the Marroc would become once Medrin finished taking out his hate on the Vathen. Sixfingers never forgot that a Marroc had nearly killed him once. It was a while before Valaric learned that it was Truesword who'd taken his hand and a while longer still before he heard the stories of how Medrin had had a new one made of iron crafted by the cold spirit of the Ice Wraiths, gifted to him along with the iron-gloved servants the forkbeards called their Fateguard but the Marroc knew by other, crueller names. The forkbeards called him Medrin Ironhand to his face, other things behind his back. Valaric called him worse and quietly carved Medrin's name into an arrowhead and kept it on a thong around his neck.

He was fingering it when Sarvic came and stood nearby in that lurking way he had where he never quite got around to saying anything, just stood closer and closer to wherever Valaric was sitting until eventually Valaric just wanted to stick a knife in his leg to make him spit it out. He never did, though. Sarvic had been at Andhun, and Andhun had turned him cold and hard. And he could shoot an arrow into a man's eye at fifty paces.

'Well?'

'Messenger from Fat Jonnic. A couple of forkbeards just wandered in from Middislet.'

'Well now they can just wander to the bottom of the swamp then, can't they? Feed them to the ghuldogs. They'll be hungry this time of year.' He frowned and looked at Sarvic hard. 'Why's Fat Jonnic bothering to tell me this?'

Sarvic shuffled his feet. 'One came with a handful of Marroc. They say the iron devil that crossed the Crackmarsh went to Middislet.'

Valaric stopped fiddling with his arrowhead. 'Middislet?' A smile spread slowly over his face. 'Nice and close. We might have to do something about that after all. Did they say how many men he's got?'

'None.'

Valaric frowned. He'd let the devil cross his swamp without trouble because none of them quite knew how to kill one, but what was he doing in in Middislet? 'Fat Jonnic did right. We'll go and see these forkbeards and ask them a question or two before we chop off their beards. And maybe pay a visit to Middislet. There's Vathen about this side of the river again. Forkbeards could get into all kinds of trouble in a place like this.' He raised an eyebrow, then saw that Sarvic wasn't rushing off to grab a fistful of swords and axes like he ought to but was doing his shuffling thing again. Valaric sighed. 'Yes?'

'Fat Jonnic got names out of the forkbeards, Valaric.'

'I hope he doesn't imagine I care. Unless one of them happens to be called Forkbeard Ghuldog-food, which I suppose would be funny.'

'No.' Shuffle shuffle.

'Oh what, Sarvic, *what*?'

'One of them said his name was Gallow. Gallow Truesword.'

Valaric shook his head. 'That Gallow's gone. Died in Andhun. But we can have some extra fun with whoever this forkbeard really is for that.'

'Thing is, Mournful, Fat Jonnic says the Marroc family say the same. They say they're *his* family. From Middislet.'

A numbness crept out from the inside of Valaric's head and crawled across his face. He nodded. 'Then, Sarvic, I think you'd better come too.' He watched Sarvic go and slowly shook his head. *Gallow Truesword? Back from the dead?*

30

OIL AND WATER

The first Lhosir to come to Witches' Reach didn't come up the track from the Varyxhun Road the next morning, but the one after. There were twenty of them from the garrison at Issetbridge below the mouth of the valley. Oribas and Achista watched together as the Lhosir crossed the bridge and rode up the Varyxhun Road, long before they turned onto the track up to the Reach. Achista smiled and took his hand. 'They're coming for us. They're coming to see.'

'How do you know?'

'I just know.'

The Marroc moved quickly. By the time the Lhosir reached the fort the gates hung open, the fire pits were stamped out and the Marroc were hidden away, the tower seemingly abandoned, all to lure the Lhosir inside. And they came, but they walked into the trap with their eyes wide open, with two men on horses outside the gates and two more further down the trail, and when the Marroc surged out of their hiding places and cut the Lhosir down with their arrows and their axes, the riders on the trail both got away. Oribas found himself busy again, stitching up more holes in the Marroc who'd been hurt. That night he heard the gates open and he knew that Achista was taking Lhosir bodies down to the bridge again to leave them where they couldn't be missed.

'Perhaps we'll have a day or two more before they come again,' she said, but they didn't.

By the middle of the next day, Addic had joined them from wherever he'd been with news that the forkbeards of Varyxhun were on the move. He'd watched them as long as he dared and then he'd ridden like the wind. They'd be at Witches' Reach the next morning, some fifty or sixty of them and perhaps more coming on behind. More still once Cithjan heard what had happened to the forkbeards from Issetbridge. Addic wandered the fortress with Achista, along the walls and in and out of the sheds and the forge and the halls inside the tower to the kitchens and the cellars and the old Aulian tomb below. Oribas left them to it. He stared at the mountains, up the Isset gorge to the snow-covered peaks around Varyxhun and beyond to the old Aulian Way. It didn't seem all that long ago that he'd thought Gallow dead and all he could think about was the spring and crossing back the way he'd come, away from all this cursed cold. Now? Now the thought simply wasn't there any more. When he looked for it, he found it didn't even make sense. There wasn't anything waiting for him back in old Aulia. No family, no friends, no people. The Rakshasa had taken those years ago. He could name three people on the other side of the mountains that he might have called friends in a pinch, the other survivors of the great hunt; and when he'd left them behind to cross the mountains with Gallow it had seemed impossible that he wouldn't come back, that they wouldn't be a band together for ever, fearless and unstoppable, hunting down shadewalkers and things far worse and sending them to their rest. Now he saw all that for the illusion it was. He couldn't imagine going back. He couldn't even imagine seeing the spring. He'd bound himself to these Marroc without seeing it happen, and now all of them were doomed. Perhaps it was as much an illusion as the one he'd left behind but that didn't matter. From where he was, it felt the most real thing in the world.

'I think my sister is in love with you,' said Addic quietly.

The words were so in tune with his own thoughts that the Marroc's silent arrival didn't even make him flinch.

'And I think I am in love with her,' Oribas replied.

'She's not had eyes for a man for a while. There was a farmhand a couple of years back. A good man, I thought. They might have been married but the forkbeards killed him. After that I think she wedded her bow instead.' Addic shook his head and then pulled a satchel off his shoulder. 'I have something for you, Aulian.' Oribas stared and then smiled. His satchel. *His* satchel. The one he thought he'd lost when the Lhosir had thrown him over the edge of the gorge back on the snowbound Aulian Way. 'One of Brawlic's men went and got it before the forkbeards killed him. I don't know how he knew it was there. He must have overheard some talk, I suppose. He was probably in Varyxhun to sell it but I got to him first.' He handed the satchel to Oribas, who looked inside. Someone had been through it, that was obvious, but everything that mattered was still there.

'Thank you.'

Addic leaned over the tower walls and stared out at the gorge. 'My sister wants to close the Aulian door so the forkbeards can't come in as we did. She'd seal us in here.'

'With me on the outside to open the door when she asks.'

'But she won't ask. And nor will I. You know that, don't you?'

'Yes, I do.'

'What I mean to say, Aulian, is that we should make the very most of the days we have left, all of us. Make her happy. Make both of you happy. You have my blessing.' He put an awkward hand on Oribas's shoulder and walked away.

'I had a thought. About the shaft and the way in through the caves ...' Oribas began, but Addic was already gone and his own thoughts were in too much turmoil. It was slowly dawning on him what Addic had meant. He stood and looked out over the river a while longer. The steep craggy sides of the gorge struck him as stern and majestic now instead of forbidding. The Aulian Bridge gleamed and the water sparkled in the bright winter sun. The Isset falls were a mile away and out of sight, but from the walls of Witches' Reach Oribas could see beyond the sudden end of the mountains to the flat brownish haze that the Marroc said was the Crackmarsh, and to the shapes of the dales beyond and around it. He tried to imagine the hills and the mountains covered in lavish green and dappled with the colours of spring flowers. Strip away all this snow and he could see that the Varyxhun valley would be beautiful. Still too cold, though. He climbed down from the walls. The Marroc were none too keen on opening the gates to let him out and made no promises about letting him back in again, but there was always the cave and the old Aulian tomb for that.

It took him a while to walk down to the forest and the old forest camp and find what he was looking for. By the time he got back to Witches' Reach, the sun was sinking. He found Achista among the wounded, bright-eyed as ever and listening to their stories, bringing them water and soup from the kitchen below. He watched her a while, marvelling at how she seemed to lift each one of them. It seemed a shame to ask her to stop and so he waited, simply looking at her until the sun kissed the hills outside. Then he touched her on the shoulder. 'I have something important to show you,' he said, and when she turned to smile at him, he led her away to the very top of the tower and its open roof. He pointed to the orange sun as it straddled the western mountains across the gorge.

'I'm a stranger from a strange land.' He took her hands in his. 'It makes me sad that I know so little of the customs of your people. Where I come from there is a proper way to this. I have no doubt there is a proper way among your people too, one that's different. I hope you understand. This is the Aulian way. One day you'll teach me the Marroc way. I have three gifts for you.' He let her hands go and forced himself to look at the sun and not at her. 'The first is this sunset and the memory of it, for the sun is always the most radiant thing bar one in any life, and that one thing that eclipses it in mine is you. When the sun sinks beneath the horizon, I will remain bathed in the light of knowing you, of being beside you, of remembering you and of the possibilities you bring.' He swallowed hard, knowing those possibilities were likely few and short, and knowing too that it no longer mattered. He reached into his satchel and drew out three of the blue flowers from the forest. 'The second are these flowers.' With delicate fingers he lifted off her helm and slipped one stalk over each ear and twined the last into her hair. 'The left is for the past we shared. The right is for the future. The third is for what matters most of all, for the now.' Last of all he offered her his gloves. He smiled and laughed. 'In my own land I would have offered you the most exquisite silk, woven with patterns of gold and silver thread. All I have here are these, which I have worn for months and are old and battered. They have served me well. They're a part of me. I offer them now to be a part of you. As I offer myself.'

He held out the gloves. Achista stared at them and then at him. Her eyes shone in the sunset. 'I don't understand, Oribas.' She cocked her head.

'I'm telling you, Achista of the Marroc, that I belong with you. And I'm asking whether you will belong with me, for the rest of our lives, however long or short they may be, whatever the dawn may bring. I'm asking you to become one with me, that we may both be the wings that the other may fly, that we might do together what neither of us could do alone, that, gods willing, we shall live long and bring great happiness to one another, that we shall raise sons and daughters together and watch them make us proud, that we shall herd our animals and grow our crops and work hard, side by side under the burning sun, and that we shall sleep softly in the same tent and hold one another in the cool hours of dark until we are old and grey and the gods call us away.'

Tears marked her cheeks. She looked away. 'Oribas, no. Whatever the dawn may bring? You know the answer to that. Forkbeards. You're not Marroc. I can't ask you to stay. I don't want you to stay.' She looked back at him. 'I want you to go. You have to close the seal and wait for—'

Oribas put a finger to her lips. 'For the signal you'll never give.' He smiled and nodded. 'I know. And I've thought about this long and hard today. I've watched you move among your kin. You bring a spark of hope to each and every one. I could never do that. Except for you. I'm not a fool, Achista. I know what awaits us. I've looked at the future. I'm a wizard, after all!' He laughed but not for long. 'If I leave, perhaps I will have a long life or perhaps not, but it will be one that is forever tarnished with regret. If my choice is between long dull empty years or one more day here with you then I will stay, and so I *will* stay, however you answer, and you cannot stop me. I will find means to make this tower impossible to enter, no matter how many forkbeards come, if that is what I must do to keep you. I would call down gods and raise up demons and fling fire from the sky if only I could find a way.'

He offered her the gloves a second time. 'I have felt this fire once before. A demon destroyed my world. I gave my life to bringing about its end. The gods sent to me what I needed, and now they have sent me to you. My fire then was vengeance but now I have another that burns with a kinder flame. My heart is yours, Achista of the Marroc, and you cannot change that, for my heart belongs always to me and so is always mine to give as I choose.'

She closed her eyes and bowed her head. Her voice broke to a whisper. 'I cannot ask you to stay, Oribas. I cannot.'

'You can ask me to stay or you can ask me to leave or you can say nothing at all, but it will make no difference. I will stand with you to the end either way.'

'You can't even hold a sword!' She shook her head, sobbing and laughing, smiling in a ring of tears.

Oribas reached a hand and lifted her chin so she was looking at him again. 'But I can hold you.'

She fell into his arms and crushed him and he held her back, long and tight. He lifted her head and kissed her, and for a long time the sunset and the glory of the Isset gorge and the mountains around them faded into nothing. Oribas thought he saw Addic poke his head up onto the roof, but he vanished again, and suddenly it was dark and cold and the sun was long gone and stars speckled the sky, and Addic really was there this time.

'Brother. I …' Oribas watched her smile, and he was right: it was every bit as warm as the sun itself.

'Diaran and Modris watch over both of you.' Addic smiled back and beckoned them away, out of the cold, down through the belly of the tower, past the kitchens and the cellars to the old Aulian tomb where a brazier now burned beside a huge pile of furs that hadn't been there before. 'There's little enough joy for us Marroc,' he said, and he hugged Achista and then Oribas as well. 'No one will trouble you here before sunrise.'

And no one did, though neither of them got much sleep that night, and it was well into the next morning before they were finally awoken after they fell asleep in each other's arms amid a cocoon of fur. When Addic came down to them again, this time there was no sign of a smile on his face.

'The forkbeards have come,' he said.

31

THE CRACKMARSH

Gallow opened his eyes. He was in a cave. Three Marroc stood looking at him. 'Well,' said the one who'd given him the worst of the kicking. The other two stared. The torchlight behind them made them into silhouettes. They were soldiers and that was all he could see.

'That's him.' He didn't know the second voice but he knew the one that came after it.

'Gallow.'

Valaric. Gallow hauled himself up to his hands and knees. 'Need your horse shod or a new blade for your scythe, do you?'

'I thought you were dead.' Gallow twisted until he was sitting up. 'Might have been better if things had stayed that way too. Better for a lot of people.' For a long time Valaric didn't move. Then he let out a great sigh and turned away. 'Go on then, Jonnic, let him loose. Then he can tell us all about the iron devil of Varyxhun being in Middislet. You're not going to tell me you have nothing to do with that, are you, Gallow?'

'He's left Middislet by now.'

Outside in the sunlight the Marroc fed him and gave him water and returned what they'd taken from him. They were none too happy about it but they did what Valaric told them. He let Loudmouth loose as well after Gallow told him what they'd done in Andhun.

'Turning into a right forkbeard-lover, aren't I?' Valaric spat, then listened as Gallow told his story. 'They turned Varyxhun upside down looking for you,' he said when

Gallow was done. 'Blood ravens lining the road. Dozens of them. All because of you.'

'If you put it that way, how many Marroc in Andhun died because of *you*, then?' snapped Tolvis.

'Was Sixfingers who turned on the city.' Valaric's eyes narrowed.

'Was Sixfingers who turned on Varyxhun.'

The two of them stared at each other, neither one giving any ground until a Marroc ran and whispered in Valaric's ear. He nodded. 'Forkbeards came past Middislet yesterday. One, maybe two dozen. They had the iron devil of Varyxhun and a Marroc woman with them.' He cocked his head, still staring at Tolvis. 'Didn't burn it down, didn't hang anyone, just passed through. Why are you here, Gallow?'

Gallow shrugged. He'd been asking himself the same thing ever since Beyard had sent him off into the night. Why? Why would a Fateguard do something like that? Because they'd once been friends? But that had been long ago and Beyard was an ironskin now, and so didn't the past and friendship count for nothing? Why all the trouble to hunt him down only to let him go? And if it was only the sword he wanted then he had that already. Why take Arda? It made no sense. No sense at all.

'Spying,' said Fat Jonnic. 'Why else?'

Valaric finally let his eyes move from Tolvis to Gallow. 'And what say you, Gallow the Foxbeard? Are you a spy?'

'I cut off Medrin's hand, Valaric.'

'So *you* say.' He leaned forward. 'But you know the Crackmarsh well enough to find these caves. Everyone in Middislet knows them. What about your friend?' His eyes flicked back to Tolvis. 'He a spy?'

Tolvis growled. 'Ask me to my face, Marroc.'

Gallow put a hand on Loudmouth's arm. 'I'd vouch for Tolvis with my life, Valaric.'

'A forkbeard vouching for a forkbeard?' Valaric sneered.

'What's a Marroc to make of that?'

'When Twelvefingers and his army stood inside the gates of Andhun, how many Marroc stood with you?' Gallow let that sink in a bit. 'I don't want anything from you, Valaric. Beyard has my wife.'

'Arda Smithswife?' Valaric chuckled and even Fat Jonnic laughed too. 'Good luck to him!'

Gallow flared. 'Mind yourself, Valaric!'

'Oh calm now, Gallow. We know Arda well enough. She'd come through the Crackmarsh now and then with a mule, heading to Issetbridge and back. She was a friend of the Crackmarsh men and did us favours now and then, and in return we kept the ghuldogs off her.' He snorted and grinned at Jonnic. 'Not that she needed much help with that, mind, not with that tongue of hers.' Then his face became serious again. 'The iron devil has a score of men with him. If he crosses the Crackmarsh again then we'll take him down this time. He might not die, but all that iron will rust if it's held under the water for long enough.'

Gallow shook his head. Beyard wouldn't be going through the Crackmarsh. 'Hrodicslet,' he said. 'There's a way into the Varyxhun valley without crossing the Aulian Bridge.' And he told Valaric and the Marroc about the trail from Hrodicslet into the high valleys and Jodderslet and the Devil's Caves while Valaric scratched his chin and began to pace. By the time he was done, Valaric was smiling.

'Show me this road and I'll take you to Hrodicslet.' He cocked his head. 'What do you say, forkbeard?'

'What about my family?'

'They can stay here with Fat Jonnic until they're ready to go home again. Safe as anywhere. Shall we go?'

Gallow nodded.

'Good.' Valaric rubbed his hands. 'Cithjan's iron devil has had it coming for a while now.' He nudged Gallow. 'You've got a forge. We'll melt him down if that's what it takes.'

32

SNOW AND FIRE

Addic might have seen fifty or sixty forkbeards riding out of Varyxhun castle but there were closer to a hundred of them around the fortress. They took their time, picking their way around the slopes below Witches' Reach, carefully outside the range of the Marroc archers on the walls. They ringed the fort with watchers and then withdrew and set about cutting wood for their fires and got a few of them going. The smell of roasting fat wafted up the mountain. Hours after they arrived two of them finally walked toward the gates with their shields raised, holding high a spear with a white rag tied to the shaft. Oribas watched them come.

'Oribas should talk to them,' Achista said.

Addic snorted. 'What's to talk about? Do you imagine they'll let us go? Either the valley will rise to our banner or the forkbeards will kill us, and I'd rather die on the end of their spears than be hung as one of their ravens.'

Achista shook her head. 'Nevertheless, Oribas will talk to them.'

Achista led them now, and however much Addic rolled his eyes, this was a thing Oribas had asked to do. He went to the gates, the Marroc opened them and he walked out onto the road, hands held high where all could see them. Fifty paces away the Lhosir stopped and waited. They looked at him in puzzlement as he drew closer.

'I am Oribas of what was once Aulia.' He stopped before them, hands still raised. 'In my own land a herbalist and a

213

healer but now a prisoner of these Marroc. They've sent me out to hear your words and receive your spears. There are many arrows pointed at my back.'

The Lhosir carrying the spear frowned and peered at him. 'Didn't we send you to the Devil's Caves once already?'

'Yes, you did. There were Marroc waiting in ambush and so I became their prisoner instead of yours. They won't let me leave because I fled with them and I have seen their secret paths between the valleys.'

The Lhosir's eyes narrowed. 'So how is it they send you to do their talking?'

'Forgive me. I've given you my name; may I have yours?'

The Lhosir glanced past Oribas to the walls of the Reach. 'Skilljan, known as Spearhoof. Tell your Marroc friends my name. Some of them will know it.'

Oribas bobbed his head. 'I am here because the Marroc have nothing to say and nor do you. If I take one step past you on this road, Skilljan Spearhoof, I will fall with a dozen Marroc arrows in my back. I have no friends among either of you. If you turn your spears on me, you save them a few arrowheads. If you take me, there is little I can reveal save how to reach from here to the Devil's Caves without walking the Varyxhun Road. The Marroc don't believe you have anything to say that could possibly matter. If I'm honest with you, Skilljan Spearhoof, nor do I. I'll take them your name. Is there anything else?'

'Who leads them here?' asked Skilljan.

'A woman. Her name is Ylista but they call her Shieldborn.'

'Never heard of her. A woman leads this Marroc rabble, eh?' The Lhosir glanced at one another. 'Here's what I have to say, Oribas of Aulia: there will be no quarter or mercy for any Marroc here. I will grant the remainder of the day for you all to make your peace with your gods. On the morrow we come. For every day that the gates of Witches' Reach remain closed to us, one Marroc farm somewhere in the valley will burn with every Marroc who lives there still within it. To those who surrender before we come, death will be quick and merciful. Those we take in battle will be raised on poles as blood ravens to keep watch over the Aulian Way and greet the shadewalkers. I will find the names of those who die on our swords from those we take alive. We will hunt down their fathers and their sons and their brothers. Sisters and wives and mothers and daughters will weep and curse and throw salt over the cairns of their sons. Tell them that, Aulian.' The Lhosir cocked his head. 'Shall we speak again? Shall we say sunrise to hear their answer?'

Oribas shrugged. 'I doubt they will open the gates for parley a second time.'

'Nor will I have aught else to say. But I'll offer you the chance nonetheless. I'll bring some shields. Maybe you'd like to run away from those arrows and speak a little more about these secret Marroc paths, Oribas of Aulia.' The Lhosir bowed and turned away. Oribas returned to the tower and told Addic and Achista what the Lhosir had said.

'I'd like to speak with them again,' he said when he was done. 'The seeds are sown. I have an idea how you might win this battle.'

'How many of them are there?' asked Achista.

Oribas shrugged but Addic answered. 'Not yet enough to take this tower by force but too many for us to face in the open. And there will be more.' He shook his head. 'I say we fight on a few days until they're ready to overwhelm us, then we leave. We slink away through the caves and strike again elsewhere. It'll gall them that we've slipped through their grasp.'

Achista shook her head. 'Every day we stay, Marroc turn their heads as they walk along the Varyxhun Road. They see our banner. They whisper our deeds where the forkbeards can't hear. If we run the whispers will be nothing more, but every day we defy the forkbeards they grow louder.

We'll stay until they're shouts hurled from every rooftop in Varyxhun!'

'These are simple men,' snapped Addic. 'They have farms and families and sons and daughters. Let them make their stand and go. Half of them are only here because they know there's an escape waiting for them.'

Achista glanced at Oribas. Oribas shook his head. 'Make ladders,' he said. 'Rope and wood. Things that can be thrown over the walls. Do that first. They will seem another means to escape. Keep them in the tomb where they can be watched with care. Perhaps some of these brave men here should be allowed to slip away once the end is in sight to spread the word far and wide of what you have done at Witches' Reach?' He didn't wait for an answer but left them and went back into the tower, down the stairs to the old tomb and the Lhosir stores. There were kegs there with the smell of fish oil to them. He opened them one by one and tested them to see which would most easily burn. When he'd found the ones that suited him best, he put them aside and returned to the Marroc above. Fire was a fine weapon in any siege. Let the Lhosir learn that when they came, if they didn't know it already. For the rest of the day he walked the walls and stood on the roof of the tower, watching the Lhosir camp. The Lhosir were busy in the woods, felling trees and building. They were careful to keep out of sight but there weren't too many things they could be making. Ladders or a ram or most probably both. Oribas watched their scouting parties circle the walls, looking for places where they might climb up the slopes under cover and bring up a ladder without being seen. There weren't any, but he thought he knew where they might try. And they had their own watchers too, climbing up the side of the neighbouring mountain where Achista had shown him her banner and told him what she meant to do. They'd be able to see down into the yard between the walls and the tower, and so

Oribas had the Marroc build a few things that might look from a distance like Aulian bolt-throwers and carry them up around the gates. He waited with the oil until after dark, rolling out half a dozen kegs while the Marroc lit fires and sang and drank.

'Be sparing,' he warned Achista. 'As soon as it's gone, that's when you'll wish you had it the most.' He took her back into the tomb with a few other Marroc and as many buckets and all the rope they could find to lift water from the bottom of the shaft, as much as they could carry. 'You have enough water in the snow here for days but there's no call to waste it. The water down here is foul. Tip scalding pots of it over the forkbeards when they try to climb their ladders. If the time comes when you must drink it, heat it over a fire until it steams. Keep it there for one finger of the sun and then let it cool.'

'It seems a lot of work when there's snow lying every-where underfoot.' They barely had enough rope.

'Pile the snow outside into a mound against the gates in the night and pack it tight. It will strengthen them and be your source of water. Make other mounds elsewhere, against the wall of the tower. That too will be your water. Who knows what will come over the walls when the Lhosir at-tack. Animal dung and their own faeces, perhaps. Although perhaps not.' He frowned. 'In the desert heat it is effective. Here perhaps less so.' He climbed down the rungs of the shaft and called to the Marroc to lower the first bucket. As each one came down, he filled it five or six times and threw the water down the tunnel that led out to the mountainside. It would freeze into ice in the night, he thought. He did that and then filled each bucket one last time and tugged on the rope for the Marroc to haul it back up. The buckets banged and clattered against the wall as they rose and most of the water spilled, but Oribas kept them at it. When they were done, he tested the level of the water in the shaft. It was a handspan down from the level of the passage now. Good enough.

'What was the point of that?' Achista asked him when he finally reached the top again. 'The buckets were almost empty by the time we got them up.'

'Fill them with snow.'

She threw up her hands in exasperation and fatigue. 'If we're going to do that, why did we waste half the night with this?'

'Do your Marroc have something better to do?'

He thought he had her there, since although the Marroc should be resting before the fight began in the morning, they both knew that most of them wouldn't be able to sleep. But when she wrapped her arms around his neck, he realised he was wrong. '*I* do,' she whispered.

They didn't get much sleep that night either, and this time Oribas was up before dawn. He showed Achista the oil he'd kept aside and told her exactly what he meant to do. Then, before he went out to parley with the Lhosir again, he opened his satchel and set to work.

33

HRODICSLET

Two days of hard walking on the heels of Valaric and his men brought them across the Crackmarsh and to Hrodicslet, where little wooden jetties stuck up out of the snow and all the houses were built on stilts for when the Isset flooded in the spring and the swamps and bogs of the marsh turned into miles and miles of water meadows and a thousand creeks and channels. Some years Hrodicslet didn't flood but more often than not it did. Boats lay scattered everywhere, resting askew in the snow, half buried, tethered to the houses and walkways, waiting for the thaw and for the rising waters that would follow. Valaric sent Sarvic ahead into the town to find where Beyard and his men were staying.

'They've helped themselves to Elder Hall,' Sarvic said when he came back. 'Can't see where else they'd go.'

'No. Don't suppose you can.'

Gallow looked over Valaric's Crackmarsh men. They were surly seasoned soldiers who'd face up to a Lhosir, but Beyard was a Fateguard armed with Solace, and every Marroc knew that the Comforter was a wicked blade.

'You can look as doubtful as you like,' Valaric growled. 'Do you think I'm going to stand outside and shout at them until they come out in their mail so we can have a fair fight? It'll be creeping in at midnight with knives. It'll be cutting throats, and the ones who wake up won't be dressed for battle. You know how much a forkbeard in a nightshirt troubles me? Not much at all.'

'I'll not be a part of murdering men while they sleep.'

'Fine.' Valaric picked up a stick and began to strip the bark off it with his teeth. 'You two go in there and ask them nicely to give your woman back, and then later after we've done with cutting throats, we'll all stand around your corpse and think what bloody idiots you forkbeards are. Or stay here and pick your noses and wait for me to bring her back to you. Your choice.'

The sun set. Winter darkness came quickly in the mountains but in the marsh the twilight seemed to linger. Valaric and his Marroc sat in a circle around a small fire, swigging beer and playing dice to while away the time. Gallow and Tolvis sat together apart from the Marroc. Gallow wasn't sure what to make of Loudmouth now he knew the truth. He should be grateful. Most of him believed that. Grateful to a man who'd walked across a hostile land to hand a purse of silver to another man's wife and not kept it for himself. Grateful to a man who'd protected his family and hidden them away from Medrin when he could so easily have sold them. Grateful to a man who'd seen to it that his children had food and grew strong, who'd taught them right and wrong as a Lhosir should know it and how to hunt and forage and the beginnings of how to fight. Grateful to a man who'd lost his own family years ago and was content to take on the duties of another. Grateful, and yet Tolvis had done more than merely care for Arda and his children as though he was a dutiful brother, and even if all of them had thought he was dead, a part of Gallow seethed at that. Tolvis had taken what was not his to take. Among the Lhosir such things were only ever settled with blood.

'I'll leave,' Tolvis said. 'As soon as she's free, I'll leave. I'll return across the sea and never come back.'

'You'll never survive. Too many people know you. Medrin will hear. He'll have you hanged.'

'I have plenty of friends.'

'You have plenty of enemies.'

Tolvis hesitated. 'And which should I call you?'

'Friend. I'll tell you if it must be otherwise.'

'Don't blame Arda.' Tolvis held his head in his hands. 'I was the one who—'

'Stop!' Again and again he remembered standing over Tolvis on the road out of Andhun, axe in hand after Medrin had sent Tolvis to bring Gallow back to join him in his hunt for the Crimson Shield. He'd looked at the soldier lying on the road scrabbling for his feet and had made up his mind that yes, he *would* go back and he *would* join Medrin and he *would* finally set his eyes on the mystic shield that had created the rift between them in the first place. He'd thought it might change something. And it did, but nothing good. He'd have given much to go back to that moment, to leave Tolvis lying there and ride on home. Leave the Marroc and the Lhosir and the Vathen to fight and fight until only one remained while he lived quietly in peace, far away from anything, drawing wire and hammering nails and hoes and ploughs and scythes.

'Stop,' he said again, more gently. He pressed his hands to his face. It made no difference now. There was nothing he could do to make those years come back and nothing he could do to make things as they'd been before he'd left. Loudmouth might go home but so what? Did Arda even still want Gallow? Did his children remember him? And even if they did, Beyard knew who he was and perhaps so did the Lhosir who rode with him. They'd seen where he lived and they knew his family, and nowhere would ever be safe again. 'I don't want to know, Loudmouth. This is how it will be. When I'm with you, I'll blame Arda and be grateful for the care you took of my sons. When I'm with Arda, everything will be my fault, since Arda certainly won't allow for anything else.'

'She has a tongue to her, that's for sure. I wondered

sometimes how you survived for all those years.' Tolvis chuckled and for a moment Gallow smiled too. Arda with her sharp tongue and Loudmouth together? Surprising they were both still alive.

'She put a spell on me, my friend,' said Gallow. 'The same one she put on you. One that never went away.'

Tolvis thought about that for a bit. 'There's more than one Marroc in Middislet who calls her a witch when they think no one will hear.'

'I remember three. Shilla, because everyone knew her brother was an idiot but Arda couldn't stop telling everyone anyway in case they'd somehow forgotten. Jassic because he was sweet on Shilla.'

'And then there's old woman Katta in her hut, who comes into the village once a week and makes the sign of Modris every time she walks past the forge.' Tolvis smiled.

'Still alive, is she?'

'I think she'll live for ever, that one. Didn't know about Jassic though. He died two winters back. Vanished. Didn't find his body for weeks. No one knows what happened.' Tolvis shrugged. 'Got hurt, couldn't get home and froze, I suppose. Shilla married Boric the spring after.'

'She was always playing those two off against each other.'

They sat in silence after that, neither of them finding anything to say until Valaric finally got up from the fire and the rest of his Marroc rose to follow him. 'You forkbeards coming or are you leaving it to Marroc to do your fighting for you?'

'I'll not murder men in their sleep.'

Beside Gallow, Tolvis shook his head. 'Nor I.' He stood up anyway. 'But you'll need someone to face the ironskin for you.' He followed as Valaric led his men into the darkness and the distant fires of Hrodicslet, and so Gallow rose too, because Arda would expect it. She'd expect him to cut throats if that's what it took to keep his family safe, but some things he couldn't do, not even for her.

Valaric knew Hrodicslet well enough to find his way around its outskirts in the starlight. With his men he crept towards the centre through the deep snow among the raised walkways until the Marroc found their way to the Elder Hall at the town's heart. Valaric led them to the small door at the back, hidden in shadows under the overhanging eaves of a house that was more like a barn. He took the stick he'd been whittling earlier and wriggled it between the door and its frame and then made a face and crouched down and wriggled it some more, trying to lift the bar that held it closed on the inside. He peered through the crack and whispered, 'Quick as you can, lads. No need for quiet. They're a-snoring on the floor in there.' Then he threw the door open and the Marroc ran inside, swords drawn, yelling and screaming, stabbing into the thick bundles of fur on the floor. Valaric grabbed Gallow's hand and pulled him, dragging him inside. 'You don't have to do the killing if it troubles you, forkbeard, but by the gods you'll be here to see it happen.'

He stopped, the two of them barely inside the door. The first Marroc were halfway across the hall, their cries dying on their lips. The Lhosir bundles of fur were thrown over not men but sacks filled with straw. And then all around the hall, the doors to the little rooms around the sides where animals were kept indoors for the winter nights were thrown open and there they were, the Lhosir, axes drawn and ready for battle. They howled and fell on the Marroc and the Marroc ran. Valaric seized Gallow by his furs. 'Forkbeard piss pot! You led us into a trap!'

A Marroc bolted through the door. Gallow pushed Valaric outside and then stood to bar the way to Beyard and the advancing Lhosir. The Marroc who'd led the way were already dead, cut down in the first charge. Two Lhosir ran at him; he blocked them both with his shield and swung his axe at their faces, forcing them back. Behind him Loudmouth tugged at his coat. 'The Marroc are running, Truesword, and we should run too.'

'No!' Beyard had seen him now. Most of the Lhosir were pouring out of the big door at the other end of the hall into the streets of Hrodicslet. 'Arda!'

'Will not be helped by our deaths! Maker-Devourer, Truesword, I'd die for her too; I'd die for both of you if it would help, but it won't, not this time. This time we must run!'

Run. A Lhosir never ran. That was what they all told themselves but the truth was that they did, more often than any of them would ever admit. He remembered old Jyrdas One-Eye, most terrible of the Screambreaker's men: he'd been happy to admit that he'd turned and run plenty of times when the odds didn't suit him. Hadn't been afraid to die when he thought it would make a difference but had no interest in it when it changed nothing. Even the Screambreaker had run once. They'd all run at Selleuk's Bridge, the one and only time the Marroc had got the better of them. He and Tolvis had run from the Vathen in Andhun. So yes, a Lhosir ran when it suited him, but Arda was in there, the woman whose memory had kept him alive for three hard years.

Tolvis pulled so hard that Gallow staggered back out of the doorway, and then Loudmouth was standing in front of him with his axe and his shield and no mail at all, facing three Lhosir who saw how easy he was going to be and grinned. 'Stay if you like, Gallow, but if you do then I won't budge from in front of you.'

So he ran, and Tolvis ran after him, and the Lhosir gave chase but Beyard called them back. 'Find the Marroc! Don't worry about them. They'll be back. I have something they want.' As the Lhosir stopped, Gallow slowed and looked over his shoulder. He could just about make out Beyard in his iron crown, striding out into the night. 'I kept my word, Truesword! I gave you a day and I've not hurt her!'

Gallow rounded on the cry with one of his own: 'Why did you let me go, Beyard? Why keep her but let me go?' But he got no answer.

They followed their own tracks back into the edges of the Crackmarsh, to where the surviving Marroc were gathering. Valaric stared at the two of them in disbelief while the other Marroc circled around, weapons drawn and faces tight with fury.

'I lost seven men tonight, forkbeards. Another man might think you knew all along that this was a trap. Another man might think you led us to Hrodicslet knowing they'd be waiting.'

'Kill them Valaric! Feed them to the ghuldogs!'

Tolvis snarled, 'Who's first?'

Gallow pushed in front of him. 'I led you to some forkbeards, that's all. You were going to kill them in their sleep. I told you not to. You did this to yourself, Valaric. You knew a Fateguard led them.'

Valaric turned away. 'Go, Truesword. You're not welcome here any more.'

'Valaric!' Two of the Marroc almost jumped at him. 'They're forkbeards! You can't just let them go!'

Valaric stilled them with a wave of his hand. He didn't look round as Gallow and Tolvis left.

34

BETRAYER

The Lhosir were waiting for him as they'd promised. The same two but now they had the rest of their men only a hundred paces further down the road. They stood in a solid rank across the track, ready for battle, a wooden ram behind them. It couldn't be anything else. They'd been thoughtful enough to put a roof over the top of it.

Behind Oribas, the gates to Witches' Reach were closed. They'd be closed for the rest of winter now – the mound of crushed snow and ice behind them would see to that. Oribas had come down the wall on a ladder.

'They've heard of you, Skilljan Spearhoof. They don't strike me as particularly afraid. Shall I give you the message I have for you? The gates tell you all that matters. Their message is the same except in words more calculated to enrage.'

Skilljan Spearhoof nodded. 'Will you stay then, Oribas of Aulia? Tell me of these secret Marroc paths and I'll give you a kind death when the time comes. Kinder than the one you'll receive when we breach the walls.'

'I'd prefer no death at all, Lhosir.'

'My eyes tell me that the Marroc have been building Aulian spear-throwers in the night. Since they're farmers, I must suppose you were their architect.'

Oribas shook his head. 'There are no spear-throwers. The Marroc have neither the tools nor the skills nor the materials to make one. What your eyes have seen are a few pieces of wood thrown together to deceive you.' He looked up sharply, catching Skilljan's eye. 'I *could* show a man how, though, given time.'

Skilljan shook his head. 'Not enough to earn you your life, Aulian. Cithjan himself gave the order to send you to the Devil's Caves. I cannot ignore my lord.'

'Would *you* send men to the Devil's Caves, Skilljan Spearhoof?'

The Lhosir started to shake his head and then caught himself and smiled. 'You're a clever one, Oribas of Aulia. No, I would not, but nor am I the lord of Varyxhun.'

Oribas turned back towards the tower. 'Do you have any words for me to take back?'

'None that any Marroc will heed.'

'There is one thing, Skilljan Spearhoof. Consider, as I leave you, whose people it was who first built this tower.'

'Oh, I know they were yours, Aulian. We all know that.'

'Our people liked to dig, Skilljan Spearhoof.'

'And what am I to take from that?'

'That I am one of my kind.'

Skilljan laughed. 'Are you offering to dig our cesspits, Aulian?'

'You may scorn me but I value my life, Lhosir.' Oribas left them in the road. The Lhosir waited for him to reach the walls and climb the Marroc ladder before they came on. They took their time and assembled on the slope below the gates, out of range of the Marroc arrows. A hundred of them perhaps, and they had their ram with its sharply sloping hide-covered roof on top and a dozen ladders. Around the back of the mountain three more groups of Lhosir picked their way through the tumbled stones. They didn't go to much trouble to hide themselves, nor would it have made any difference if they had.

With a howl the Lhosir raised their shields and ran at the wall, a tightly packed mass of them. The Marroc loosed a hail of arrows and a few of the Lhosir fell, but most of the arrows found only shields and mail. The Lhosir reached the wall and hurled their ram at the gates while the ladders came up from among them and tipped against the walls. Now on the tower roof, Oribas tensed. The first minutes mattered more than anything. The Lhosir were what they were and it would take a very bloody nose indeed for them to lose the will to fight, but the Marroc were flighty. They weren't soldiers seasoned in the blood and fire of battle, these men. If the Lhosir gained a foothold on any part of the wall then the Marroc would break and it would all be over. He closed his eyes and said a prayer to the gods. He wasn't sure which gods he should talk to on this side of the mountains, whether Marroc gods would even listen to an Aulian, but he prayed to them anyway. *Let the ice behind the gates hold. Let the Marroc trust in it and turn away the ladders. Let them win!* He might have added, *Let them keep back the burning oil until it would make the most difference and use their pots of boiling water instead*, but that seemed a strangely cruel prayer to any god, save perhaps the Weeping God of the Vathen.

Oribas couldn't see the gates themselves, only the Marroc on the walls over the top of them hurling spears and shooting arrows at the Lhosir trying to work the ram. He saw one ladder crest the wall only to be thrown back, and another and another, and then in one place further around a Marroc tumbled into the yard with a spear through him and then a second, and a moment later a Lhosir helm and shield appeared over the battlements. But then Addic was there. He drove his sword at the Lhosir and kicked him back down, and the ladder was quickly gone.

On the other side of the mountain the three groups of Lhosir were approaching the wall. Oribas shouted down to the handful of Marroc keeping back from the fight around the gates. They ran up to where he pointed and peppered the Lhosir with arrows. Among the rocks, the Lhosir were having a hard time holding their shields up as well as climbing and carrying ladders. The first group gave up after two of them were stuck with arrows fifty paces short of the walls. The second group got a little closer. The third, Oribas saw, tried a good deal harder: they almost reached the wall before they dropped their ladder, turned and fled, three arrow-pierced corpses littered among the boulders and the snow.

Around the gates the Lhosir pulled back, but then a rock the size of a man's head flew over the wall and smashed into the yard. Oribas squinted down the trail at the trees beside the road from where the stone had come. He couldn't make out what the Lhosir had there until it jerked and fired again. A simple onager and not a particularly big one, not even quite out of range of the Marroc archers, but that didn't seem to bother the Lhosir. The second stone was low, thudding into the slope beneath the wall. The third and the fourth hit the wall, and then suddenly three ladders came up at once at the same place, arrows showered the wall and half a dozen Marroc fell at once. Lhosir with bows! They almost never used them, but now they'd taken the Marroc by surprise and Lhosir were cresting the wall with no one in their way. Two of them reached the battlements and turned to face the Marroc running along the walkway. Three more scrambled up the ladders, lowered themselves to dangle off the walkway and jumped down into the yard. They ran for the gates to throw them open while arrows flashed past them, but then saw the ice and snow and stopped, unsure what do to. The Marroc on the battlements pushed back the Lhosir and threw down their ladders. The three trapped inside were scythed down, a few Marroc running across the stained snow to finish them off. Three more heads for Achista to mount on the Aulian Bridge.

The Lhosir withdrew not long after that. Oribas came down from the tower to tend to the wounded but there were few. Eight Marroc were dead and six injured, three with simple cuts that would mend easily enough if they didn't turn bad, one with an arrow though an arm that would probably mend, and two for whom the best Oribas could do was make them comfortable and hold their hands together while they prayed. As well as the three Lhosir in the yard Achista said she counted thirty dead outside. Oribas, when he looked for himself, thought it more like twenty, but he kept quiet. It didn't matter. The Marroc had beaten the hated forkbeards again, and whether there were fifty or sixty or seventy of them left outside on the ridge, it made no difference.

She caught him at twilight and pulled him down to the Aulian tomb and they made love for an hour as the sun set. 'Tonight,' she told him as they lay together afterwards. 'You go tonight.'

Oribas said nothing. The Lhosir would grow stronger and stronger. It made sense, before going was no longer possible. 'I wish you would come with me.'

'You know I must be here.' She kissed his ear and stroked his hair. 'I'll send the men who are too wounded to fight but who can still walk out through the passage. They'll hang our three forkbeard heads over the bridge and seek Valaric the Mournful in the Crackmarsh. Then the doorway must be sealed. If they're caught, the forkbeards will find it.'

He held her tight for a long time. They both knew it would be the last night they had. 'I will not die first,' he whispered in her ear as they rose and dressed.

'I'll hold you to that.' They both knew it would be her.

'The Lhosir will come in the night.' Oribas was thinking of the three groups that had attacked the wall at the back of the tower earlier in the day, particularly of the band that had pressed harder than the rest. 'The south-west corner. They left a ladder there.'

Later they stood at the top of the shaft and watched the wounded Marroc climb down, three of them, each with a

Lhosir head slung over his shoulder. They kissed and held one another and then Achista stepped back through the round stone door and together, one either on side of it, they rolled it back into place until it lay between them.

'Goodbye, Oribas. Fare well,' he heard her call on the other side of the door, then heard her walk away. He turned the four seals, stood and looked at what he'd done and almost opened them again. It felt as though this was *her* tomb, that he'd sealed her in to die.

She'd left a torch burning at the edge of the shaft to give him some light. He moved it carefully away and waited until the other Marroc had gone ahead and then threw a few things down into the water. Easier that way than carrying them. By the time he reached the bottom, the faint flicker of orange light from the top was dim and fading. He worked quickly, doing what needed to be done, and then waited for the fire to go out. In the darkness he left, picking and sliding his way through the caves to the mountainside. The other Marroc were already long gone. They'd each choose their own path lest the Lhosir catch them and none of them would know that he'd followed. Achista's last try at keeping him safe.

But he didn't follow. Instead he turned the other way and trudged as quietly as he could around the edge of the mountain, towards the Lhosir camp.

35

THE AULIAN WAY

Skilljan Spearhoof had a few hours of bad and uncomfortable sleep. He'd started the day with some hundred fighting men and now he was down to more like seventy if you included the ones with wounds trivial enough to keep going. Bloody bastard Marroc with their bows. They were supposed to be farmers and beggars but half of them were in stolen Lhosir mail with shields and helms and swords and they didn't seem to have any shortage of those cursed arrows. Worse, the gates were stronger than he'd thought, which left scaling the walls and he'd already seen how badly *that* was going to go. He'd sent a rider back towards Varyxhun to say he was going to need more men – a lot more men – and that left him seething. Yes, there goes Skilljan Spearhoof who couldn't deal with a few angry Marroc farmers even with a hundred hardened Lhosir warriors at his back. And if it was true that the Marroc were led by a woman … He held his head and shuddered.

He led the night-time sortie himself, creeping up the mountain round the back of the tower in the dark to get to the ladder than Foddis Longbeard had left for him and lost three men doing it. And it seemed as though the Marroc had crept into his thoughts and read his mind. They let him climb all the way up the blasted crags and set the ladder against the wall before a dozen of them popped up over the top and threw a hail of arrows at them and he was lucky to get away with no worse than his tail between his legs and two more men sent to the Maker-Devourer's cauldron. In the middle of the night he finally he got to his tent and tried to sleep, and tossed and turned and set his plans as best he could. The Marroc hadn't left him with much of a choice. In the morning he'd build his pyres for the men he'd lost and lick his wounds, and then he'd wait and pen the Marroc inside Witches' Reach until he had another two hundred men. After that he'd go for the walls again. It would be a bloody business scaling them, but with that many men he'd do it and then the Marroc could see what it meant to defy him.

'Oi! Spearhoof!'

Skilljan felt as though he'd only closed his eyes a minute ago. When he looked it was still dark, so maybe he had. He recognised the voice. Hardal Daggereyes. 'This had better be very important.'

'Oh, you'll like this.' Hardal didn't sound like *he* liked it. Skilljan sat up and rubbed his face and then wished he hadn't. His skin still stung like the lash of a whip from when he'd been working the ram and the Marroc had poured scalding water over them all. The hide roof had kept the worst of it off, but by then it had had its fair share of rents and tears from all the arrows and spears the Marroc kept throwing at it. There weren't many who'd worked the ram who'd come away unscathed.

'Well, what then?'

'Best you come out.'

His legs didn't like it much, nor the rest of him either, but Skilljan hauled himself out of his nice warm tent. The furs he'd worn all day still kept him warm but on bare skin the cold at this time of night was like being flayed. Hardal had two of the night sentries with him and three others. Two battered-looking Marroc down on their knees and whimpering and – Skilljan blinked – the Aulian.

'These two we found near the Varyxhun Road.'

'Runners.' Skilljan nodded. He'd expected a few, which

was why Hardal had been out there in the first place. He'd hoped for more than two though.

Hardal shook his head. 'No. Look what this one had on him.' He held up a severed head. It took Skilljan a moment to realise he was looking at Geryk Frostbeard. Or what was left of him.

Skilljan growled and drew his sword, then stilled himself. He bent down and grabbed the Marroc's face instead, twisting it to look at him. 'We'll make a raven of this one in the morning.' That would make him feel better. It would make the others feel better too.

'On his way to cross the bridge, he was. Taking messages to the outlaws in the Crackmarsh. So was the other one. Apparently there were three, so we missed one.'

Skilljan clenched his teeth. So be it. He'd have more men before any band of outlaws could come crawling out of the swamp and maybe that would be just the thing to lure them. He frowned. 'I count three, not two, so how did you miss one?'

Hardal shoved the Aulian forward. 'We found this one on the way back, creeping into the camp. He says he wants to bargain with you.'

'I wasn't creeping, Skilljan Spearhoof. I was walking as any man would in the dead of night across moonlit snow.'

The Aulian looked scared, though, despite the defiance in his words. After the day Skilljan had had, anyone within range of his spear had a right to look scared. He laughed. 'There's no bargaining now, Aulian. We're long past that. Your Marroc are all dead men.'

'I wish to bargain for myself. For my own life. The Marroc inside Witches' Reach may all be dead men but I'm not Marroc, Skilljan Spearhoof.'

Scared, but he wasn't quivering and he stood still and spoke for himself, which in Skilljan's eyes spoke of at least *some* courage. 'I have to suppose that Cithjan sent you to the Devil's Caves for a reason, Aulian, even if I don't know what it was. For myself, I have no grudge against you.'

'I'll tell you why your ram failed if you like. The Marroc have piled up all the snow from the Reach against the gates. They packed it down hard and poured water over it through the night. The gates are frozen shut with a block of ice behind them as large as a shed.'

Skilljan looked at the Aulian and then turned back to his tent. Ice! Clever little *nioingrs*. So much for making a bigger ram. Maybe the Maker-Devourer knew how to smash a way through, but Skilljan didn't. 'Make those Marroc as uncomfortable as you like, Hardal, but don't let them die. I want their screams to reach the river when we gut them in the morning. The Aulian can have a clean death. Feed him.'

'Don't you wish to hear what I have to offer, Skilljan Spearhoof?' asked the Aulian.

'Not unless you have a way to get me into Witches' Reach.'

There was a long silence before the Aulian replied. 'And what, Lhosir, if I do?'

Oribas sat bound beside a fire in the Lhosir camp. Fear didn't stop him from sizing up their numbers and it didn't stop him listening either. They were angry, simmering with rage and impatient to avenge their fallen. In the morning they walked to the walls and waved a flag of parley to ask for their dead but the Marroc had already crept out in the night and hauled the bodies closest to the walls back inside. Skilljan's face turned thunderous. They all knew what that meant.

They tried a second time, easing into reach of the walls behind a line of shields and with one of their Marroc prisoners held in front of them. The Marroc asked for their man to be set free and then the Lhosir could have their bodies. When Skilljan refused, the archers in the fort killed the Marroc and drove the Lhosir away. Oribas's face went white when Skilljan told him that. 'They're madmen,' he whispered.

The Lhosir built their pyres and dragged away all the bodies they could reach. When they'd done that, they started on the last Marroc, and Oribas realised then why Achista had killed the first prisoner when she'd had the chance. For most of his life Oribas had been proud of his knowledge of the human frame. He'd worked with skeletons of men and cadavers. He'd been taught what organs were what and where they were to be found and what their importance was and what would happen if they were to fail. Now he tried to close his eyes and forget. The Lhosir stripped the last Marroc and laid him on his belly in the mud, close enough to one of the fires that the snow had all melted away. They held his arms and his legs while one of them took a knife and opened the skin on his back, one long deep cut on each side of the spine. They opened the cuts up wide and deep until bone showed beneath, and the screams were a thing Oribas knew he'd never forget. Then one of the Lhosir brought a strange-looking tool like a pair of long-handled tongs with cutting blades instead of metal fingers. One by one they pushed it into the screaming Marroc's wounds and pulled the handles apart, and each time they did, bone cracked and splintered. They were separating the Marroc's ribs from his spine. Oribas shut his eyes then and clamped his hands over his ears but he couldn't stop the sounds, couldn't stop that awful screaming. Worst of all though, he couldn't stop himself counting, to see if the Lhosir snapped every rib or only some, and he couldn't stop himself from wondering how many they'd cut before the Marroc could no longer breathe and so died.

The screams slowly faded. When it had been quiet for a while he opened his eyes and wished he hadn't. The Marroc was lying where he'd been before, only now he was lying on a wooden wheel with two fat stakes driven right through him and sticking out of the gaping wounds on his back near the shoulder. The dead man's lungs had been drawn out through the wounds and the Lhosir were draping them from strands of wire to make them look like wings. The blood raven. He'd heard Gallow talk of them.

When they were done they ran ropes around the two stakes and hung the dead Marroc from a pole. Three Lhosir carried him up towards Witches' Reach. Oribas didn't see what they did with him. Dangled him from a gibbet like the Marroc he'd seen in Varyxhun, perhaps.

They burned their own dead after that, standing beside each pyre to speak the deeds that each man had done in life and offering their souls to the cauldron of the Maker-Devourer. Skilljan Spearhoof had ignored Oribas until now, but as the dead burned and the Lhosir settled to an afternoon of feasting and remembering and watching the walls of Witches' Reach, he came at last. An old Lhosir came with him.

'Well then, Oribas of Aulia. Speak.'

'Witches' Reach was built by my people. There is an old Aulian tomb beneath it.'

Spearhoof looked to the old Lhosir. 'Sharpear here has been inside the tower. Tell us what you know.'

So Oribas described the parts of the tomb the Lhosir had turned into a storeroom and the round stone door they'd never been able to open. He told them of the caves on the other side, how the Marroc had made him open the door for them and entered the tower and taken it. How these men that Skilljan had caught and killed had sealed it shut again.

'So you're the one who let them in?' Skilljan bared his teeth. 'I should make a raven out of you too, Aulian.'

'I will open a door to anyone who has a knife at my throat and offers to remove it. The Marroc were good to their word. They meant to leave it to you to kill me.'

'Careless of them to let you go, then.'

Oribas shook his head. 'They didn't let me go, Lhosir. They were careless with the ladders they were using to go over the walls and rope up all your dead so they could cut off their heads and scatter them on the Varyxhun Road. Tonight I dare say they'll slip over the walls again and deliver their presents to you.'

Skilljan's eyes narrowed. 'Why did you come here, Aulian, when you could have run away?'

'And go where?' Oribas shrugged. 'I have nothing to do with this fight and no wish to be a part of it, but between you and the Marroc I have no choice but to choose a side. So I choose the side that will win. I will show you the way into Witches' Reach and open the door for you if you will swear in blood two things. You will let me live. I did nothing wrong but befriend a *nioingr* without knowing who he was, and for that I was sent to the Devil's Caves. You will become my kinsman and speak for me. You will swear in blood and I will lead you into Witches' Reach. Afterwards, while you bask in your victory, I will help you as best I can and you will shelter me until the snows melt in the spring and the Aulian Way is clear. Then I will go home.'

Skilljan Spearhoof laughed. 'I'll do all those things, will I? I have a different offer. You show me the way into Witches' Reach and I won't kill you as I killed that Marroc.' He crouched in front of Oribas and glared.

Oribas met his eye. 'I spent a year with a Lhosir, Skilljan Spearhoof. He was brave and strong and good to his word, and he taught me your ways well. I'll take you to the door. We will make a blood oath in front of your men. I'll open it and you'll lead your soldiers into the Reach and you won't look like a fool beaten by a few Marroc farmers.' Skilljan ground his teeth. Oribas smiled at him. 'When you see what I have to offer, you'll agree it was a small price, and so I'll have one more thing too. You'll give me one of the Marroc to do with as I see fit. Whichever one I choose.'

36

THE CHIMNEY

As the sun set, Oribas led Skilljan and three of his men around the mountain to the crack in the crags that led to the tomb beneath Witches' Reach. They crouched inside and Oribas fiddled with the flint and steel in his satchel until he had a tiny lamp burning. The Lhosir wrinkled their noses. 'What's that smell?'

Oribas began up the passage as far as the shaft. 'The cess of Witches' Reach makes its way down here.'

One of the Lhosir slipped and fell. 'Cursed greasy ice! I can't see a thing.' He made a retching sound. 'Stinks of fish.'

'Bring torches down the mountainside and the Marroc will know your purpose.' They pressed on all the way to the shaft, guided by the Aulian's tiny flame until Oribas stood in the mouth of the passage and pointed up. 'There are rungs set into the far wall. It was a long climb and slippery. One of the Marroc fell.'

'Show us.'

Oribas pursed his lips. 'At the top of the shaft is a door made by Aulian priests. I can open it. Go and look if you like. It's a long way and I'm not sure I have the strength to climb it twice in one night.'

'Twice, Aulian? The three of us will be enough to open the gates.'

Oribas laughed. 'You won't open any gates, Skilljan Spearhoof. I told you: the Marroc have sealed themselves in with ice and only the goddess of spring will open those gates now. That is unless you mean to light a fire beside them and hold off fifty Marroc archers for as long as it takes for that ice to melt.' Skilljan growled at him. The problem took him longer to mull over than Oribas liked. 'The Marroc came in this way, all of them. A cautious man like me would wait until he had more swords to follow him.'

'You're not as cautious as you'd like me to think.' Skilljan shook his head and stared up at the shaft.

Oribas withdrew a little way down the passage. 'The door is closed,' he whispered, 'but the Marroc aren't stupid. They may still have an ear to it. They'll know by now that I am gone.'

'But not that you came to me.' The Lhosir whispered among themselves and then Skilljan and one of his men crept away, leaving Oribas behind with the others. While he was away, Oribas and the two Lhosir sat in the pale light of his Aulian lamp. The Lhosir barred his way out, but it didn't seem to trouble them when he left the lamp beside them and moved back to the shaft, and so they didn't see as he circled the stone walkway, sprinkling powder from his satchel into the oily water. Oribas was half minded to climb the shaft without them, but would they follow? So he waited, and from their numbers when Skilljan returned, Oribas guessed he must have brought very nearly his entire band, what was left of them.

'You first, Aulian,' hissed Skilljan. 'I'll follow.'

Oribas gave Skilljan his lamp. 'No sound. No light. I'll take you to the door. You can stand there and see it in front of all your men, and then you can murder me and grind your teeth in frustration or you can whisper your blood oath and I will open it.'

'We'll see, Aulian.'

It was a long slow climb, every bit as hard as Oribas remembered. Worse for thinking of what waited at the top. He'd never done a thing like this. A horrible, terrible thing by any reckoning. There would be no forgiveness, not from those he crossed. And it was strange, because the Oribas who'd left the desert would never have done what he was about to do now, would never have considered it, would have thrown up his hands in horror at such a betrayal, and yet he felt no doubt. He would die for Achista, he'd known that for a while, but then he would have died for other things too – for Gallow, for the shadow-stalker and the sword-dancer he'd left behind who'd stood with him against the Rakshasa, for many others too. But for this Marroc woman he would do things far worse. For her and only for her.

Below him, Skilljan Spearhoof snarled and snapped at him to climb faster. Oribas kept his pace measured, though he was as eager as the Lhosir to reach the top and be done with this evil. The damp walls of the shaft glittered dimly in the lamplight, the only light any of them had until they reached the top and Skilljan climbed over the ledge and gripped Oribas and shook him. 'If you've brought us all this way for nothing …'

Oribas pulled himself free. 'Light a torch, Lhosir. We will need one.' Quickly, before too many of the Lhosir could follow Skilljan over the edge, he snatched his lamp and ran to the door. When Skilljan had his brand burning, he followed. 'Your oath,' hissed Oribas. 'And quickly, lest they hear us.' He started to turn the wheels.

'You have it.' Which only made it worse.

Skilljan lit a second torch and held them both so Oribas could see. The wheels moved more easily this time and it was done in seconds. Oribas bowed his head and took back the torch. 'Then the way is yours.' He stared at the look of glee on the Lhosir's face as Skilljan put his shoulder to the stone door and felt it begin to slide, then quietly walked away. There were six Lhosir up, then seven, and each one ran to the door with sword at the ready to race into the tower and fall upon the sleeping Marroc. None of them paid any attention to Oribas, their eyes focused on the slowly moving door, not even when he knelt down by the ledge to help one of them up and accidentally knocked over a bucket of foul-smelling oil that happened to be sitting by where he'd left it the day before. Nor as he stumbled back, holding his hands up in apology, and a piece of paper fell from his fingers and into the oil he'd spilled. Nor as he took his torch and lowered its flame to the ground. They only really noticed him again when the cavern lit up in a flash of light.

The oil he'd spilled over the edge caught alight and the fire began to spread across the floor. A Lhosir looked down to find his boots burning and tried to stamp them out. But it wasn't the Lhosir who'd already climbed the shaft that Oribas was looking at. He was crouching, making himself as small as he could, looking into the shaft.

The fire ran down the wall. It was slow, not as quick as Oribas had hoped, but the Lhosir clinging to the rungs had nowhere to go as the flames trickled towards them and the stones around their hands and in front of their faces burned. A gobbet of flaming oil dripped down the shaft, a bright falling star vanishing into the darkness. But only so far. For waiting for it was the rest of the trap Oribas had laid. The drop of oil hit the surface of what had once been water but was now oil laced with saltpetre. Oribas looked away as the whole shaft bloomed into bright burning light and the Lhosir began to scream.

In the old tomb Achista heard the stone move and the Lhosir's whispers grow louder. Through the cracks at the edge of the stone she saw the first flash of light, the signal Oribas had promised her. Thirty Marroc men gripped their spears and swords while a couple helped the Lhosir pull the stone door aside.

*

Skilljan Spearhoof froze at the first flash of light. He knew at once he'd been betrayed but he didn't yet know how. The hairs on his back prickled like a creeping spider. He let go of the door and turned to see the fire. The flames didn't seem like very much.

He turned back. The door kept moving even though no Lhosir was pushing it any more. He caught a glimpse of a face coming at him from the other side. What he didn't see was the spear point that came at him too, and so he died as steel pierced his eye and deep into his skull, the first fork-beard to fall but not the last.

The Marroc burst out from the tomb. Oribas stayed very still, face turned away from the flames, crouched in his corner, losing himself in the flickering shadows. The Lhosir could have found him if they'd chosen to look but most of them had no idea what has happening. It was over in a dozen heartbeats. The Marroc slammed into them and cut them down or pushed them back. Two ended up thrown over the edge. The Lhosir below were still climbing as fast as they could, roaring and swearing and howling as flames licked at their hands and reached for their faces and burned their forked beards. The Marroc waiting for them at the top were merciless. The Lhosir who fell vanished into the inferno at the bottom of the shaft. The last few started to climb back down but all they had waiting for them were flames and a thickening fish-stench of choking smoke.

Oribas turned away and then forced himself to turn back. There was nothing here he wanted to see but he needed to. He had to. Had to be sure he would remember what he'd done. He felt a presence at his shoulder. 'Come away.' He knew it would be her.

'I can't.'

'Yes, you can.' She leaned into him, wrapped her arms around his neck and nuzzled his ear.

'I will not forget that I have done this.'

'All they ever had to do was go. You've spared so many of us who never had that choice.'

Oribas followed her away, certain that he hadn't saved anyone at all, that these Marroc would stay here until the Lhosir starved them out, or burned them, or laid them low with axe and sword. But it was easier to listen to Achista's whispers than to the lost ghosts of the men who'd taught him how to do these things.

A few of the Marroc stayed in the tomb, watching. The rest crept up onto the walls of Witches' Reach and threw down ladders and slipped away into the night. They encircled the Lhosir camp and tore through it, pulling down the men that Skilljan Spearhoof had left to stand watch over his wounded and slaughtering the Lhosir to the last man. They took the heads of the men they'd killed and carried them down to the Varyxhun Road and the Aulian Bridge and once again left them there, another Marroc message of triumph.

Through it all, Achista held Oribas tight. Sometimes he hardly felt her. He sat in the tower, rocking back and forth. Every breath carried the smell of burning fish and burning fur and hair aflame. Between her soothing words he heard the Lhosir scream, howling with rage and fury and pain and, at the very last, a deep and horrible fear.

He didn't close his eyes to sleep that night. He was far too afraid of what he might see.

SOLACE

37

THE VARYXHUN ROAD

Beyard paused and stared at the Marroc woman Arda and wondered what he was doing. Only the Fateguard themselves could understand what it meant to be made into an ironskin, a man who served the Eyes of Time. Much was lost, many things that other men took for granted and would never willingly have forgone, and almost all those the Eyes of Time chose were given no say in becoming a Fateguard. Yet it was not all loss. With the iron and the sleepless eyes and the ever-present chill and the little need for food and rest there came an instinct for what was proper and what was wrong, what was fated and what was chance, what was a man's destiny and what was not. This was the instinct that had made Beyard let Gallow go in Middislet, the same instinct again in Hrodicslet. Something lay between them. Their fates had been entwined for a full score years and would not unravel so easily.

So he told himself, and he told himself too that it couldn't simply be that Gallow had once been his friend or that he was a better man than Sixfingers and always had been. The Fateguard had no friends, and fate cared nothing for right and wrong.

He followed the trail from Hrodicslet up into the mountains, tracing the path Gallow had made coming down. Snow began to fall, and for two nights and one day they were forced to wait in a Marroc farm while a blizzard wiped away every trace of every track that had existed before. When it was gone and the last snowflakes had settled, Beyard looked up at the sky, at the parting clouds, and smiled and followed anyway. Gallow had walked this road. He'd carried Solace for three long years and he left traces of his fate like a wounded man dripped blood.

He wasn't sure what it meant, this thing that lay between him and Gallow now. He passed through Jodderslet and didn't have all the Marroc there killed, even though he knew he probably should. His thoughts were distracted, and the more he sought for meaning, the more it seemed to elude him. He crossed into the Varyxhun valley through the Devil's Caves with every intention of returning to the castle. Gallow would come. He would come for his Marroc wife as surely as the sun would rise each dawn but the walls of Varyxhun would make him pause.

In sight of the city he stopped. Between him and the castle stood a host of Lhosir warriors. There must have been almost a thousand of them, and that, by Beyard's reckoning, accounted for nearly every Lhosir man in Varyxhun and almost half in the entire valley.

He stopped and watched. He was still watching when two riders broke away and galloped straight to him. 'Ironskin,' they called, breathless. 'Cithjan summons you!' And when Beyard stood before the man he was supposed to serve, Cithjan looked like he didn't even begin to understand why everything had turned out the way it had. Beyard pitied him for him for that.

'My Fateguard vanishes and now the whole valley is on the brink of revolt! Where in the Maker-Devourer's cauldron have you been?'

'Hunting Gallow Foxbeard.' Beyard gave that a moment to sink in. He drew Solace from its scabbard and held it up for Cithjan to see.

'Is that …?'

'Yes.' Beyard put the sword away. 'I will leave the valley

and take it to King Medrin when I can take the Foxbeard to him as well.'

'The Foxbeard is *here*?'

Beyard bowed his head a fraction. 'I have something he wants and so he will come to me. As I no longer need to hunt him, I am at your disposal until he does. Is there a war? Have the Vathen entered the Crackmarsh again? Has Valaric the Mournful called us to the field at last?'

Words tumbled out of Cithjan's mouth as he spoke of the Marroc of Witches' Reach – how they'd taken the tower and slaughtered two Lhosir attacks almost to the man. How they'd held the Reach for twenty days and sent messengers across the bridge to the outlaw Valaric to call for his aid. How Varyxhun simmered with discontent.

'Let Valaric come. I have a prisoner to be taken on to Varyxhun ...' He hesitated. Was that best? Foolish not to send her, but Gallow would go to her, not to him. 'No. I will keep her close.' He felt the uncertainty drain away. This was the right thing. 'I will lead your army, Cithjan.' Beneath his iron mask Beyard almost smiled.

The Marroc had wiped out the Lhosir in the shaft under Witches' Reach without losing a single man. When it was finished, Achista sent the last of the walking wounded with the severed heads of the Lhosir to the Aulian Bridge and on across the river, past Issetbridge, which guarded the mountain road to the Varyxhun valley, searching again for the men of the Crackmarsh. Addic went up the valley, murmuring and whispering in every tavern and inn where there were no forkbeards watching. The other Marroc Achista released were never meant to come back, but Addic wouldn't allow himself to be sent away and so Oribas went with him, and everyone knew that Achista had sent them both so they wouldn't be in the tower when the end came – all except Oribas and Addic, who had every intention of defying her.

They passed a few small bands of Lhosir heading for the tower but not enough to take it. They watched a party walking down from the Devil's Caves with a Marroc woman and the iron devil at their head and kept well away. They passed along the valley in secret, spreading their word until they found the Lhosir army from Varyxhun and then they watched it. In the valley Marroc came and went without being seen. In the winter chill, wrapped up in furs, even an Aulian passed unnoticed.

Addic watched the forkbeards trudging the Varyxhun Road. 'They're scared,' he said.

Oribas thought the Lhosir looked more angry than scared, but he kept this to himself. For the next three days the army moved slowly, swamping every village it reached. Most of the Lhosir slept in tents, which it seemed none of them liked. They crept along, stripping the valley of food and firewood as they went, almost deliberately slow. Addic and Oribas kept behind them, riding stolen Lhosir horses and covering five times as much ground, sweeping from side to side, heading into the high valleys the army left untouched. The Marroc were scared, everywhere scared, but angry too, and Oribas felt that more and more as they drew close to Witches' Reach again. People had seen the forkbeard heads strewn across the road, had heard the tales of bodies left out on the bridge night after night. Everywhere they went Addic spread the call: *Rise and throw the forkbeards down!* He burned with a barely held hunger. 'They're ready, Oribas. Just one more spark to light their fire, just one.'

Oribas wasn't so sure that a mere spark would be enough, but he kept that to himself too.

'Do you have any tricks to defeat this army?' Addic asked when the Lhosir were only a day away from Witches' Reach.

'I might suggest ways to defeat a few dozen here, a handful there, but this many?' Oribas shook his head. 'Melt away. Burn the tower for all to see and leave them with nothing.

Take your secret paths and ways through the high valleys and strike at them somewhere else. They've made this army now and so they must use it. Strike them again and again, always out of reach. You have the speed, they have the strength. Take their city, take their castle, any town you wish. Draw them hither and yon and never face them. Make them look like fools.'

After the sun had set and they were left to stare down the mountain at the Lhosir fires, Addic chuckled and shook his head. 'You're right, Aulian, but you also haven't been here very long. Do you know what they'd do? Everywhere we went, they'd burn it flat. They'd burn Varyxhun. If they had to, they'd burn every Marroc out of this valley and simply leave.' He bared his teeth. 'What use am I inside the walls now? You go back to her, Aulian. You'll be her strength. You'll show her ways to kill forkbeards that I'd never see.' He stood up.

'This many of them?' Oribas shook his head. 'It'll be over in the first day. They'll swarm over the walls in a hundred places at once.'

'Then I'm glad I won't be there to see it.' He stood up. 'If every Marroc kills a forkbeard before he dies then the valley will be free of them quickly enough. Cithjan is here. I mean to take him. Another spark struck at the waiting fire. Tell my sister I love her. Get her out of there if you can. Drag her if you have to. Farewell, Oribas. It was good to know a proper wizard.'

He walked away down the mountain towards the Lhosir and Oribas watched him go. He felt lost. Bereft. They'd have no chances to flee after this. He'd go back to the tomb, back to Witches' Reach; he'd stand by Achista and they'd either die together or the miracle she hoped for would come and the Marroc would rise before the Reach fell, but Oribas didn't believe in miracles.

Or he could walk away. Not like Addic, but the other way.

Turn his back on Witches' Reach and the Lhosir who surrounded it. It deserved a thought, at least, and yet if it did, he couldn't come up with one. The idea of not going back was inconceivable. Perhaps that was the most frightening thing of all. He'd rather die under a storm of Lhosir swords even though those swords terrified him.

He reached into his satchel without really knowing why and pulled out a tiny leather pouch closed tight with twine and sealed with wax. He only understood when he stared at it. A soporific. He started to laugh. The most preposterous idea of them all, that he might slip a poison into Achista's drink and put her to sleep and then carry her away past Marroc and Lhosir alike. Absurd, and even if he managed it then she'd hate him. Besides, he couldn't possibly get her down the Aulian shaft. He shook his head, put the pouch back into his satchel and looked around for anything else that might magic away a thousand Lhosir soldiers. Nothing. Yes, he might poison a few of them, make a few dozen too ill to fight. He might conjure fire a few more times before his powders were gone, but to what end? He couldn't save her, not this time.

He held his head in his hands. Addic had gone to his death in the Lhosir camp because he couldn't bear to see his sister at the end. That was one thing Oribas could do. He could make a poison so that when the end did come the Lhosir wouldn't have her. After a while he rose and left, traversing the mountainside. A part of him said he should go after Addic, as if that would somehow do some good, and he was too busy wondering about that to notice when he crossed tracks in the snow where two other men had come down the mountain a little earlier in the twilight.

Addic slunk down the mountain and stopped a hundred paces short of where the Lhosir sentries should be. He couldn't see them though, which troubled him. He could see the forkbeards' fires and the edge of their camp and knew their sentries should be out in the darkness beyond. So he *ought* to be able to see them.

He was in the middle of frowning about that when he saw a subtle movement on the slope ahead.

He wasn't alone.

38

THE LHOSIR CAMP

'She talked about you all the time.' Tolvis Loudmouth knelt at the fringe of the Lhosir camp beside one of the sentries he'd killed and beckoned Gallow forward. Loudmouth was dressed in mail under his furs now, with a helm and a shield and a spear all stolen from the sentry. 'Always, Gallow did this, Gallow did that.' He put the other sentry's helm on Gallow's head and wrapped his furs around Gallow's face.

'Did she talk about Merethin?'

They looked each other over to be sure their faces were hidden. 'Never.' In the darkness no one would know them, but a beardless Lhosir wouldn't pass unchallenged. Beardless *nioingr* had no place among real men.

Gallow stood up and walked brazenly towards the edge of the camp. 'I heard about him all the time. Jelira's father. You'd think he was both a prince and a priest from the way she'd talk about him. He was Nadric's son, but Nadric told me once, when he was drunk, that she despised him. That's just the way she is.'

Tolvis didn't reply and Gallow supposed that was for the best. Better not to talk about Arda, not now. Was she pleased that he'd finally returned? He thought not. He'd been away too long. She'd given up on him and moved on. He was an inconvenience now, but however she really felt, she'd never let any of them see it – not him, not Tolvis, no one. She'd do what was best for her children, for her family.

They walked among the fires, heads bowed, moving quickly, two Lhosir soldiers on some irksome errand. They talked to one another about nothing very much: Gallow's boys and little things they'd done and how they'd grown while he'd been away. Jelira, and how she was the one who'd never let Tolvis touch her, who never let go even though Gallow hadn't been her real father either. Middislet and the tiny changes the village had seen. Things that didn't matter. Things to keep their minds away from Arda and from the thousand Lhosir soldiers around them.

Tolvis stopped beside a fire where six men were passing around a keg of Marroc ale. He crouched down beside them, back a little, face kept in shadow. 'What's that Marroc woman doing here, brothers?'

The Lhosir stopped their talk to look round at him, and when Tolvis asked again, Gallow watched where their faces turned. They laughed and shrugged and offered to share their fire and their drink – Tolvis and Gallow were brothers from across the sea after all, and even if their faces were hidden by the furs they wore against the cold, it was in their voices, in their words, in the way they spoke and moved. They were Lhosir and so they were friends, and the world was that simple. Tolvis shook his head and thanked them. The two moved on, easing closer to the centre of the camp. 'Your Fateguard friend has kept her close. We find him, we find her.'

Gallow hissed, 'He's drawing us to him. He knows we're coming.'

'He's an ironskin, Truesword, not a witch.' Tolvis clucked, shook his head and stopped another Lhosir to ask which way to the iron man. The Lhosir pointed and Tolvis thanked him. 'Is it true the Fateguard never sleep?' he asked. The Lhosir shook his head. To Gallow's surprise he made the sign of Modris to ward away evil as they parted. Modris, the Marroc god.

'How long did you wait?' The question hung in the air between them. It wasn't the sort of question that ever had a good answer.

'Before I gave up hoping you were still alive? A few months. Before I did anything about it? A year. Does it matter, Truesword? I watched over your wife and your sons when I thought you were alive and I watched over them when I thought you were dead.'

'You did more than watch over them.' Couldn't let it go. Here of all places, in the middle of the Lhosir camp.

Tolvis grabbed Gallow by his furs. 'You were *dead*. What would you have preferred? That I abandon them?'

A soldier glanced their way. Tolvis let go. Gallow clenched his teeth. 'I knew Beyard once. He'll have her in one of the tents close to a fire to keep her warm. He'll look after her as though she was a lady and he'll watch her every second. And yes, it's true that the Fateguard never sleep.'

'They must get very bored at nights then.' Tolvis stopped and nudged Gallow, pointing through the darkness to a larger fire in the middle of the camp and a big tent beside it where a banner flew. 'Cithjan. What did the Marroc do to drag even him out of his hole?'

'Beyard will be close.'

Tolvis changed course, skirting the Lhosir sentries around Cithjan's tent. 'Now there's a Lhosir I could do without. I came to thinking for a bit that when the Maker-Devourer made Sixfingers he must have spilled a bit, and that when he scooped it up, something else got in. Maybe he picked up one of the old hungry spirits from the Marches that he'd turned away long ago – maybe that's why Sixfingers has such a bitter streak inside him. Whatever he did with Medrin, he did it with Cithjan too. More and more of us from what I saw after you … after you left.'

'It's not the Maker-Devourer's brew, Loudmouth. It's a disease. A disease of the memory. We're forgetting who we are.' Gallow fell silent as Tolvis pulled him behind a tent.

'Fateguard.' Gallow peered past Tolvis's shoulder. It took a while for his eyes to pick Beyard out, but there he was, sat still in the shadows. 'Don't they feel the cold either?'

'Beyard said he always felt cold. That nothing made any difference.'

Tolvis shivered. 'They're not natural.'

'No.'

They watched for a while but Beyard didn't move. After a time Gallow took a deep breath and made to walk towards him. Tolvis caught him before he could take more than a step. 'So.' His voice was urgent, as though he'd guessed what Gallow meant to do. 'I'll create a distraction. You slip inside and bring her out while they're all looking the other way. Right?'

Gallow laughed. He slapped Tolvis Loudmouth on the shoulder. 'She's yours now. I saw how she looked at me and I saw how she looked at you.'

Tolvis shook his head. 'She will choose you, Gallow Truesword. Always.'

'I'm going to challenge Beyard. I have to. If he wins, he has me and Arda goes free. If he loses, he lets us go, all of us. For ever.'

'What makes you think he'll agree.'

'Because a part of him remembers that he was my friend once. Because of what happened in Middislet.'

Loudmouth shook his head but Gallow moved too quickly. Before Tolvis could stop him he was out in the open, lit up by the fire at the heart of the Lhosir camp. He threw back his hood. 'Beyard of the Fateguard! I challenge you! Gallow Truesword is here. You have called me *nioingr* three times and I will take what I am owed from you for that. My life or hers, Beyard. Kill me if you can, ironskin!'

Tolvis slunk off into the shadows. It wasn't the distraction he'd had in mind, but it *was* still a distraction.

Oribas circled half the camp before his legs finally agreed with what the rest of him had realised far sooner – that he could never poison Achista no matter now much it was the right thing to do and that he had to go back for Addic after all. They were shaking by then. All of him was shaking and it wasn't only the cold. He'd had enough courage, barely, for the burning of the Lhosir in the shaft under Witches' Reach and now, it seemed, he'd used it up. Or maybe the shaft had been different because it had been a trap laid with thought and care, a plan he could see even before he started, step by step from start to finish. Here … Here there was nothing but madness and the conjured thought of Achista's face when she heard that her brother was dead. The light going out of her. The hardness coming down like an armour he'd never pierce.

He had no idea how to stop Addic when he turned to-wards the camp. All he knew was that if he didn't turn now then he never would. He had no idea how he'd even find the Marroc, nor how to slip past the Lhosir pickets. The last, though, wasn't a bother. He didn't try. He walked straight at the camp until someone challenged him and then turned to-wards the Lhosir, hands held up to show he meant no harm.

'I have knowledge of a secret entrance into Witches' Reach.'

The Lhosir didn't seem to hear. He grunted at Oribas, 'What are you?'

'I'm an Aulian.' Oribas bowed. 'I know the secrets of Witches' Reach,' he said again. He had to try two more times before the Lhosir understood what Oribas was telling him and that it wasn't some trick or a joke. Once they got that far, Oribas didn't have to worry about slipping through the rest of the camp. They walked together straight to the heart of it, Oribas in front, the Lhosir behind, poking with his spear.

'Kill me if you can, iron man!'

The challenge came, welcome and wanted. Beyard looked up and then slowly, as though it pained him, he rose. Metal ground against metal as he stepped out of the shadows beside Cithjan's tent. Gallow was on the other side of the fire, spear thrust into the air. A dozen Lhosir were staring at the Foxbeard, faces in the shadows of the night lit up by the dancing flames of the fire. Most of them looked bemused. Beyard looked past them, looking for Tolvis Loudmouth but seeing only darkness. But Loudmouth was there. Beyard knew it.

Cithjan stumbled out of his tent rubbing his eyes. Beyard moved quickly before anyone could say something stupid and insulting. He strode out into the open, drew Solace and raised the cursed sword into the air, slashing at the stars. He roared and felt the watching Lhosir flinch. The Fateguard rarely spoke, and when they did their voices were low grinding whispers. Not one of them had heard a Fateguard roar, but this was Gallow and Gallow deserved it. 'Gallow Foxbeard! Here I am!' And the Lhosir flinched at that too, not at Beyard's voice this time but at his words. At the name, for there wasn't a single Lhosir here who hadn't heard of Gallow the Foxbeard.

An old anger swept through Beyard. *Foxbeard?* He lowered his sword and swept it across the watching men. 'Called Truesword by the Screambreaker himself. Braver than any of you. Stronger than any of you. More a Lhosir than any of you. He chose the wrong side but did no worse than that.' He roared again and strode around the fire watching Cithjan's Lhosir step hurriedly back to give him space. The warriors he remembered from before the Eyes of Time took him would never have moved. Yurlak and the Screambreaker. Lanjis Halfborn and Jyrdas One-Eye. Thanni Thunderhammer and yes, even Farri Moontongue before he went stupid and tried to defy not only his king but the very will of the world. *Especially* Farri Moontongue. True Lhosir. Names and stories burned into his memory too deep for even the iron witch of the Ice Wraiths to wipe away.

'Gallow Truesword!' he cried again and saw him, the only Lhosir not to back away. Beyard saluted. No mercy this time. Quick and brutal. Solace would cut through wood and steel and flesh and bone and be done with it, and Beyard wouldn't feel a jot of joy at what he'd done.

Gallow levelled his spear and crouched behind his shield. 'If I beat you, I take the Marroc woman with me and I leave. If I don't, I'll be dead and you can let her go because you'll have no use for her.' The Foxbeard bared his teeth.

Beneath his mask Beyard grinned back. 'Someone get the Marroc woman!' He looked around, pointed his sword at a Lhosir who happened to be close and waved him on his way. His eyes flicked to Cithjan, who was starting to think. Beyard could see it happening and nothing good was going to come of it. He levelled Solace at Cithjan's face. 'This one belongs to the witch of the north. He's belonged to her for seventeen years. Keep your mind on crushing the Marroc, Cithjan. Truesword is mine and I will do with him as I please and answer to Medrin when I'm done, not to you.'

Cithjan's face darkened but he kept his mouth shut and that was all that mattered. Beyard turned back to Gallow and then knelt in the mud beside the fire. He was so close that the flames sometimes licked the iron of his armour but he felt as cold as ever. Always cold. 'I called you *nioingr*, Gallow Truesword, but you are not. Let all here witness my words. I spoke falsely of you.' Behind him they were dragging the Marroc woman out into the night.

'Then you owe me a boon.' Gallow still aimed his spear at the spot between Beyard's eyes.

'Speak it.' Beyard stayed as he was. On his knees, head bowed.

'Let her go.'

Beyard rose and turned and she was there, wrapped in furs, held between two Lhosir guards. To Beyard she seemed small and unremarkable. Nothing about her stood out at all. He walked to Arda, took her arm and, shooing the other Lhosir away, dragged her towards Gallow, Solace still in his other hand. He felt for the weave of her fate and even then found nothing. For a moment he pressed the point of the cursed sword up against her throat. Gallow didn't flinch.

'As you wish, old friend.' Beyard let her go, lifted his hands away from her and turned to the watching Lhosir. 'Let her walk free. Do not follow her. She is not to be touched by anyone here.' When she didn't move he pushed her, hard, away out of the space between him and Gallow. She stopped at the edge of the circle surrounded by uncertain Lhosir but they let her be, and Gallow and Beyard locked eyes at last. Gallow's spear point twitched, a flicker of a hair's breath.

'I thank you for that kindness, old friend.'

'And you're welcome to it.' Beyard swept an arm around at the Lhosir crowded around them. 'This time I will kill you, old friend, and you know it's for the best. But you will be remembered.'

39

FIRE AND LIGHT

The Lhosir shoved Oribas towards the heart of the camp. The blaze of fire cast everything else into mercurial shadow. Outside its light he couldn't see what was happening. Something, though. Over the crack and snap of burning wood he heard shouting. One voice and then another. A pause and then the second voice came again and Oribas's heart jumped. *The iron man.* Beyard. Gallow's friend. Was he too late, then?

He stumbled on, eyes glued to the ground for each footstep, stealing glances where he could but there was little to see. He heard another exchange of words and then a shout and a battle cry he knew well: *Gallow!*

Three more Lhosir stepped out from among the tents, faces taut, spears lowered, barring his way. They spoke in murmurs, all of them pressed close around Oribas as though he wasn't there.

' … claims he's Gallow the Foxbeard.'

'He's called out the Fateguard.'

'It can't really be him.'

'The ironskin thinks so.' There was fear there, but disdain too when it came to the iron man.

'Cithjan's in a foul mood.' The Lhosir sentry prodded Oribas with a spear. 'I don't fancy your chances, Aulian.'

Another shout and then a gasp came from among the watching crowd and a chorus of jeers. The Lhosir pushed Oribas on towards the central fire and then stopped, and at last Oribas could see what was happening. Gallow was on his hands and knees, struggling to get to his feet. His shield was split in two. The ironskin was waiting for him to rise while the Edge of Sorrows in his hand gleamed like fresh blood in the firelight. Oribas steeled himself. All this way to stop Addic from getting himself killed and now it was Gallow about to die instead. He held up his hands again, the universal gesture among Aulians, Marroc, Lhosir, Vathen and probably every other people under the sun. Showing he meant no harm, that he held no weapons. But although he held no steel, neither hand was empty and he still had the pouches at his belt.

'Gallow!' he cried. His voice sounded thin and weak amid the hooting and jeering of the Lhosir. One hand tossed a swan's egg emptied and refilled and then sealed with wax. He threw it up high into the fire and followed it with the pebble-like thing in his other hand, straight into the flames. 'Beware the sun!'

Oribas turned away. He closed his eyes, waiting for one of the Lhosir to cut him down.

The fire exploded.

Tolvis stopped listening to whatever the Fateguard had to say. They were living monsters, tolerated because they served fate and because the Lhosir believed in that sort of thing. As long as they stayed in their temple on Nardjas and watched over their mysterious artefacts and didn't interfere with the way of the world, Tolvis supposed they were harmless enough, but ever since Sixfingers had taken Yurlak's crown they'd come out to serve him. He probably wasn't the only Lhosir who didn't much like it, but three years hiding among the Marroc made it hard to be sure.

He skirted the centre of the camp. Beyard and Gallow were making it easy, drawing the eyes of every Lhosir who could be bothered to come out of his tent. He moved among them and no one looked at him twice, even as he sidled up to where the Fateguard had been sitting.

He watched two Lhosir march in and drag Arda out and watched Beyard let her go, and he wondered what he was supposed to do now. *Slip back and leave the camp with her? Yes. Get her out of here.* That's what, otherwise why were they here? He paused, looking at her and then at Gallow. He saw her eyes linger on the Foxbeard and felt a sharp pang of guilt. Gallow was putting himself out of the way – letting the two of them be free together – but that wasn't right. It should be him in there facing the Fateguard. He moved back behind Cithjan's tent and past it. And froze. Someone was creeping among the shadows, easing himself towards the circle of firelight. The man moved oddly, not strutting like a Lhosir but shifting furtively. Tolvis crept closer, shuffling sideways through the snow until he reached the tracks that the other man had left behind and then planting his feet in them, step for step so the sound of snow crunching under his boots wouldn't give him away. He came soundlessly up behind the man and put a knife to his throat. No braids in his beard.

'Hello, Marroc.' He pulled back the man's hood with his teeth. Warily he loosened his grip. 'Say something, Marroc, but say it quiet.'

'Kill me quickly, forkbeard.'

The voice was full of bitter hate. Tolvis withdrew his hand but his knife stayed at the Marroc's throat. 'How many of you?'

'Would I tell you if it wasn't only me? But either way that's what it is.'

Tolvis lowered his knife. 'That's a bit disappointing. I was hoping there might be hundreds of you slipping in for a good fight. I'm going to leave you be now. I'd been thinking of opening a vein or two on Cithjan while I was here but I'll leave you to it. You can nod your head now if you like.'

The Marroc didn't move. Tolvis was about to let him go when he heard another cry over the commotion of the fight: 'Beware the sun!'

An instant passed and then a light as bright as midday bathed the Lhosir camp.

Gallow came at Beyard low and fast. They smashed into each other, shield against shield, so hard that Gallow reeled, almost dazed. He stabbed down at Beyard's feet and felt his spear point scrape and slide off the Fateguard's iron skin. As they separated he stabbed again, this time straight at Beyard's face. Beyard saw it coming. He brought Solace down on the spear as it thrust forward and the red blade snapped the shaft in two. Gallow barely had time to draw his sword before Beyard shield-slammed him again. The air moaned as Solace licked at his face. He staggered under another blow. When he stabbed back, Beyard's shield was already there, but instead of rushing him the Fateguard paused. 'You cannot win this fight, Gallow.' He sounded almost regretful. 'Not even you. But I know you must try. I will make it worthy of you.' Gallow slashed at him. Beyard stepped back and caught Gallow's sword on his shield again. 'Why, Gallow, if all you ever wanted was to be left alone? Was that what you were thinking when you took Medrin's hand?'

Gallow lunged. Beyard blocked easily and hammered Solace into Gallow's shield. 'He had a become a monster!'

'But he is your king.'

Gallow rushed in behind his shield once again and they crashed together. Bones jarred; but Gallow dropped at the last moment and hooked one foot behind Beyard's leg and shoved. The Fateguard staggered and went down. Gallow jumped at him, swinging his sword. Beyard took it on his shield. The blade skittered up and across it, scoring a deep mark in the wood. It threw sparks as it struck Beyard's iron mask. 'Yield, ironskin!'

'I cannot.' Beyard kicked at Gallow's legs and rolled onto all fours as Gallow jumped away. For a moment he was defenceless. Gallow leaped, dropping his sword and pulling out his axe as he landed, hammering the blade down into the iron on Beyard's back. It bit deep, splitting the Fateguard's armour, and stuck fast. Beyard grunted but he didn't fall. Gallow scooped up his sword.

'You see, Truesword.' Beyard was on his feet now. He took his time, the axe still sticking out of him. 'You cannot win, but when men speak your name in times to come, they will remember you for this. I'm sorry, old friend. I have nothing else to offer.' He ran at Gallow again and this time there was no holding back. They smashed together, shield on shield, once, twice, a third time, each blow knocking Gallow back. After the third, Solace came down like a hammer. Gallow threw up his shield and the red sword split it in two. Beyard kicked him, knocking him down, then waited for Gallow to rise again. An honourable fight to the bitter end. Gallow spat blood. 'When it comes, make it sure and quick, old friend.'

Beyard lifted off his crown and mask and threw them to the ground. For a moment they met each other, eye to eye. 'I'll do that much for you, Gallow Truesword.'

Someone was shouting his name over the ringing in his ears. A voice he knew. *Beware the sun!* Oribas! And he'd heard that cry before.

He drew himself to his feet and closed his eyes.

The first flash was the pebble, a crumbly cake of saltpetre wrapped in dried sheep's intestine. It flared strongly enough to dazzle the Lhosir already looking at the fire and to draw the eyes of the ones who weren't. It was bright in the night, but not as bright as what followed. The swan's egg was filled with desert oil, and when it broke it turned the fire into a tower of flame, a searing flare of light and heat that scorched the back of Oribas's neck. The Lhosir in front of him reeled, blinking to try and regain their sight as Oribas ducked between them. The fire roared, stretching for the sky. Oribas kept his eyes averted. The flames would die in a few seconds but the Lhosir didn't know that. They backed away. Oribas sneaked a glance towards Gallow. The big man was on his feet and had grabbed hold of the Marroc woman's arm. He buffeted and barged through the dazed Lhosir and they vanished into the shadows. The only one who didn't seem to be blinded was the iron man himself. Oribas dashed straight across the open circle beside the fire, taking a handful of salt out of his satchel, and as the flare of the fire died back he reached the Fateguard. Running past him, Oribas threw the salt straight into the ironskin's face and this time the ironskin had no mask to cover him. Beyard howled and clutched at himself with his iron-gloved hands and staggered to his knees. Oribas didn't know whether to be glad that salt had brought the iron man down or whether to be terrified.

The flames died and the camp fell into darkness once more, no deeper than a minute before, but to those who'd looked at the fire it seemed an inky black. Oribas caught up with Gallow. He was running, pulling the woman after him. She was slowing him. 'Gallow!'

'Oribas.' He didn't look round. 'I heard your warning. How did you know?'

'How did I know what?'

'Where to find me?'

Oribas didn't answer. He tugged on Gallow's shoulder, pulling him until he stopped, and they crouched down together in the shadow between two tents. He put a finger to his lips. 'They'll be getting back their eyes now,' he whispered. 'No more running. Now we slip away in the shadows and in the quiet.' He looked from Gallow's face to the Marroc woman and back again. Gallow nodded. The woman looked bewildered and frightened, wide-eyed like a deer about to bolt. Oribas put a hand on her arm, and when she looked at him, put his finger to his lips again.

But she wasn't looking at *him*; she was looking past him, and when Oribas turned there were two Lhosir looking back. For a moment no one moved, all as surprised as each other. Then the Lhosir went for their axes.

Addic froze at the first flash. The forkbeard froze too so Addic jabbed an elbow hard into his chest and jumped away. The flash faded. He was about to run out from behind Cithjan's tent when the fire flared up a second time. The forkbeards around it reeled and the one who'd grabbed him staggered back, eyes squeezed shut against the light. Addic saw that his chin was ragged stubble, no forked beard at all.

He ignored Tolvis then and instead drew a knife and stabbed it into Cithjan's tent. He ripped a savage hole in the fabric and slipped through, and there was Cithjan himself, standing outside the front, silhouetted against the flaring flames, forkbeards all around him shielding their eyes and yet staring at the fire, and all with their backs to Addic. Addic rose out of Cithjan's tent, stepped up and slid a blade across Cithjan's forkbeard throat and then stepped away again, and it was over and done and Addic was back in the shadows before anyone even knew.

When he scrambled out the back of the tent again, the other forkbeard was gone. He saw a shape on the far side of the fire fling something at the iron devil, something that brought the devil screaming to his knees. His heart pounded, filled with fear and elation at what the wizard had done and with the thought that he might not die here tonight after all. As the flames subsided, he slipped away, circling the fire, following in Oribas's wake.

40

ONE MUST FALL

Tolvis blinked, trying to get the sparks out of his eyes as the fire died away. He looked for Gallow but the big man was gone and Arda with him. Outside Cithjan's tent another commotion broke out. Beside the fire a small figure raced past the Fateguard and the ironskin was suddenly staggering and howling as though someone had set him on fire. Tolvis started to move and then stopped as he saw the Marroc again, hurrying out from a hole in Cithjan's tent that hadn't been there a few moments ago. The Marroc took one glance over at the fire and hurried away. Cithjan was on the ground with two Lhosir crouched beside him and the fire was still bright enough for Tolvis to see the fury on their faces as they turned to look for his murderer.

The Marroc was circling the camp in the direction Gallow had gone. Tolvis set off after him.

Oribas looked up in horror. He scrambled to his feet as the Lhosir roared and swung but Gallow was up first. The Marroc woman screamed curses. Then a shape appeared behind the two Lhosir and one of them fell and warm sticky blood sprayed into Oribas's face. An axe bit into what was left of Gallow's shield, knocking it sharply sideways. As Oribas rose, the iron rim smashed into his temple.

Addic raced after Oribas and never mind the shouts from the bewildered forkbeards. They'd been blinded, dazzled, they'd seen their iron devil fall and then their leader and Addic planned on making the most of it. The Aulian was running too, though he was taking more care not to be seen. There were two others with him. They suddenly ducked down and vanished into the gloom amid the forkbeard tents and Addic lost them there, but not for long before a pair of forkbeards found them and shouted and a fight started. A woman's voice swore. In the gloom it was impossible to see much but he knew forkbeards when he saw them. There were two, with more coming from the other direction, but the first two had their backs to him. Addic ran up behind them, wrapped a hand under one forkbeard's chin, pulled it up and rammed his knife into the man's neck. Blood fountained across them all. The other forkbeard stepped back as a shape emerged from the shadows to face him. He slammed his axe into the other man's shield hard enough to stagger them both. Addic blinked as the man in the shadows rose. The forkbeard from the Aulian Way! Another figure started to his feet beside Gallow, caught Gallow's shield in the face and dropped down. Gallow slammed into the last forkbeard, shield against shield, knocking him back. Addic dropped to one knee and stabbed his knife into the fork-beard's calf. Enough to stop him. The forkbeard howled. More were coming the other way but suddenly they fell to fighting among themselves. For a moment Addic's path was clear and Gallow and Oribas were behind him, ready to run.

So he ran.

Tolvis rushed through the snow. Gallow and Arda and the Marroc already had one pair of Lhosir on them. He saw one fall and heard the other scream but now three more were running at them from behind. Tolvis threw himself after them, hauling two of them down. He twisted so his weight landed on one, knocking the breath from his lungs. As the other started to rise, Tolvis punched him in the face, knocking him back again. He didn't wait for any more but rolled to his feet and ran on. The third Lhosir was still ahead of him, chasing Gallow and the others. He'd catch them too. Arda couldn't run like a Lhosir soldier. No Marroc could.

'Marroc!' he shouted. 'Cithjan is dead! The Marroc attack! To arms! The Marroc have come up the mountain! The Marroc of the Crackmarsh!' Anything to add to the confusion. The Lhosir were stirring anyway, woken by the sounds of fighting and the shouts and now the horns blowing from the centre of the camp. The more they milled around the better. With a spurt of speed he caught the last Lhosir and pulled alongside. 'Hello!' he said.

The Lhosir glanced at him, face set and determined. A flicker of confusion crossed his eyes before Tolvis elbowed him hard in the ribs and, as the Lhosir stumbled, stuck out his leg and sent him sprawling in the snow. The Marroc was at the front now, running with purpose up the slope through the fringe of the Lhosir camp and towards the silhouette of Witches' Reach. Tolvis caught up with Gallow and Arda and took her other hand. 'Truesword, when I said I'd create a distraction, what I meant ... Oh, never mind.' He kept his breath for running.

Gallow pulled Arda after him. For all Loudmouth's shouts about the Marroc and Cithjan being dead, the Lhosir weren't stupid. Some of them would give chase if only to see what the chase was for. And he and Tolvis might outrun Lhosir soldiers freshly roused from their beds but neither Arda nor Oribas had legs for the long chase. Although at least whoever was running ahead – and who else could it be if it wasn't the Aulian? – looked as though he knew where he was going, fast and full of purpose.

'Truesword, when I said I'd create a distraction ...' Tolvis took Arda's other hand and for a moment the three of them were running abreast, Gallow and Tolvis almost pulling

Arda through the air. Behind them more Lhosir gave chase. Gallow had no idea why they were heading for Witches' Reach but it was maybe half a mile away and up a steady slope from the camp. The Lhosir would catch them first.

'Tolvis, look after Arda!' he said. He let go of her hand and fell back. He wouldn't have to slow the Lhosir too long for Arda to make it to the tower. What Oribas meant to do when he got there Gallow had no idea, but he was Oribas and he always had a plan, and Gallow trusted him for that.

As the first Lhosir caught up, he slowed, coming at Gallow cautiously, peering past at the fleeing figures.

'And who are you?' Gallow asked.

The Lhosir's eye snapped back. He saw where Gallow's beard was missing and his stare hardened. '*Nioingr*.' He nodded. 'Hrek Sharpfoot. And I mean to kill you, Foxbeard.'

'I don't doubt it.' Gallow charged and Hrek Sharpfoot charged him back, but Gallow had the slope in his favour and he was the heavier. They smashed into one another and Gallow kept on going, bull-rushing Sharpfoot back down the slope until he stumbled and fell and almost took Gallow with him. The next two Lhosir were on them now, slowing. Gallow bellowed a battle cry and waved his axe and then turned and ran again. A few dozen heartbeats, that was all he'd given Tolvis and Arda. It wasn't enough, not this time, but he'd do it again and again until it was. Until Arda was safe.

Tolvis ran in the wake of the Marroc, who didn't seem interested in waiting for anyone. Arda pulled her hand away. When he glanced sideways at her, she was looking back at him. 'Don't let him die,' she gasped. 'Not now. Not again.'

Tolvis nodded. He turned at once, mostly so she wouldn't see the pain her words caused him. That answered that then.

'Go, Gallow,' he cried as Gallow reached him. 'Be with her.' But Gallow only slowed. Tolvis swore at him. 'I said be with her, you wooden-skull!' But Gallow shook his head.

'There's no door to hold shut, Loudmouth. This time we face our enemies together.'

Arda glanced back once and only once and her heart beat hard and fast because they were both as stupid as each other and yet she loved them both in their own very different ways, one as the father of her children and the most fierce and unexpected soulmate, the other as a kind and tender friend and sometimes more, and now they were both going to get killed because a part of each of them was the same stubborn pig-headed idiot. She might have cried, but life was a hard thing and she'd seen her share of horror, and so she'd save her tears for later when she was somewhere she could spare some time for them. She ran after the stranger in front of her, abandoned to him by the men she knew, but she'd seen him kill forkbeards and so she took him for a friend. Shouts reached her from behind. The clash of swords. She didn't dare look back. Didn't dare because she owed it to them to run as hard and fast as she could. They were buying her seconds. Buying them with their lives.

'Achista!' screamed the Marroc in front. He was a good way ahead of her now, racing for the tower of Witches' Reach. She remembered seeing that tower for the first time, looking over the Varyxhun Road not far past the heights of the Aulian Bridge over the Isset. Fenaric the carter had brought her here. She tried not to think about that too much. Maybe she'd never know whether what she'd done had been stupid or right, taking the blame for Nadric's moment of madness. It had probably saved Nadric's life and maybe Fenaric's too, but it had driven Gallow away and in time she'd regretted that more than anything. 'Achista! Marroc! Lower the ladders!' Last she'd heard, Witches' Reach had been full of forkbeards.

Torches appeared on the walls. She was tiring. The Lhosir

behind her were getting closer despite Gallow and Tolvis. She heard their shouts, both of them. They felt sharp inside her.

The gates to the Reach didn't open but a ladder came over the wall. The Marroc in front of her reached it and started to climb. Arda couldn't help herself: she let out a low wail. A ladder! Someone would have to stand at the bottom and hold the forkbeards off while the others climbed. Whoever did that would have no chance to climb it themselves. *No. No no.* Not Gallow, not after he'd come back after so many years, yet she couldn't bring herself to want it to be Tolvis either. *Do I have to choose?* But no, she didn't. She didn't ever get to choose. The men would do the choosing. And most likely, since they were cut from the same idiot cloth, they'd choose to stand together and she'd lose them both.

She reached the ladder and started up. The Marroc was standing at the top. As he reached to haul her up, he stared at her in horror. 'Who are you? You're not Oribas!' He looked aghast.

Arda grabbed his shirt and pointed at Tolvis and Gallow running towards the wall with a dozen Lhosir behind them. 'Help them!'

Another Marroc woman pushed along the wall. 'Addic! Where's Oribas?' A look went between the two. The woman's face turned ashen and then a tight mask of fury settled on it. 'Archers! Kill the forkbeards.'

A rain of arrows flew from the wall at the Lhosir, at Gallow and Tolvis and the forkbeards chasing them alike. Arda screamed at the archers, 'Not the two at the front! Not the two at the front!' The forkbeards kept on coming though, all of them, right up to the walls. Gallow was first. He dropped his broken shield and threw himself at the ladder, pulling with his arms. The Marroc on the walls kept loosing arrows, mostly at the chasing forkbeards but not all. One arrow hit Gallow on the head, bouncing off his helm and almost knocking him off the ladder. Two or three flashed past Tolvis.

Gallow screamed up at them, 'Friend! Friend!' and the Marroc who'd led them here roared at the archers to let him climb. More arrows flew into the onrushing forkbeards below. One fell and then another and the rest slowed, crouching behind their shields. Gallow reached the top. Arda wanted to rush to him but Tolvis was at the ladder now and Gallow was leaning over, urging him on.

Another forkbeard fell. The edge of panic had gone from the Marroc on the wall and now they took their time, picking their targets carefully. As the first forkbeards ran at Tolvis to haul him off the ladder, a dozen shafts hit them, cutting down two and staggering the rest, making them cower behind their shields again; and then Tolvis was out of their reach and Gallow was pulling him over the wall and they were grinning at each other and grinning at Arda and she wanted to run over to embrace them both and bash their stupid heads together but she just couldn't.

Instead she walked up to Gallow and brought her fist like a hammer down on his chest. 'Where were you?' There was a catch in her voice. She hit him again. 'Where were you? Where? What were you thinking! That you could leave us for year after year and then just come back again?' She had tears in her eyes and there was nothing she wanted more than to hold him and cry and laugh and perhaps hit him a few more times, but there was a wall inside her that wouldn't let her, a wall that had never let her show him how she really felt. She stepped away and looked at Tolvis instead. Did what she always did when she was angry, turned away to someone else.

Tolvis had an arrow sticking out of his side. A Marroc arrow. His face was pale and gleamed with sweat in the starlight. Arda jumped. 'Modris and Diaran!'

Loudmouth grimaced. 'It's going to hurt,' he said, 'but

it's not going to kill me.' He turned her around and pushed her at Gallow. He took her hands and put them on Gallow's shoulders. Panic started to burn inside her and she didn't know what to do. Then Tolvis cracked his hand sharply across her buttocks and walked away, laughing. The shock paralysed her and for a moment the wall had a crack in it. Gallow wrapped his arms around her and she reached for him and they held each other close for a very long time, not saying a word.

'Where's Oribas?' he asked as they finally pulled apart.

41

AN AULIAN INTERROGATION

For most of the first hour after Gallow fled, Beyard stayed where he was, crouched beside the Lhosir campfire. He had no idea what it was that had burned him, nor who had thrown it in his face, but he wasn't surprised when three Lhosir showed up dragging the Aulian between them. He had Cithjan's men tie Oribas up and put him in a tent and watch him, constantly. He also had them empty his pockets and take away anything they didn't understand and lock it up in Cithjan's strongbox. For most of the morning that followed he contented himself dealing with Cithjan's murder.

A message would go to King Medrin Sixfingers to say Cithjan had been killed while putting down a Marroc insurrection and that he, Beyard, had assumed command. He thought long and hard about what to say about how it had happened and what had led up to it but there was no pretending now. He'd been protecting Gallow ever since his old friend had returned. Not in any useful, meaningful way, but little things. Not telling Cithjan about Gallow when he'd taken Solace. Not calling him by his name outside the Devil's Caves. Going alone to Middislet. Most of all, letting him go. A life for a life had seemed fair and due and fated to be, but Sixfingers would never see it that way and nor would Cithjan if he'd lived to hear of it. Even in Hrodicslet, not giving chase: time after time he'd held his hand but last night he'd meant it. A good fight, a fair fight, a fight to be remembered. A better end than Sixfingers would have given him. Last night he would have killed Gallow, and Gallow had understood and so he'd named himself in front of a thousand Lhosir.

And despite the pain that still burned his face, he was smiling because Truesword had escaped anyway and there was a part of him that was glad. Truesword. Now there was a thing. In Beyard's thoughts Gallow had changed from being Gallow the Foxbeard to being Gallow Truesword again. He tried to remember where and how it had happened. In the bottom of the ravine. *I will not forget …*

He looked at the messenger he meant to send to Sixfingers. 'Ask him on my behalf for a new governor. Tell him …' Even now he hesitated. 'Tell him that Gallow Truesword has returned with the red sword the Aulians call the Edge of Sorrows and the Marroc call Solace and the Comforter. I will send both to him together.' Not that Gallow would be taken alive. He'd see to that.

After the messenger there was the matter of command. Beyard dealt with that by telling the Lhosir that he would be in charge until the Marroc of Witches' Reach were crushed and responding to all objections with a malevolent silence. Cithjan had already sent half his force down to the Aulian Bridge to guard it against the outlaws and rebels in the Crackmarsh. He'd hoped the pleas from Witches' Reach might lure them out to where he could slaughter them. Beyard supposed it was a good enough plan to follow, and it left him with five or six hundred Lhosir against a few score Marroc. Good enough. He told everyone to go and make ladders and a ram and whatever else they usually made when they were attacking a walled fortress, and then at last he went back to the Aulian. He'd put it off because it was the part of the day he was most looking forward to and also the part that made him afraid. He couldn't remember being afraid since the Eyes of Time had given him his iron skin.

The Aulian was awake. Droopy-eyed and with a great

lump on his temple, bruised and bloodied but awake.

'Again, Aulian.' Beyard sent the other Lhosir away, and when he and the Aulian were alone he took off his mask and his crown. He saw the Aulian's eyes widen for a moment. 'You were never meant to be sent to the Devil's Caves.' His voice was as dry as desert sand. 'Cithjan should have let you go. Or kept you in the castle as his guest until the pass opened in the spring. I dare say there's a great deal we could have learned from a man like you. How many Marroc are there in Witches' Reach, Aulian?'

'Sixty. Seventy. I didn't count them exactly.' The Aulian was terrified and was right to be. A Fateguard stood before him, an iron-made man, and the Lhosir were not known for kindness to their prisoners.

'Food? Water?'

'Whatever you Lhosir once stored there. I saw enough to know they have food for two or three months. Water? They have the snow. You won't starve them out in a hurry.'

'I never thought I would, Aulian. But I have to ask. What have they done to the gates?'

'Piled up snow behind them and packed it tight. It is as good as placing a block of stone behind the doors.'

Beyard nodded. He tried to smile, a thing he was never very good at since the Eyes of Time had made him into what he was. 'I would have let you go still, even after the Devil's Caves. I suppose it was your doing to bring an avalanche down on us.' The Aulian lowered his head, which was enough of an answer. 'Cithjan underestimated how many Marroc were in the Reach. He sent a smaller force first. Not all of them died but I would like you to tell me, in your own words, how most of them did. I know you were there.'

The Aulian bowed his head. 'You must give me a day, shadewalker. That is the Aulian way of these things. One day, and then we will imagine that your torturers have plied their trade and done terrible things and that I screamed and bled and begged for it all to end, and at the end of that one day I was broken. We shall both imagine this thing and then I shall tell you without the pain, and you will hear it without the unpleasantness and the expense. That is the Aulian way.'

Oribas was quaking where he sat but his voice was strong and resolved. Beyard lifted his mask back over his head. 'But we are not in Aulia and that is not the Lhosir way, and there is no expense, nor is there unpleasantness.' He sighed. 'I would like to send you back to Varyxhun to hang. But I can hand you over to the Lhosir here to take their time over you if you like. You're a foreigner, as good as a *nioingr*, so there's nothing they won't do if it amuses them. We are not a civilised people. Not in your way. So tell me about the other way into Witches' Reach you claim to know, or all those things you wish only to imagine will be visited upon you, one after the other. Or …' he paused and leaned in closer '… worse.'

'Bird, fish, bear, dragon,' said the Aulian. 'There. I've told you the piece that matters. The thing you want to know. But they will be watching. The shaft is death to you now.'

Beyard lifted the red sword and grated the edge of it against his iron-gloved hand. The Aulian whimpered. His words tripped over one another in their eagerness. The cave in the mountainside, the passageway, the shaft and the old Aulian tomb. The sealed door – bird, fish, bear, dragon – and how it led into the cellars of Witches' Reach. How Oribas had opened it for the Marroc and how he'd lured fifty or more Lhosir into that same shaft and then burned them alive. The Aulian almost wept when he spoke of it, and there was more to his tears than fear: he was ashamed. Beyard understood. He almost reached out a hand, but they were cased in iron and were hardly things of comfort. So he let the Aulian speak on until he was done, and when at last Oribas fell to silence, Beyard let it hang between them for a long time.

'I know what it is to have shamed yourself,' he said at last. When the Aulian didn't reply he got up and looked outside the tent. The day was fading, the sun already low over the mountains.

'I was taught to battle monsters,' whispered Oribas. 'Not men.'

Beyard kept staring out at the orange sun hanging in a deep blue sky. The mountains before it were in shadow, a deep purple, almost black. He felt a terrible truth coalescing inside him, as yet unheard but demanding at last to be told. 'Why did you call me shadewalker.'

The Aulian didn't answer.

'What did you throw in my face, Oribas of Aulia?'

'Salt.' The word was a whisper, so quiet that Beyard barely heard.

'Salt. Again?'

'Yes.'

'*Just* salt?'

'Yes.'

Beyard let that linger a while. 'Why, Aulian? Why would you throw salt in a man's face? Why did your salt burn so?'

The Aulian didn't answer but by then he didn't need to. The iron skin, the ever-present sense of cold, the ambivalence to food and even water, the sleepless nights and salt that burned. He'd been what he was for seventeen years and had never understood, and yet this Aulian had seen through it in days. If he'd still been able to cry, Beyard might have shed a tear for himself.

'No need, Aulian. No need.' His voice was like the grinding of stones. 'I am like them, am I?'

'Yes.'

'I am no longer alive.'

'No.'

The Eyes of Time had done this to him. He'd stolen into the Temple of Fates, for which the price was always death, and thought he'd escaped his punishment, but he hadn't escaped at all.

He slipped the crown and mask over his face once more. 'They will hang you in Varyxhun. It will be clean.' He strode out into the sunset, leaving the Aulian behind.

42

A SPEAKING OUT

The Lhosir took their time. They stayed in their camp on the first day of the siege and Achista stood on the walls watching, wondering whether Oribas was a prisoner among them or whether he'd found his own path to slip away. She couldn't bring herself to think of him held by the forkbeards, but nor could she bring herself to think of him simply walking away.

'We have to suppose the forkbeards have him,' whispered Addic. He stood beside her, looking down the slope of the mountain saddle to the Lhosir camp. 'We have to suppose they know about the tomb.'

'He wouldn't tell them!'

'But perhaps they knew already. Is it sealed?'

'If you sealed it when you left.' Achista couldn't remember what they'd agreed. Whether they'd even spoken of it. 'How many forkbeards this time?'

'More than enough.' Addic put a hand on her shoulder and squeezed.

'The Wolf will come out of the Crackmarsh.' She tried to sound as though she believed it. Not a word had come back, not one of the messengers they'd sent. She didn't know if any of them had even reached Valaric. The Crackmarsh was a hostile place, filled with monsters that only he and his men had learned to master.

Her brother stroked her hair. 'Cithjan sent as many men

again to the bridge to guard against that. If Valaric comes, he'll have a hard fight to even get here.'

'Then there's no rescue and no escape.'

'Win or lose this day, sister, we've already won this war before a sword was drawn. I've ridden across the valley, back and forth. Men will see what we've done. They'll rise as we did, not a few score as we are but in their hundreds and their thousands, from here to Andhun, in Sithhun itself. I've seen it with my own eyes and heard it with my own ears. The Marroc of Varyxhun are ready for you, Achista.'

'If they're ready then let them come.' She turned away.

Gallow and Arda spent the rest of that night together. Neither said much. 'I don't want to hear,' Arda told him when he started to speak. 'I don't want a word. You can tell me why it took three years to walk from Andhun to home when there's no forkbeards out there and I can get properly angry with you again. I don't want to be angry with you now.' And there were tears in her eyes, and Gallow didn't understand but he held her in silence as she'd asked, and it was beautiful because it was a closeness that had always been unacknowledged. Eventually they fell asleep holding one another, and in the morning light the Marroc looked at him askance, trying to work him out, this man who looked like a forkbeard but wasn't.

Some time later Gallow sat with Tolvis. Loudmouth's pain ran deeper than the Marroc arrow in his side and for once there was nothing Gallow could do. Late in the afternoon as he crossed the yard with a bucket of water, he found Addic coming the other way. They glanced uncertainly at each other. Each had been in the Lhosir camp that night for something different. Both had got what they went for and both now had a hole in them where Oribas used to be.

'I thought you were him,' said Gallow. All the way from the Lhosir camp to the walls of Witches' Reach he'd thought they were following Oribas. He'd never seen the skinny little Aulian run so fast, but then he'd never had a dozen Lhosir chasing him. In the dark he simply hadn't noticed. And Addic had thought that the Aulian was Arda.

Addic looked at his feet, at the ground, all around, anywhere but at Gallow's face. 'Oribas married my sister.'

'Oribas?' Gallow struggled to imagine Oribas even interested in a woman. Before they'd crossed the mountains every drop of his life and passion had gone on hunting the Rakshasa. After they'd defeated it he'd just seemed empty. Then Gallow started to laugh. Oribas, looking for something to fill the place where the Rakshasa had been, had found a fiery Marroc woman had he? Achista. The Marroc called her Huntress now. She was their voice and their fire, and who was he, Gallow, to say anything to that but *Well done*?

'Why are you laughing?' Addic looked stricken. 'I thought he was your friend.'

'The only one I had for a long time.'

'And now he's gone and you're laughing?'

'Because he came from another land and fell in love with a Marroc, just as I did.'

Then Addic smiled too as he understood. 'We make good women. Will you talk to her? Tell her something about him? They had so little time.'

'He might not even be taken, Addic, and taken is not the same as dead.'

'Cithjan sent Oribas to the Devil's Caves simply for knowing you.'

'But Cithjan is dead. You killed him. If the Lhosir have him then Beyard will decide his fate, and Beyard isn't Cithjan.' Perhaps they should leave the Fateguard as master of Varyxhun castle. Beneath the iron he was still the man he used to be, and that was why Medrin Sixfingers would never have it. Gallow passed the bucket to Addic. 'Here. Take this to Tolvis. Arda will be there. Perhaps she should talk to your sister. I was lost to her for years so I suppose she has some wisdom when it comes to waiting.'

Addic chuckled. He took the water. 'Don't say that to Achista.'

Gallow climbed the steps to the wall. He passed along the walkway over the gates where the mound of ice still lay pressed up against them. If the Lhosir brought up a ram and it was anything short of a whole tree, they'd be wasting their time. But if they knew how many Marroc were inside, they'd bring ladders. One between three. One man to climb, one man to hold the ladder steady and one to hold a shield and throw the occasional spear.

He stopped beside Achista. She seemed too small and young to lead these Marroc, and yet she did. He told her about the ladders, how the Lhosir would overwhelm the wall with sheer numbers by coming at it from everywhere at once. 'You can't hold it,' he said. 'You don't have enough men.'

She replied to the wind in a whisper barely heard. 'Oribas would have found a way.'

'No. Not even Oribas.'

'He was a wizard.'

'He still is.'

She shook her head and started telling Gallow of all the things Oribas had done, of all the miracles he'd worked. Laying a shadewalker to rest, the avalanche outside the Devil's Caves and the victory at Jodderslet even though Gallow had seen both for himself; then in the woods below Witches' Reach and opening the Aulian seal, luring Skilljan Spearhoof's Lhosir into the shaft and burning them there. Gallow understood. She didn't know it, but she was speaking him out, letting him go in the Lhosir way and reminding the gods of his deeds. When she paused, Gallow took over. He told her of the scared twitchy desperate man who'd found him washed up on a sandy beach a thousand miles to the south of the Aulian mountains. Of the determination that had kept him going after the monstrous Rakshasa, relentless and remorseless and unstoppable as the old Screambreaker himself. How he'd hunted the Rakshasa for year after year and never stopped until even the gods themselves had seen the strength of his heart and answered his prayers. 'He wasn't the one who laid it to rest, not at the end,' he told her, 'but Oribas was the one who laid the traps, who followed its trail, who saw through its tricks and disguises and in the end fooled it into its doom. I've never met a man who was so driven to his end, and the end he's chosen now is you. He will find a way, Achista of the Marroc. There's no man in the world who'll try harder and few better equipped to succeed.' He could feel the lightening around her, the shedding of her burden. She would still grieve, but it wouldn't crush her now.

'It was even his idea to mound up the snow behind the gates.'

'If he was here now, what he'd tell you to do was take as much snow as you can up to the roof of the tower and as many stones as you can carry.'

'Why?'

'Beyard will take the walls tomorrow, and quickly. Ladders won't help him get into the tower, though. He'll need to force the door. He'll have a ram but since the doors are a full man's height above the ground with steps that come at them from sideways, he'll have to build a ramp to use it. In time he will, and he'll get in – don't be mistaken about that. But the Lhosir with him, they'll be impatient and looking for a quicker way. They'll go at the tower door with axes and fire. The snow is for the fires, the stones for the Lhosir who try to light them or bring their axes.'

'Once they have us penned in the tower, we'll all die.'

'You set that to be your fate long before today, Marroc. Oribas may yet outlive us all.'

She laughed, a harsh broken sound. 'Oribas will arrive on the back of a dragon that he's awoken with some ancient Aulian spell to burn the forkbeards? Perhaps the dragon buried under Varyxhun!' She shook her head. 'No. It's done. We'll fight and shed our blood and die, all of us, and it will be the telling of our courage that will live on. We won't win, but our story will eat you forkbeards one by one, until none of you are left.' She twisted suddenly to meet his gaze. 'Why are *you* here, forkbeard? How is this your fight?'

Gallow stared down at her. So fierce. 'I had a dozen angry brothers of the sea chasing me and you lowered a ladder for me to climb and so here I am. When they come, I'll hold your wall for you as best I can. If the chance comes, I'll seek out Beyard and we'll finish what we started. I don't expect to live either, but perhaps he'll spare my Arda. Would you believe me if I told you he's a good man? Brave and honourable.'

Achista laughed and turned away. 'The iron devil of Varyxhun? He's a monster.'

'Can he not be both? He'll be fair, Achista. If he offers you mercy, at least listen. He'll be good to his word. Better than most.'

'There'll be no mercy.' Her eyes settled back on the Lhosir camp. They'd been busy with their axes today. They'd built a pyre for Cithjan and burned him, but Gallow was sure they'd built other things too. She was probably right. Beyard might give them quick clean deaths to honour their courage, but not mercy. That wasn't what the Fateguard were for.

'Tomorrow you'll need small groups of men around you, Addic, Tolvis and me. Four to each of us, the best swordsmen or axemen you have. Station the rest of your men evenly around the walls. We'll go to wherever the fighting is most fierce, wherever the Lhosir get a foothold on the battlements. It will come to us to try and drive them back. Someone must take charge of calling a retreat to the tower.

These same four groups of men will keep the Lhosir at bay. Tell your Marroc that when the call comes to abandon the walls they must do it at once. They must turn and run as fast as they can with their bows to the tower and then stand at the doors. The Lhosir will take the walls faster than you can imagine. Those with swords will keep them back long enough for the men with bows to get to the tower but they'll not hold for long. Then the bowmen must hold the Lhosir in turn while the men with swords withdraw. Many will die when the walls fall, but if your Marroc don't understand that they must run like the wind when the signal is given, the Lhosir will take the tower too and it will all be done and gone in a day. You need to last. To be seen.'

'As long as we can. Will they really take these walls so quickly?'

Gallow looked out over the encamped Lhosir. 'Yes. There's only one thing you have in your favour.'

'One thing?' she asked.

'Beyard.'

'The iron devil?' She turned to glance up at him as though he was mad.

'He'll do his best to break you and he *will* win. But I think he'd be pleased if you somehow beat him.'

The Marroc woman shook her head. Definitely crazy. And maybe he was, and Beyard too, and all the old Lhosir who thought that way. Gallow raised a hand to slap her shoulder, one soldier to another. Paused, as he remembered she was a woman, then did it anyway.

'Rest well tonight,' he said. 'Tomorrow they come.'

43

THE WOLF

Valaric rolled his eyes. The Marroc was the third messenger from the idiots in Witches' Reach to get to him.
There might have been more, but if there were then they'd
fallen to the forkbeards watching the Aulian Bridge or the
ones who patrolled the fringes of the Crackmarsh near
Issetbridge or, most likely of all, to the ghuldogs. Valaric
had no idea how many ghuldogs lived in the Crackmarsh
but it was probably thousands and he only had a few of the
packs tamed. The wild ones suited him. They all had their
territories, loosely marked and understood, and Valaric's
was more or less in the middle. If the forkbeards got ideas
about coming in after him they'd have to pass a night amid
the wild ghuldogs first. So far that had been enough to keep
them away.

Eventually the messenger finished. In a grudging way
Valaric admired the man. A Marroc who'd stood up to
the forkbeards, who'd fought them and won and more
than once. From what the man said, whoever was leading
at Witches' Reach was a true Marroc hero, even if he was
doomed. Valaric forced back a laugh. Trapping the forkbeards in a cave and then burning them? No wonder they
were like angry hornets.

'I admire what you've done,' he said. 'But a horde of
forkbeards is about to fall on your stronghold. You ask for
my help yet at the same time the forkbeards are strength-
ening their garrisons all along the Isset valley, from the

Crackmarsh to Andhun. The Vathen are mustering. In the spring they'll come again and the forkbeards know it. They might leave me alone in my swamp but they're all around it. They'll know if I come out.'

'Then what's the point of you?'

Valaric stiffened. The messenger limped from a cut on his leg that was slowly going bad. Likely as not he faced a slow and miserable death. Maybe that was what gave him courage. 'The same point as you, you daft bugger, except I'll still be here a month from now and you won't.' He heard Sarvic mutter behind him and wasn't sure whether it was a murmur of disapproval or of agreement. 'How loud do you suppose the forkbeards would cheer if they can get rid of all of us before the Vathen sweep across the Isset again?' He sighed and beckoned the Marroc closer. 'Do you think I want to sit idly by and do nothing? No, but between me and Witches' Reach lies the garrison of Issetbridge and then the river itself. I have spies of my own, and what they tell me is the forkbeards have been watching the bridge like eagles ever since you started leaving their severed heads littered about the place. There's no other way to enter the Varyxhun valley. The forkbeards know this. I'd have to fight past whatever men they put on the bridge and with the Issetbridge garrison at my back. I'd be out in the open. They could slaughter us all. Not one of us would reach you, and then what?' He shook his head. 'Do you have a way to take word back to your friends in the tower?' The Marroc nodded. 'Then I'll do this much for you. I'll take the fight to Issetbridge. That might draw some of them away. If I find the bridge clear, I'll consider crossing it.' Not that there was any chance of that.

The messenger didn't like what he was hearing but it was all he was going to get. Valaric sent him away to be fed and watered and to have one of the Marroc who knew about herbs and things see whether his leg could be saved. The next morning they guided him to the edge of the Crackmarsh, which was as far as Valaric's men went. The leg, it turned out, was beyond help. In a way that made Valaric feel a little better about what he'd just done.

'Issetbridge then,' growled Sarvic eagerly after the Marroc had limped away.

'Don't be an idiot. They'll know we're coming and they'd shred us.' Sarvic looked confused. Valaric sighed. Sometimes Sarvic could be a little slow. Brave and deadly these days but still not so bright. 'Sarvic, how's he going to get across the Isset, if he even gets that far?'

Sarvic sounded surprised. 'Across the bridge of course!'

'Yes. The bridge. The one the forkbeards are watching like eagles. That bridge, and he can't even run. Maybe he'll get back to Witches' Reach but more likely the forkbeards will get him. Not that we're going to Issetbridge anyway.'

'But you said we—'

'Yes, I lied.' Valaric smiled at Sarvic. Such a lot still to learn, but he'd come a long way in the three years since they'd fought the Vathen at Lostring Hill and then the forkbeards in Andhun. 'I'll send a dozen or so men with a pack of ghuldogs to make a nuisance of themselves. See if we can't provoke the wild packs to come out after us and stir something up. Maybe that'll draw away as many of the forkbeards as they think they can spare.'

'And then we're going to sit here and do nothing?'

'No. Go back to Fat Jonnic and tell him to muster his men. I'll be waiting for him at Hrodicslet. I'll tell Stannic and Modric the same. No, we're not going to do nothing.'

'But?' Sarvic screwed up his face. 'I thought you said … So we *are* crossing the bridge then. Are we?'

'No, Sarvic, because that way into the Varyxhun valley will just get us all killed, fun as it might be to have a good old spat with the forkbeards out in the open. But we don't have to go that way any more, do we? Because Gallow said there was another way: out from Hrodicslet and up into the high valleys and across and through some caves.'

Sarvic just stood there looking stupid. Valaric sighed again and shook his head. 'Just go and tell Fat Jonnic to get his men to Hrodicslet, will you?'

'Oh!' Understanding lit up Sarvic's face. 'So Gallow came down a different way from the mountains?'

'Yes.' Valaric shooed him away. Gallow had come down a different way and had gone back again, and he hadn't been the only one either. That had probably slipped Sarvic's mind, but then a lot of things did.

44

THE BLOODY WALLS

The Lhosir came at first light with their ladders. They didn't try to hide. They spread out, picking their way across the steeper slopes to the northern and western faces until they'd made a ring around Witches' Reach out of range of the Marroc bows. It took them almost until midday and they arranged themselves slowly and carefully as though they were in no hurry at all. Little fires sprang up here and there. The smell of cooking meat wafted in on the breeze. An old trick, although not much use when the Marroc had such a storehouse beneath their feet. As the sun reached its zenith, Beyard walked out from among the Lhosir barring the road and strode clanking to the gates.

'Marroc!' he cried. 'I promise you one thing. There will be no ravens. You have been brave and I will honour you for that. Your deaths will be quick and sure. Make peace with your gods, Marroc of Witches' Reach. I know of your tunnels and your caves and I am not interested in your surrender.' He turned to go and then turned back. 'Are you in there, Gallow? If you are, we weren't finished two nights back. Face me as you did then and I'll let your woman live. I'd do the same for your Aulian friend but he has Lhosir blood on his hands now and so he must hang.'

As he walked away, Achista sprang up behind the battlements over the gates. 'May you wander the Marches for ever, iron devil!'

Beyard didn't look back. He raised a hand as he went, and

when he dropped it again a horn sounded over the valley. A great roar went up from the Lhosir, and on the western and the northern slopes they began to move, clambering through the rocks with their ladders and shields. The advance swept around the tower like a slow wave. On the steeper slopes they came with caution, taking cover behind the stones and boulders there from the archers on the walls, shields held over their heads. On the flat ground to the east and the south they yelled their battle cries and charged.

Arrows flew from the walls to meet them, but these were warriors in mail, with iron helms and broad round shields, and only a handful fell. The Lhosir reached the walls and the ladders came up. The Marroc pushed them back, but every Marroc pushing at a ladder was a Marroc not shooting a bow and the rain of arrows eased to a drizzle. The Lhosir put more of their men to holding the ladders and fewer to holding shields. They started to climb. As the first man crested the battlements, Gallow howled and raised his axe. The Lhosir lifted his shield to catch the blow and Gallow kicked out instead, blooding the warrior's face and sending him sprawling down the ladder into the men below. A few feet further on he knelt and heaved with two Marroc at another ladder. A spear stabbed up at him. Its point hit the stone beside his face and struck sparks across his eyes and then the ladder fell back into the sea of men around the walls. Another Lhosir screamed at him and then Gallow had that ladder falling back too, the Lhosir still clinging to it as he fell into the snow. He floundered and the Marroc archers saw an easy target. An arrow hit his head and creased his skin in a flurry of blood. A second hit the snow an inch from his face but then a wall of shields closed around him.

A hand reached up and grabbed a Marroc by the belt, pulled and hurled him over the wall. He screamed pitifully as he fell; a moment later a Lhosir warrior was scrambling onto the battlements. A Marroc swung an axe. The Lhosir caught the man's arm, twisted and tipped him off the wall. Gallow roared and charged, shield up, axe over his head. The Lhosir saw him coming and the two of them crashed together. Gallow twisted and tried to swing his axe round the Lhosir's shield. The blade caught the Lhosir on the shoulder, digging into his mail, and Gallow felt him flinch, and then a Marroc came from behind and rammed a spear into the Lhosir's back, shoving him into Gallow. If he wasn't already dead, Gallow's axe smashed into his helm and made sure. The man's eyes rolled back, his knees buckled, and he tipped sideways off the wall into the yard below.

The air stank of hot pitch. On the far side of the gates the Marroc were scattering. Lhosir carrying bladders on ropes crested the battlements. They hurled the bladders at the nearest Marroc and splattered them with steaming tar. On the western wall soldiers had topped the battlements and were holding Addic and his men at bay while more climbed up. More pitch-throwers climbed over the parapet, threw, and then and barged into the Marroc with their shields, drawing their swords. Gallow yelled at his band to follow and raced to stop them. He spared a glance for the tower steps, where Achista and three Marroc archers were watching for any Lhosir who reached the yard, all the time shooting at the Lhosir on the walls.

'The horn!' Gallow cried. 'Sound the horn!' The walls were lost. There were so many Lhosir on them now that hardly any Marroc could use their bows any more, and without arrows to keep them under their shields, Beyard's men were swarming over.

The last Marroc in front of him spun and fell into Gallow with half his face smashed in by a Lhosir axe. The Lhosir shoved him out of the way and swung an overhead cut. Gallow stepped back and levelled a backhand slash of his own but the soldier saw it coming. He was too unbalanced to get out of the way, but he turned his shield enough to catch it and staggered against the parapet. Behind him three ladders were against the wall and more Lhosir were already hauling themselves up. One fell almost before he could stand, an arrow through his neck from Achista's archers. Gallow slammed into the soldier in front of him and sliced a low cut at the man's ankles, shattering bone. The Lhosir screamed and swung back, a wild blow, then fell forward. Gallow shouldered him aside, tipping him off the battlements into the yard below, and moved to meet the next who was already lunging with a spear. On the eastern wall Tolvis was holding the Lhosir back, racing up and down the battlements even with the arrow wound in his side, hacking and slashing and shouting at the Marroc.

'For the love of Modris sound the horn!'

The Lhosir held the wall in two places now. More were on the battlements in front of Gallow, forcing him back with spears and shields, content to block him while others climbed up behind them. Further round they were sweeping the Marroc aside. Some of Achista's men had already turned to run. Arrows lashed the Lhosir on the battlements and some fell, but not as many as climbed. One Lhosir vaulted over the ramparts and dropped to the yard below. A spear lashed at Gallow's face and another stabbed at his feet. He hooked one of the shields facing him with his axe and pulled it back, and if there had been another Lhosir beside him with a spear, a lunge would have gone through the gap and struck home. But Gallow's men were Marroc farmers and hunters, unskilled in war. Another Lhosir jumped down to the yard and then another, and at last Achista blew the horn and everywhere the Marroc turned and fled, even the swordsmen who were supposed to hold the Lhosir back while the others escaped. The Lhosir howled and pressed forward. Terrified Marroc jumped down to the yard, taking their chances with the drop instead of running for the steps. Battle-mad Lhosir leaped after them. Men screamed as legs twisted and ankles snapped. Gallow stepped back and stumbled over the body of a dead Lhosir. One of the spearmen lunged at his face. He lifted his shield, pure instinct. He knew at once that he'd been drawn into leaving an opening, but before he could do more, he felt a second spear point slam into his ribs and something crack. His mail held. He stepped back again. The dead Lhosir slowed the spearmen too. It gave him a moment. He took it and ran.

The yard was a horror. Achista had waited too long. Marroc were reaching the tower but more were still leaping from the walls and there must have been a dozen Lhosir already in the yard now, screaming and swinging their blades. Men of both sides limped and hobbled and tore each other down. For now the Lhosir were too consumed by killing to make a wall of shields and charge the steps to the tower. The moment they did that, the battle was lost. Gallow glanced over the side of the walkway but the drop was the height of two men and he didn't dare, not in mail. He ran for the steps, the last man, half a second ahead of the Lhosir behind him. He turned in the air as he vaulted down, swinging his axe, taking out the soldier's feet, tipping him over so that the surging men behind tripped and they all tumbled together. An arrow flew past his head – Achista's archers at the tower door. As he looked back he saw a Lhosir slide to his knees with an arrow in his face and fall dead with a spear still clutched in his hand. Marroc cut off from the tower were being slaughtered but there was nothing anyone could do for them now. A hundred Lhosir were inside the walls, more coming every moment. Gallow reached the steps and found only Tolvis and three Marroc in a wall of shields and spears, holding the way. The wall opened to let him through.

'Here.' Tolvis passed him a spear so he could stab past their shields. A wild-eyed Marroc ran into them and then another, and then suddenly there were no more and they were facing Lhosir instead. Through the open doors at the top of the steps Marroc archers still fired into the yard.

Gallow shook his head. He ran up the steps, grabbed Achista and almost snatched the bow out of her hands. 'Get inside and close the doors!' He threw her in and glared at the other archers until they turned and then he ran back down the steps. He yanked Tolvis. 'Just run!'

They ran. The Lhosir bellowed and charged after them. The last defenders skittered into the tower through the closing doors and hurled themselves down to slide across the stone floor to the feet of a dozen Marroc archers with bows drawn. As the Lhosir threw themselves after the Marroc the archers let fly and the Lhosir fell back. Everyone inside raced to the doors, stabbing at the Lhosir, pushing them back or pulling them in and dragging them down, and then at last the doors were shut and the bars were dropped. They shook as the first Lhosir threw themselves against them.

'Up!' bawled Gallow. 'Up to the roof!' He led the way, a dozen and more weary Marroc following in his wake until they'd climbed to the open roof of the tower where Achista had had snow and stones piled as he'd asked. 'Bows! Shoot them now! While they're in their frenzy.' It wouldn't take the Lhosir in the yard long to gather themselves and hide behind their shields but every one the Marroc killed now was one fewer for later. Not that it would make any difference to the end.

He left the Marroc to their arrows, ran to the stones and picked a decent-sized one, peered over the edge and dropped it on the head of one of the axemen hacking at the door. They stopped after he felled a second; and then suddenly all across the yard the Lhosir were falling back to the wall, raising their shields. Achista yelled at the archers to save their arrows. The Reach fell still, the air quiet enough for Gallow to clearly hear the last screams and wails of the men left dying in the bloody snow. There were dozens of fallen in the yard and most of them were Marroc. He had no idea how many Lhosir they'd taken with them out of sight beyond the walls. He saw a few scattered in the snow below, but however many Lhosir were dead, half the Marroc defenders were dead too, the walls were lost and they hadn't even reached their first sunset.

Down in the yard a dull glint of iron caught Gallow's eye. Beyard. He walked among the fallen Marroc, lifting each one as he reached them. One moved as he approached, hauling himself away on his arms and leaving a wide smear of blood in the snow. Beyard reached down and picked him up. He looked at the tower roof – straight, it seemed, at Gallow – and drove a knife into the dying Marroc's neck. 'Quick and merciful,' he cried. 'I promised you that.'

He moved on to the next.

45

CAGED

Just as they did before the attack, the Lhosir took their time. A dozen of them made a wall of shields while others took it in turns to hack away the ice behind the outer gates. Once they had the gates open they left, and all Gallow and the Marroc saw of them for the rest of that day were a few scouts and sentries, watchers left on the walls behind barricades of shields and out on the trail down the mountain. That night they heard scrapings beyond the Aulian tomb door in the cellars and the steady strike of pickaxes on stone. None of them slept much.

The Lhosir were quiet the next day too except for the pickaxes in the tomb. When Gallow asked how thick the stone door was, none of the Marroc seemed to know. Addic thought about a handspan and it was hard stone too, but the Lhosir would be through it in another day. Outside the tomb, the Lhosir were busy in the woods, felling trees and cutting planks.

They broke through the Aulian stone that night and Gallow and most of the Marroc were waiting for them. As the first crack came and the stone began to crumble, the Marroc archers drew their bows. A large piece of the door fell away and a dozen arrows flew through it. Then Addic and others threw pots of oil through the hole. The next volley of arrows were flaming ones, and the space beyond the door where the Lhosir were at work lit up. The Marroc shot more arrows and poured in more oil and the Lhosir withdrew. When they were gone, Addic took a pick of his own and hammered at the door until the hole was large enough for the smallest of the Marroc to climb through and keep watch. When the Lhosir came again a few hours later, the Marroc set the last of their oil alight and poured it on the men climbing up the shaft. Beyard didn't try a third time.

'I still don't want to know.' Gallow wanted to tell Arda about the years he was away but she wouldn't listen. Something had changed inside her, something that had stood between them that was now gone. She slept curled up beside him, and when they found a place to be alone they made love the way they always had. She sat for long hours with Tolvis too, nursing him, and Gallow found no jealousy there any more, no envy, only pity for his friend, whose wound had been worse than any of them had known and who seemed to have lost the will to fight it.

The Lhosir brought up wooden shields and started work on a platform for the ram that would smash in the tower door. The Marroc sniped at them with arrows and stones, but they were short on both and the last oil had gone on burning the Lhosir in the shaft. The Lhosir were still down there too, the light of their torches and the sounds of their voices floating up now and then. For two more days Beyard's men worked on their ram and on the ramp that would let them drive it at the raised tower door. Now and then a few of them came with axes or tried to set a fire, and the Marroc on the tower roof threw rocks and snow and the last of their arrows until the Lhosir withdrew or Beyard came and ordered them back with his iron voice.

'Do you feel the death in the air?' Addic stood on the roof beside Gallow as the two of them stared at the Lhosir below. Beyard's shields kept the Marroc arrows at bay but they could see well enough what he was doing. Once the ram was in place it would smash the tower door to splinters and crush anyone caught behind. Beyard worked as though he had all the time in the world. The Marroc of Varyxhun hadn't risen after all.

Gallow nodded. They were going to die here, in vain, and everything would return to the way it was. Despair was a disease spreading among them, sapping their will. If Beyard hadn't gripped them so tightly, most of the Marroc would have run by now. He could hardly blame them.

'Is this what you came back for, Gallow the Foxbeard?' Addic laughed bitterly.

'No.' He'd come back for Arda, and now he had her that made every second worth living.

'I envy you.' Addic smiled as though he'd read Gallow's mind. 'This is how you forkbeards want to go, isn't it? Down fighting.'

'I'd prefer to grow fat and old watching my children, hammering ploughs and horseshoes.'

'I wish the Aulian was here with us. He'd find a way to win. Or a way to slip out at the last.' Addic laughed. 'Let the Lhosir smash their way into an empty tower.'

Gallow looked at the enemy below. 'Even Oribas couldn't find a way where there is none.'

'He would. He'd show us how to fly.'

'I wish he was here for your sister. But not for him. He'd weep, knowing there was no trick to escape this cage. Beyard will finish his ram tomorrow or the next day and then he'll smash our door. All that's left is to give a good account of ourselves before we fall.'

Addic spat over the edge of the tower. 'Doesn't it make you angry?'

'It's fate, Addic. Rail against fate if you will, but in the end it makes no difference. I spat at fate once, and all it did was tear me away and torment me for years in the wilderness and then throw me back right where I would have been anyway. Perhaps if our deaths are bright enough you'll light a fire in the hearts of your Marroc at last.'

'Perhaps.' Addic didn't turn away from the Lhosir below. 'But who will know, Gallow? Who will know?'

All told there were some five hundred Marroc hiding in the Crackmarsh. A surly bitter lot, Valaric's kind of Marroc, the sort of men who'd spit in a forkbeard's eye as soon as they saw him. Men who'd lost a little, men who'd lost a lot, all of them with nothing left but a hunger for forkbeard blood. Valaric waited for them in Hrodicslet and made the little town his, and then he marched them up the old track into the mountain valleys. They stopped at farms and the Marroc there gave what little they had. Not much food to spare, not with winter setting in, but a little, and most of all they pointed out the trail. At Jodderslet there weren't any forkbeards waiting for them, but Valaric was a cautious man and so he left the others to wait and took a handful of his best along the track up into the ravine and out again, across the mountain slope and into the back of the Devil's Caves. Still no forkbeards, so he sent a runner for the rest of his men. The caves made a good place to hide.

The messenger from Witches' Reach had had the right of it. What use was he sitting in the Crackmarsh, a whispered name and nothing else?

Addic left Gallow on the roof of the tower and went back inside. He crept down to the Aulian tomb and looked at what was left of the Lhosir supplies. He searched for anything that might burn the forkbeard ram and the ramp they'd built but they'd used all the oil driving them out of the shaft. He found rope, though, still a lot of that, plenty enough to climb down from the top of the tower and out to the mountain slopes if the forkbeards hadn't been keeping such a tight watch on them.

After that he walked among the Marroc. When the

forkbeards smashed in the door, the Marroc were going to die. They knew it. He picked two men he trusted and made them each an offer: still a way to die but a different one, one that served a bit more of a purpose. He waited until dark and climbed up to the roof to join the watchmen there, made sure his rope was carefully tied and lowered it over the edge and watched the others go, one and then the other, climbing barefoot. He'd be last down, the one most likely to be seen, but as he reached for the rope a shadow came across the roof. At first he thought it was Gallow but it turned out it was the other forkbeard instead. Tolvis put his hand on Addic's shoulder.

'I can shout for your sister to come and scream at you,' he said, 'or I can go in your place. You choose.' And for a long moment the two of them stared at each other, and then Addic let go of the rope because here was a forkbeard who looked like he was wanting to die.

The wound in his side was a constant pain now but Tolvis Loudmouth ignored it as best he could. The two Marroc were almost down. He followed quickly. No mail because mail made noise. No swords or axes to scrape against the stone as they climbed down. No boots, even. They went barefoot, muffled in furs, each with a knife between his teeth. They didn't go over the north side of the tower because the Lhosir kept watch out there on the mountain slopes. Not the south side either, because that was where the gates were. Over the east side, where the tower cast a shadow in the moonlight, and when he reached the walkway of the wall below with no cries of alarm, Tolvis knew they'd almost done it. He slipped like a shadow down from the wall to the yard and crept behind Beyard's wooden shields. The two Marroc had already set to work, knives sawing at the ropes that held together the struts and beams that the Lhosir had built. Tolvis cut a rope and felt a piece of wood shift. He went to another.

'Who's there?'

He ignored the challenge and kept on cutting. The light of a torch flickered nearby. He shifted. Stopped for a moment, crouching in the shadows, gasping at the pain in his side. 'Oi! What are you doing?' The sentry had seen one of the Marroc. Tolvis darted from his hiding place, knife ready, but he was too late. 'Marroc! Marroc under the ramp! To arms!'

Tolvis silenced him anyway, taking him from the side and opening his throat. The Lhosir sentries around the Reach were already coming, calling out, rousing others. Tolvis took the dead man's axe for himself. No need for subtlety now. He swung the axe into the wooden pillars of the ramp.

A Lhosir ran at him. He let the man come, dodged aside and swung his axe again, still hacking at the wood, then ducked around it. 'I was Tolvis Loudmouth!' he bellowed. Ducked and swung again. The wood was starting to split. More Lhosir were coming. He saw one of the Marroc up and fighting, saw the other one fall. 'The Screambreaker named me. I fought at his side for five long years. I've done many things, some that were good and some that were bad, and all that time I've stood by—'

A spear plunged through him from behind, deep between his ribs, and ripped out again. He spun round. Blood flowed out of him like a river and the axe fell from his fingers. The Lhosir who'd killed him was hidden behind an owl helm. Not a man Tolvis knew. For a moment they stared at one another, then the Lhosir drove the spear into Tolvis again, into his belly, twisting hard. Tolvis staggered. His hands reached out and grabbed the man who'd killed him.

'By what was right,' he gasped. With his last strength he dragged the Lhosir over, throwing them both against the wooden beams beside the ram. As his eyes closed for the last time, he heard the crack of splitting wood, and then a great and sudden weight pressed down and he heard nothing more.

46

FLAMES AT TWILIGHT

A corner of the platform in front of the tower doors sagged, then cracked and fell. The sounds woke Gallow, but when he climbed to the roof to look he felt no joy, only a heaviness. The Lhosir were swarming like ants around their ramp and everyone knew that the Marroc who had gone down there wouldn't be coming back. He heard the last one scream, 'For King Tane!' He'd walked this valley years ago with Screambreaker, chasing that old Marroc king. In the years since then he'd come to think that it was the Lhosir who'd changed, that they'd somehow lost what had once made them noble, and perhaps there *was* some truth to that, but mostly what he thought now was that they'd never been all that noble in the first place. Savages who fought better than the rest, that's all they were.

He never heard Tolvis fall. What did his life buy? Another day?

In the morning Beyard came to the tower doors, waving a flag of parley. 'Gallow Truesword! I would speak with you.' In the yard the Lhosir were cutting away the broken wood of the ramp. New beams already lay in wait outside the gates. When the Lhosir tried to make their repairs, the Marroc would use the last of their arrows and stones. When those were spent, they'd wait because there wasn't anything else they could do. The Screambreaker had finally got into Varyxhun castle because the last of King Tane's huscarls had killed themselves rather than be taken. Would that be what happened here? 'Gallow Truesword!'

Gallow looked down from the tower roof. 'Up here, Beyard!'

'Tolvis Loudmouth lies dead. At dusk I send him to the Maker-Devourer as befits the warrior that he was. He died well. Will you come to speak him out, Gallow Truesword?'

'What of the Marroc?'

Beyard put his hands on his hips. 'What of them, Truesword? I honour a Lhosir.'

Gallow paused. What did he know of Marroc burials? Almost nothing. Eight years living among them and he hadn't much idea how the Marroc made peace with their dead. 'Bury them!' That was all he knew.

Beyard shook his head. 'No one will bury anyone here, Truesword, not until spring, not unless you want to have at the ground with a pick.' He turned away. The Lhosir started rebuilding their ramp and raising their ram, and the Marroc went back to throwing stones and shooting arrows made from the crates and barrels in the cellars of the Reach. As the sun dipped towards the horizon, the Lhosir withdrew and Beyard returned. The ram was ready and Beyard stood beside it. 'Gallow! I mean to burn the dead tonight before I smash in your doors.'

Achista stopped him. 'It's a trap, forkbeard. The iron devil means to snare you.'

'Whatever you think of him, Beyard will honour his word.'

'I will not open the doors for you to do this.'

Gallow sighed. 'Yes, you will, because he has Oribas and I will ask for the Aulian's life.' He saw her face as she crumbled inside. It was a terrible thing.

The Lhosir left the yard until Beyard remained alone. 'Let us understand one another, Marroc,' he called. 'I withdraw my men so you may open your doors. This is no truce.

When Gallow crosses the Witches' Reach, we will be as we were. Die well, Marroc. You've earned your places in the Maker-Devourer's cauldron.' Beyard turned and walked away.

Achista's eyes were red. Tears and not enough sleep. Gallow looked for Arda. She was staring at him from across the hall, but when he caught her eye she folded her arms and turned away. The same look he'd seen when he'd left her to fight the Vathen, years ago. *Give me a man who has enough of the coward in him to stay at home and keep his family safe.* Gallow took Achista's hands. 'If I don't come back, find a place for her to hide and make her stay there. I'll trade my life for hers and for Oribas if I can.' He bowed his head. Beyard might give him Arda, but not Oribas, not after what the Aulian had done.

Two Marroc pulled back the bars, Achista opened the tower doors and Gallow stepped outside. He'd barely taken a step when he heard it slam behind him and the bars grind back into place. It felt strange to be on the outside – as though he'd been set free of something.

Across the yard at the outer gates Beyard was waiting. The pyre was a little way beyond him, and there they stopped. Tolvis lay atop the wood, arms folded across his chest, eyes closed. His furs were dark and matted with blood. 'He bought you this day,' Beyard said. 'If it wasn't for him I'd have smashed my way in this morning. So honour him. Tolvis Loudmouth. I never knew him, though I heard his name after what he did in Andhun. Reviled below only yours. Why was he even here, Truesword? Why did you come back, either of you?'

'For Arda.'

'Both of you?'

'Both of us.'

Beyard shook his head. 'I'm told my heart stopped beating seventeen winters back. Sometimes in the dead of night when the silence is so thick it's suffocating, I close my eyes and listen for it. I hear nothing, so forgive me if I don't understand how a heart works any more. Your Aulian friend showed me a mirror that I should have seen a very long time ago.' He took off his mask and crown and Gallow saw that his face was burned and scarred as if by fire. 'You and Tolvis Loudmouth. Two fine brothers of the sea. Speak him out then, old friend, and let us all be back to killing each other.' He sounded sad, like the Beyard that Gallow remembered.

Gallow spoke of Tolvis then, of the life he'd led, of the battles he'd seen and the deeds he'd done. Of his years when he'd fought in the Screambreaker's war. He'd been there at every turn as the Marroc were crushed, and now he was dead so that a handful could live another day. As Gallow spoke, Beyard took a torch to the pyre and lit it. A few other Lhosir paused and stood, listening sombrely. Maybe they were old warriors who'd known Tolvis once, or maybe they simply respected the old way of speaking out an enemy who'd died well in battle. 'We're lessened by his passing,' breathed Beyard when Gallow was done. They were the old words for bidding farewell to a fallen friend but Beyard gave them a weight as though he truly meant them. 'Tonight we will be lessened by yours. I will speak you out myself.'

'I have a favour to ask, old friend,' said Gallow. 'Oribas.'

'The Aulian.' Beyard shook his head. 'He killed, Gallow. Many men and in bad ways. I've sent him back to Varyxhun to be hanged.'

But by now Gallow was looking at the mountainside beyond the pyre. In the twilight it seemed that it was moving.

A dozen Crackmarsh men hung back, armed with bows to take down any forkbeards travelling the Varyxhun Road from higher in the valley – messengers, perhaps, from the castle. The Marroc would shoot the horses out from under the forkbeards to stop them, whether one came or a hundred. Valaric took a handful of men ahead in case any came the other way. The bulk of the Marroc travelled in between, moving down the valley in secret. Surprise was a weapon Valaric couldn't afford to lose. An hour up the Varyxhun Road from Witches' Reach he stopped and left the vanguard with Sarvic and led his main force up the mountainside instead. It was slow going through the snow. The air was bitter, a harsh biting cold far worse than wintering in the Crackmarsh. He hadn't meant to, but Valaric saw now that he'd brought his men to a choice between victory or death. They'd either overrun the forkbeards and their camp and relieve the Reach or they'd die in the night, frozen in their boots. He called a halt on the side of the mountain as the sun began to set and they caught their first sight of the Lhosir camp. The Marroc couldn't light any fires of their own but the sight of so many enemies was enough to keep them warm. They strung their bows and sharpened their swords and their spears and their axes; they tightened the straps on their shields and their helms and rubbed their hands and paced back and forth. There were no fine words, not from Valaric. They all knew what they'd come for, why they'd gone to the Crackmarsh in the first place, and here it was.

The mountain darkness came quickly. A pyre burst into flame up by the gates of Witches' Reach. It was a sign, Valaric decided: Modris telling him that now was the time. There was no great shout, no wild charge, but as one the grim-faced Marroc of the Crackmarsh poured down the mountain towards the Lhosir below.

Beyard faced Witches' Reach. He had his back to the mountain where the shadows had come alive. Gallow slowly drew his sword. 'Can we not settle this between us, old friend? One against another?'

Beyard looked sad. 'But I will win.'

'Perhaps.'

'What do you ask, Gallow? Beat me and I will let these Marroc go? I cannot. And what do you offer? If I bring you to your knees, will they meekly open their gates? No. Those days are gone.'

Gallow shook his head. 'They're not gone for as long as we remember them, old friend. For as long as we live.'

Beyard laughed, bitter as poison. 'Did your Aulian not tell you what I am?' He looked at Gallow's confusion and shook his head. 'I am dead, Gallow. The Eyes of Time took me in the Temple of Fate. The Fateguard sent me to the Ice Wraiths and the Eyes of Time gave me this.' He beat his fist against the iron he wore and looked up at the mountains around the Reach. 'I have liked these mountains ever since I saw them. Their cold unforgiving majesty reminds me of the last journey I took as a man, with blood that ran warm and a heart to beat and a soul that burned.' Venom filled his words. He took off one iron gauntlet and drew out the red sword, but instead of coming at Gallow with it he slid the edge across his palm. The flesh beneath his pale skin was dark but no blood dripped into the snow melting around Tolvis's pyre. He sheathed Solace and stared at his hand. 'I feel no heat from these flames, nor do I have warmth inside me.'

Abruptly he picked up his mask and crown and put them on his head. He paced back and forth and then drew Solace again. 'There's no happy outcome here, but an outcome there must be. Let's be at it, old friend.'

From the roof of the tower Achista peered towards the pyre. She watched Gallow and the iron devil stand beside it. She saw Gallow, lit up by the flames, draw his sword, and the iron devil too, and watched them begin to circle. The forkbeard wouldn't be coming back. Nor would Oribas. Most of the Lhosir were further down the ridge, sitting around their fires, warming themselves for the fight to come. She ran down the stairs that circled the inside of the tower, shouting to the Marroc to rise. Thirty men perhaps, no more, against five hundred forkbeards, but when she called them to arms they followed her gladly, the weight of waiting lifted from their shoulders, a burden pulled away. They threw down the bars and hurled open the doors and spilled into the night onto the Lhosir ramp, voices strong and clear, swords and helms gleaming in the light of the torches that lit up the walls of Witches' Reach. They would die but they would not be meek.

47

MEN OF FATE

Gallow and Beyard circled each other. Neither carried a shield and so there were no rushing charges to knock the other man down. For once they were wary. Gallow's eyes stayed on the edge of the red sword. So many names among the different people of the world – Solace, the Comforter, the Peacebringer – but the Aulians had the right of it: the Edge of Sorrows. For all the sharpness of its terrible blade, it carried a curse.

He put his back to the pyre and sprang, arms wide, sword out to swing at Beyard's head, and then changed into a chop to the hip where Beyard's armour seemed weakest, but the iron man held out the red sword like a spear, pointed at Gallow's chest. He stepped aside and Gallow had no choice but to cut at the sword or else impale himself on its tip. He'd seen it shear through mail in a way no sword should ever do.

Beyard whipped Solace at Gallow's legs. Gallow jumped away and turned, and now it was Beyard who was looking down the slope of the mountain saddle towards his camp. Shouts echoed up the ridge. Beyard took a step back. For a moment his head craned forward as if he was trying to see what was happening. Gallow flung himself at the iron man and brought his sword down as hard as he could. Beyard, half off guard, brought up Solace, but too slowly, and Gallow's blade cracked into the iron armour around his collar, into the space between shoulder and neck. Gallow felt it strike, felt the edge of his steel bite into metal, felt it stick and wrenched it free before the sword was torn out of his hand. He jumped away. Beyard swayed. Where Gallow had struck, his armour was cracked and misshapen, a large dark scar cut into it that ought to have cracked bones and drip with seeping blood. For a moment the two of them stared at one another. Then Beyard bowed his head.

'A well made blow, old friend.' He looked past Gallow towards the camp, towards the sounds of fighting. 'I wish I'd known you for longer.'

He took one step closer and then another, an iron-gloved hand held out before him, the red sword raised and poised. He snarled and the steps turned to a charge.

The Crackmarsh men slammed through the forkbeard camp like a herd of charging bulls. Valaric screamed at them to keep running, to smash down the forkbeards as they rose from their fires. Some stopped anyway, pausing to finish a forkbeard they'd dazed and left helpless, and Valaric was happy enough with that. Others stopped to fight other forkbeards who hadn't been knocked down and got themselves caught in duels, one against one, two against one, two against three. Keep moving, that was the thing. Tear through the forkbeard camp. Scatter them. Fight them in ones and twos, and whatever you did, don't let them gather together. He had no illusions about his men. They were hard and bitter fighters but they weren't forkbeards. If the Lhosir formed ranks behind their shields then the battle would be over.

He scooped up a burning branch from one of the fires and hurled it at three forkbeards standing together, then charged into them, battering one man down, veering away before the other two could stab him with their spears. He wheeled and ran straight into a forkbeard fighting toe to toe with one of his Marroc. Valaric rammed his spear into the back of the forkbeard's thigh and ran on. A pair of Lhosir with axes were racing across the camp, coming his way. He dropped into the shadows of a tent, stuck out his foot and tripped one and then surged up and brought his spear down with all his strength, splitting the mail that protected the back of the forkbeard's neck. He yanked his point free, blade dark with forkbeard blood. The second axeman skidded to a stop and spun to face him. Valaric bared his teeth. *Modris, but it feels good to be doing something at last!*

Gallow stepped aside as the iron man hurled himself forward. He struck Beyard in the side with all the strength his arm could muster. Beyard turned and stood for a moment, lit by Tolvis's pyre, armour gleaming, shoulders rising and falling with each heavy breath. He came more slowly now, with the patient purpose of a Fateguard, driving Gallow back towards the heat of the fire. The red sword arced and swung and the air moaned under its blade. Gallow raised his own sword to defend himself. Sparks flashed as steel touched steel. Beyard lunged, driving for Gallow's heart. Gallow leaped sideways, almost falling into the pyre in his desperation. He hurled another swing at Beyard but the Edge of Sorrows caught it easily and almost wrenched his sword out of his hand. Beyard swung and lunged again. This time Gallow stepped inside the blow and barged Beyard with his shoulder, staggering him back. He lifted his sword to drive it between the bars of the iron man's mask, but Beyard smashed the blade aside. The ring as the two swords struck sounded oddly dull. The red sword slashed at Gallow's face. Gallow stumbled again, and this time when the red sword came down and he blocked it with his own, his blade shattered. Gallow rolled away, snatched a brand out of the pyre and jumped to his feet, waving it at Beyard's face. The iron man caught it in his fist and held it. For an instant their eyes met, the fire burning between them, then Beyard punched

Gallow with the hand that still held Solace. As he reeled, Beyard pushed him to the ground. A moment later the tip of the red sword rested on the back of Gallow's neck.

'Yield!' rasped Beyard.

The Marroc raced out of the tower, howling and screaming, hacking at the ramp the forkbeards had built, drawing them from where they stood watch. They came slowly, distracted by the fight at the pyre, but they came, and Achista and the Marroc fought them as hard as they could. But there were dozens of them, soldiers born and bred, and slowly they drove the Marroc back into a tight circle of shields and spears just outside the gates, pressing in, killing them one by one with no way out.

Valaric took the forkbeard's axe on his shield and rammed his spear point into the man's belly – maybe not hard enough to pierce mail but hard enough to wind him. As the Lhosir doubled over, Valaric lifted his shield and smashed its rim into the back of the forkbeard's head. He went down.

'Next!' In the darkness, amid the litter of campfires and the scurrying of men here and there, it was impossible to tell who was who and who was winning. It was everything Valaric had wanted though – a wild swirling melee with every man for himself. The forkbeards hadn't formed their wall of shields because he hadn't let them. He crouched down in the shadows. A Lhosir ran out in front of him. He sprang and brought him down, banging the forkbeard's head into the frozen ground and holding it there until his struggles eased enough for Valaric to get out a knife and open his throat. Not ten feet away a Marroc was fighting another forkbeard, the two of them locked together, grunting and swearing, the forkbeard slowly bearing the Marroc down. The forkbeard wasn't wearing his mail though, so Valaric ran to them and knifed him in the liver.

317

'Look!' The Marroc pointed up the slope towards the Reach. In the dim light around the gates Valaric saw fighting. 'They've come out for us,' said the Marroc.

'Crazy fools.' They were surrounded. He could see that even from here. He could see the pyre as well and two men fighting around it, and as he watched, one of the men fell. A savage growl prowled inside him, looking for an escape. 'Round up some others,' he snarled. 'Not too many. But we came here for Witches' Reach.'

'Yield.' Gallow was kneeling now. 'Yield and I'll give you a clean death.'

'Let the Marroc go. Let Oribas go. Let all of them go. End it all, old friend.'

'Look around you. It's ended already.'

'Yet still I will not yield.' Gallow started to rise.

The tip of the red sword pressed into his neck. 'Your Marroc are beaten, old friend.'

Gallow kept rising though the sword's edge cut into his skin. He could feel the blood trickling down his back. Beyard could kill him with a flick of his wrist yet he didn't. 'No, Beyard. Lost is not beaten. You're Lhosir. You of all of us understand the difference.' He walked away and picked up the jagged stump of his broken sword. 'I'll fight you until you kill me, old friend.'

Beyard kept the red sword held out before him. Gallow walked calmly towards it. He swatted the Edge of Sorrows aside with his half-sword. Beyard stepped away. 'Stop,' he hissed. He sounded hoarse. 'Just go, Gallow.'

'I will not.'

'I don't want to kill you, old friend.'

Gallow flicked the red sword aside again. 'Then take your Lhosir and walk away.'

'I cannot.'

'Then I have no other choice to give you.' Gallow lunged

and Beyard only moved at the very last moment. The jagged edge of Gallow's steel slid off the side of the Fateguard mask. The iron man stayed where he was. He didn't raise the red sword. Instead he lifted the mask and crown off his face and looked Gallow in the eye.

'There would be tears in my eyes if I could still weep.'

'Yield, old friend.'

'I cannot. No more than you.'

They looked at one another a moment longer. Beneath the pale scarred skin and the hollow cheeks and the red-rimmed eyes, Gallow saw the Beyard who'd stood beside him in the Temple of the Fates, holding closed a door, young and strong and fierce, the best of the three of them by far.

'Don't let him lessen us,' Beyard whispered and put back his mask and crown, and Gallow knew he meant Medrin. Medrin, who'd been with them that day and had run away.

The iron man lowered the Edge of Sorrows and was still. Gallow drove the spike of his broken sword through the bars of the iron mask. Beyard spasmed. The red sword fell from his hand. His weight sagged forward and Gallow eased him to his knees. 'Farewell, old friend.'

Beyard still had some strange strength to him. He knelt, head bowed, a spike of iron through his skull, and yet for a moment he didn't die. He gripped Gallow's leg.

'Peace.' Gallow pulled away. He picked the red sword out of the snow and brought it down with all his strength on the back of Beyard's neck. Solace. The Comforter. The Peacebringer.

Achista knew she'd die. The last dozen of the Marroc from the tower were pressed together. She'd never even fought a man with a sword and half the other Marroc were the same – pathetic, desperate – while the forkbeards were forkbeards. Even as she dodged and ducked and lunged, inside she cringed, waiting for the end. And then suddenly the forkbeards were drawing back. A score of them and they were pulling away, all of them staring down the trail from the gates of Witches' Reach to the pyre where one man stood holding the sword of the Weeping God. Gallow.

Slowly, with their shields still high and their spears still raised, the forkbeards drew away and melted into the night. They were Lhosir, after all, men of fate, and fate had spoken. Achista stared long after they'd vanished into the darkness. Stared as a horn sounded in the distance, deep and mournful. Stared at Gallow as he stood there doing nothing but looking down at the fallen iron devil. Then figures appeared out of the shadows heading up from the forkbeard camp – Marroc, led by a man with wild mad eyes, scarred and spattered with blood. He looked at her and at the others and then back again and held out his arm. 'Valaric,' he said. 'They call me Mournful.'

It was a miracle. She clasped his arm. 'Achista. They call me the Huntress.'

'Why did the forkbeards run? They never run.'

She pointed at Gallow. There was the answer, somehow. "But they didn't *run*. They just ... left.'

Valaric nodded. 'Well get your men together, Achista whom they call the Huntress. We've work to do. There's plenty more forkbeards left where they came from.'

He ran back yelling orders and Achista watched him, too dazed by fate's sudden turn to take it in. The forkbeards would come again. Another army, bigger. But this time there would be enough Marroc to hold the walls for months.

She left the gate and walked to the pyre. Gallow was dragging the body of the iron devil towards the flames but it was too heavy and awkward for one man to lift alone. She took the iron devil's feet. Burning it felt right. Burning it into ash. Together they heaved it into the flames. 'You won,' she said. 'I don't know how, but you won.'

Gallow picked up the iron devil's head, still with the spike of his broken sword driven through its mask. He threw it into the flames and whispered words amid the crackling heat. Achista stared into the pyre, lost. It was like watching all the forkbeards she'd ever known burn, all the things they'd done and all the bitterness they'd wrought.

When she turned back to Gallow to ask him what he would do, he was gone.

48

READY TO DO WHAT A HERO CAN

Gallow stared at Beyard, wreathed in fire, his head still mercifully cased in iron, the crown and mask of the Fateguard pinned in place by the spike of his broken sword. He'd been a man once. Even at the end neither of them had forgotten. The right thing now was to speak out his deeds, shout them to the sky loud and clear so the wind would carry his words across the world and through the Herenian Marches to the Maker-Devourer and his cauldron, but what was there to say? 'Beyard. A Lhosir of the old way. The best of us all. Maker-Devourer, take him to your cauldron. A friend once.' That was what mattered the most.

Achista was staring, mesmerised by the flames and their ever-fickle meanings. Her eyes were black and wide. Words grew in his throat and then died on his lips. He almost reached out to touch her, to bring her back from wherever she was, and then stopped. He was a forkbeard and she was a Marroc, and that would never change. Only Arda ever saw past to the man inside. Arda, who'd kept his heart alive for three long years, and now he had to leave her again.

The heat of the pyre burned his face. He stepped back, and then turned away and slammed the Edge of Sorrows down. Its point bit deep into the frozen earth, ever hungry for the piercing of things. He left it there and walked through snow pounded flat by a thousand fleeing footfalls. The Marroc from the keep were out by the gates now, the few that were left, dancing and singing and whooping. Addic was there and somehow Valaric too, Addic drunk with delight that he was still alive, Valaric yelling orders at his men who'd come from Maker-Devourer-knew-where on this night to save them. A miracle? A sign from the gods? Luck? Fate? Gallow passed them by and felt none of it, no joy, no pride, no glory, just the weight of a lot of dead men whose blood had spilled for no great cause one way or the other. He walked up the steps to the keep, and there she was in the shadows beyond the doorway, looking out. Watching. Arda. He opened his arms to her and she walked to him and let him hold her tight. In his mail and his furs he felt like a bear and she so fragile.

'Arda.' He nuzzled her hair and held her, and for a long time that was enough.

'I know that look.'

'I killed a friend tonight.'

She didn't say a word.

'You are ...' He shook his head. Oribas would have found words of magic power, drawn patterns in the air with them, made them dance and sing to the tune of his heart, but that was Oribas, whose art was knowledge. Gallow had no idea how to tell Arda what was in his heart. Neither of them had ever been good at that.

Oribas, whom Beyard had sent away to be hanged, whom Gallow had walked away from once back in Varyxhun.

'Clod-head. I know. Come.'

She led him away to the cellars, to a quiet place where the Marroc left them alone and kept him there until the creeping grey of dawn spread across the mountain sky to the east. And when he thought she was sleeping and turned back the furs to slip silently away, she looked him right in the eye. She'd known all along that it would come to this.

'You're going to go again, aren't you?' She tried to sound like it didn't matter but she couldn't. Her voice was flat and dead.

'Yes.'

The Arda he'd left behind three years ago would have sworn and shouted and thrown things, screaming about family and loyalty, but now she only looked at him. 'Why, Gallow? Why?'

'Oribas.' And that was all. As if that should be enough. She stiffened, the old anger and resentment and all those other things still burning away inside her, hard to push away.

'Pursic doesn't even remember you.' She knew he'd seen back in Middislet: Pursic at the top of the cellar stairs staring at Tolvis. *Dada!*

Gallow closed his eyes. His voice broke to a whisper. 'I know.'

She snorted, and for a moment she was herself again, the old Arda who was used to being around mud-brained forkbeards. 'Well, if you're going then you'll be not much use if you freeze to death.' She picked up a handful of furs and threw them at him. 'At least keep yourself warm.' She waited while he put on his mail and buckled his belt and arranged his furs, and then when he was dressed she led him by the hand to the gates of Witches' Reach and handed him his spear. 'I won't be here when you come back. Three years was enough. I'll not do that again.'

'They're going to hang him. He was my friend. I have to go.'

Her lips were dry. 'I know. And so do I.'

'If you ask me to I'll stay.'

She didn't doubt he meant it but it was such a stupid thing to say. She pushed him on and then stepped back. 'You stole my heart with all your forkbeard pride and your courage and your strength. I love you for what you are, Gallow, but what I need is a man who'll feed my children and protect them. Someone who's there. War clouds are coming. I need a man who'll stay at home and that's not you. So yes, Gallow

Truesword, Gallow the Foxbeard, I want you to stay, I want that more than anything, but I'll not ask it. Only you can say which matters to you more. And if you ask me to wait, I won't. Not again.' She stepped back into the shadows of Witches' Reach.

'There's no peace for us, Arda.' Gallow shook his head. 'No peace. Not while Medrin lives.'

Arda nodded and turned her back and walked away because hell would freeze over before she'd let a forkbeard see her cry. Gallow called after her one last time but she didn't dare look back, and then he was gone. She climbed to the top of the tower and looked out over the dawn and saw him again, standing by the pyre of Tolvis Loudmouth, and she watched him pull a sword out of the ground where he'd left it the night before and turn and go. Watched until she couldn't see him any more, until she saw that he didn't look back, not once.

When he was gone, she dried her eyes and went looking for Valaric the Mournful, the Marroc whose men had her children back in his hideout. There were things to be said about that and in no uncertain manner.

More Lhosir came later that day, the half-an-army that had been waiting by the Aulian Bridge to fall on Valaric's Crackmarsh men. They were righteously furious, and from all the stories told afterwards it was a vicious and bloody little siege until the forkbeards finally took the walls and built the iron devil's ram again and smashed down the gates and stormed inside. But at the end, the stories said, all they found was an empty tower. And Arda heard those stories too, but she couldn't have said if they were true because before the first of the forkbeards came up from the bridge, she was already gone.

*

No one had taken the red sword. A hundred upon a hundred Marroc plundering and looting the dead, and not one of them had touched it. Gallow pulled it free and sheathed it at his side. The cursed blade. His and his alone, stained by the blood of his oldest friend. He turned to face south, the road to Varyxhun, and when the Lhosir came later that day he was long gone too.

EPILOGUE

There were riots in the city. Oribas couldn't see but he could hear them and he could smell the smoke. The Marroc had been restless for days. Something had happened but no one would tell him what. Down in his cell he picked up rumours now and then and saw the odd Marroc being dragged off to the torturer and then later he heard their screams and sobs. He heard everything they cried, not that it added up to much, but there were more every day.

His cell was underground, but on the day they hanged him they hauled him up to the castle yard and he could hear and smell the turmoil clearly at last. He could see it too, written on the Lhosir around the castle, on their faces and in the way they held themselves. He looked up at the gallows and he could see it even there. They were going to hang him but he wouldn't be the only one. There were some Marroc to die too. Out here in the yard, pressed together with the other prisoners, he'd heard what it was that had the streets of Varyxhun filled with revolt. The forkbeards were beaten. The iron devil was dead and Witches' Reach still held.

Witches' Reach still held.

He stared up at the waiting gallows and knew that Achista was still alive. He would hang a happy man.

ACKNOWLEDGEMENTS

When Simon Spanton, who commissioned this and with whom I war perpetually on the subject of prologues, called me up to ask if I could do fantasy without any dragons, he didn't know I was surrounded by Vikings at the time. If there are a lot of axes in this, that's probably why. So thanks to Simon for his endless faith, sometimes rewarded and sometimes not, and to Marcus Gipps for his editorial input, to Hugh Davies who did the copy-edit and to the proof-readers, even if I never know who you are. Thank you in particular to all the booksellers who are are real people with real enthusiasms and not an algorithm in Luxembourg.

And thanks to all the crazy people who thought the best way to spend a week in February was to strut though York in mail carrying an axe. And thank you too for reading this. As always, if you liked this story, please tell others who might like it too.